PENGUIN BOOKS

CHILDREN OF A HARSH WINTER

Janet Cohen is the author of *The Highest Bidder* (Penguin 1992) and, under the name of Janet Neel, four highly acclaimed crime novels: *Death's Bright Angel*, *Death on Site*, *Death of a Partner* and *Death Among the Dons*. The latter two were shortlisted for the Crime Writers' Association Gold Dagger Award for 1991 and 1993 respectively.

Educated at Cambridge and qualified as a solicitor, Janet Cohen was an industrial relations specialist for John Laing Construction before spending thirteen years in the Department of Trade and Industry. She is now a director of Charterhouse Bank, a member of the Board of Governors of the BBC, a board member of the Sheffield Development Corporation and a non-executive director of the Yorkshire Building Society, John Waddington plc and BPP Holdings plc. She started Parsons restaurant in the Fulham Road, London, and created Café Pelican in St Martin's Lane, London, and its sister restaurant in the City. She is married with three children and lives in London.

JANET COHEN

Children of
a Harsh Winter

PENGUIN BOOKS

PENGUIN BOOKS

Published by the Penguin Group
Penguin Books Ltd, 27 Wrights Lane, London w8 5TZ, England
Penguin Books USA Inc., 375 Hudson Street, New York, New York 10014, USA
Penguin Books Australia Ltd, Ringwood, Victoria, Australia
Penguin Books Canada Ltd, 10 Alcorn Avenue, Toronto, Ontario, Canada M4V 3B2
Penguin Books (NZ) Ltd, 182–190 Wairau Road, Auckland 10, New Zealand

Penguin Books Ltd, Registered Offices: Harmondsworth, Middlesex, England

First published by Michael Joseph 1994
Published in Penguin Books 1995
1 3 5 7 9 10 8 6 4 2

Copyright © Janet Cohen, 1994
All rights reserved

The moral right of the author has been asserted

Filmset by Datix International Limited, Bungay, Suffolk
Printed in England by Clays Ltd, St Ives plc
Set in 10½/12½ pt Monophoto Sabon

For my daughter, Isobel

CHAPTER ONE

November 1965

'Wait for me.' A small, fair child rushed across the sea of mud and weeds, yards behind four bigger boys, straining to keep up, squealing with excitement and fear. He failed to see a pothole, caught his foot, went over and shrieked as the leg cracked. He lay on the rough ground screaming in short, panicked bursts, stopping the fleeing children ahead of him in their tracks, and causing passers-by a hundred yards away to peer uneasily through the November dusk. A larger fair boy, shouting with fear and rage, led the charge back to the injured child, under a hail of stones thrown from the corner of a digger. He squatted, clasping the little boy, now grey with pain and shock, mouth rounded in a series of screams.

'Stop that noise, Mickey. Tell me where it hurts.' He flinched as a stone caught him on the cheek, and started up to deal with this menace, but his brother's hand clamped on his, trapping him. 'Davey, it's my leg.'

'Stop it!' another boy screamed anxiously from their left. 'You've killed someone.'

The hail of stones slackened and stopped, and confused shufflings could be heard from the huge digger, as shadowy, small figures slid off their various vantage-points and made for a gap in the fence, grey in the increasing dark.

'That's Paul Seles' gang,' the voice said, its naturally shrill quality underlined by tears of rage. 'I'll tell my father.'

'Shut up, Peter.' David Banner, agonized, held his small brother's hand.

'We'll have to get an ambulance.'

'My father will kill me,' David Banner said, horrified.

'He'll kill you even worse if Mickey dies,' Peter, a round, plump boy, a natural second-in-command, pointed out. 'Look here.' The four boys stared at the lights swinging and bobbing two hundred yards away by the gate, and heard the squeal of a police siren.

'We're all in trouble,' Peter observed. 'Look, look, they got Paul Seles, that's him! Over there!' His voice cracked with excitement and alarm as David Banner stared down at the small boy who clung to him, wailing and hiccuping. 'It's the fuzz!'

'You lot run,' David Banner said, estimating the distance between the oncoming lights and the group. 'You'll just do it. Oh, no!'

The small party fell silent as they all saw the lights divide and fan out, one lot moving towards them, the other towards the enemy group. They huddled together by the injured child, hoping to share in his presumed immunity from the wrath of the adult world.

'Over here!' called David Banner, the natural leader of this or any other group of his contemporaries. 'My brother's leg's broken.' He stood up to greet the oncoming adults, as he had been unfashionably taught to do, a tall, strongly built ten-year-old with the promise of startling good looks in the regular, blunt features, wide blue eyes and bright blond, curly hair.

'And how did all this happen, then?' The policeman was no more than ten years older than the boys. 'We'll need an ambulance. Young man with a broken leg – how old are you, son?'

'He's five.'

'You're his brother?' The policeman looked from one blond head to the other. 'Your mother'll play war with you.'

'Not my mother, my father,' David said, pulled involuntarily into speech as police reinforcements gathered around the group.

'You come along with us, and tell us who you are, and we'll

get your mum along to the hospital. Your brother will be all right – he won't know whether it's Christmas or Friday until his leg is fixed.'

'That's not true.' The policeman turned with a start to find a small, thin, dirty child, on closer scrutiny probably female, in the custody of one of his colleagues from the other group who had a firm hand on her shoulder. 'The hospital will need parental consent before they can do anything to a minor.'

The assembled police force gaped at her.

'How old are you, missy?' a sergeant inquired severely.

'Nine,' the clear voice said defiantly.

'No, you're not, you're only eight,' a bigger boy, heavy, dark and thick-set, who looked much older, said accusingly.

'I shall be nine tomorrow,' the grubby child said with dignity.

'You hurt my brother.' No one had been watching David Banner, who threw himself at the dark boy, hands reaching for his throat. He was beaten off by the larger boy with contemptuous ease and thrown sprawling on the ground, weeping with rage.

'Now, that's enough.' One policeman grabbed David, and another the dark boy who snarled at him, causing him to flinch back momentarily.

'No he didn't, you stupid git,' the clear female voice said, shaking but determined. 'I saw it. We were all throwing stones and your silly little brother tripped over all by himself. You shouldn't bring babies like that into this sort of fight.'

David Banner, on his feet again, spoke for the meeting. 'If you weren't a girl I'd hit you.'

'You and whose army?' the girl asked sharply, tilting her chin to look up at him, nearly a head taller than her. 'It wasn't Paul's fault.'

'None of you children ought to be here, and especially not you, missy. I don't doubt your parents will feel the same when we fetch them to take you home,' the sergeant said firmly. 'You'll all come along to the station and we'll see what's what.' He turned sharply at the sound of feet sliding on stone;

3

the dark, heavy Paul was yards away and going fast, running for a corner of the site, and two of the younger policemen set off after him, their extra length of leg giving them the advantage.

'Leave him alone.' The girl tugged at the sergeant's coat and he looked down severely, to see her face twisted in agony. 'You don't understand. He gets beaten all the time.'

The sergeant hesitated and opened his mouth to call, but the lead policeman had floored the flying boy and was slowly getting up with his captive. The girl broke free and ran over to the pair, and could be seen trying to reassure the boy, bobbing about to get him to look at her, as he was dragged back, his large, dark head sullenly bowed.

The sergeant considered his situation. There were four constables with their hands full with seven boys, roughly of an age between ten or eleven, all dressed in the ubiquitous jeans, and one small, dirty girl, aged nearly nine. No charges could be brought against them, but he stifled the temptation just to tell them all to go home so he could get on with some real work. There was a child – and a middle-class child at that – on his way to hospital with a broken leg, and, more importantly, the local juveniles needed to be shown that this patch was off limits. It was a long narrow rectangle, perhaps a mile long by two hundred yards wide, cleared so that a road could be driven through this crowded part of West London. In one way the clearance had been of great assistance to the police; the four square miles through which the road – the first urban motorway – was to run, was a thieves' kitchen; malefactors had always slipped through houses and back gardens like water through sand, and these rat runs were now abruptly curtailed. But in two weeks' time the area would be full of holes dug for the foundations of the road and covered in dangerous, heavy and expensive equipment. It was absolutely essential to check incursions by juveniles bent on mischief, or worse accidents than this would follow.

'Right. Who's the leader, then?' he asked.

'I am, of my lot.' David Banner held his chin up and the sergeant considered him measuringly.

'What does your father do?'

'He's in the Navy.'

'Right then, lad, you collect your men and come along to the station.'

'He's nothing to do with us,' the girl said sharply, brushing away tears. 'We're different. Paul here . . .' She stopped, bit her lip and shifted out of range of the dark boy. '*I* am our leader.'

'I see,' the sergeant said indulgently, catching the eye of the three boys at her back and inviting them to marvel, but they all firmly avoided his speculative gaze. He considered them; two were known to him already, he'd met them accused of shoplifting or darting through the crowds of the local market. The shrimp-like little girl was new to him, as was the dark Paul. He placed a fatherly hand on her shoulder and got a look that made him remove it for fear of being bitten. He collected the children, observing *sotto voce* to one of his constables that one group came from Barton Hill, a big primary school which drew from one of the bleakest council estates in that area of North Paddington.

'Which school do you go to, young man?' he asked the good-looking David, who lifted his chin defiantly under the pallid streetlights.

'St Peter's.'

Would be, of course, the sergeant thought. There was an ongoing daytime battle between local estate children and the privileged, blue-uniformed St Peter's boys who, weighed down by the accoutrements of middle-class education like the satchel, the clarinet and the games bat, were hopelessly handicapped against the lightly armed troops of Barton Hill. The battle tonight, which had left a five-year-old with a broken leg, and all eight children here present with marks of injury, was an unfortunate and threatening extension of a local difficulty that had hitherto been confined to the daytime, flaring only during the hours of arrival and departure from school.

'What about you, missy?' They were walking back to the local station, only fifty yards away now, with young constables flanking the group.

'I'm at Barton Hill. In Form 2.'

The sergeant blinked thoughtfully. The clear, self-assured accent did not go with Barton Hill, in fact the child did not go with Barton Hill. He looked at her again, small for eight or nine, dark, very thin, the ancient jeans she was wearing slipping towards non-existent hips. She was improbably dirty, they all were, and he realized that they were all wearing a primitive camouflage of mud on their faces and hands, in approved military style. He wondered if she was lying and was in truth a refugee from one of the local girls' uniformed preparatory schools, but discarded the idea. She was not the leader of this group; that was, of course, the dark, awkward boy, who had made a run for it, but she was very much part of it. She was walking very close to her leader, coming as near to holding his hand as she dared. She was flanked by a big Jamaican boy whom he knew as one of the notorious Miller extended family, and a small, neatly made Irish boy, Pat McCarthy, who had not been out of trouble since he left his crowded pram. The girl probably came from a middle-class single-parent family, who found themselves on the Barton Hill estate, he decided, as he shepherded the children into the police station and found them a room, summoning a woman PC in the interests of the only girl present. He watched, intrigued, as she refused utterly to leave her leader, even to be escorted to the lavatory.

The WPC shrugged and bent to the task of getting the child to open her clenched left hand long enough to let her get embedded gravel out of a nasty graze. Three other constables were similarly deployed, and the sergeant passed among the children collecting names, addresses and telephone numbers, drawing a blank with the dark boy, who would not speak. He returned to make the necessary phone calls, including one to the headmaster of Barton Hill who reluctantly identified a dark ten-year-old boy called Paul as Paul Seles, living with relatives, not his parents, in one of the precariously respectable little roads threatened by the redevelopment which would be necessary to accommodate the new road.

'Hungarian child. Came over as a baby in 1956 after the revolution. No, no mother. Lives with a cousin.'

6

'We've also got a little girl, Jennifer Redwood. Say she's one of yours?'

'She is. Father's an economist. And a councillor in the Labour interest.'

Not likely to be much else round here, the sergeant thought silently. 'I'll be a bit careful then.'

'You need to be. The man's an idealist, that's why he sent his daughter here rather than to St Edith's, or somewhere like that. I'd just as soon not have that kind of child.' The weary voice paused. 'How many of mine have you got? Four? I'd come down, but it's my wife's evening class and I'm babysitting.'

'There's not much I can do to them, Mr Edwards,' the sergeant pointed out drily. 'The wee girl's only nine and the others only ten. I'm just going to send them home, after a caution, that's all we ever do until we persuade the social workers to do something with the Miller or the McCarthy families. Pat's father's in jail anyway, did you know?'

'Again? No, I didn't. Look, thank you, sergeant . . . oh, blast it . . . sorry, I have to go, my seven-year-old just knocked over a saucepan. Can you pop in at school tomorrow? Thanks.'

The sergeant finished his phone calls; he had been received with middle-class horror and subsequent apology in the households of the St Peter's boys, dithering panic by Jennifer Redwood's mother and with the expected earful of abuse from both the Miller and McCarthy households. He detoured past the police canteen to buy snacks for the children; experience suggested it would be a little while before their parents managed to get themselves or an envoy to the station. He handed out sausage rolls to the young criminals, who fell on them with the fervour of the starving. They'd had a busy afternoon, hadn't they, he thought wearily; ten minutes later he heard loud, middle-class voices in the hall and went out to confront a man who had to be the father of David and the injured Michael. Strikingly good-looking, like his elder son, and just a little too conscious of it, he was a tall but compact man, bursting with ill-directed energy and giving a peculiarly nervous impression.

'I'll skin that boy of mine,' he said to the sergeant, who observed neutrally that none of the children should have been on the site. He watched as father and son were reunited; the boy was watchful but not frightened, looking at his father in a way slightly chilling in a ten-year-old.

'Well, we didn't start it, Dad,' he was saying carefully, his voice lowered.

'Bloody liar.' It was the nine-year-old, Jennifer, blazing with contempt and indignation, left hand now thickly bandaged, the only clean thing about her, chocolate round her mouth, adding to the general disorder. Commander Banner glanced at her dismissively, writing her off as a child of the slums, but she stood her ground.

'Your boy set the whole thing up,' she informed him coldly. 'I am sorry that he does not now feel able to take responsibility for his actions.'

The sergeant tried unsuccessfully to suppress the grin spreading over his face; Commander Banner was so openly wrong-footed by this little tough with the vocabulary of a much older child and the manners and accent of the confident middle class.

'You were there or thereabouts, missy,' he intervened in the interests of justice.

'I never suggested otherwise.' The child was in a cold rage, and David Banner had gone pink with confusion and guilt. Into this complicated scene waddled Mrs Miller, all fifteen stone of her, who seized her son, cuffed him soundly, voice rising in a paroxysm of complaint and rage against the difficulties of a mother's life and the provocation offered by the police force of North Paddington. Commander Banner's face was eloquent of horror at finding himself in this company, and another St Peter's father, diffidently putting his head round the door, plainly would have liked to turn and run.

'Good evening.' The sergeant glanced up to see a tall, thin man, leaning against the door jamb. The small Jennifer ran to him, precocious dignity abandoned, and he staggered slightly under the onslaught.

'What has she been up to, and can I take her home?' It was a voice as clear as his daughter's, but utterly weary, and the sergeant looked at him again. And could not look away; the tall man was not only thin, he was skeletal, the shadow of a much bigger man, the cheek-bones standing away from the flesh of the face, the ugly blue suit falling loosely from the hunched shoulders, both long, painfully thin hands resting gently on his daughter's shoulders. The man was ill unto death, he thought, transfixed; he was holding himself very carefully, the dark blue eyes resting on him with no curiosity, all emotion turned inward. The man glanced down at his child and smiled, the sinews in the throat standing out like cords, then looked wordlessly back to the sergeant.

'Sir. Yes. She'd better go home, she's had a long day.' He recovered himself and managed to lead Commander Banner and Councillor Redwood out of the room, leaving a constable to contain Mrs Miller's diatribe as best he might. He delivered a suitably reproving homily to both children to which David Banner attended with every evidence of soldierly attention, and to which Jennifer Redwood straightforwardly did not listen at all. She was tugging at her father's jacket, desperate to communicate, but Councillor Redwood waited courteously until the sergeant had finished, before squatting stiffly beside his daughter, who pulled his head towards her and whispered impassionedly in his ear. He waited until he was sure she had finished, then pulled himself to his feet, leaning on her.

'Sergeant, could we have a word privately about one of the other children? No, not your boy, Commander, one of my daughter's associates. I understand it was your younger one who got a broken leg? I'm very sorry to hear that.'

The sergeant, watching, understood that Banner, of the type to make a self-important fuss in ordinary circumstances, had been as taken aback as himself by Councillor Redwood. His son, less sensitive to atmosphere, unwisely stuck his tongue out at Jennifer Redwood who kicked him promptly on the kneecap. Commander Banner opened his mouth in outrage, but Redwood was too quick for him.

'What happened, Jens?'

'He stuck his tongue out, the stupid pillock.'

'Not very ladylike language, Jens, and no need to kick him.' He gave David Banner a thoughtful look as he turned a slow scarlet. 'Sergeant?'

Galvanized, he showed the Redwoods into a small interviewing room and offered the councillor a chair, into which the man folded himself. He was in pain, the sergeant realized, accustomed and habitual, steeling himself to endure for his daughter. 'Jens is concerned for one of her friends, Paul Seles. The cousin with whom he lives is apparently rather heavy-handed.'

'He beats him with a strap every time he does anything.' Jennifer was staring at the floor, scarlet with misery and embarrassment.

'She is worried that he will be punished this time.'

The sergeant met the councillor's eye. 'I'm not sure how much I can do about that, sir.'

Redwood shifted painfully. 'Let me have a word, Sergeant, when he comes to collect Paul.' He tucked his daughter's hand into his, and they both looked up, startled by the banging of doors.

'I come for Paul Seles,' they could hear, and the sergeant rose, momentarily uncertain what to do first.

'We'll come with you.' Councillor Redwood clawed himself to his feet, his daughter clinging to his hand, and the sergeant rushed to the door to hold it for him.

The reception hall was now heavily overcrowded. Commander Banner was struggling with the telephone, hand over his free ear to shut out the noise, with David Banner tucked in beside him as close as he dared, staring wide-eyed at a harassed young desk constable, and a squat, middle-aged man who was making all the noise, listening to nothing but his own voice. Even the dauntless Jennifer Redwood was keeping her father between herself and the shouting as he advanced calmly into the fray. 'Mr Seles.'

The man swung round in mid-sentence, ready to start shouting again, but was silenced as the sergeant had been and stood, mouth still half-open, gaping at Councillor Redwood.

'You've come to fetch Paul? My bad child is in trouble too.' Redwood was sounding, at God only knew what cost to himself, relaxed and amused, and the fraught atmosphere in the room lightened abruptly. David Banner moved out from behind his father and, seeing Jennifer emerging from behind her father, retreated again. Paul's guardian was not tall, only about five foot six, but square, with dark, short hair and almost neckless with heavy shoulders and long, powerful arms ending in huge, wide hands. He had arrived straight off a site, wearing an ancient suit thick with mud, and heavy boots. There was no colour in the sallow skin, but he had to be a drinker, the sergeant thought, considering the overhanging beer belly under the short, too tight jacket.

'I 'ad to come off work,' he said, recovering his voice and addressing the group generally.

'So did I, and I expect Banner here did too. Do you know each other? Commander Banner, Mr Seles, is it? Sorry, Mr Vazarely.'

The sergeant watched, fascinated, as Banner was impelled into extending a hand which Vazarely looked at doubtfully before taking.

'How is your younger one?' Redwood asked.

'He's been settled for the night, thank you.' Banner was edging towards the door. 'I'm afraid I have to go and pick up my wife from the hospital.'

Vazarely considered him. 'You not worry. I beat Paul.'

Banner murmured something unintelligible and reached for the door-handle, but a look from Redwood stopped him in his tracks. 'Not on my account or my son's. From what I understand all our children were in the wrong. And my boy fell over, no one pushed him.'

He looked, the sergeant thought, like some character from one of those war films where the captain rallies his men as the ship goes down. And knew it; just a bit pleased with himself, aware he was showing himself in a good light. Nothing moved in Redwood's drawn face, but the sergeant felt a wave of fellow-feeling. He led the way into the main room, housing the rest of his juvenile crime wave. The other St Peter's fathers were huddled crossly in a corner with their sons, while Mrs Miller had been joined by a slight Irishwoman, mother to Pat McCarthy, and a young woman trailing files and scarves, known to the sergeant as an employee of the council's Social Services department, an organization of which he had the poorest possible opinion. Paul Seles, sitting with his head down, gazing doggedly at his feet, looked up, startled, jerked his head back and made a small, pitched, involuntary animal noise in his throat. His guardian stared across at him wordlessly, the smile with which he had entered the room gone, and hatred crackled in the air between them. The sergeant drew breath carefully; he had seen confrontations like this before but between grown men. The child was outgunned and outweighted, physically half his cousin's size and with no adult resources, and he was afraid, but when he grew to manhood there would be murder done if something or somebody did not intervene.

'Hello, Paul.' Councillor Redwood's clear, relaxed delivery eased the tension. 'Well, you *are* a nuisance, you and Jens. *And* you, Pat, *and* you, Jimmie. Good evening Mrs Miller, Mrs McCarthy.'

The Barton Hill boys grinned at him, in no way abashed.

'You lookin' tired, Councillor,' Mrs Miller said, voice lowered to gentleness. 'You need de chair more than me.'

Vazarely jerked his head at Paul, who took a deliberate time about obeying the summons, leisurely collecting himself while his guardian fidgeted, the powerful muscles at the back of the neck tense. The sergeant realized Redwood was ready to go, his daughter anxiously close to him, and followed them out.

Redwood asked, over her head: 'You're taking no action? Against the children, I mean? No. I agree, no point. I'll have a word about all that' – a jerk of the head indicated the room they had just left – 'with Mrs Richardson in Social Services . . .' He hesitated, then stopped, eyes closed, and the sergeant looked up, alarmed. 'It's all right, it passes ... sorry.' The bright eyes opened, unfocused. 'I must get home,' he said, in quite a different voice, and the sergeant understood that he and the anxious child might as well not have been there; this man was already far away.

'We'll drive you,' he said urgently, from a dry throat, and summoned a constable.

'That would be very kind.' Redwood was with them again, pale as death itself, a fine rim of sweat standing round his hairline. Mercifully there was a car and a driver and they shepherded Redwood towards it, uniting to help him gently into the car. The car pulled away and the constable, white-faced, looked at his sergeant, who turned away, choked and cold, his hands remembering the feel of Redwood's sharp bones under the good suit.

Paul walked along, a cautious yard away from the Bastard, or Cousin Franz as he was required to call him, the familiar sick anxiety churning in his stomach, wondering if his best bet were not to run for it and hole up somewhere in the hope that Franz would be less angry by tomorrow. On the other hand, perhaps it would be better now, when he just wanted to get to the pub, than later when he'd been there. And yet, through sick fear, he was cautiously savouring the memory of Franz in the police station; he had been shitting himself when the sergeant had lined them both up with the Millers and the McCarthys and delivered a ticking-off. It had washed off the Millers and the McCarthys, but the Bastard had hated being in a police station, looking awful in his scruffy site clothes and muddy boots, surrounded by people in uniforms. And he'd been frightened of Jens's father too, like the bog-ignorant peasant that he was. He'd had to give his name, and he'd been alarmed by *that* too; if he'd had to sign anything, well, that really would have been good. He couldn't read and could barely write, as Paul was not supposed to know, but had known from the time he had come to live with them when he was four and already able to do both.

He glanced cautiously sideways and his heart sank. The heavy muscles at the edge of the Bastard's jaw were clenched and moving in the way they did when he was working himself up. Paul glanced to his left, braced to run, looking for the alleyway which led through to the next street, but a wire gate had appeared there since that morning with a contractor's notice: something to do with access works to the road. The Bastard had felt him move and took hold of him, the big hand biting into the muscles of his upper arm, and he clenched his teeth in order not to cry, as he was pushed up the narrow path to the run-down little terraced house he so hated.

'Elisaveta, come here. See what this boy has done now.'

His mother's cousin – and how his mother had ever had such a stupid woman as a cousin he could not see – slunk out of the kitchen, hardly daring to look at her husband. 'You bad boy, Paul,' she said, meaning it. She was no use at all as an ally, too frightened of the Bastard. 'I wish we never had you.'

'Why did you bother?' he shouted, suddenly enraged by her whining rejection. 'Why not put me in care or let someone else adopt me? I didn't want you either.' He ducked expertly away from the Bastard's clumsy swing.

'Nobody didn't want you,' the Bastard shouted at him, and he was not quick enough to avoid him this time, cornered as he was by the bannister in the mean, narrow hall, so that he fell over, his head ringing, seeing stars. He was just crawling to his feet when he was felled by a sickening pain as the Bastard put his heavy, mud-stained work boot into his ribs and for a moment he could do nothing but hunch over, dumb with pain and shock. But then it happened, as it had happened before, the pure transcending rage which got him on his feet and snatching up a chair and battering at the Bastard with it, feeling the flimsy, cheap thing shatter. He saw the heavy face contort in fear, just for a second, before the pain started again and he was beaten to the floor with the back of the chair. Through a haze he could see the Bastard start to loosen his belt, then he heard through Elisaveta's feeble screams a heavy banging on the wall. Then he was cowering, arms over his head to save his face, trying to squeeze himself into the corner between the door and the wall to get some protection from the merciless flying buckle, when he heard shouting outside the house and saw the Bastard freeze, belt raised to strike.

'You in there! Mr Vazarely! If you don't stop that noise I'll call the police. My wife's ill and she's trying to get some rest, so just shut it!'

A door banged savagely and the Bastard shouted at it to mind its own bloody business, but the magic had worked and he banged out of the door, crushing Paul between it and the wall as he went, buckling on his belt.

About ten minutes later Paul had managed to get on to his hands and knees and crawl up to the cold, miserable first-floor bathroom. The Bastard earned good money, he knew, but none of it ever got into the house, it dribbled itself away in the pub and the betting shop, and the household was actually maintained on his child allowance and Elisaveta's wages as a cleaner. She helped him this time, give her credit, she cleaned him up, she gave him supper, not that he could eat much, his mouth was too bruised, and she shared with him her stock of Anadin which she bought with her wages, so that the pain reduced itself to something tolerable.

'Why don't you leave him?' he asked her, in the moment of warmth engendered by this minimal nurturing.

'Where would I go?' She poured him some tea and glanced at the clock, both of them conscious that in a couple of hours he would be back and that he would probably have a go at her, not Paul, this time.

'To a hostel. Like Mrs McCarthy does sometimes.'

'He would kill me.' It was said without any particular stress and Paul, was silenced by her conviction. The Bastard probably would kill her, as he would kill him one day if he hit back. He sat silent, woozy from the pain and the pills, facing a monstrous reality.

'Why did you – why did you ever marry him?' he asked at last, uncomprehending.

'I thought he would look after me. You do not understand,

Paul, we were alone. I came in 1956 with your mother and you. She tell me, she say, I should not go with Franz, but I could see what hard time she had and I was scared. I get these black days, I always had them. And I thought he would be all right.' She had never talked to him like this before, so exhausted by her life that he might have been anyone, another grown-up rather than a beaten ten-year-old boy, and he sat transfixed, watching her drawn pale face and her thin shoulders in the shabby cardigan she always wore. 'Then Susanna died and I took you. I shouldn't never have done that, better for you if I hadn't, but Franz wanted it. He said it would be shame if we let a Hungarian boy be adopted and he wanted a son, and I wasn't getting pregnant.'

But not a son who could read and write at four and who had cried for his mother every night and wanted to cling to Elisaveta, as neither of them said.

'I don't get a baby now, Paul. I had to have an operation.'

'I'm so sorry.' He had heard Jens Redwood say that, like a grown-up, when one of the kids in the class had told her his brother had killed himself in the nick, and had remembered it as the way you greeted a disaster.

'Better you go, when you can.'

It was offered without either hostility or sympathy, out of exhaustion as if they were prisoners in the same cell.

'I know,' he said, in the voice of a much older boy. 'I'll work on it.'

'Better go up now.' She glanced at the clock and her mouth twitched nervously. His guts twisted.

'Make a noise if he gets after you,' he said urgently. 'Wake the neighbours. They'll get the police.'

'They don't usually bother. But I try. Goodnight, Paul.'

He flinched as she kissed him awkwardly, unaccustomedly, just to the left of the worst of the cuts caused by the buckle of her husband's belt.

The sergeant was on duty two weeks later when he saw the paper. He had gone down with 'flu the day after the building-site skirmish and been back at work, feeling well below par, for just a day. He had gone to the canteen for his dinner and was eating without appetite when he saw a familiar name and craned to look.

Local man to command naval training school, it said above a picture of David Banner's father. The sergeant considered the picture, trying to work out what it was that was putting his back up, and decided it was the theatrically narrowed eyes and the lifted, defiant chin. The Banner child had the same manner-ism and it had perhaps been that as much as his sticking out his tongue which had infuriated the little Jennifer Redwood into kicking him when it would have been wiser not to. But the Banner family was moving on; the commander was now a full commander rather than a lieutenant-commander, and he was to be in charge of one of the naval training establishments on the south coast, HMS *Dreadnought*. The sergeant knew just enough about the Navy to understand that it would not be a ship but a house or barracks, securely anchored to dry land, several miles from the sea. Wherever the Navy was it lived in a ship in defiance of the actual facts. A smaller picture of the Banner family also appeared; three children in all, David, aged ten, then Mickey, aged five, self-consciously displaying a leg in full plaster, and a smaller boy, Thomas, aged four. A good-looking lot, he conceded, wondering about the five-year gap between David and the rest, but all three boys looked like their father. Well, Mrs Banner would be glad to have her husband at home with that lot, he thought, more kindly. Perhaps, indeed, an absent father was the reason that the two elder boys had been running wild on the site.

He turned the paper back to the front page, tidying it to return it, and stopped, transfixed. 'When did that happen?' he inquired of the air, and two constables looked at each other anxiously. He spread the paper flat, pushing his plate aside. *Funeral of popular councillor*, it said, over a picture only just recognizable as the man he had met. It was a three-quarter face, obviously taken at some social gathering, before Redwood had become ill. He was smiling, amused. It had been a long face with a heavy jaw, but not gaunt and strained as it had become, and the blue eyes were deep-set but not sunk back in his head as they had been two weeks ago. And the suit fitted him and the tendons in the neck barely showed rather than standing out like knotted ropes, and the smile was full of charm, not a rictus of the muscle. He looked happy and carefree and communicative, and the sergeant stared at the picture for a long time, feeling the infection he thought he had shaken off in his bones and behind his eyes.

He read the text and counted on his fingers. Redwood had died a week after the incident on the building site, having been in hospital for several days. We should have called an ambulance for him that night, he thought, not that it would have done any good. A long illness, the article said, a tragically early death, a brilliant man, an economist with a stream of publications to his credit. He turned the page and stopped at a picture of Jennifer and her mother. The child's face was clean and the wild hair suppressed under an unbecoming round brimmed hat. She was looking straight at the camera, head held well up, glaring into the lens, desolation in every line of the small face. He looked at her, heartsick; a child whose world had gone. The mother was looking down; the shoulders bent, supported by a strong masculine arm belonging to someone out of camera, Jennifer's hand clenched in hers. No other children. *Survived by his wife Mary and daughter Jennifer, nine, at Barton Hill School.*

Shaken, he read slowly to the end of the long list of dignitaries and friends who had attended, and a name jogged his memory. He got up from the table and swayed slightly; he should have taken the extra days off that his wife had wanted, but there was one thing he could do in memory of Councillor Redwood and he would do it now, even if it was of no use at all, as it likely would not be, given that useless lot in Social Services. He shut the door of his office and worked his way doggedly through the council's switchboard until he reached Mrs Richardson in Social Services and shyly explained his errand.

'Oh, *dear*,' the pleasant, harassed voice said anxiously, 'Jim Redwood did ring, but I couldn't ring him back – I forget why – and I rang him back the next day but he was in hospital, his wife said – no, it wasn't his wife, it was the child, and she was obviously trying not to cry, so I just got off the line.'

'He never came out, I take it.'

'No. It was cancer, of course.' They both let a silence fall, in tribute. 'Well,' Mrs Richardson said, gathering pace, 'so it was a boy, Paul Seles, at Barton Hill he was worried about. With a stepfather?'

'No, a relative. A Mr Vazarely,' he added, reading it off the records. 'A foreman brickie, working on the clearance for the new road. Beats the boy, apparently, and I believe it, having seen them together.'

There was a pause while they considered the problem.

'Badly enough to leave scars, or just to terrorize?'

The sergeant blinked at the matter-of-fact question, and bent his mind to the answer. 'Probably bad enough to show,' he said slowly. 'He's a big chap, heavy. Looks like a brute. The cousin, I mean.'

'And the child is ten? In for a school medical with any luck – I'll get in touch and tell the doctor to look. He will anyway, at Barton Hill; there's a lot of it. I'll let you know.'

She rang off crisply, leaving the sergeant to reflect that Redwood had known his stuff: that woman would do what she promised and do it efficiently. He looked again at the laughing, charismatic, handsome face, so different from the grim mask he had met, and turned over to look again at the survivors, gaining a tiny crumb of comfort from the conviction that he had done his best to finish the job that Redwood had started.

CHAPTER TWO

February 1969

The big blond teenager pounded down the field, pursuing the long ball, going like the wind, head back, leading with his chin. He changed direction smartly to avoid an oncoming back and slipped on the thick mud, but got the ball past the goalkeeper as they went down together in a heap. He got up slowly, spitting mud, to a rattle of applause from the thin line of people by the goalmouth: an excited group of small boys, a bored group of much larger boys and a scattering of women. He swaggered slightly as he walked back to the centre, nodding to a slight, fair-haired boy, very much younger but recognizably his brother, and casting a shy, sideways glance at a young woman just in her twenties with thick ankles and a pretty face, cheeks reddened by the raw winter cold, her dark, curly hair blowing in the wind: Mary Gardener, the under-matron for the junior school.

'Well played, Banner.'

He graciously acknowledged the call from his housemaster, a brisk, square man of no academic talent whatsoever, whose House always won all the team sports.

'Tea in twenty minutes, junior boys.' Mary Gardener was a West Country girl, a farmer's daughter, and you could hear it in her voice, which was slow and heavy, promising cream teas in lush, warm valleys. She paused to ruffle the hair of the fair boy, tall already at nine, but with none of his older brother's heavy muscle structure. 'Mickey Banner, you come as soon as the match is over. No nonsense now!'

The grey afternoon darkened rapidly, so that by the time the whistle blew the players' muddied white shorts were showing ghostly clear in the fading light. The teams gathered into two bunches of sweating, muddy adolescents under the charge of their respective masters, who cheered each other dutifully and hoarsely before going to the showers, the Ashford boys, as the home team, pairing off self-consciously with the visitors.

'Very promising forward, the fair lad, I mean – the one who got two of your goals,' the visiting master, whose team had won, said politely.

'Banner. Yes. And a year young for the team. He's fourteen. I can't get him to train, though. He plays everything, including the fool.'

'Oh, one of those. They grow out of it.' The visiting master, older and more experienced than his host, looked indulgently at the group ahead, David Banner at its centre, all conversing at the full pitch of their adolescent voices. 'Noisy as well, I see. Well, that's normal.' 'Service child, is he?' Ashford, like his own school, had a substantial clientele from the Armed Forces, having special fee arrangements with the Ministry of Defence.

'Yes, Navy. Father's a commander.'

The group in front, having reached the games block, recalled themselves and stopped, as they had been laboriously trained to do, and let the staff through. As the visiting master was wont to observe, to fathers if not to mothers, either you beat some elementary deference into adolescent boys or you got trampled underfoot, and both schools were run on that basis.

The masters shepherded the teams to the showers and retired themselves to the decent privacy of the staff showers. Ashford's scientific facilities were a touch old-fashioned, but they had four football pitches and a magnificent gymnasium block with enough showers – and boiler capacity – to turn out fifty clean adolescents every ten minutes, all day if need be.

And the tea was particularly good, the visiting master thought with pleasure, accepting a fourth scone with jam and cream, politely pressed on him by the captain of the home team. A young woman, introduced as 'our Miss Gardener', came in bearing reinforcements, a pretty, pink creature, and he beamed at her, relaxed by warmth and food. The adolescents in his charge, still at the age where they were stimulated rather than made sleepy by an hour and a half's exercise and a good tea, sat up as one boy. He scowled repressively at the biggest of the fifteen-year-olds from his own school, whose mouth fell with unconcealed, raw longing. The girl, unperturbed by male admiration, distributed platefuls of scones. She stopped by the big fair boy, Banner, and reached past him to deposit a plate, touching his shoulder. The boy blushed; he was strikingly good-looking, now that he was free of mud, even with a cut swelling above his right eye; just as well that Ashford was not the sort of school where attractive fourteen-year-olds were courted by older boys.

The teams devoured almost the last ounce of food and the visiting master rose to collect his group, hoping against experience that no one was going to be sick in the bus on the way home. He packed his boys in quickly to prevent everyone getting a cold, and smiled in farewell to the pretty Miss Gardener, who was carrying two substantial tea-pots back to some fastness. As the bus pulled out he looked back to see the home team move *en masse* to help her. Wouldn't have needed to tell them to do *that*, he thought, amused, and turned his attention to a scuffle at the back of the bus.

In the brightly lit kitchen, Mary Gardener encouraged the volunteer labour to eat the odd remaining sandwiches and to help her load the big washing-up machines.

'You'd better get back now, or your housemaster will be looking for you.' She watched indulgently as they scuffled at the door, biding her moment. 'David. David Banner.'

The fair boy, who had hung back, turned.

'Matron'll want a look at that eye – it's swelling right up. You wait and I'll take you over.'

Two of the older boys giggled enviously, digging David in the ribs, but she ignored the by-play, telling them sharply to get on back, now. They clattered out, and she waited for the sound of their voices to die away. 'Come over here, David, and I'll take a look. Might save bothering Matron. Here, under the light.'

The boy came over slowly, watching her, and she waited, unmoving, till he stopped close to her and looked down at her.

'You're too tall for me,' she said calmly, looking up at him. 'You'll need to sit down.'

Checked, he found a chair and sat, lifting his chin self-consciously, the fair skin reddened with exercise and tea, and she moved round behind him and tilted his head firmly towards the light.

'It's only a bruise, come to look at it closely,' she said, consideringly. 'Nothing to do, really, except maybe put a cold flannel to it.'

The boy sat still, his head held gently in her hands, his heart thumping, but she moved away quietly and came back with a cloth wrung out in cold water which she pressed to the swelling above his eye, standing close to him so that any movement would bring him into contact with her. He sat frozen in self-consciousness, breathing in the soft, pleasant smell of her, very conscious of the tension between his legs.

'Better?'

'Mm,' he said, too self-conscious to look at her, but she tipped his chin with her finger and he found himself looking into her eyes. She looked back at him straight and he waited, heart thumping, but determined not to blink. She smiled slowly and, taking her time, bent to him and kissed him lightly on the swollen patch above the eye. He clutched at her clumsily but held on, and she smiled. 'What about a proper kiss, then?' He pulled her on to his knee awkwardly, and wrapped his arms round her and kissed her, missing her mouth, then finding it, in a long minute of pure pleasure. She broke free, and he looked at her helplessly, not knowing what to do next, but unwilling to let go of the warm, soft body.

'Would you like to?'

'Oh yes. Oh. Yes, please.'

'Come on then.' She disentangled herself gently, and took his hand, and led him through to the small room where a boy after sustaining a minor injury during games would be put to rest until the master in charge had time to deal with him. It was sparsely furnished with two beds and smelt of gym-shoes. 'We can't put the light on. But we don't need it, do we?'

The boy gulped. 'I never have before.'

She stopped to hold him to her, pressing the whole length of her body against him, and he folded his arms round her like a drowning man.

'It's lovely. And you're ready, aren't you?' She pressed her stomach against his and he drew breath sharply and bent to kiss her.

'Here. Take my blouse off.'

He fumbled his way down the buttons, gathering confidence as he went, hearing her breathe in sharply as he touched her breasts, cautiously.

'And the bra. It does up at the back.'

'I know *that*.' His hands were at the clasp on her back, and he gasped as her breasts swung loose.

'Do you like them?'

'Oh, they're wonderful.' He was acutely conscious of his erection, and the whole of his back felt rigid with tension. She laughed softly, and took off his tie for him and slid her arms up his shirt. He reached hesitantly for the button at the back of her full skirt and, gaining confidence, undid it and the zip, so that it fell to her feet and she stood back from him to step out of it. Hands trembling and praying that he would not come where he stood, he unzipped his own grey flannel school trousers and pulled off his underpants, sighing with relief as the pressure on his cock eased. He gasped as he felt Mary's hands on it and managed with a violent effort to get control again.

'Mary . . .'

'Come and lie down.' She peeled off her light knickers and he drew a sharp breath at the sight of the dark patch of hair where her legs met, and followed her obediently on to the bed. He grasped luxuriously at her comfortable soft buttocks and buried his head in her breasts, then felt cautiously between her legs.

'Here, like this, see.' She guided his hand, and his fingers felt into the warm, wet place. 'You put him in there, now.' She turned on to her back and spread her legs for him, and he rose on his knees and approached carefully. He felt her hand on him, guiding him, and he cried out in excitement and pleasure, and then he was pushing at the entrance and was suddenly inside, where it was warm and embracing and wet. He moved, groaning with pleasure until an enormous embracing wave overtook everything else and he plunged frantically in a long spasm of ecstasy.

'Oh, God,' he said, into her cheek, lying on her, every bit of him throbbing still with pleasure. 'Sorry.'

'Well, it was your first time,' she said, breathless.

He moved hastily over on to one elbow, then stiffened in horror. 'Mary, I . . . we didn't . . . didn't use anything.'

'Well, I'm on the Pill, Davey. And you haven't been with anyone else, have you?'

'No. Never. Oh, Mary.' He embraced her in an ecstasy of pleasure and relief and wonder. 'It was easy. It was wonderful.' He kissed her and she laughed at him. 'Now you have to teach me what to do. For you, I mean.'

'I will. See, I need to come too. Give me your hand.' She guided him and he propped himself up on his side so he could watch her while he did as she directed. 'That's right, Davey. Oh, goodness me, what's happening here?'

'It'll wait,' he said confidently and bent his head to suck her nipples.

'Davey.' She was twisting towards him with pleasure, and with growing confidence he went on with what he was doing. He moved his hand between her legs, pushing them apart, and came into her again, knowing this time what he was doing, and felt her shudder and heave under him as he pushed in. A minute later he came again, triumphantly, arching his back in pleasure.

'Thank you,' he said soberly into her shoulder.

'You didn't need much help.' She was sounding resentful, he realized, puzzled.

'When can we do it again?' he asked hopefully, and she relaxed.

'We have to get up now or they'll be looking for you.'

'I haven't done my prep.' He had rolled off the bed in automatic obedience and was crouched on the floor looking for his underpants. He pulled them on and stood facing her, gazing down at her proudly as she did up her bra.

'Oh, Christ! Look at the time.' She scrambled into her clothes, urging him to hurry, but he was so happy and so pleased with himself that he was slow, and she finally pushed him out of the pavilion with one sock on and the other in his hand, so that he had to stop on the darkened field path to put on the other sock, and to have a long, luxurious pee.

A hundred miles away, a thin, anxious girl sat exhausted on her bed, looking out of the window, where day was reluctantly breaking, wondering whether she could last out until the end of this term. Every day had seemed long, but Thursdays stretched to eternity, each minute laden with some new misery. The old building which housed the Fourth Form boarders was endemically cold and draughty; it was a painful fight to get out of bed, and barely tolerable to wash in the freezing, shabby communal bathroom. Momentarily she longed for the bathroom at home which was hers and which had a lock, but stopped her thoughts at that point. She was here in this draughty hell after a year's planning and manoeuvring, at huge expense to her grandparents, and here she had to stay. She stood up carefully; she had grown five inches in the last year, and gone up six places in the gym line in the five months since she had arrived at Wanstead Abbey, and this spurt of growth was accompanied by exhaustion and a tendency to black-out if she got up too fast in the morning. She subsided again, warned by the faint ringing in her ears, and waited anxiously, listening to the breakfast bell tolling a hundred cold yards away. The three girls with whom she shared this cramped bedroom had gone, leaving her. She understood that she had offended against the canons by which they lived their life, by being so totally uninterested in the prospect of meeting the local boys' school. They were cold-shouldering her again today, giggling and refusing to speak to her directly.

The door opened on one of the Form Prefects, a solid, contained girl of her own age, an inch or so smaller than herself, unfashionably plump. 'Jennifer. You'll be late.'

'Sorry. I'm feeling dizzy.'

'Is it your period?'

There was only one girl in this class, Jennifer Redwood decided with respect, who could ask that question without giggling or becoming over-confidential. 'No, I haven't started,' she said, feeling a fundamental sense of relief at having someone to whom she could state, without shame, that at nearly fourteen she was behind her contemporaries in this crucial respect.

'Lucky you. I started at ten and it could not have been more of a nuisance, or more embarrassing. So, are you all right? Shall we go over together, or would you rather wait a bit? I have to go, I'm afraid.'

Jennifer's shoulders relaxed and she breathed in properly for the first time that morning. 'I have to stand up slowly.' She cautiously put her feet flat on the floor and stood up, gathering confidence.

'You probably have low blood pressure,' the dark girl said with interest. 'In which case you'll be fine after breakfast. And if this place had any pretensions to civilization you would get a cup of tea before you even tried to get out of bed.' The detached, confident, adult observation almost stopped Jennifer in her tracks, but as she followed the dark girl – Sofia – she felt a surge of hope. Outside of this awful place there was a real world which she would inhabit again. She shut down hard on pursuing that thought and hurried to keep up with Sofia, tongue-tied but wishing desperately that the walk to breakfast were longer. It was still dark and foggy, and she coughed in the raw February morning.

'I can't seem to get warm here,' she ventured.

'I know. My father, who is a doctor, says that cold air in the lungs when you're straight out of bed is a bad idea.'

'But he sent you here,' Jennifer protested, feeling she had not had a straightforward conversation with anyone in the six months she had been at Wanstead Abbey, but Sofia was neither offended nor defensive.

'We live in the country, you see, and he didn't like the local school. Mum was here, and it is academic.'

Jennifer Redwood, who, to add to her miseries, was struggling in both maths and English, agreed, grimly, that it was.

'Was your mother here?' Sofia asked.

'No. My grandmother on my father's side.' She hesitated. 'My father is dead.'

'Oh, I'm sorry.' It was said matter-of-factly, but Jennifer felt tears behind her eyes. They had reached the door of the big dining-room, and she waited resignedly for Sofia to go through and join the little group who were waving to her. 'Would you like to come and sit with us?' Sofia said, with that courtesy which belonged to an older, quieter generation.

'Oh, yes, please,' Jennifer said, and blushed scarlet at this gaucherie, but Sofia looked mildly pleased.

'I always have a decent breakfast,' she said placidly, so that Jennifer, permanently hungry and the recipient of much snide teenage sniping, could pile her plate high as well. She was introduced around Sofia's group and acknowledged with the same slightly old-fashioned politeness, and ate her breakfast luxuriously, expanding in the warmth and the unexpected, sudden matter-of-fact friendliness with which she was being treated. They had asked her what she preferred to be called, why she was here and whether she had brothers and sisters, appearing to be genuinely interested in the answers and not to feel the need to comment or compete or mock. It was a different world, and her heart sank as breakfast ended, but the group swept her along with them and she entered the classroom in good heart, momentarily undaunted by the knowledge that she had written a poor essay on last week's poem. She took her place in the third row, close to the back, three rows away from Sofia's gang; her essay was waiting for her, marked 'C + – please see me' for the third time that term. She looked at it despairingly, resting her head on her hand to hide the tears.

'What did you get, Jens?' Sofia was somehow beside her and she showed her the comment wordlessly.

'Well, it's a very C+ sort of poem,' Sofia said calmly. 'I wouldn't waste any more effort on it.'

'What did *you* get?' Jennifer managed to ask, warmth spreading through her spine at the casual dismissal of one of the more famous works of literature, and the use of her father's diminutive.

'She didn't mark it. I wrote a different poem.'

Sofia's group were laughing, and Jennifer looked at them cautiously and saw that they were laughing not *at* her, but in pleased anticipation of whatever Sofia had done.

'Read it, Sofia.'

'I couldn't bear to, but you can see it, after Jens.' She started to unpack her books, dumping in front of Jennifer a single sheet written in her large, slanting, left-handed script.

> Time, you old gipsy man,
> *Do* go away,
> The grass is all *gone*
> Where your caravan lay . . .

It started briskly and went on for eight irritable stanzas. Jennifer read it three times, for pleasure, with other girls pressing easily on her shoulder to read it too, anxiety, competition and teenage quarrelsomeness forgotten. The English mistress had not given it a mark, but there was a large single tick in red at the bottom of the page, and Jennifer understood in a expanding flash that the grown-up academic world was not immutably hostile and impenetrable. The English mistress arrived. Jennifer passed Sofia's paper back reluctantly, and set herself with a sudden access of confidence to cope with *Romantic Poetry of the Nineteenth Century*.

Five weeks later it was the end of term and Jens had imperceptibly become a core member of Sofia's little group. There had been four of them, held together primarily by affection for Sofia, and now there were five. Jens had had a little difficulty with Louise, a tall, insecure child, the only girl in a family of brothers, who had resented Sofia's bringing her into the group. But Louise was not an ill-tempered girl and Sofia in any case raised the moral tone of any group in a way rare and welcome in the affairs of teenage girls. The only daughter of a well-off, eccentric country doctor, she had been brought up in a dated, calm home, more reminiscent of the thirties than the frenetic sixties, and was not expected to bring home boys, take drugs, or go to pop concerts. Those of her contemporaries who were not baffled by her found her utterly restful. So, curiously, did the school staff. Sofia did not exactly break rules, she simply questioned them in a way that did not seem threatening. In reply to Sofia's gentle inquiry as to whether it might not be more rational to allow everyone to return to the dormitories after breakfast to 'attend to nature's other demands rather than have adolescent girls fidget through the first lesson, dying for a pee and picking cornflakes out of our teeth', authority had laughed and yielded. Similarly, Sofia's designation of the indigestible porridge as 'a character-forming challenge to which I am sure we will all rise' had somehow resulted in this dish vanishing from the menu.

In the hall the group were waiting, bags packed, for the school bus to take them to London, and Sofia and Jennifer for car-borne parents.

'Dad will be late,' Sofia said cheerfully, settling down with a book. 'He'll have stopped to see a patient. Is your stepfather coming, Jens?'

'I expect so.' Jennifer felt the familiar painful twinge in her stomach; she had been getting this reaction in the last week, and had, without realizing it, been increasingly irritable. The group considered her silently, and Sofia looked up from her book, but decided to leave it.

'Sofia French.' The second games mistress, bouncing with youth and pent-up energy, clipboard clasped to her non-existent bosom, peered into the throng.

'Good heavens,' Sofia said, packing her book. 'Come on, let's see what the old man is driving this time.'

The group clattered to the door and Jennifer hung back to

see the contained Sofia swept into the arms of a great bear of a man, rather older than she had expected, with thick, untidy grey hair cut *en brosse*. He swept the other three impartially into the same embrace, shouting greetings, totally unselfconscious, then advanced, beaming, on Jennifer, hand outstretched in welcome, tie pulled askew and jacket half off.

'Heard all about you,' he assured her, in a voice that carried down the hall. 'Knew your father – lot younger than me, of course, but my eldest sister was a friend of your granny's. How's your mother?'

Jennifer, dazed, was trying to tell him, overcome by the size of him and the mass of information, when she saw behind his shoulder her stepfather's big Jaguar slide into the car park, driven bad-temperedly but stylishly. She watched him, stomach clenching, as he stamped up the steps, balding, assured, expensively dressed, and she realized with a shock that she was not far off his height. She opened her mouth to introduce him but Sofia's father, quick for such a big man, was there first, booming a greeting and extending a vast hand. 'William French. Father of one of this lot here.' The wave encompassed them all.

'Joshua Logan. Jenny's stepfather. How are you, pet?' He reached to kiss her, which she endured and looked up to see William French watching them.

'We were hoping Jens would come and stay with us for a week or so if you can spare her,' he said easily. 'Huge house, lots of room, always like to have an extra girl. Make them do the garden. Can't do that with boys.' He scowled theatrically round the group who laughed in recognition of a familiar joke.

'We'll all come,' Louise said confidently.

''Course you shall, if your parents say you can. Bring your overalls or whatever you girls wear to weed a gravel path.' He patted Jennifer's shoulder. 'Just ring us up.' He swept Sofia off, the group following to the car, leaving Jennifer on the steps gazing longingly after him. If only her mother had found someone like William French. The problem was, of course, that people like William married young and stayed married;

31

they weren't available to a widow in her mid-thirties. It was men like Joshua (she had persistently refused to call him Dad, Josh, Jo or indeed anything at all other than his given name, which he disliked, in full) who were around, having been divorced by his first wife and no wonder.

He had, she supposed, looked all right when he first turned up, carefully escorting her mother through the door and demurely accepting coffee and an introduction to the bony, anxious eleven-year-old she had then been. He certainly didn't look any worse than the other suitors her pretty mother had attracted and, indeed, a good deal better than the ill-at-ease married accountant who was trying to get up the courage to change wives, or the very much older deputy head of the local PE college. At eleven, two years after her father's death, she had accepted that her mother would have to remarry. There had been no money, that was one of the problems; her father had got cancer when he was thirty and had not been able to buy any more life insurance, so they had never been able to move out of the small flat they were in. Or, as she now understood, have the further children her mother had longed for. And brilliant though he was, and although they had saved hard, there were limits to what a man of thirty-six, mortally ill since he was thirty, had been able to achieve financially. All this had been made more difficult by her mother's absolute lack of any qualification, which would have enabled her to get a well-paid job, and her objection to taking any job that meant that her daughter would have to come home to an empty house. It was just one of the many ironies in the situation that for a pubescent girl no empty house could have held anything like the terrors of a house full of Joshua.

But Joshua had his own well-established contracting business, was apparently the innocent party in a recent divorce since his wife had left him for another man, and very much wanted more children to replace the two his first wife had taken with her. Her mother, by then thirty-seven, had admitted to feeling time going away from her; Joshua, well able to provide and wanting very much to do so, a suitable five years older than her and blatantly, embarrassingly, sexually attracted, looked like a good idea. Jennifer had been cautiously adjusting herself to the prospect of sharing her mother with a new man and probably with babies, weighing in the balance her mother's obvious happiness against the load of responsibility that slid from her own shoulders, and the chance of a bigger house and a larger room for herself.

Only it had not worked like that. The first year was all right, just. Joshua was rather given to wet kisses, and wanting her to sit on his knee, but she had evaded these demands without much problem, just as all the local girls avoided similar demands from the tall, haunted man who ran the greengrocery. But after a year her mother was four months pregnant, and having a bad time of it physically, sick all the time in a way she had not been with Jennifer, as she tearfully assured all who would listen. Then it started; Joshua took to staying out, or when he was at home would corner her, carefully and furtively, squeezing her waist or stroking her bottom, demanding a kiss in the morning and when she came back from school. She had not known what to do, and there was no one she could tell; her mother was sickly and distressed and in love with Joshua, and she loved her and would willingly have died before indicating the problem. She took to spending long hours at school, but there was no close friend; she had gone on to a big, competitive, all-girls North London grammar school and, in the distress of her father's death, had not made new friends. Her primary school friends were scattered; Paul Seles had vanished, and the rest of the gang, to whom she had never been so close, had been firmly discouraged by her mother, who had always hated having the children of Paddington's minor criminals in the house.

She had endured until Christopher was born, when the situation had improved sharply. She realized why, painfully, when she found Joshua coming out of the bedroom that had been allocated to the young maternity nurse who was there for six weeks to get Christopher started off properly. Joshua had seen her too, but had banked, correctly, on her silence and had left her alone. He and her mother had gone back to sharing a bedroom shortly after the girl left and *that* had been all right for several months. Then it had started again and she had known she must get out. So she had gone to see her Redwood grandparents, pocketing her pride, and slandering the reputation of the excellent day school she was at, in order to get herself off to boarding school, allegedly in the interests of her academic future. This fiction was based on fact; what with grief for her own father and the nagging terror of Joshua, she was falling behind at school, so her grandparents had rallied to the middle-class colours and were making the substantial sacrifice of savings necessary to get her to O-level and the first rung of a conventional future. So she was safe, at least in term time, her mother was happy and well and contented, and if she could just get through a week of these holidays she now had a friend, and a refuge.

She turned reluctantly to find Joshua's bright brown round eyes fixed on her.

'You've grown again,' he said, putting an arm round her. 'And you've filled out a bit.' She pulled away but his arm tightened. 'Your mother's looking forward to seeing you.'

'Why isn't she here?'

'She was a bit tired this morning, so I said I'd come by myself and get you.' He gave her a bold sideways look and she realized, with a sick feeling, that he was pleased with himself, freshly showered and bouncing with confidence. She waited, sullen and anxious, longing for her mother but dreading the car ride.

'Doing well, are you, pet?' he asked.

'Not very, but it's getting better.'

'You should have let me send you to St Aloysius.'

'This is a better school.'

'Not much to look at.' Joshua stopped, the better to size up the building. He caught her eye. 'Don't worry, Jenny, I'm not planning to buy it.'

She stopped herself from observing that the school's trustees were there to prevent people like Joshua getting anywhere near the place. It had occurred to her, in a small moment of revelation, that she liked the businessman Joshua; careful, decisive and reliable, and if he owned the place it would be comfortable and the plumbing would work. He took her bags impatiently and shut them into the boot, then saw her into the front seat, where she pulled the seat-belt round her, forestalling his help.

He settled in his seat and turned to her. 'Give us a kiss then.'

She proffered her cheek but he leant over and kissed her on the lips, his hand on her right breast.

'Growing up, aren't you?' he said, the bright brown eyes intent and rapacious, watching her as she sat flushed and miserable in the familiar trap of not being able to defend herself against her mother's husband and sole source of financial support. He gave her breast a farewell nip, and withdrew to his side of the car, fastening himself in, openly shifting the crotch of his trousers, while she prayed that there would be no traffic lights in the hundred miles to London.

'Seles. You're one of the London group, aren't you, Paul?'

'Sir.' The boy got up slowly from his position, sprawled in front of an inadequate fire in the reception area.

'Well, you need to get outside. The bus is here, and if it leaves without you, you can walk it. You don't want to stay with us *that* much, do you?'

'No, sir.' The pause for consideration before the statement was just this side of insolence, and Roger Caldwell, the Deputy Warden, gave him a careful look, wondering what had soured the day for this lad. He had taught at Wellington before he had come to this job at an LCC boarding school for 150 boys between the ages of eleven and eighteen, all of whom had been deemed to be in need of boarding education. Some had no family, but most had been snatched from the bosom of criminal or non-functioning families, and all were there as an expression of hope that the cycle of criminality or poverty or abuse could be broken. He had come, twenty years ago, because he shared this hope, and in this time had found it broadly justified. Most of these boys flourished, removed from their criminal associates and teeming, restless households with only the streets as a playground. Their energies were diverted to games or destructive but socially harmless activities like damming streams or shooting rocks with an airgun, which did the rocks no harm at all. Most days only their accents distinguished them from the equivalent age group at a public school. But among their number were always some violent ones; you tried to keep them, of course, rather than throw them back, but this term they had a few too many of the lads needing very special attention, and the atmosphere had been very tense. And now Paul Seles was obviously working up for trouble.

'We'll see you back in three weeks' time. Don't do anything I wouldn't do.'

Half a dozen hoarse adolescent voices suggested that this left them a fairly wide scope, which Roger Caldwell received with a grin. He shepherded his flock outside where the buses waited, checking addresses.

'Paul, Islington, right?'

'Blackstock Road. Just by Highbury Barn.'

The poor lad lived in a children's home when he wasn't at school, of course. Not much of a life, though better than being brutally beaten every other day. But he was tense and anxious; perhaps there was something wrong at the Home.

'How's it going, then?' he asked the boy, as they waited in the sun.

'Orright, I suppose.' He waited patiently; the boy had something to say. 'It's a lovely place here. I mean, posh, and there's space. I got my own room.'

'Well, when you're old enough you can work in the country, or in a country town. Get the space that way.'

The boy was Hungarian by birth, he remembered, wondering if he had lived in the country there.

'Yeah, I'd like a house like this, though.'

Roger Caldwell gazed silently at Woolverstone Hall, which had been an ostentatious nineteenth-century mansion, built by an industrial millionaire. The original house had had fifty bedrooms and supplementary housing had grown up around it, ranging from converted stable blocks to a neat row of ugly little houses, built for resident staff. Under a cold April sky with blowing clouds the house looked imposing but hardly comfortable or charming.

'Bit big,' he ventured, not wanting to discourage confidence from this heavy, clumsy adolescent. He had had Paul Seles in his English and history classes for the last two terms and had been impressed by him. On a good day you could see a quick mind and a wide-ranging intelligence there, and an unusual ability to see one thing in terms of another, the mark of an academic boy. But on a bad day, when the demons of his childhood clasped at him, the lad was unteachable, locked in himself, emerging only to commit some act of mindless, tiresome violence, which caused endless trouble every time. It was a very distressing history; he had been lifted from his home at ten years old under a court order, and the cousin in charge of him jailed, and it was clear that he had been seriously and continually beaten for six years. But there were lads with worse stories here; Paul at least had had four years with a loving mother, whereas some of the boys had literally been born to abuse, sexual as well as physical. Patient, slow therapy had made him easier to deal with, but the onset of adolescence had set the whole process back again. Roger Caldwell, professionally as well as naturally optimistic, hoped that in six months' time when the hormones had settled down a bit this lad's natural and considerable intellectual gifts would flourish.

'Yeah, you wouldn't need all this. But it's nice. Specially in the summer.'

'Yes, it is,' Roger Caldwell agreed tranquilly, and felt the boy relax fractionally.

He determinedly ignored the intent profiles of the group at the bus door, heads in a circle, bent on some mischief. It was probably only an adult magazine or a packet of fags that was receiving such detailed attention. Paul was kicking the bus tyres, repeatedly. Roger Caldwell suggested they might walk a bit, save them freezing to bloody death, and was relieved to see the boy laugh and turn explosively on his heel.

'I don't want to go back to the Home,' he said flatly, after they had walked once round the bus. 'I wanted to go somewhere with a family but there wasn't one.'

There never was when you needed one, the man reflected. Curious that the boy retained a slight foreign accent, having arrived in England as a baby. He'd been brought up by Hungarians, of course, but he did not seem to have adjusted in three years away.

'I'll have another try at Social Services, Paul. I agree with you about the Home, you need something different.' They were crossing the car park.

'I'm a bit old now for a family. I'm going to have a flat when I'm eighteen.'

It was, of course, more likely to be an impersonal room in a hostel, but there was no need gratuitously to discourage him, let the world do that. It was hard for boys who had been carefully looked after and coached through exams here when they found themselves without any of this kind of support, expected to get jobs and find their own accommodation. No middle-class family would expect that of their kids; he himself had none but he was watching with sympathy and amusement his brother's eldest at twenty being patiently levered towards the edge of the nest. No institutional Social Services structure could provide that sort of help, which was why Woolverstone Hall would try to push the more vulnerable of the pupils into somewhere like the Armed Services where they were looked after. But the Services were picky about who they took these days, and the lads who needed it often weren't accepted; in that context it was impossible not to regret the passing of National Service which had provided support, re-education and a home for two years for many a rootless, vulnerable teenager.

'Thought at all about the Services? The Army?'

'Not really. Don't want all that bullshit.'

'Perhaps not the Services, then. The advantage is you get your living while you get a training. But you've got a while yet before you need worry.'

They rounded the corner of the bus; the conspiratorial group had all lit up and a drift of smoke hung in the still air over their heads.

'That's your bus.' Roger Caldwell hesitated. 'Come and talk to me next term, will you? We've got plenty of time, but we'd better start thinking about what you want to do. Have a good time.' He nodded and turned away, unable to suppress the thought of the Home's holidays, featuring bored staff, dying to get off, and far too much TV. You can't save them all, he reminded himself, and he desperately needed the two weeks in Wales he had arranged for himself.

CHAPTER THREE

July 1971

'Shall I ask Mrs Banner to come in now?'

The headmaster hesitated, but decided there was no point in trying to postpone this interview further. The mother of three pupils, David, Michael and Thomas, was a paying customer, and for that reason, if no other, had every right to his time. 'Give me a minute,' he suggested.

Mrs Banner had rung up in an agitated state, his secretary had reported, and he needed time to think if there was any obvious clue to her troubles.

Commander Banner was in the Navy, no, hang on, he had resigned the year before and gone to an industrial job. No trouble with fees; the Navy had paid for all three boys until a year ago, then cheques had arrived from Commander Banner on the first day of term, the last day of grace before the school charged interest, so *that* was all right. The boys were doing quite well – David rather better than that, nothing special academically, but likely to get seven respectable O-levels in the exams he had just finished. He was, however, the best all-round games player the school had produced in years. Forward for his age, he recalled drily, but then Mary Gardener had had that effect on several of his young men. He spared Mary a thought; a neat solution had been achieved there with no bones broken, and a colleague running a preparatory school near Mary's calf-country had acquired an excellent junior matron who had settled down and was just about to marry a fellow staff member. Better for her than teenage boys, not that she had done any real harm to David Banner, starting him only a year or so early on his way, and indeed with those blond good looks an interest in women saved trouble in an all-male school. Michael Banner, on the other hand, aged eleven, was reported by the headmaster of the junior school to be something of a problem; young for his age, some trouble with bullying, both as victim and as perpetrator, work and marks all over the place – a middle child, of course – with Thomas, aged nine and a half, rather close at his heels. Thomas, it seemed, was another David, heedless, noisy and a superb games player who was in all the under-eleven teams, though fully eighteen months younger than most of his team-mates.

He pressed the bell and rose to greet his visitor, sustaining a shock as he did so. He remembered Mrs Banner as a smart, confident, rather noisy mother, pleased with herself and her three good-looking sons and handsome husband. The woman before him seemed to have both shrunk and aged. She was carelessly dressed, with a stain on the front of her demure, round-collared blouse, and her skirt was crumpled and the hook on the side not properly done up. She sank into a chair and blew her nose, loudly, obviously uninterested in any impression she might be making.

'I had to come,' she said, with a final sniff, stowing the handkerchief in her sleeve and looking at him defiantly. 'You see, he's left us. My husband, I mean.'

The headmaster, who had been expecting this, or something like it, from the moment she had walked in, made a noise expressive of sympathy and inquiry. This was an increasingly familiar scene for all senior teachers these days: a parent, sometimes alone, sometimes accompanied by a hangdog spouse, explaining with undertones of rage and bafflement that they had been abandoned and, of course, the children must be told. His heart always ached for his charges, who invariably wanted passionately, whatever the history or the facts, for their parents to stay together. And why ever couldn't they, he thought, momentarily furious. Why have children if you are going to put them through this? But there could be no point in saying this to the pathetic, angry creature in front of him, since the trouble was clearly not of her making. So he was gentle and sympathetic, causing her to burst into further floods of tears over the coffee and tell him more than he wanted to know. She had not had an easy time; David had apparently been followed in the family by a longed-for daughter, who had died in infancy, a cot death. A miscarriage – rather late – had followed before Mickey had finally arrived successfully.

'You must have been thrilled,' the headmaster said, hoping to keep her mind on happier days.

'Patrick was over the moon, and we were *both* pleased when we found Thomas was on the way.' She blew her nose again, while he noted automatically that she had not been as pleased as her husband about the long-awaited Mickey.

'Well, Thomas must be a great pleasure to you; a lively boy, by all accounts.'

'Yes. He turned up very quickly after Mickey, of course.'

And Mickey had found that difficult, he thought. Mrs Banner started to cry again, and he waited, embarrassed but steady, while considering the next problem. Banner was out of the Navy, but he was making a good salary; hopefully this was not going to be difficult.

Mrs Banner managed, finally, to stop gulping and weeping and took a substantial mouthful of her coffee, heedless of the fact that she spilt a bit on her skirt. 'And he's lost his job,' she said baldly, fresh tears brimming. 'Oh dear, I'm so sorry.' She pulled her handkerchief from her bag and blew her nose again. 'This . . . this girl was his secretary, and, of course, she's lost her job too. So there's no money, and *he* says he can't find next term's fees, and the boys will have to go to a day school.' The last words were a wail of distress, and this time the headmaster's sympathies were engaged.

It would be appallingly disruptive for the boys to lose their school at the same time as a no doubt much-loved father. In the old days it had usually been possible to find a scholarship for a year or so for a boy whose father had died or gone bust, or vanished, but increasingly, as after the Divorce Law Reform

42

Act people felt free to leave each other with the children inadequately provided for, these cosy arrangements were no longer possible. There was little hope that anything could be done for three boys, already on reduced fees.

'Perhaps the Navy would help?' he ventured, following that train of thought. He had agreed, a little reluctantly, to maintain the discount originally demanded by Her Majesty's Government.

'I don't suppose so. They made it very clear that there are no further claims – I remember Patrick signing all the forms ... and it's not as if I'm a widow.' She groped for her handkerchief again while the headmaster silently agreed with her. Widow was a much better position than divorcee from which to tackle the Navy.

'I could try,' he volunteered unhopefully.

'Oh, would you?' She stared at him, as if at her saviour, and he sighed inwardly; the stuffing seemed to have leaked from her with her husband's desertion, but she must be rallied for her children's sake.

'We need to think about telling your boys,' he suggested, gently emphasizing the personal pronoun.

'Patrick said I should do it, he's too busy trying to get another job.' She examined her handkerchief. 'That's not true; he's busy trying to get his firm to take him back. He thinks it's unfair to have fired him.'

'Usually they just fire the woman in question,' the headmaster agreed drily.

'Oh, *that* wasn't why they fired him. He's always had ... well ... the odd little *excursion*, you know. He was rude to someone they were trying to sell to. He didn't like being told he was wrong.'

Not a useful characteristic for a naval officer, the headmaster reflected, and indeed this cast a new light on Banner's departure from the Service. Conscientiously he considered his charges; young David didn't particularly welcome criticism, but he took it. Michael now, he recalled uneasily from his discussions that morning, was said to add to his own difficulties by being

43

totally unable to receive criticism, however well meant, alternately collapsing into tears or hitting out. However, no one appeared to have anything to say against Thomas. He returned his attention to Mrs Banner and steered her to the question of telling the boys – how, where, and whether all together or separately. It took a patient half-hour to organize her and he passed a note to his secretary to get the Deputy Head to take the general studies class which he normally enjoyed teaching, deciding that his duty lay here rather than to the Lower Sixth.

'So, while you talk to David, I'll get Mrs Smith to round up Michael and Thomas from the Junior School, yes? Where is David Banner, Mrs Smith? No, he'll be second set maths, I'm sure. Will you ask Mr Judd to excuse him, please, and send him over?' He did not need to tell her not to explain to young Banner that his mother was here; better by far that the boy should spend an anxious five minutes examining his conscience to decide why the headmaster wanted him than that he should have to run over in the sure knowledge that only disaster could have brought his mother here in the middle of a school week.

'Could you possibly stay with me? Just for the first five minutes?' Mrs Banner said, suddenly desperate, and he agreed, feeling that she should not have to confess failure to a nearly grown-up son without the support of a man. If her husband could not face it, then it fell to him, *in loco parentis*; it was part of his job.

He looked up to see David Banner in the doorway; the lad seemed to have grown again, but he had the athlete's lightness of foot, and he had not heard him come down the corridor. The boy stood, transfixed, eyes on his mother, the fair skin beneath the bright reddish-blond hair flushed pink.

'Mum? Is it Dad?'

His mother rose and cast herself into his arms and the boy looked frantically over her head.

'Has he had an accident?'

'No, no,' the headmaster said quickly. 'No, your father's all right.'

'He's left us, Davey,' Mrs Banner said, weeping ungracefully.

'He's gone off with his secretary, I'm afraid.' She looked finally at her son's face and made a huge, visible effort to pull herself together. 'I'm sorry, darling. I wanted him to come too, but he wouldn't.'

'Sit down, David, and have some coffee,' the headmaster intervened.

The boy had gone from pink to white and he sat and drank the coffee without acknowledgement.

'He's also lost his job.' Mrs Banner had recovered herself, blessedly. She straightened her cardigan and, with a frown, did up the errant hook and eye at the side of her skirt. She sat up, straight-backed, and accepted another coffee. 'So I have had to say to the headmaster that he may not be able to find the fees for you three next year. I'm very sorry, Davey.'

The boy's face was wooden with shock and the headmaster quietly poured more coffee, loading in sugar. He waited while mother and son watched each other.

'Why?' David, flushing, asked baldly.

'Why did he leave or why did he lose his job?' his mother asked sharply.

'Both.'

'He went off with his secretary – and he's done that before – but he lost his job because he quarrelled with someone. As usual.'

David and the headmaster both winced, but she was implacable. 'And this secretary is a lot younger than me, if that's an answer.'

The headmaster cleared his throat warningly, but the other two ignored him.

'Well, I'm not letting him mess up my life. I'm going to stay here for A-levels.'

'I really don't know how.' Mrs Banner, the headmaster observed, fascinated, had been quite restored by this tussle with her son; she was sitting up properly, tears banished and colour in her cheeks.

'I must.' The boy was openly desperate.

'I think you may be trying to rush ahead, David,' the

45

headmaster said in warning, measured tones. 'I'm sorry you've all had this shock. Your mother would like you all home for the weekend, and that's time enough to think about the future. Your brothers will be here shortly.'

'Mickey,' David Banner said, and glanced at his mother. It was an uncomfortably calculating adult look, of inquiry and warning. There was a light tap on the door and a young woman teacher appeared shepherding in the rest of the Banner family. Mickey, a tall, dark blond, frail creature, went straight to his mother, barely acknowledging the headmaster, and kissed her longingly. Thomas, almost exactly the same height as Mickey, but with David's strong shoulders and reddish hair, threw himself unself-consciously into her arms, leaving Mickey to edge over to David, looking up at him anxiously.

'Mum.'

'Yes, sorry.' She disengaged herself from Thomas gently and told both the younger boys of the disaster, doing it better this time, tempering the wind to their youth, while the headmaster sat and watched sombrely. It was at least an hour later that he finally managed to shepherd the family out of his office and into the custody of his secretary in a small ante-room, so that he could manage to arrive, just in time, to take current affairs with the Fourth Form.

Jennifer Redwood sat at breakfast diagonally opposite her stepfather, as far away from him as she could achieve. Next to her, crowing contentedly in his high-chair, was her brother, Christopher, now nearly two. Normally she was cheered by his presence, but this morning a boil was all too obviously forming on her left cheek in addition to the clutch of teenage spots disfiguring her chin, and she had other reasons for despondency.

'Come on, Chrissie,' she said irritably, hunched forward over the pain in her stomach which was bad enough to make her feel sick. At fifteen years old, two years after she had gone to Wanstead Abbey she was five foot seven, three inches taller than her mother and a scant inch smaller than her stepfather, but her periods had only started six months ago. Presumably her system could only do one thing at a time as William French had suggested, when, six months before and driven by anxiety, she had managed to ask him. She had been so surprised that she had laughed before listening carefully to his patient, unembarrassed explanation.

'It's the *last* manifestation of puberty, Jens. Everything else, hair, breasts, all that happens first and that's all in place, isn't it? Yes, well, your periods will turn up one of these days and then you'll probably wish they hadn't.'

She had kissed him, with simple relief. From the first term at Wanstead Abbey she had managed to spend over half the school holidays with the Frenches, who were unquestioningly welcoming of all of Sofia's friends, and William had become the missing man in her life. Her periods had started a month after that conversation, giving her considerable trouble, just as William had predicted. They had, however, one distinct advantage which could not be admitted even to William; pale, spotty and blatantly adolescent, she seemed momentarily to have succeeded in discouraging the attentions of her mother's husband. It was less necessary to avoid all encounters with him, and the advent of her periods had enabled her to insist to her mother that she must have a lock on her bedroom door. No one was to be allowed in, she had insisted, she would clean her room herself, and her mother had given way, reluctantly, in the teeth of her determination.

It was just before she had got away to Wanstead Abbey, when her mother was pregnant with Christopher and had gone to bed early, she had been standing in front of the mirror in her room, stripped to her knickers examining her developing breasts, when her door had opened silently. She stared at it, stupidly, hands clasped over the small soft swellings of flesh, and Joshua had sidled in, his bright brown eyes feverish and unfocused.

'You're lovely,' he had said breathlessly, and then seized her, hands caressing her bottom, feeling inside her knickers. She had fought him off after a moment's bewildered paralysis but his hands seemed to be everywhere, inside her knickers, pushing into her and on her breasts, and she found herself pushed towards the bed so that it caught her behind the knees and she fell back, Joshua on top of her. He took his left hand off her breast and fumbled at his waist, and she felt the fleshy pressure of him so that everything she had half understood snapped suddenly into place. As if someone had spoken to her, she had gathered the clarity and the sense to scream the house down, waking her mother to whom she had explained apologetically that she was sure someone had been trying to get into her room. She had sat in the safety of her mother's arms, watching Joshua check the doors and explain, flustered, that it must have been a bad dream, refusing to meet her eye. He had understood that message and she had had reasonable peace for weeks, but since then she had never gone to bed in her own home without dragging a chest of drawers across her door. Joshua had not been permanently discouraged; he still took every opportunity to feel her breasts or crowd her on the stairs or seize a wet kiss, knowing somehow that she would not be able to tell her mother about any of it. It felt most days like a guerilla war, fought against a determined, cruel and cunning opponent, and it exhausted her. She spent as much time away as she could, but the long school holidays were a problem; there were limits to the amount of time she could spend either with her grandparents or with the Frenches, and in any case, she thought resentfully and miserably, she missed her home.

She looked across the table at her mother, who was watching Chris with obvious affection. Her stomach crunched as she thought of the simple impossibility of destroying that happiness, as she would have to in order to get herself back into her house. She got up to go to her room; she was due to leave for the Frenches early the next day and she had not yet packed, or rather had not repacked from her stay with her grandparents. She needed to hang up the tidy clothes necessary for a visit to the quiet, ugly, cavernous flat in Worthing, and substitute the ancient jeans and sweaters that all Sofia's friends wore all the time. William French was going to drive her back to school with Sofia a week later and her heart lifted at the thought of him, large, untidy, deeply academic, interested equally in all the children his daughter brought home, and fundamentally his own man. She had slowly come to understand that the Frenches were rich by middle-class standards. Trusts for children and grandchildren set up by Victorian forebears underpinned their life-style and explained why William, who had trained obligingly as a doctor, because he felt he ought to be useful, was able to live in a sparsely inhabited patch of Hampshire with not very many patients. Not that he was a bad doctor, careful, learned, patient and conscious of where his knowledge stopped, but he was deeply interested in his wife and daughter and did not want to be kept from their company.

Jennifer was smiling as she went upstairs until she understood, nerves instantly alert, that she had walked into a trap. Joshua had slid quietly out of the breakfast-room after her and was crowding her in the corner of the stairs. She tried to squeeze past him, working her way round the walls, but he was too quick and she felt his hand between her legs on the seam of her jeans. She jerked away, miserable, furious and self-conscious about the sanitary pad which was frustrating his groping fingers.

'Why do you do that when you know I hate it?' she found the courage to hiss at him, glancing downstairs to make sure her mother was safely ensconced in the breakfast-room. His swift look downstairs mirrored hers; it was as if they were in a dreadful conspiracy together, and she felt sick and helpless.

'You don't hate it. You just won't relax,' he said, his eyes very bright and watching her mouth as he reached for her again, and she saw, again, that this was a version of bullying, the tormentor assuring a smaller boy that he would like being beaten. For a moment her head cleared of anxiety and confusion and she pushed his hand coolly away.

'I just don't like it with you,' she said sharply. 'Excuse me, please.'

He grabbed her by the upper arms and shook her, and she realized she had hit home and was frightened. The pain in her upper arms was acute and she was helpless.

'Mum!' she called. 'Mum! I can't find anything.'

'Coming, darling,' she heard her mother say, and Joshua released her with a final painful squeeze of the biceps muscles so that she could run downstairs and stick closely by her mother's side until Joshua slammed his way off to work. She stood in the kitchen, listening to the echoes of the house, watching Chrissie picking his way into the saucepan cupboard and hauling pans on to the floor with a satisfying crash.

'He gets into everything. Just like you at that age.' Her mother, pretty in the pink and white housecoat Joshua had chosen for her, bent hastily to remove a heavy frying-pan from his ambit.

Jennifer's arms ached and her throat swelled. 'Mum?'

'What, darling?'

'Would you mind if I went to the Frenches today rather than tomorrow? If they can have me.'

'Oh, darling. Joshua is taking us out to dinner. It's his last night with you before term. You're always with the Frenches.'

'Mum,' Jennifer said, desperate, 'you know Joshua and I don't get on.'

'Jennifer!' Her mother sat down, outraged. 'He's devoted to you. He'd pay your school fees if your grandparents didn't. In fact, I think he'll have to soon, the old things are getting very worried about money, particularly with Grandad Redwood's sight getting so bad. Jennifer, what's the matter? Sit down. Is it your period?'

'Yes. No. I didn't realize they were short of money.'

'Well . . .' Her mother bustled over to put on coffee. 'Plenty of sugar for you, I think. They're not short exactly, but £3000 a year out of taxed income is a great deal of money for older people. Joshua has offered to take it over. He went to see Grandad the other day. I wasn't going to tell you, but I can't have you thinking he doesn't like you.'

'I *don't* like him. I *don't* want him to pay my school fees.'

'Jennifer. If you're going to behave like that you can go to the new comprehensive. I will not have this. Joshua has treated you like his own daughter.' Her mother was an unbecoming pink, clashing with the housecoat.

He gropes me, he pinches my breasts, he puts his horrible great hands between my legs, he'd be in my bedroom if I didn't lock the door every night and now he's hurt me, Jennifer screamed silently, as flushed as her mother, staring across the table, willing the words she could not speak to get through the air into her mother's mind.

'The trouble is, you get spoilt at the Frenches,' her mother said in righteous anger. 'I've a good mind to stop you going.'

Jennifer glared back across the table, sick with anxiety and grief, deciding that if her mother were to make a serious attempt to stop her she would go, now, with no cases, with her hoarded savings, and somehow manage to tell William French about it all. Her mother's eyes dropped.

'At any rate, you are absolutely not going tonight, and you are going to behave pleasantly to Joshua. Without him, we wouldn't have any of this.' She indicated with pleasure the comfortable kitchen bristling with expensive equipment.

'I hate this house,' Jennifer said bitterly. 'It's pretentious and ugly and much too big and I wish we were in the old flat.'

Her mother rose to do battle. 'We could not have stayed there. Your father took out a mortgage to buy it and there wasn't enough money to pay the interest, never mind repay the capital. But for Joshua we would have been on the streets.'

'You could have got a bloody job,' Jennifer, exhausted and in pain, screamed unforgivably, and hardly flinched as her mother slapped her face. She sat shocked but unmoving while her mother burst into tears.

'You *know* I couldn't. You know all I could get was rotten little jobs serving in shops, and I'd never have been home when you came back from school, and I was no good at them anyway. I just was not educated to work and your father never wanted me to.' She reached down to pick up Christopher, who had started to cry, and cuddled him to her as a shield against her daughter.

Jennifer sat stony-faced. Never, never, never, she vowed. 'I must finish packing,' she said when she could speak.

'And you're not to try and go away tonight,' her mother

said sharply, through tears. 'Joshua would be very disappointed and angry.'

It was a plea and Jennifer understood it as such, and she leaned over, forcing her mother to look at her.

'Mum, I don't want to be left alone with him. No little talks, nothing like that. There'll only be a row and he'll be even more grieved and difficult. Can we get that clear?'

Her mother's eyes dropped. 'I think you're very ungrateful. But yes,' she added hastily, 'if you'll stay and talk to both of us rather than rushing off to your room. I'm going shopping in a minute. Can I leave Chris with you?'

'Yes, of course.' She carted him upstairs on her hip and watched him with amusement as he crawled under her bed to find the ancient toys that she kept for him to play with. She saw him safely established and started to pile her school uniform into her trunk, then stopped, sickened by the sudden realization that this might be her last term. It was simply not possible to allow Joshua to pay her fees, the price he wanted would be too high. And she was only fifteen, a year before O-levels – a minimum qualification – and a year under the official school-leaving age. She sat down, winded, realizing the full extent of her troubles. She was, quite simply, unemployable; no one respectable would take her on without a National Insurance card, and she could not earn enough to keep herself living away from home. She sat, sick with fright, feeling the walls of her room close in around her. Chris started to scream and she snatched him up and confiscated the mouthful of carpet fluff on which he was trying to choke and sat, soothing him, understanding in her bones what it was to be helpless and encumbered.

They were eating that evening at the restaurant of the big London hotel in which Joshua's company had a shareholding. Chris had been left with a babysitter – interestingly, her mother had not been prepared to have a young nanny living in the house – and Joshua was exerting himself to be pleasant while she, slightly sick with apprehension, was wearing her school-outing dress and her least becoming pair of glasses, and had made no attempt to conceal her spots. Her mother had sighed and tut-tutted, but had felt unable to say a lot about any of it. The meal had progressed pleasantly enough and Joshua had called for the bill, put on his glasses and was sitting squarely, patiently checking every item.

'They're hardly going to cheat you, are they, given that you own the place?' Jennifer, who had had a whole glass of wine rather than her usual half, asked in genuine inquiry. He looked up at her thoughtfully, just as if she were a real person, she thought, surprised.

'We don't own all of it. And even if we did I always check the bill. You never know who's up to what, and in any case people make mistakes.'

'Yes.' Her tone invited him to go on.

'You've got a lot of people working bloody hard to make a profit in the kitchen and everywhere else. You need to make sure it's not being thrown away.'

'I do see,' she assured him, and she did, admiring the careful, businesslike approach.

He smiled at her briefly and they considered each other momentarily with real fellow-feeling. Then she felt his foot touch hers under the table, and she withdrew her own feet sharply. 'I need a little talk with you, Jennifer, when we get home,' he said.

'Why not here?' Jennifer settled into her plush seat and looked to her mother, who avoided her eye. She fought back sickness.

'It's a bit personal,' Joshua said reluctantly.

'If it's about my school fees, Mum has already told me about your most generous offer.' She watched his quick, irritable glance at her mother, who made a careful little deprecating movement. 'I rang Grandad this afternoon and he says he can easily manage another year, till I get my O-levels.' She watched Joshua flush slowly red, and clenched her hands in her lap. 'I told him that if it came to Sixth Form or other further training I would not come down on him for fees, but would ask you.' She contrived a graceful smile.

'You never told me you were going to see them, Jennifer. Why did you do that?' Her mother was scarlet with embarrassment and confusion, looking anxiously at Joshua.

'Grandad and I talked about it when I first went to Wanstead Abbey. He always said he could get me to O-levels,' Jennifer said steadily. 'They're leaving me all their money, anyway, what's left, and I felt Joshua had done enough.' She brought herself to look into Joshua's brown eyes, dark with rage, and noticed how tight his mouth was set. Deliberately, shaking, she reached out for the mints, pushing up the short sleeve to show the bruise on her right upper arm that had ripened along with its companion on the left since the morning. They stared at each other, neither of them listening to the burble of anxious protest from the other side of the table, and she understood that she had managed a powerful and dangerous counter-punch in the war between them.

At Woolverstone Hall, a staff meeting was in progress. The Sixth Form – small as always, given the unacademic background of most of the children – were engaged in private study, supervised by the latest trainee from a London borough's Social Services department, a scant three years older than his charges. Older and more hardened men were escorting the Fourth and Fifth Forms on a ten-mile hike, and the more docile, or at least younger, Third Form on a visit to Hawley Castle. It was a warm day; the sun was percolating with difficulty through the double thickness of nineteenth-century brick of what had once been the music-room, when its Victorian owner, his wife, eleven children, a couple of maiden aunts, and fifteen indoor servants had lived there.

'Leavers,' the Warden said unhopefully. It had been a very difficult year, and while he was not yet prepared to articulate his worries, he had lost much of the optimism which he had brought with him when he had come from the Prison Service. There were thirty boys, aged sixteen, leaving this year; too young to be cast into the world, as everyone round the table knew, but that was the school-leaving age, and it had been possible to build some kind of support system by way of a job, or a training course, and somewhere sheltered to live, round less than two-thirds of these boys. The other twelve were plainly going to be vulnerable; either their families had totally collapsed, leaving not even a grandmother capable of housing and nurturing a working grandson, or, just as bad, the family octopus was waiting to turn them into the next generation of unemployment, sexual deviation and criminality.

'I found Jimmy a live-in job in a hotel a hundred miles away from the lot of them,' one of the social workers charged with liaison was saying bitterly. 'All fixed. They liked the lad, due to go there in August . . . just give him time to say goodbye at home . . . but yesterday I get a phone call. His brother Danny – no, you wouldn't know him – is out again and Jimmy's going to work in the North Star in Kilburn and live at home – "Thank you very much for your trouble" – he'll be passing betting slips by next week.'

Heads nodded gloomily round the table and the Warden moved on doggedly. 'Seles.'

'That's another whose family disintegrated, right?'

Roger Caldwell nodded in confirmation. 'Seles was taken away from them on a court order.'

'So he can't go back there?'

'He wants to go into the Army, I understand. He fancies the SAS . . . yes, well . . . I know they all do, but his O-levels ought to be all right, oughtn't they, Roger?'

'You can never tell. But he's very clever and his maths is good. They mind more about that than English, where he's not so good. But, Warden, he shouldn't be there. The Army, I mean.'

'What, because of the incidents we've had?' The Warden knew that the quiet, sallow bachelor, Roger Caldwell, with twenty years' teaching here, was always worth listening to. 'What have we had? Three this year? Do you find him less able to control himself than some of the others?'

Violent flare-ups were endemic at Woolverstone Hall; many of the boys came from homes where violence was the normal currency. A good deal of their emotional education was totally inadequate so that frustrations which would cause no more than a momentary sulk in boys from more stable households unleashed explosions of rage. It was like dealing with toddlers, only instead of being able to pick up and remove a small, rigid, shrieking bundle, you were facing a big, heavy, senselessly enraged teenager with adult muscle power, willing to use any weapon at hand. Paul Seles had always been too quick with his hands, or feet. And as Roger Caldwell was right to remind the meeting, the violent incidents had become more serious as Paul got older and bigger. He was not particularly tall, but was very strong, built like a tank, round, heavy shoulders, bull-necked with arms a little too long for his height, and powerful legs. And a dirty, effective fighter, no going in with arms flailing for Paul Seles, just a savage, punishing attack delivered where it would do most harm.

'What do you think triggers him?' the Warden asked; if anyone could get near the truth it would be Roger.

There was a pause and the resident psychiatrist took it upon himself to answer and treated them to the familiar disquisition about frustration, no normal tolerance of, for which you really did not need two degrees and five years' personal analysis to see for yourself if you worked at Woolverstone Hall.

'Roger?' the Warden said patiently. He had been watching his man and understood that he was in no doubt about the answer to the question, he had merely paused to consider how best to convey the truth he knew.

'I would say the trigger for Seles is pain, Warden. Pain inflicted on him, I mean.'

'But isn't that so for most people?'

'No. Pain quietens a lot of people down; they creep away and hide, hoping it will go away. That's why people beat each other, after all, you make the other person go away or shut up. But for Seles it is intolerable and he has to hit back.'

'That's true,' the senior PE coach said, sitting upright. 'When he half-killed Jackson last term, you know why? Jackson trod on his calf muscle when they went down together, by accident, he says. He won't do that again, not that what Seles did wasn't over the top. But Seles surprised himself, I saw that. Didn't mean to hit Jackson so hard, and he was sorry after.'

'Did he say so?' Roger Caldwell asked, leaning forward.

'Not then. Bit later.'

The psychiatrist cleared his throat. 'I would suggest that what Roger has observed is a reaction to humiliation rather than pain.'

The rest of the table looked at him balefully, but Roger Caldwell nodded. 'Pain *is* humiliation, and most of us react by crawling away to recover. Seles hits out, hard and uncontrollably.'

There was a discouraged silence round the table.

'Intelligent boy, I thought,' the psychiatrist said hopefully.

'Yes.'

'I could explain the mechanism to him – I'm sorry, I've only had one session with him, what with the various other demands.'

And the fact that we share you with Hallwell nick and you're not that much given to doing a proper day's work anyway, and you skive off whenever you're asked to appear even on the late night news round-up of the local television, the Warden thought wearily.

'Perhaps you could talk to Seles, Roger?'

'Of course I will. But, Warden, any scheme which involves sending him into the Army would be a serious mistake. And we need to keep him here for a bit longer if we can.'

'Point taken.'

Two hours later Roger Caldwell walked sadly back across the grounds, worrying about his leavers. You had in the end to say to yourself that at least these boys had had a break from their violent, abusive, disorganized backgrounds. They had lived to a routine, they had got a great deal more useful education – formal and informal – than they could have received by going to a disorderly city school from their disorderly homes. However vulnerable they still were at sixteen, there was some

57

foundation there; the habit of work, clean clothes and regular meals had been established, and a lot of them would find their way to a life with those things in it.

Just then, he saw Paul Seles, by himself, sitting out of the sun under a tree, reading a book, and his heart lifted. There was no way Seles would have been able to engage in such an ordinary, non-destructive, contemplative activity if he had remained with a bullying monster in the inner city. The book was probably *The Story of O*, or similar, but none the less ... He changed course, clearing his throat, so that Seles would have time to hide the book if his worst fears were justified but the young man greeted him easily with a smile that transformed that heavy, sullen face.

'You ever been to Hungary, sir?'

Caldwell dropped down beside him. 'No. The Russians liberated Budapest, not us. We stopped in North Italy. Not very close. And, of course, it's difficult now.'

'My dad was killed in the uprising in 1956. That's why I'm here. My mum came over here but she died in 1960.'

'I remember. You could go back there some day.'

'Yeah. Our name was spelt different. A single "S" is "Sh" in Hungarian; we were Seles with the hard "S" which is spelt "Szeles". I might change to that.'

'Difficult for people here to spell, perhaps?'

'They may have to learn.'

Roger Caldwell sat quietly, deciding how to start.

'I've decided to give the Army a miss,' Paul Seles said, putting his book down, face downwards. *Guide to Hungary*, it said, and had been written by two people with Russian names.

'Ah, well, I ... we ... were wondering whether that was a good idea in any case.'

'Why?' Seles sounded defensive but interested, and Roger Caldwell inched his way forward.

'We'd all noticed you hit out if someone stands on your foot, even by accident. And they do it on purpose in the Army, or did when I was in.'

The boy had gone rigid and his hands were clenched.

'Paul, you can talk about this rather than get upset. I'm not trying to make you miserable, just to see if we can work out why these things happen.' He watched the hands relax marginally. 'It's when someone hurts you, isn't it?'

Colour washed up from the boy's neck into the sallow skin.

'Most people don't mean to hurt, and what we want you to do is wait – just a minute – to decide whether it mightn't have been an accident.'

The big hands uncurled slowly, the colour subsided and the rigidity went out of the shoulders. 'I could wait, couldn't I? Like Robbo – Jackson, I mean. *He* didn't mean to kick me.'

'No. It's difficult, mind you, for any of us, to remember that if someone hurts you they may not have meant to do so. And that's not just physical hurt.'

There was a long silence, which he was sufficiently experienced not to break.

'But if they *do* mean it . . .'

'That's different. You may still not want to savage them because *you'll* get into trouble, but it's different. And if you wait a minute you can decide.'

Paul Seles sat so still that Roger Caldwell glanced cautiously at him to see if he was all right. 'Could I stay here next year?'

'I don't see why not. We'll have to fight to get the cash, but I really don't see why not. Provided your O-levels are all right. Damn, that's the bell.' He placed a hand on the boy's shoulder and scrambled to his feet, exultant to have snatched one more brand from the burning.

CHAPTER FOUR

February 1972

David Banner stopped by the Sixth Form pigeon-holes to take out two envelopes. He knew the handwriting on both of them, and decided to leave the letter from home until last. He walked out into the cold, bright February morning, tearing open the other, and read it walking across the edge of the first team soccer pitch, the frost crackling under his feet. Everything that the school mythology had said about girls at Catholic boarding schools seemed to be true, though in practice this particular girl was more explicit about her sexual needs on paper than she found it possible to be face to face, or with him having her from behind which she had plainly wanted but had not found herself able to do other than hint at. He grinned to himself, finishing the letter, conscious that he might need a wank as well before he was going to make much sense of Maths 1 this morning. He hesitated; there was a first team match this afternoon and he half believed that wanking took the edge off your game, and *that* could not be afforded, or at least not today, not against Marlborough. He decided to confine himself to the most pressing need following the vast school breakfast and headed for the lavatories.

'Good one, was it, Watling?' he shouted to a fellow member of the Army set, who was emerging, slightly flushed, from one of the stalls. 'You'll go deaf.'

'Fuck off, Banner.'

He remembered his mother's letter, as he washed his hands with the finicky carefulness that she insisted on, and extracted it with hands still damp from one of the thin, permanently wet squares of towel that hung, depressed, from a hook in the yellowing wall.

It started all right, as a letter, the usual wittering about what she was doing and who she was seeing. He scowled at the plans for his next exeat weekend; what made her think he would want to drive forty miles each way to see her old friend Lucy and meet the daughter again? He intended to sleep all day and meet up with Teresa in the evening, and now there was going to be a wearying argument. Reluctantly he turned to the third page of the letter. He was not naturally analytical, a quick, physical adolescent who lived very much within his own strong body, but his instincts were cat-like and sound. If there were a real difficulty or disaster his mother always left it until the end of a letter, or until he was just leaving to go back to school, as if she could not bear to let him go without shifting some part of her burden on to him.

'I want you to talk to Mickey,' the letter said. 'He doesn't like the school and he seems very unhappy, and I can't do anything with him. He *is* looking forward to seeing *you*. Thomas is very happy at the school – it is rough, of course, but he seems to like it. He is captain of one of the junior football teams.'

David thought about his pale, anxious brother with an uprush of guilt and resentment. Mickey had always been his particular responsibility ever since Thomas was born and had become instantly the apple of his mother's eye. Mickey had been a gentle, rather helpless little boy, desperate for attention. Thomas was quite different: a capable, cheerful, secure little menace, who had suffered very little from the upheaval in their fortunes.

It had, of course, proved impossible to keep the three of them at Ashford. In the agonized negotiations which had raged through last summer holidays, it had become quickly clear that the Navy had no formal powers, and not much informal desire, to help the sons of one of their officers who had resigned to go to a much richer job and then made a mess of it.

The school had done its best, offering a further reduction on fees for all three boys, but it had still left an unbridgeable gap, or at least one beyond the resources of his mother's middle-class Scots family. His father's family were scattered, mostly in the Services, and had unanimously taken the line that they wouldn't bother with boarding schools if they were settled in one place instead of being whisked hither and thither in the Queen's Service. So in the end it had been decided that David, being within two years of the end of his education, should continue at Ashford, on reduced fees grudgingly paid for by his Scots uncles and the two younger boys would go to the local boys' grammar school. Mickey had taken their father's departure hard, had been wretched at leaving Ashford, and had made absolutely no attempt to make the best of any of it. The tough little Thomas, on the other hand, was flourishing.

David re-read Teresa's letter, just to cheer himself up, then turned to go into the main classrooms, pausing to look at himself with satisfaction in the aged yellowing mirror. He had never had the spots or the acne which made other adolescent boys' lives a hell of anxious pressings and scrutinies. He needed a lot of physical exercise and took it; he ran every morning, was never ill, bouncing with health and conspicuous among his pale, blemished fellows in the Sixth Form, and girls responded to him partly because of this bounding energy as well as his blond good looks. Pleased with his reflection, he ran out of the door to join the stream of passing boys on their way to classes, all hoarse, loud voices and huge feet, a wholly masculine, savagely competitive world in which he was perfectly at home.

Three days later, David walked soberly up from the station, wondering why Mickey had not come to meet him; Thomas, it being Saturday, would be playing in a team somewhere, but Mickey was not much use at anything except swimming.

He opened the gate into the neat suburban front garden. It was a good house, in a pleasant part of Esher, thirties-built but substantial, with almost an acre of garden. He paused at the gate, frowning; the place looked untidy, the path needed weeding, there were odd garden tools scattered about, and the brass on the front door was dull and stained. He put down his light overnight bag and picked up the tools to put them away, so that he was encumbered by a hand-fork, a pair of secateurs and a rake, as his mother rushed out to embrace him.

'Darling, how nice. I hadn't realized it had got so late, or I would have walked up to meet you. You've grown – no, perhaps you haven't, but you look very well.'

He kissed her back, sniffing the Chanel No. 5 which she had always worn, glad to be home and looking forward to lunch with her.

'I haven't been able to get Mickey out of bed yet, he is naughty. But he'll get up now you're here.'

He drew back a little, alerted by something in her voice. 'Is he ill?'

'No, no.' The denial was a little too emphatic, and he looked at her sharply. 'He's being rather difficult, as I told you, but he'll be very glad to see you. Come in, never mind those – oh well, yes, they do go in the shed, I was just going to pick them up.' She hovered by him while he put the tools away, automatically clearing up the shed which seemed to be also in a mess.

'I'll be there in a minute, Mum,' he said impatiently.

'Yes.' She waited, irresolute, making little anxious fidgetings with her hands, and he straightened irritably.

'I did wonder,' she said, in a burst, 'whether I should take Mickey to Dr Macdonald, but I thought I would wait to see what you thought.'

He looked at her warily. 'What's wrong with him?'

'He's very unhappy.' She moved closer as he backed out of the shed, swearing as a nail caught his sleeve. 'I meant to hang that wire up, but I've been rather worried and somehow I haven't managed to tidy up.' She saw his face. 'I'm sorry, I shouldn't worry you with all this, on your exeat weekend home, only I don't know what to *do*.' There were tears in her eyes and he sighed and put an arm round her.

'Is it only Mickey?'

'No. It's the house as well. We can't afford to keep it.'

'This house? But I thought it was yours – I mean, I thought Dad handed it over.'

'Well, he did, but there's a mortgage on it, and this little job he's got means he can't keep up the payments. Or so he says.'

'Bloody hell!' David was outraged. 'He isn't paying school fees any more. Why can't he pay the mortgage? I know it's less than our fees were.'

His mother looked anxious, hunted and furtive, the blond hair looking faded and untidy. 'Well, I don't know, but I can't manage on what he gives me to keep us, and he says he can't afford the mortgage, and we'll have to sell the house.' Her face crumpled and he pulled her to him.

'Mum, don't cry. Stop. Was he late paying this month?'

She snuffled into his shoulder, and he thought that if he had not grown she had shrunk. 'Well, only just, darling, he's actually not too bad about paying when he says he will, it's just not *enough*.' It was a wail of distress. 'I mean, naval officers aren't well paid, we *never* had enough money and I was really so happy when he got this job – the one before this, I mean, because we could live like other people and have a proper house. And now he says we can't keep the house.' David watched, aghast, as she reached for a handkerchief and stuffed it into her mouth. 'Oh dear, oh, I'm so sorry, but with Mickey too . . . I don't know where to turn.'

'Davey?' It was a small, tentative, hopeful inquiry, and David threw open the shed door, shielding his mother behind him.

'Mickey, old son.' He moved towards his brother, but the boy stepped sideways, clumsily, and he stopped, disconcerted. His first thought was that Mickey had shrunk since the Christmas holidays, but actually if anything he was taller. But, Christ, he was thin, the wrist-bones like chicken bones, with the family's large square hands ridiculous on the end of his arms. He looked ill, David thought, appalled, he looked – if you really faced it – slightly mad, his eyes not meeting yours and that hangdog, superior half-smile which he'd begun to do at

Christmas, but which was much more obvious now. He felt a wave of pure rage, which he suppressed, horrified. This was illness he was looking at, it was something not normal. He looked sideways for guidance to his mother who was stuffing gardening gloves on to an overcrowded shelf, but all she did was say, 'Oh good, now we can have lunch,' and she led the way into the house, with him following after her and Mickey dragging his feet and then wandering off out of the kitchen.

David watched him cautiously, trying to understand what was happening. The boy turned into the spacious cloakroom, which was one of the things his mother liked so much about the house, but he didn't shut the door and he evidently wasn't going for a slash. He was running water and washing his hands, over and over, rocking slightly on his feet, his lips moving. It was somehow intensely annoying to watch as well as very frightening.

'Mickey, what are you doing, trying to wash them away?' He laughed shortly, to show it was a joke, but his brother turned, looking agonized.

'They're dirty. Germs all over.'

'Not any more, Mickey, not now.' David dropped his voice into gentleness and went and stood beside his brother. 'Show me. Very clean, much better than we ever did at Ashford, not that you could ever find the soap there.' He turned off the tap sharply, snatched the towel and dried his brother's hands forcefully. 'Come on, it's lunch now.'

'I haven't finished.' Mickey stood his ground, looking out of the corner of his eye, his mouth distorted in a terrified half-smile. 'They're not clean yet.' He turned back to the taps and David, without thinking, smacked his face. Mickey flinched but went on, twisting his hands under the water, not looking at his brother, a red mark made by David's hand clearly visible on the pale skin.

'Jesus! *Stop* that, you little shit. Come out of there.' David felt quite seriously that he might kill his brother if he did not stop this rocking and washing, all with that little smirk at the corner of his mouth. He dragged him out of the cloakroom and banged the door and marched him into the kitchen. His mother had her back to them, stirring something on the stove, but he understood from the rigidity of her shoulders that she had heard exactly what was happening.

'How long's he been doing this?' David pushed his brother in front of him, unable to avoid feeling how pathetically thin he was.

'Doing what, darling?'

'This hand-washing.' He would willingly have slapped her as well at that moment.

'Not long.'

He waited, red with anger but disciplined until she had to turn and face him, looking both defiant and furtive. 'I *told* you.'

'No, you didn't.'

'Well, I couldn't, you had to see for yourself.' Her face puckered, and with an exclamation she turned back to the stove where she had managed to let something boil over.

Standing with his hands on his brother's stiff shoulders, David breathed in carefully and told his mother that if lunch was ready they would eat. She gave him an unreadable look under her eyelashes and put plates of soup in front of him and Mickey, whom he had pushed into a chair. He sat down himself and was halfway through his plate before he realized that his mother was rigid with tension, barely eating, watching Mickey, who had not even picked up his spoon but was staring out of the window, looking frightened but still with that contradictory little smirk at the corners of his mouth.

'Mickey, eat!' he said, in tones that would have commanded instant obedience anywhere at Ashford.

His brother turned and gave him an agonized look, and picked up a spoon, then put it into the soup, looked at it, and gagged.

David stopped eating, appetite banished. 'Does he not eat either?' he snapped at his mother.

'He's very difficult about it,' she said, head down, avoiding his eye. He watched her deliberately until she had to look up, and he saw, sickened, that although she was distressed, she was also triumphant; here was proof of her trials.

'How long has he not been eating?' David asked grimly.

'Well, why don't you ask *him*?' she said petulantly. 'It's not *me* doing all this.'

'Mickey, how long have you not been eating?'

'I can't eat soup.'

'That's not true,' their mother said sharply, sounding no older than Mickey. 'He won't eat *anything*. He says it has germs in it.'

'Mother. Mum, have you taken him to see the doctor?'

She shook her head wordlessly, fighting tears.

'Why not? He's ill.'

'He won't come. And I can't drag a great boy like that.'

David thought of the thin shoulder-bones he had felt under his hands, and shut his mouth hard. 'We'll go this afternoon.'

'There isn't a surgery,' his mother said, childishly triumphant, then met his look. 'I could ring up.'

'Will you do that, please?' It was his most chilling tone, the one used to warn someone at school that one more false step and they'd be in for a beating, and his mother went straight away to the phone, leaving him with the silent Mickey.

'It's all right, Mick, old son,' he said gently to the working face with the wide, frightened eyes. 'You're ill and we need some help.'

'I don't want to go.'

'You don't have a choice. I'm big enough to carry you, remember.'

In the event he nearly had to break down the cloakroom door and was tight-lipped and flushed on the cheek-bones as he stuffed Mickey into the heavy school coat which hung limply on him. The bloody kid must have lost a stone, he thought, horrified and repelled. Mickey's lips were moving in what he recognized, irritably, as the Ashford Grace, and his hands moved continually, clasping and unclasping. David, putting Mickey firmly between himself and his mother, nodded curtly and dismissively to a neighbour, who made as if to advance on them.

He was tense with Dr Macdonald too; he had never met the man because he was never ill in the ordinary way, and the minor cuts and sprains sustained on the games field were always dealt with at school. But the man had dismissed both himself and his mother from consideration and had his whole attention on Mickey, who was sitting like a loony, not looking at any of them, his lips still moving, answering at random. His mother was in one of her fidgets, desperately embarrassed by Mickey and replying to questions whether put to her or not, and appealing to him for help. Dr Macdonald tried to ignore her, but when for the third time she tried to answer a question addressed to Mickey, he gave her a long, thoughtful look and said to the space between her and David that he thought this would be easier if they sat in the waiting-room or went for a little walk while he talked to Michael. He just glanced at David but he was on his feet, holding out his hand to his mother, before the words had settled in the silence, desperate to get her out.

He bustled her past the waiting-room, realizing that she was near tears, and afraid that there might be other people there. He had decided twenty minutes was the right sort of time, although if Mickey was going to sit in that frightening, exasperating way, muttering to himself and twisting his hands and not answering when you spoke to him, then it was difficult to see what a doctor would be able to do. He turned his mother firmly away from her automatic path to the town centre, and from any possible contact with other people. She was sniffing and mopping at her face and he was overwhelmed by exasperation.

'Mum, look, here's a bench. Come and sit down. You're not helping Mickey by crying.' He sounded exactly like his father.

'I can't help Mickey, I've tried. He's gone religious, as I tried to tell Dr Macdonald, but he wasn't listening to me. When he isn't washing his hands, he prays, he does really, David, he kneels by the bed – for *hours*.'

The Banners were Church of England, in much the same way as being members of a tennis club, and David shared her incomprehension. 'Does he say why?' he asked carefully.

'He says he's a sinner and everything is his fault.'

'Probably started to wank and someone's told him he'll die.'

'David!' She surveyed him over her handkerchief with a gleam of hope. 'It couldn't be as simple as that, could it? *You* could talk to him.'

'Thanks, Mum,' he said, relieved to have distracted her. 'But you're right, I do know you won't die from it.'

His mother was herself timid and tentative about matters sexual, but his father had always been open and easy and he had observed that his mother enjoyed his casual vulgarity. She looked at him pleadingly.

'Oh darling, I'm so glad you're here, I've been at my wits' end. I tried to tell your father,' she said hastily, forestalling his next question, 'but he won't listen, he's too busy with that girl . . . I *don't* know what he sees in her.' The tears started to flow again and David sought for something to distract her. He had refused to meet his father's inamorata, out of genuine outrage as well as a wish not to distress his mother, and he had therefore nothing to offer on the question of the attractions of the other woman, other than an uneasy understanding that sex, easy, pleasant and satisfying, had a lot to do with it. He steered her on to the subject of Thomas, who was, he knew, enjoying his new school and presumably not causing anxiety, but this was not a success either.

'The thing *is*, darling, it's very mixed.' He understood that this meant the school was not middle-class. 'A lot of the boys are Indian or Chinese and, of course, the *local* boys all go there.' She hesitated, struggling to say what she meant, the straight blonde hair, fine like Mickey's, rather than thick, curly and tinged with red like Thomas's and his own and his father's, blowing round her face. The sun was shining but it was too cold to stay sitting long and he urged her to her feet. 'I'm frightened,' she said baldly. 'I'm afraid for them. It's a very different world now, with all this unemployment, and if Mickey and Thomas don't get a proper education at a good school I'm afraid they'll never get decent jobs and they'll just drop out. Of our class, I mean, and I *don't* mean that

69

snobbishly, you know I don't. I always hated all that nonsense in the Navy, I just mean, well ... professional people with proper jobs like the Services, or medicine, or law.'

He knew exactly what she meant. It was precisely the postulate of the education he was himself receiving and the statement of his school's position; its old boys were not expected to become distinguished artists, politicians or men of the theatre, but they were expected to qualify to man the ranks of the comfortable professional classes. He was, after all, on his way to that destination, that was why he had accepted the humiliation of having his fees paid by his uncles. He chose the easier ground.

'Thomas can go into the Services too, provided he gets O-levels.'

'*If* he does at *that* school. And there's Mickey.'

He tucked his arm in hers, protectively, unable to think of anything useful to say about Mickey in his present state.

'Well, you're a great comfort to me,' she said, patting his hand, so that he smiled down at her and nodded to an older woman whose face he knew, seeing reflected in her eyes the attractive mother/son cameo presented to her.

As they pushed through the door to Dr Macdonald's house they heard Mickey laugh, like an ordinary boy, and checked, looking at each other in hope and pleasure. The doctor summoned them in and they stood side by side looking at Mickey. He was white and exhausted and there were tear tracks down both cheeks, but he was there, inside his skin, and Davey went forward instinctively to embrace him. He looked at Dr Macdonald, to try to see what had happened, but he was standing on the balls of his feet, a small, compact, greying man, watching Mickey very carefully, eyes narrowed.

'Michael,' he said, 'will you wait for your mother? I need to talk to her for a minute. Your brother will stay with you. It's all right.'

Mrs Banner turned anxiously to David. 'I'd like my eldest son to be with me too, Doctor.'

The doctor hesitated and David straightened up protectively

and moved towards his mother, but Mickey's face tightened up again, so all the lines of anxiety were back. 'I'd rather David stayed with Michael.'

So he had to go crossly off with Mickey; he would get it all out of his mother afterwards, but he had wanted to be there, as her support, treated as a grown-up. It was not even as if Mickey seemed pleased to have him; he was sitting tensely on a chair, winding his hands round each other, staring out of the window, so David picked up a car magazine and read about the new Ferraris . . . dream on, Banner.

He had finished the article by the time Dr Macdonald put his head in and asked if both young men would join them, please. His mother was sitting awkwardly in an uncomfortable high-backed chair, very pale, looking older and tired and defensive, the lines round the mouth very deep; just as she had looked when Dad was going on about something, he thought anxiously, and looked accusingly at Dr Macdonald.

'Mickey, are you with us?'

Mickey nodded, hunched forward, his eyes on Dr Macdonald's face. 'I've told your mother that I want you to see a colleague of mine, another doctor, who will help you feel better. As I told you, I think he'll want you to come into the little hospital – the one in Furlong Lane – for a bit to make it easier to see you.'

David waited for Mickey to protest or vanish back into himself, white with misery, as he used to do when they all went back to school, but he only nodded, never taking his eyes off the doctor's face.

'I've explained that you can't go to school for a bit, and I will write to your headmaster. All right?'

David opened his mouth to protest, or ask a question, but found he had nothing to say. Mickey and the doctor seemed to know what they wanted and his mother had that peculiar stunned look she had had when his father had first left home.

The doctor turned to David. 'And you're at Ashford?' They were all standing up now, and he felt much too large and healthy in the small room. 'Due back on Monday?'

'I could stay if it would help.'

The doctor glanced at Mickey who was standing slumped in the hall, waiting to be told to move. 'Mickey is too ill just now to be anywhere but in a hospital and I hope he'll be there on Monday. But he will need you. He needs his father too, and you may have to help with that.' The cool, considering look flicked over Mrs Banner who was emerging from the cloakroom.

'What's wrong with him?' David asked urgently.

'My good colleague, Dr Daiches, will have a better idea. But it's a complete breakdown. You've been away, of course.' There was no criticism in the dispassionate tone, but it silenced David and he only just managed to return his thanks in his father's best naval manner for the man's giving up his Saturday afternoon.

'Not much of a weekend home for you,' Dr Macdonald replied disconcertingly, and David shook hands wordlessly, realizing that any plans he might have had for his own comfort or pleasure, including time with Teresa, were going to have to be junked.

CHAPTER FIVE

April 1972

Jennifer Redwood squinted out of the kitchen window to see a corner of William French's big old Bentley outlined against the shrubbery and smiled to herself. Her hands were covered with flour but there was no need to rush to the door; William would find his way to the kitchen inside two minutes. The door flew open and he edged in sideways, carrying a briefcase, his medical bag and a pile of magazines, balanced insecurely, which he let fall on to the kitchen table.

'Morning, Jens.'

'Morning, William.' She beamed at him, watching with love as he added the magazines to a vast, untidy pile in the corner. He had hoped, they all knew, that he was influencing the rabble of teenage girls in his house in favour of medical careers by leaving his magazines around. His own daughter had been the only one who felt able to point out that the only articles they all read avidly, sprawled around the big table, were those about sexual deviation. William had defiantly taken the line that that was useful too, it would tell them all what to avoid, but they had all noticed that he now went carefully through his literature, removing any articles of that nature.

'Killed anyone this morning?' she asked, in the traditional greeting to Father in the French household.

'They were all looking fairly perky when I left them.' He scowled at the magazine he was inspecting and dropped it back in his briefcase.

'More unpleasantness with sheep?'

'Worse. Never marry a farmer, Jens. Though come to think about it, it's the wretched chaps who are too shy to talk to women, or who can't afford to marry, we have to thank for all this. Is there coffee?'

'On't stove, Feyther.' A recent TV serial, costumed to the nines, had left them speaking BBC Yorkshire for weeks.

'Nay, lass, 'tis not a man's place to be fettling wi' wimmin's tasks.'

'That's true, isn't it, even though I don't think fettling is right. Sit still and I'll pass you some.'

'No, no, I'll get it. I just didn't want you slipping out of period, as it were. Where are the rest of the mob? Where's my wife?'

'Lucy's being a Girl Guide with Sofie and Petra, so I'm doing lunch. Ali's still in bed and Louise is picking raspberries.'

'Ah, good.' He got up, poured himself some coffee and peered out of the window, restlessly. He would be off in a minute, she knew, to see the rest of his girls, and she felt the usual pang of jealousy. They all wanted William to themselves sometimes; Lucy, because she had been married to him for twenty years, Sofia because after all he was her father, and Ali and Petra and Louise because they all had unsatisfactory fathers. Ali's father shared his life between Ali's mother and a long-standing mistress, Louise's father was a remote, rather stiff academic, and Petra's was a war correspondent. And she herself was worse than fatherless; she had Joshua. She remembered an infallible way of detaining William for a bit longer.

'The Hollandaise is a bit runny. Could you come and look?'

He appeared at her elbow and took the pan. 'The egg needs to cook a bit more. Take a few risks.' He patted her shoulder, returned the pan and stood beside her as she whisked the mixture furiously over the heat. 'Leave it at that. It'll thicken a bit while it sits. What are we eating?'

'*Filet de bœuf en croûte*, broccoli with Hollandaise, raspberry Pavlova for pudding.'

'Just something simple and light, old boy? Sounds good.'

It was a symptom of William's uncritical affection for the young that he appeared occasionally to forget which sex they were. Lucy would remonstrate with him, pointing out that these were young women he had around him, but she missed the point. All four of them in different ways were anxious about growing up and more than happy to relapse into a sexless childhood happiness when they could, and none of them minded being called 'old boy'. Ali, the prettiest and most sexually advanced of the group, had brought a boyfriend with her for the weekend last summer, a clever eighteen-year-old on whom they had all exercised their wiles in vain. He had also fallen in love with William and prolonged his stay to five days in order to go everywhere with him. He was now at medical school, and William was still writing to him on his own account, long after Ali had lost interest.

Jenny rolled out the puff pastry, spread the garnish of mushrooms and sauce on it and picked up the beef, while William reached over her for a spoonful.

'Oh, *excellent*, Jens,' he said warmly, extending the spoon for some more sauce.

'William! *What* happened to food hygiene?'

'It's only us. Small group, all got the same germs and immunities. Anyway you're going to cook it.'

He checked, nonetheless, and took a clean spoon, as befitted the man who had not only taught her to cook to *cordon bleu* standard but had instilled, casually but thoroughly, the rules of hygiene in kitchens. Early in her friendship with Sofia, desperate to find a place in this household, she had found her way to the kitchen and shyly offered to help Lucy with anything. Lucy had accepted, placidly, and Jennifer had spent the morning picking and cleaning vegetables for the next two meals, a chore which to a town child had all the charm of novelty. William had appeared as she was finishing and announced he was going to cook his 'special', so she could sit down with a drink and watch him. He had poured them both white wine, filling her glass right up with soda water, so that she could be a grown-up without the consequences, and had started to chop the vegetables into immaculate, tiny cubes. Flushed, even by the small amount of wine she had drunk, she asked to be allowed to help, and he had stopped, wound her into a huge apron, issued her with a heavy steel knife and showed her how to chop parsley and slice mushrooms, on the basis that she should start with something soft that didn't bite back. She had loved everything about that day, the neatness with which William worked, the colours and textures of the vegetables and the miraculous way in which a delicious sauce was created under his direction. He was an inspired teacher, patient, didn't intervene too much and had somehow left her and everyone else with the impression that the meal had been created by her alone. Watching the whole table clean their plates, she understood she had found something she really liked doing, and was deeply relieved. Housework she had always hated and her ironing was a disaster. In any case people did not greet a clean bath or an ironed shirt with cries of pleasure and requests for a second helping, but if you could cook, she understood, you were welcome anywhere.

'William,' she said warningly, 'we are nine for lunch, and if you eat any more there won't be enough.'

'Why nine? There were only five girls when I left this morning.'

'Lucy is bringing home two Guide Commissioners.'

'I don't think *that's* right – I mean, there's only one Guide Commissioner in this county and Lucy is it.' He peered through the glass door of the oven where the meringue circle was drying.

'Don't open that. Well, Lucy's found two more.'

'They'll be starving,' he forecast gloomily. 'Good women always are. They live on boiled eggs if *they* have to cook, but offer them a decent square meal and you'll be lucky to get any yourself. We'd better do a first course quickly, or the family will have to hold back on the *filet de bœuf*.'

Jennifer and he considered the supplies. 'Artichokes?' she suggested. William had found them in the market, imported from France.

'They'll be wearing Guide uniforms and won't want to eat with their fingers.' One of the best things about William was the way he considered other people; he might be bored by the idea of having two 'good women' to lunch, but these were Lucy's colleagues and guests in his house and their interests would be carefully considered.

'Soup, then, but vegetable, not meat stock.'

'No, that's right. Too rich with the *filet* otherwise. I'll do it.'

'Nah. It won't take but a minute. You sit and drink your coffee.' She started to dice vegetables, fast and easily, with a sharp knife. She and William were both agreed that they were not the same done in one of the new food processors. She was pleased to exercise her skill, but was also in the state of welcoming any activity that staved off her combined anxieties about O-levels next term and the even more pressing worry of the following year. Her mother had refused to give the school the statutory term's notice of withdrawal of a pupil, pointing out that Joshua was keen to pay her fees through the Sixth Form. She had moments of wondering whether Joshua would be any worse if she let him pay for her, or whether he would accept this as a victory in the deadly subterranean war between them and leave her alone for a bit. She knew that her refusal to accept him as anything, be it sexual partner, father, or provider, infuriated him; he had been fit to be tied last year after she had persuaded her grandfather to produce another year's fees. Indeed, she had sometimes wondered whether if she actually let him have what he seemed to want he would shut up and go away. There were two difficulties about this approach: first, nothing in the magazines William was now hiding from them suggested that it would work; according to them, men seemed to want to go on with their daughters or the sheep, once they had started. Secondly, and critically, she simply could not do it, it was beyond imagining. She pressed down on the knife and sliced the edge of her finger. 'Damn.' She sucked it and reached for a Bandaid.

'Come here, Jen.' William took the plaster from her and held her finger under the cold tap, matter-of-factly, like a father, and she leant against his chest feeling dizzy, which he accepted equally calmly. All four of his adopted daughters draped themselves over him, or sat on his knee, or held his hand with the same ease, and in her dreams she sometimes had a stepfather who was like William, not like Joshua. Suddenly, unwarned and unheralded, tears came to her eyes.

'What is it, Jens? Onions? No?'

'Sorry. No good at blood,' she managed to say, and had an enormous sniff and tore off a bit of kitchen towel to blow her nose.

'Wash your hands,' he said automatically, and the matter-of-fact patient piece of direction was too much for her. The desert that faced her was suddenly overwhelming, and she stood rigid by the stove, her throat swelling, nose blocking and eyes filling. She turned, overwhelmed by misery, trying not to let William see, burying her face in another bit of kitchen towel, but there was no stopping the flood and with a feeling of immensely painful relief she let it all go. It was like being sick when you had eaten something rash; you tried not to be but the relief of succumbing finally was enormous. She sat down, put her head down on her arms and wept and wailed and snivelled, while William, falling over his size-twelve feet as usual, made a rush to the stove to turn the gas down under the soup and shift pans out of harm's way. She banged her head on the table in long-suppressed grief for her own lost father, and in rage and frustration at her loved mother for having presented her with a poisoned substitute.

'Can you tell me?' William was beside her now, patting her back anxiously, and she thought through her misery how threatening the same gesture would have been from Joshua, being a prelude to trying to get his horrid hands down the back of her jeans or under her blouse.

'No,' she said wretchedly.

'Sit up, Jens, there's a good girl.' The familiar authority pulled her upright, and he turned her face towards him, and tore off some more paper towel with the other hand. 'Blow.'

She did, obediently, like a child, still hiccuping.

'It's time you told someone,' he said, gently but implacably.

'You're always like this the day before you go home. Is there trouble there?'

Sheer surprise stopped her hiccuping. 'Am I?'

'Oh, always. As if you had something very difficult to do which you are nerving yourself for – for which you are nerving yourself.' William was picky about grammar, and her marks in English language had improved steadily since she had known him. 'So what is it?'

She looked at him hopelessly, unable to risk losing him by the story of her and Joshua, but he was not looking anxious or fatherly or interested, or any of the expressions they all knew so well. He looked, well, like a doctor, impersonal and detached, and suddenly she was able to speak to that calm, professional face. She poured out the whole, horrible secret history, amid disgusting tears and snufflings and handfuls of paper towel. Nothing could stop her, even though William had to get up twice to bar other members of the household from the kitchen. She wound down finally, exhausted, her head aching all the way round the top of her skull. She looked shyly at William and quailed; the calm mask had vanished and he was scarlet with anger.

'God, you poor child,' he said quietly. His hands were shaking, she saw, awed. He shot out of his chair, scattering papers and banging his knee; William had always accepted that his large frame and what he referred to as the excess baggage brought him into collision with inanimate objects. 'And you can't tell your mother?'

'No,' she said, and started to cry again, staring into that darkness. She felt his hands on her shoulders as he stood behind her.

'It would destroy her marriage, of course.' He wasn't talking to her, it was an observation, and she found it oddly calming.

The sound of a car drawing up in the drive froze them both.

'Oh, God, the Girl Guide Movement. Stay here, Jens, I'll deflect them to sherry.' He plunged out of the room, leaving her limp, cried-out, aching, but with her head suddenly clear. She got up and drank two glasses of water straight down, relit the gas under the soup, finished rolling up the *filet* and got it into the oven, and had filled the kettle to boil water for the broccoli by the time William got back, holding a bottle of sherry in one hand.

'Well done, Jens,' he said, taking a comprehensive look. 'Ali and Louise are laying the table and I've told them we're not to be disturbed. And Sofie and Petra are sorting out the wine, God help us all.' He poured her a sherry, then looked at her carefully. 'You've got a headache, haven't you?'

'It's easing.'

'Better not sherry, I'll drink it. And lay off the red at lunch.' He placed a heavy hand on her shoulder. 'When the Commissioners of three counties – which is what is honouring us – have left, we'll talk ways and means, but let me say now that whatever needs doing, we will do, including adopting you if that's what you'd like.' She felt the tears prickle again. 'You should have told me before, you shouldn't have had to put up with all that.' His voice shook and she turned, horrified, to console him.

'It wasn't so bad. I had you to come and stay with.'

'Mm.' He was looking wretched. 'Lucy always said that there was a problem at your house; I should have pressed you before.'

Somewhere in all this, she thought, turning to stir the soup, something had changed for ever; William was speaking to her as a fellow adult, sharing his own pain. 'Don't tell Lucy,' she said.

'I must.' He was sounding fatherly and definite again. 'Married people do tell each other those things, they have to.' He hesitated awkwardly, while they both thought about a married couple who emphatically did not tell each other that sort of thing. 'Anyway, Lucy is bound to have a good idea about what to do. Jens, you need to wash your face. Nip out the side door and up to the bathroom, I'll hold the fort here.' He looked at her carefully. 'Don't be longer than you have to, I'll never get this lot on to the table by myself.'

*

80

Paul Seles swung off the train and looked for the Woolverstone Hall bus. There it was, with Old Caldwell leaning against the door, coughing in the cold spring air, looking like an old age pensioner as he always did. He swaggered across the station car park, nodding graciously to smaller boys.

'Sir?'

'Paul, my boy, how was the holiday?'

'Great.' He waited, savouring the moment. 'I was in Germany – Berlin.'

'Good heavens.' Old Caldwell was really impressed, you could see. 'How did you get there?'

'In a car. And a boat.'

'Come *on*, Paul, tell me all.'

There was a gratifying audience of his contemporaries; that idiot Wilkins was open-mouthed, and he settled to tell the story.

'I've got this mate, see, who's German. Met him in a caff here, by the . . . by where I live.' He was still at seventeen ignominiously housed in a children's home while the useless Social Services tried to find him a place in a hostel, but he wasn't too fussed. He had his own key and the staff left him alone, he could come and go as he wanted. 'He comes from Berlin. West Berlin – his grandma managed to get the family over there in 1945 when the Russians came, but *she* lived in Dresden.' Old Caldwell was interested in history, so he'd remembered to tell him that bit. 'Günther, this mate of mine, was working in the caff at Islington and he wanted to go home for a wedding, so he says why don't I come too.' He paused for effect. 'So we went over on the boat to Ostend and hitched, and his family were dead nice to me. I stayed and we both worked in a caff there. In Berlin. After the wedding.'

'Did you find you could use your German?'

'Yeah. It was easy. By the end of three weeks I couldn't even speak English.' He grinned at the group around him in remembered pleasure. 'Nearly didn't come back,' he boasted.

'That's wonderful, Paul.' Old Caldwell was really pleased, you could see. Woolverstone Hall mostly kept the education to basics: English, maths, history, and a lot of woodwork and craft skills, but Caldwell had been a linguist at one point in his career and had seen no reason why he should not be allowed to offer French and German to any boy who wanted to learn. Some years some boys would manage a year or so of a language. Paul Seles had opted to do both French and German and had stuck with them and got 78 per cent for German and 74 per cent for French in his O-level examination, some of the best marks ever recorded at the school. O-levels themselves were not all that common; the school aimed at CSE, the Certificate of Secondary Education, or the technical examinations set by the City and Guilds or the Royal Society of Arts. It was not that the boys were particularly slow, but they had their hands full emotionally, and were all there because they had no habits of industry. Paul's performance had been matched only by an Irish boy who had turned out to be a mathematician.

'How did you manage, though?' Caldwell was sounding anxious. 'You didn't have a work permit, though of course *that* should be all right next year when we're in the Common Market.'

'No one asked. Günther – my mate – said I could easily be one of the *Gastarbeiters von der Türkei*.'

The boys in his audience looked blank but Caldwell liked that one and burst out laughing, dropping fag ash everywhere. 'Paul is saying they thought he was one of the Turks who came over to work,' he said informatively. 'You've got the right colouring, Paul, but your hair should be straight.'

'That's true,' Paul conceded, thinking of the Turkish chef. 'But there was lots of foreigners. There was another bloke from Hungary – I mean, he was German, or rather his mother was, but they'd lived in Hungary for years and they only came out in 1956. He taught me a bit of Hungarian.'

'Listen to this, you lads. Remember I told you that under the West German constitution everyone of German origin is German and has the right to live and work and be a citizen of Germany?' Old Caldwell was dead excited; well, it *had* been

82

interesting seeing a current affairs lesson come to life in the person of Max, who was working his way up as a waiter.

'How did you get on with Hungarian?' Caldwell was asking, actually standing up, not leaning on the bus, he was so keen. 'I understand it has nothing in common with any European language.'

'It's not that difficult.' Nor had it been. Max's sister had joined them for a drink, very late one night after the shift had finished, and the two had dropped into a language in which he recognized not just words but whole phrases. He had deliberately blotted out much of his childhood but his adoptive parents had often lapsed into Hungarian to each other and to him. For a moment the memories had been painful but that had passed, in the company of friends, with money in his pocket, pleasantly tired after a heavy shift, and he tried out his half-remembered vocabulary. He didn't find that sort of thing difficult, indeed he could not understand how some people were unable to hear the difference between one sound and another.

'It has a Finno-Ugric base, apparently,' Caldwell said inquiringly, and his audience considered him with tolerant affection.

'I expect so, sir. Probably both of them.'

'I wonder if we could find someone to teach you. Hungarian, I mean.' Caldwell was off, away with the fairies, he thought, touched and amused. 'Don't look so sceptical, Paul. The Hungarians have been scattered several times in their recent history. I read somewhere that there are more native Hungarians in New York than there are in Budapest. There might easily be a Hungarian speaker in Milton Keynes.'

His audience was sniggering now, and Paul decided to turn the conversation. 'I reckon the oral is a doddle for the German exam, anyway.'

'Oh, I should think so. *Du hast das Kunstmuseum in Berlin gesehen, oder?*'

'*Nein, ich hatte keine Zeit, wissen Sie. Ich musste zuviel arbeiten – von neun Uhr früh bis abends um acht. Dann haben wir viel Bier getrunken.*'

Caldwell beamed at him. 'Oh yes,' he said, 'I see. Your pronunciation is very much better. Of course, you've always had a good ear. Well now, what have the rest of you been doing? Mark?'

Paul was angry; he'd wanted to go on talking in German and telling Caldwell all about the holidays. He slumped crossly into a seat, banging his case down on the toes of a boy a form below him, daring him to complain. He stared out of the window, lower lip stuck out. None of these wankers would have done anything half as interesting as he had done, but there was Old Caldwell listening to the rubbish about a day out in Margate with Uncle and Auntie. That was the trouble with Woolverstone Hall, they wasted their time on dossers or hopeless cases, people who were never in a million years going to do anything other than maybe work as a postman.

'Am I so fortunate as to have most of the first football team here?' Old Caldwell had stopped asking people about having their grannies to tea and returned to the real world. He was attended by groans and jeers. There were three football teams but none of them was up to much. There were only ten boys in the Sixth Form and five of them did not voluntarily play anything. Such as the first team was, however, it was on the bus, now lurching down the school's pockmarked drive.

'We've got one final match, a friendly, on Saturday, so I hope you've all got your boots. We're playing Ashford. No, not their first team, their sixteen-and-under team. That makes it about right; most of our team is not more than sixteen.'

'That's a posh school,' Paul objected, needing to make himself heard.

'It's a boarding school. Like us and like Abbeyfield, which we played last term.' Old Caldwell was sounding a bit defensive; Woolverstone Hall normally played the local comprehensive, the local grammar and, by long tradition, Abbeyfield, a private school, which took almost as difficult a collection of misfits as Woolverstone Hall. Ashford was a new departure and Paul viewed it with mistrust, but he was the mainstay of the first team's forwards and was not about to withdraw. He looked to the front of the bus; Caldwell was boring on with some little Third Form kid, so he occupied himself with threatening his neighbour across the aisle until he reluctantly produced a cigarette.

Two days later, the Woolverstone Hall first team was gathered on the pitch, awaiting the emergence of Ashford's sixteen-and-under from the changing-rooms.

'Big blokes, weren't they?' one of his fellow-forwards said warily to Paul. The Wolves team generally and the forwards in particular were of very uneven size and weight. They included Paul at centre forward, who at five foot ten inches and nearly seventeen, was a big bloke himself, including where it mattered, he thought, pleased, remembering Max's sister in Germany, who'd even taught him the Hungarian for it. Next to him at right half was Sean Kelly, a thick-set Paddy, who turned out to be a mathematician, a midget at five foot three inches with his boots on, but a God-given footballer; and the left half was Daniel Scota, who had grown to six foot two inches in the last year and lost a lot of strength with it. The rest of the team was pretty uneven too, well outweighed by the heavies they'd seen getting off the bus, and their best winger was only just fifteen. The Warden and Roger Caldwell, whose idea this had been, were chatting up the other side's Sirs. They were big blokes as well and looked up to putting the boot in if it were needed. Let them try any of *that* and they would see where it got them.

The Warden walked over and they watched him anxiously. 'They too are under strength today,' he reported cheerily. 'Measles – so they're playing a couple of fifteen-year-olds, like us. So, we'll just have a nice game, and nobody loses their temper, right?' He scowled at Danny Scota, who was chicken in addition to being built like a stick of spaghetti, and wouldn't have dreamt of taking on anyone anywhere near his own size, but it was Paul, understanding where the warning was directed, who was offended. It was nearly a year since he'd lost his rag with anyone, but they still expected him to start kicking and biting any minute. He ought to have been captain, but he wasn't, because they didn't think he could control himself.

The Ashford team emerged from the changing-rooms, clumped together in little groups. It was a bright, clear, sunny day, uncomfortably warm for football, and both teams were fidgeting and rolling up their sleeves. Paul had his sleeves rolled up and his socks rolled down, in imitation of the Arsenal forwards in extra time. He watched sardonically as Danny lost the toss with the other side's captain, a tall, fair bloke, very pleased with himself, whom he disliked instantly. He looked useful, though, and fast, not too heavy, and he was fit, you could see from the way he moved. Uneasily conscious that three weeks in smoke-filled cafés had not contributed much to his own ability to get down the field, he decided that they might just have to frighten this lot, because there was only him and Sean who could score.

'They're never all sixteen and under,' he observed *sotto voce* to the Warden, who was hopping uneasily from foot to foot, dressed in a referee's black strip.

'Bet you they're saying the same about you, Paul,' the Warden said, and he laughed, his black mood dispersing.

He ran off to get into his place, opposite the fair bloke, their captain. He'd be a striker too, then, at centre forward. He held his hand out – why? Paul looked at him blankly, then understood, that was the thing with posh schools, all these phoney manners. You shook hands before you put the boot in. He touched hands reluctantly, with an odd sense of recognition teasing him, then the bloke kicked off. A quick through ball, but the Wolves' back was awake for once, and managed – just – to slip the ball inside before the Ashford winger was on him. Paul swore, dropped back to help, stopped the ball dead and looked for his own winger, but saw that Sean was up with him and found the space to pass to him. They almost got through the Ashford backs between them but the fair bloke came whistling up out of nowhere and took it off them narrowly avoiding a corner, cursing at his team in the poncey accent that set Paul's teeth on edge. 'Come on, lads,' he mimicked savagely to Sean as they took the throw in and attacked again, this time getting through the backs with a neat display of cross-passing which wrong-footed the goalkeeper, so that was one up for Woolverstone Hall in the first five minutes. He and Sean touched hands, running back like the professionals did. You couldn't throw your arms around Sean, he'd half kill you, but you could slap his open palm. He'd never talked to Sean about how he'd come to be at the school, but he knew as surely as if he had been told that someone had hurt him badly.

They were in with a chance, he realized ten minutes later. The Ashford lot were bigger, man for man, and fitter. That fucking centre forward was in better nick than anyone on either team, he was everywhere at once, on spring heels, but the Wolves were the better team, better footballers, even the fourth-year kids, they had more idea of what they were about. It was just a question of holding out and popping another one in quickly to discourage the opposition.

He and Sean almost managed it, just before half-time, but the Ashford defence had got its act together and that centre forward was invariably back with them when the Wolves' attack threatened. The teams gathered in separate huddles, both sweating in the warm April air.

'One up's nothing,' Paul said generally, since you couldn't rely on Danny to point these things out to the lads. 'They could score any time.' He glanced interrogatively at Sean who was scowling and muttering something. He always spoke without opening his mouth or moving his lips, and only under pressure, as if he did not mean any observation of his to be heard. He cupped his ear and looked inquiringly, and Sean managed to raise his voice to audibility. 'That centre forward! Doesn't know how to put them in.'

Now that was right, Paul agreed. The fair boy was so busy playing every place on the field he was not concentrating on the striker's main task, that of actually scoring goals.

'It's the winger you need to watch,' Sean muttered. 'On the left.'

A silence greeted this analysis, while Danny cleared his throat and tried to think of a captain's contribution to the debate.

'The bugger at centre forward's in me way!' It was Sean

again, unusually communicative. 'Next time me or Paul has the ball with a chance, one of you get him off us. We get another one, we've got it won.'

Sound, Paul agreed, and even Danny seemed to have grasped the idea. They trotted back again as the whistle blew. The Ashford team had also rethought their tactics; the centre forward intercepted the ball off the Wolves' kick, burst through at speed and, instead of trying to go it alone, passed smartly to the winger who sliced through the Wolves' defence to score. One all, and the Wolves ran back swearing at each other; the team tended to go to pieces under pressure, consisting as it did of too many boys for whom co-operation was always going to be difficult.

Paul lined up, facing the fair-haired centre forward, reading his mind. He was going to try the same again, bang the ball down the field where the winger could run on to it, and get down there himself so that the bloke had someone to pass to. He turned and glared at the Fifth Former, just fifteen, who was the back on that side, and saw him nod and move up. The fair bloke had missed all this, too busy making captain-type noises of encouragement to the rest of the field. He kicked the ball exactly where Paul had predicted, but the kid got there first and cleared fast to Sean, who danced round the big Ashford bloke who was marking him. Paul was running beside him, heart hammering. Two Ashford blokes bore down on Sean who looked up, fractionally, and passed it to him, perfectly placed for him to run on to it, but his legs went from under him and he hit the ground hard in a knot with the Ashford centre forward, who had brought him down. Pain shot through his hip and he smacked a punch instantly and unthinkingly into the bloke's gut, then felt for his throat.

'Paul! Leave dat, you stupid bugger!' He flailed at Sean but that little Paddy was strong – they rose out of the Irish mud built like brick shithouses, was the school's view – and he found he was pinned down. As the pain ebbed and the pressure on his head eased, he could hear angry voices raging above them and see that the fair Ashford bloke was on his knees, throwing up and gasping.

'Off!' It was Old Caldwell, well out of breath, and well angry, and Sean interrupted unintelligibly.

'Banner fouled your man,' the Ashford PE bloke pointed out in tones of Olympian fairness.

'Dat he did. We'd de goal made.' Rage had rendered Sean suddenly intelligible, but Roger Caldwell was implacable, and Paul was a burning heap of misery and humiliation, wanting to kill the Ashford boy who had robbed him of the goal and was now about to take the match from them. He got shakily to his feet, unwilling to sit in the mud surrounded by heavy boots and knees, and found that his opponent was trying to do the same. He narrowed his eyes, calculating his chances of flattening him again, might as well be hung for a sheep as for a lamb, but failed to shake off Sean's hands, like steel bands on his right arm.

'Sorry. My foul. I slipped,' the Ashford boy said between gasps.

Bugger that for a lie, Paul thought, the pressure in his head painful again, he meant to bring me down, he never stopped. He glared at the Ashford boy, who had made it to his feet, still slightly bent in the middle, his face covered with mud.

'Paul, we've got dem beat.' Sean spoke into his shoulder, and he felt the eyes of the team on him. Well, the fucker had had to apologize, publicly, after all, he thought, and looked over to Old Caldwell, who stared back at him. Well, what did he want now? It struck him like a blow; he was expected to say *he* was sorry for clobbering the bloke who'd fouled him deliberately, knowing exactly what he was doing. He stood in the warm air boiling with rage. What did they expect? The bloke had wound him up, he'd meant to foul him.

'Two minutes, can we?' It was the Ashford referee, and he didn't wait for an answer, just put an arm under his bloke's shoulder and took him off, limping, Paul was glad to see. The rest of the Ashford team, who had been in an angry clump, got told sharpish to kick the ball about and not get cold, and trailed off, leaving the Wolves.

'Everyone except Seles, go and have a kick-around.' Sean reluctantly let go and went, and Old Caldwell came close to him. 'Bad luck, Paul. Are you going to manage to climb down or is it too difficult?'

The entirely matter-of-fact question winded him and he felt the ground shift. 'It was *him*.'

'It was, in the first instance. And he apologized.'

'Only after I hit him. He was shit-scared.'

'No, he wasn't. He had the whole team to his back by then.'

That was unanswerably, unquestionably true, but there was something in this situation that was wholly unfair. He struggled for words. 'He only did it to make himself look good. He wasn't sorry.'

Caldwell thought about it, then grinned slowly, and Paul felt the knot in his chest ease. 'Something in that, yes. But he did apologize, and in public. And you can do the same.'

'I'm not sorry.'

'Doesn't matter. You can make yourself look good, so you're even with him. And we can get on with the game.'

Paul stood, choking on the necessity, but suddenly it seemed to him that it wasn't *that* difficult and it would show that wanker that the Wolves could behave just like any poncey schoolkids. He glanced across the field to where the bloke was huddled in a sweater, drinking something hot. 'You coming?'

'Yes, of course.'

Old Caldwell walked over with him and he stopped a yard short of the bloke and spoke, gabbling to get the words out. 'I'm sorry I hit you. It was a reflex, I didn't mean to.'

'I'm sorry I fouled you.'

He saw with exhilaration that the bloke had understood a good deal, that he wouldn't mess with him again, he'd stay well clear for the rest of the match. And Old Caldwell had been right; by playing it civil he had snatched back the advantage, he hadn't been humiliated and thrown out of the game.

'Right.' Old Caldwell was sounding openly relieved and Paul felt a dizzying sense of power. The game could go on, he was still a player and he hadn't let the situation really wreck him. He smiled exultantly at the fair bloke. Bit pleased with himself but no real harm in him.

'Don't I know you from somewhere?' he said, something about the lifted chin and fair curly hair catching his attention. '*I* know,' he said, in amazement. 'You was at St Peter's.'

'Christ!' The bloke gaped at him. 'Yes, I remember you now. Paul. I'm David Banner. You broke my brother's leg – no, hang on, sorry, that's wrong, he fell. God, my father was furious. Was yours?'

'My guardian. Yeah.' He felt sick suddenly, remembering himself huddled in the hall, bleeding from the beating he had been unable to avert or deal with, and the pain and humiliation of it.

'Come on, you two.' Old Caldwell sounded nervous and both boys grinned.

'I wasn't going to do it again,' David Banner said drily.

'Nor was I.'

They nodded to each other as equals and rejoined their teams.

They sat next to each other at tea an hour later, and Paul understood that something had happened to the cocky boy he remembered. 'Your father still in the Navy?' he asked experimentally.

'No. Divorced my mother and remarried.'

'Sorry.'

'What about your people?'

'My parents died when I was a baby.' That usually stopped questioners in their tracks but this Banner bloke went stamping on in a way that no Woolverstone Hall boy would have, for fear of getting a real sorting-out, and asked who he lived with, so he had to tell him about the Home, daring anyone else at the table to comment. But Banner was all right, he didn't sympathize or anything bloody stupid, just went on to ask what A-levels he was doing and what the Sirs were like, so that he was able to relax and remember a few of his own questions. 'Your brother at the same school, is he?' he asked, and was sorry he had, because the brother was plainly not all right, poor little sod, and both of them fell silent, not quite knowing how to go on.

'The girl who was with you . . .' David Banner said into the awkward silence, '. . . forgotten her name.'

'Jennifer. Jens,' he said, suddenly seeing her, covered with dirt and chocolate, half the size of the boys, shouting the odds to this lad's snotty father.

'Do you still see her?'

'No,' he said, with a painful sense of loss. 'No. We was real mates but they moved. Her father died and she didn't come back to school for a bit, and then . . . then I changed schools. I never saw her again after that,' he said in bewildered memory.

'We moved about a month later too.' David said. 'My father was sent to command a naval training school, so we went to Surrey and I went to Ashford Preparatory, because I was ten by then.'

'You remember Jens telling the police she was nine?' He was warmed by the memory. 'Bloody liar. She wasn't nine for at least another month.'

They lapsed into speechlessness again, but it was an easier silence.

'How's your leg?' Banner asked, turning pink on the cheek-bones, and he took a chance.

'Fucking worse than before you hacked at it.'

'Same with my gut,' Banner said, quick as thought, and they considered each other, grinning, not quite knowing how to go on. 'Do you play cricket? Here, I mean?' Banner asked.

'Well, yeah. Some of us,' he admitted, cautiously.

'Maybe we could organize a friendly for next term?'

He meant it, Paul saw. 'I'd like that. I'll get Old Caldwell – that's our Sir – on to it.' He cleared his throat. 'Good to see you after all these years.' He reached out a hand and they solemnly shook on it, just like in the books, and in the end he took him over to Old Caldwell and the Ashford Sir to get the preliminary arrangements in place.

CHAPTER SIX

August 1972

David pulled open the passenger door for his mother ill-temperedly, ignoring Mickey's pleading look. He absolutely did not want to waste one of the last days of his school holidays driving forty miles on a family expedition to see his mother's boring friend, Lucy, but he had promised. He was not, however, feeling benevolent enough to ask his mother to let Mickey have the front seat; he got car-sick, but their mother had thought that he could overcome it by will-power and had never accepted that there might be a simple mechanical solution like letting him ride in the front seat. David preferred to have his mother beside him but he felt a pang of conscience as he glanced in the mirror at Mickey's white, miserable face. Thomas, of course, was impervious to all this, settled behind him with comics and several bags of sweets. David switched on the engine and scowled as it choked and finally caught.

'Did you have the service done?' he asked his mother sternly, knowing the answer.

'No, I'm sorry, darling. We can't afford it just yet.'

'I just hope it'll start again to come back. What time are you supposed to be meeting Dad?'

'Oh, not till eight.'

Thomas had taken the earphones off cautiously and both younger boys were alert, he saw. Their father had come to see them at the beginning of the school holidays, taken them out for the day and stayed the night afterwards, quite unexpectedly. A week or so later their mother, pink and pleased, had left

David in charge of his siblings while she had gone off for the weekend. And then their father had stayed another odd night, so that all three of them had begun to hope. He had himself cautioned against optimism, not wanting to destabilize Mickey, but secretly he hoped too; he missed his father and desperately wanted him back in place, to hold his mother together and support the household and turn them back into a normal family. He knew that his father's job was not all that well paid or high status, but it had to be better to have him home. He looked sideways at his mother; she had the little wrinkly lines over her nose that she always got when she was anxious, and the corners of her mouth were tight.

Ten miles later he heard a scuffle in the back and felt a sharp kick in the back of his seat as Thomas's oversize feet flew everywhere.

'Oh Christ, Mickey!' His brother had been silently sick on to the space between him and Thomas, and was sitting hopelessly.

'I'm sorry, I didn't realize I was going to.'

'Oh God, Mickey, you are such a *nuisance*.' His mother had gone red, in patches, in the way she did when she was angry.

He cursed both boys out of the back seat, cleaned up grittily and left the car doors open to get rid of the smell.

'I'm sorry, Ma, but if we're going to go on, Mickey had better sit in the front.'

She was furious, he could see, but had heard the implied threat; if she didn't co-operate he would insist on turning back. The trouble with old Mickey was he didn't know how to tell her the odds, but she reacted better to being told than being asked.

'Or you can drive and I'll ride in the back,' he suggested, as she hesitated, and she climbed sulkily into the back as he had known she would. She felt vaguely that it was improper for her to drive when she had a grown-up son to do it for her.

'Cheer up,' he said quietly to Mickey, who was looking hangdog and unhappy. 'You'll be all right now.'

It was a bit of a risk taking him anywhere, as his mother did

94

not quite accept. He had been in hospital for four months until June, when the famous psychiatrist who was looking after him had recommended that a smaller, less demanding school, and one which didn't contain Thomas, be found forthwith. David had had to come back from school to fix that too; his mother, who had grumbled about the last school, had hated this one even more and had been held back from refusing a place only by the psychiatrist's quietly expressed threat to give up treating Mickey if his advice on this point were not taken. She just wasn't very good with old Mickey, he reflected heavily; she liked her men dominating and successful and cheerful and was plainly both alarmed by and scornful of the poor kid. Mickey would be a lot better off if their father came back. He clamped down hard on this hope and drove on doggedly, glancing at his watch, not wanting to be late because it offended his sense of order. And the sooner they arrived, presumably the sooner they could get away.

'Tell me about these Frenches,' he asked his mother, in order to lighten the atmosphere in the car. 'And why are we going there?'

'They've got a tennis court and I thought it would be fun for you. Lucy is something in the Girl Guides. And there's a daughter for you, Davey, called Sofia, who is your sort of age.'

He nodded; he was interested in meeting girls and they always turned out to be interested in him. At all events, a game of tennis would be fun.

'William, we're having who for tea, sorry? And how many of them?' Jens, wrapped in a vast apron over a grubby pair of jeans, was sprinkling flour on a working surface.

'Lucy's old acquaintance Elisabeth Banner and three assorted sons.'

'How old sons?' Ali, sitting in a chair, long brown legs stretched out, looked up hopefully.

'Only one any good to you lot. Seventeen or eighteen, something like that, and his little brothers, aged twelve and eleven.'

'So four extra, all up, three of them starving boys. Wait a minute, is there a father?'

'Glad you asked,' William said, tripping over a chair leg. 'Forgot. Problem about father. He apparently left the family a year ago but may be coming back.'

'Don't ask,' Jens and Ali said in chorus.

'Absolutely right.'

'Scones and drop scones to go with the gooey cake, yes?' Jens asked.

'Thank you, Chef. Have you time to do that chocolate cake as well?' William French seized a biscuit from the rack and retreated, taking Ali with him to do some shopping, and Jennifer looked after them, momentarily envious.

Ali at sixteen and a half was beautiful: long black hair, wide blue eyes, slightly sallow skin and endless perfect legs. She had passed through every teenage stage without as much as a spot or an ounce of puppy fat; Jens and Sofia by contrast were both dieting furiously (or as furiously as William would allow) and Jens was trying to conceal an incipient boil on the side of her nose. She sighed and turned firmly back to work, choosing her ingredients. The boil apart, life looked remarkably much better than it had done, and she was approaching the autumn with real confidence.

She and the Frenches had conferred on the night of her revelations to William. He had still been furiously angry and had wanted to confront Joshua and her mother. Lucy, to Jennifer's enormous relief, had insisted that nothing could be done which involved breaking up a workable marriage, and incidentally damaging Jennifer's half-brother. William had wanted her to go on at Wanstead Abbey, having a good opinion of her intellectual ability, but they had all had to agree that an academic education was not possible in her circumstances, at this stage.

'Even if we could get a scholarship for Wanstead Abbey and I got to university, I couldn't get a grant. Joshua's too rich,' she had pointed out unregretfully, since she had started to see her way clear. 'What I'd like to do is a proper cookery training, so that I can work and have my own restaurant.'

So they had agreed that what was needed was a good technical college where the fees were low and near enough for her to live with the Frenches. Lucy had proceeded to recruit fellow-Commissioners into the search, coming up with two local authority technical colleges where there were no fees. A decision on the course was easy; one was an hour away from the Frenches' house, the other twenty minutes on quiet roads on which she could bicycle, or be driven by William on a bad day. Two days after the summer term of her O-level year had started it was all fixed, she had been interviewed and accepted by the principal of the college, a senior Guide who had eaten many a meal cooked by her after a day spent telling other women how to put up tents and dig latrines.

Joshua had been furious, an anger fuelled by guilt, as she had by now understood, but she had met it steadily. She had waited till he had stopped ranting – and there were tears in her mother's eyes – before she offered Joshua lunch with William French to discuss the whole issue. She had watched him, sick with fright, but it had worked, the coded message had got to him and he had backed off. It had been William's plan, of course. 'These grubby things go away if you shine a light on them,' he had said, very late when the three of them had drunk too much and talked too long. 'He won't be able to acknowledge or deal with what he's been doing but he will understand that you have told us all about it. I won't be asked to have that lunch, more's the pity.' Nor had he been, and Jennifer was still incredulous at how easy it had been to defeat the monster who had terrified her for five years and finally forced her out of her home. Joshua resented her and had been sullen at home for weeks, but he had kept his hands off her. Her mother was still unhappy and uncomprehending about her daughter going to live in another part of the country before her seventeenth birthday, but *that* was a price which had to be paid, and it left them all with a recognizable family situation: a daughter away finishing her education.

Joshua had tried to insist on paying for her board and lodging with the Frenches, but William had dismissed the suggestion. 'Child's the best cook here,' he had said. 'We ought to be paying her for what she does at weekends. One more doesn't cost anything, all these bedrooms eating their heads off. Glad to have her, she can do the weeding as well, it'll save a gardener somewhere. Lives on air, anyway.'

None of this was true of course, Jennifer thought with love, whisking flour into the egg and sour milk mixture for the drop scones; she helped at weekends, but in all the three years she had spent around that household there had never been the smallest suggestion that help was a condition of remaining a guest. The beautiful Alison, in an indeterminate teenage crisis, had lain round the house for a full three weeks of the Christmas holidays, eating, sleeping and playing tennis obsessively without a word of reproach spoken by any adult. And Lucy indeed had strictly forbidden any of her contemporaries to rebuke her, saying that she needed to lie about for a bit and she would stop doing it soon. Moreover, to the others' ill-concealed jealousy, both William and Lucy had spent time every day sitting with Ali, chatting to her and lending her a handkerchief when she wept. The idea of either of the Frenches demanding gardening or cooking services in lieu of payment for board and lodging was simply ridiculous. Jennifer did cost money to feed, she was always hungry and was uneasily conscious that any exercise she took was simply laying a foundation of solid muscle under the flesh. But as her friend Sofia observed, she was tall with good legs and no one would notice or care that she was not reed-slim like Ali. She smiled at the thought of Sofia going her iconoclastic way through A-level Latin, English and History, too secure in her parents' affections to mind that Jens would be effectively the daughter at home. Sofia was destined securely for Cambridge, even perhaps for William's old college, King's, which, in his view, was showing a sad want of principle in threatening to admit women undergraduates. Or perhaps Girton, which was run by another Old Guide; every female academic establishment in the United Kingdom was probably run by a Girl Guide colleague of Lucy's.

At three o'clock that afternoon Jennifer was smugly regarding two racks of fresh tarts and a plateful of drop scones, all still warm, and two large cakes. The thought was, according to William, that the young would play tennis, family holding back in order that all three young men could play with whichever of his girls seemed most appropriate. Some of them could play croquet with Lucy, or shoot clay pigeons with him. Tea would be served at 4.30 and the party would depart at 6 p.m.

'Right. Stand by.' William had seen the car coming up the long drive and he and Lucy went to the door to greet them with Sofia and Jens behind them, and Ali in exiguous shorts in front. Lucy and William advanced while the girls watched to see what was emerging from the car.

'Good-looking lot,' Sofia observed detachedly, and Jens nodded, considering the fair boy standing behind his mother, hands behind his back like Prince Charles. 'Bit conventional.'

The boy, who could surely not have heard them, looked over in their direction, and they both blushed guiltily.

'Oh, wow. Where has *he* been all my life?' Ali said, awestruck.

He was very good-looking, Jens conceded, edging backwards into the doorway, while Sofia advanced with Ali to inspect this phenomenon. Tall and blond, dressed in the boring public-school uniform of jeans and what was obviously his school sweater, he was brown from the sun and bouncing with health and energy. He lifted his chin self-consciously as Ali and Sofia were introduced, and Jens blinked, walking forward in obedience to William's impatient signal.

'David, this is Jens Redwood. David Banner, Jens.'

'Good heavens,' he said, letting go of Ali's hand. 'But we've met. On a building site. You were nine years old and wearing camouflage on your face and you were much smaller.'

'I remember.' She forgot to be anxious, remembering with total clarity the darkening sky and this boy kneeling in the mud. 'You've got a brother.'

'Two. Here's Mickey. Mickey, come here. This is Jennifer Redwood. Broke your leg for you.'

'Did not,' she said, outraged, and hated David Banner heartily as his whole face split in a grin.

'Actually, that's not true,' he said, turning to Ali, smiling into her eyes. 'Mickey slipped and fell and we all ended up in the nick.'

William was looking at her inquiringly, eyebrows raised, and she rose to the occasion.

'Perfectly true, and I had quite forgotten it,' she said quellingly, shaking hands with the younger boys. 'Who is playing tennis?'

Ali and David, it turned out, whoever else wasn't. William made a swift judgement and took the youngest boy, Thomas, who looked just like his big brother, down to the annoying habit of lifting his chin when challenged, off to shoot clay pigeons. Jens, it appeared, was to play with Mickey against David and Ali; she would much rather have shot, but you did not argue with William in full hospitable flight.

They knocked up and she understood that David Banner, who had protested modestly that his game was cricket, was a natural at this or any other ball game; he had no technique at all but he had a superb eye and was untiring. It was very hard to find a place on the court to put the ball where he could not get to it. She herself was a good, well-trained player, Ali was a rabbit and Mickey had the makings but was wildly erratic, easily tired and even more easily discouraged, so that despite her steady serve they lost the first set 6:1. Or rather David Banner won it, with minimal assistance. She thought about it as they changed ends, and considered her partner; he was breathless with apology and looked miserable.

'Mickey,' she said, cutting short an anxious regret, 'we'll change sides. You've got a good forehand, use it, run round your backhand and I'll get anything that comes down the middle. OK? And if you can, hit it back to Ali. She'll miss it.'

The boy stared at her, then giggled. 'That's not sporting.'

'Ali won't care.' She watched him digest this thought. He nodded slowly, took a grip on his racket and changed places with her, and she saw, across the net, David Banner's chin go up. They won the next set, 6:2, and she grinned conspiratorially at Mickey as they stopped for breath. 'Nicely,' she said, noticing that he appeared to have grown a couple of inches. 'You're doing very well, outweighted as you are. Remember, put it to Ali.'

They lost the final set but not by much, and in good heart. David Banner had been absolutely determined to win and had adopted Jennifer's strategy of banging the ball back to the weaker partner so that his twelve-year-old brother was having to bear the brunt of the attack. She took everything she could but she was tiring, as was Mickey who looked to her as if he might have outgrown his strength.

'Sorry,' he said sadly, as a blistering shot from his brother took the set. She told him warmly that he had no need to apologize, he'd done exceedingly well against a heavyweight five years his senior, and had the pleasure of seeing the confident David blush to the ears. She took Mickey with her to the kitchen to get a drink of water and let him help with the scones, feeling that he was in some ways not much older than her four-year-old half-brother.

'Food by Jens,' William stated as she and Mickey carried in plates, and she grinned at him, unembarrassed. William's pride in them all was so transparent and so easy that none of them was self-conscious about being held up for show, publicly. She settled down with two drop scones dripping with butter and a slice of chocolate cake, deciding that the spot at the side of her nose would just have to look after itself and observing sardonically that Ali was picking at a tiny crumb of cake. At a warning glance from William she put her plate down and went round with the tea-pot. Mickey, awkwardly poised on the edge of a chair, started and spilt his tea, and watched, horrified, as a whole cupful seeped into a sofa cushion. He looked to his mother, stricken.

'Oh, Mickey, for *God's* sake,' she said furiously, spots of red appearing in the cheek-bones. 'Goodness, I am so sorry, he's so *clumsy*.'

'Doesn't matter at all. Good for the cushions. Give me that cup, old boy, and I'll fill it again.' William as usual moved faster than anyone else when a child was in need of help. 'Jens, give Mrs Banner another slice of cake.'

Trying not to giggle at William's totally transparent line of thought, Jens solemnly ladled a slab of very sweet, very sticky chocolate cake on to Elisabeth Banner's plate, ignoring her protests. She stepped over David's feet; he had arranged himself at Ali's side, his shoulder just touching her knee, and she scowled at them both. Ali, gazing dreamily at the curly head so close to her, noticed nothing, but David pulled his feet in and smiled at her.

'I've just thought,' he said. 'I met Paul Seles in the spring. Do you remember him?'

'Paul,' she said, putting the tea-pot down hard on the nearest surface, and dropping to the floor to get closer to him. 'Where? How was he?'

He told her, making a good story of it, and she listened, eyes on his face but not seeing him at all, remembering the feel of Paul's solid shoulder against hers, and his speed of mind, and the way he sometimes looked on a bad morning.

'Is he . . . does he still live in the same place?'

'No. His stepfather, or whatever, died, apparently.'

'What was the school's name again?' She nodded, a memory of her father jolting her. 'It's an LCC boarding school. He's probably in care. But he's doing A-level? He was always clever. I must write to him.'

'We played them at cricket last term too. He's not bad.'

'No. We used to play in the street. He's a bowler.'

'What about you?' He was, she understood, intent on charming her too, even though he had Ali mooning over him.

'Well, I was a bat.'

'Oh, I *see*.' And now the conceited sod was laughing at her. She got up abruptly and retired to the kitchen from which she had to be coaxed by William with a promise of a go at the clay pigeons. She and Mickey made an unexpectedly good team; her eye was only fair, but he was a natural, and when six o'clock came and it was time to go, he was sparkling with pleasure and deeply reluctant to leave.

'Come again, laddie,' William French said warmly, patting him on the shoulder. 'Drive carefully, David, the traffic's a bit dodgy at this time, all those people who had too much lunch fighting their way home through a hangover.'

They all watched, beady-eyed, as David self-consciously said goodbye to Ali; the dreadful, noisy Thomas had confided, generally, that Ali and David had been snogging in the shrubbery by the tennis court. David held the door punctiliously for his mother, who was making a performance of giving Mickey the front seat, and Jens went round to say a particular goodbye, seeing the boy was dashed.

'A very good-looking young man,' Lucy observed kindly to Ali, who was staring after the car.

'He's going into the Army,' she said dreamily.

'He'll look wonderful in uniform,' Sofia said, interested, and Ali turned to her gratefully.

Jens sniffed. 'The mother's *awful*. Horrid to Mickey.'

William looked at her reproachfully; unkind comments on guests were forbidden in the French household. 'Well,' he said reluctantly, 'she's under strain.'

'Why?' Sofia had walked off with Ali, patiently listening to a word-for-word account of everything that had passed between her and David, leaving Jens and William together.

'Hoping for a reconciliation with her husband, but as I hear it's not at all clear that's on the cards. And Mickey has been a great worry.'

'You talked to her?' Of course he had, everyone in distress came to William. 'What was wrong with Mickey?'

'Oh, a complete nervous breakdown; pre-adolescent depression and stress. These things do happen – he's being looked after by my old friend Bob Daiches. Only sensible psychiatrist I know. So. Not to be too critical, Jens. You never know quite what's going on.'

'Indeed. You want to play tennis?'

'I'm too *old*. Or at least I'm too old to play singles. Here, Ali, Sofe, come along, it'll stop you moping.'

Mickey Banner sat tensely in the back seat of his father's Rover, immaculately clean, tidy and smelling of polish, as his father's cars and personal things always were. Both his parents were in the front seat, his mother rigid and angry. He feared her disapproval more than anything; he was scared by it. When he had been so ill, paradoxically, it hadn't mattered, he hadn't noticed what she or anyone else had thought, and then when he was getting better it had been good for a while. She had been more gentle and his father had come to see him too. But things were changing again, she was cross and bitter and bored by him. He'd asked Dr Daiches what he had done, assuming it to be his fault, and had been deeply relieved to be briskly ticked off for thinking he was that important. 'It is part of the teenage condition to feel that you are the centre of the universe, but you'd be more comfortable and understand more of what was going on if you would just remember that the grown-up world mostly isn't worrying about you, it's getting on with its own lives as best it can.' Mickey tried to hang on to this thought as he watched his mother, who was getting into one of her fusses, her neck turning pink, feeling incompetently for a handkerchief. He tapped her on the shoulder and passed her one of his as he had seen Davey do, and she turned, surprised, to thank him, mercifully distracted from whatever had been agitating her.

'It's on the left here, Patrick,' she said, in that cold voice she used all the time now to his father. All through July and August he and Thomas had hoped they might be getting back together; but during the four weeks of September his father hadn't been around, although there had been all these phone calls.

'Are you sure this is right?' His father was using a different voice, exaggeratedly patient but angry.

'I come here every week, Patrick, as you seem to have forgotten.'

'Well, here we are, old boy.' His father had evidently remembered that he was there and was making an effort. He slid the big car neatly into the car park; Mickey got out of the back and opened the door for his mother. She kept both of them waiting while she re-did her lipstick and checked the contents of her handbag. His father opened his mouth to snap at her to hurry up, closed it again and gave Mickey a look of chronic exasperation which he loyally declined to return.

'What's the chap's name?'

'Daiches,' Mickey said quickly, before his mother could start another row. 'Dr Daiches.'

'He is a medical doctor, is he?'

'Yes.'

Dr Daiches had been through this with Mickey at the beginning and explained that it had been thought wiser that Mickey, who was physically as well as emotionally ill, should be in the care of a psychiatrist rather than a lay therapist or analyst.

'Sensible man, is he?' His father was clearing his throat and fidgeting inside his jacket in the way he did when he was nervous.

'I like him. And he's famous.'

He was, too, an internationally known writer on his subject, and this had been useful inasmuch as it gave his mother the ammunition to repel her family's anxious questions. It was also, he had realized, a source of personal gratification to her that a well-known name was treating her son; it made the whole painful experience more tolerable. His father had been so angry and anxious that he had so far avoided seeing Dr Daiches at all.

They filed into one of the grey prefabs which housed the psychiatric wing of the big general hospital. He was on familiar ground; he had spent four months in one of these prefabs, being escorted every second day to see Dr Daiches, to whom at first he had been hardly able to speak. He smiled at the receptionist who beamed back at him and greeted his parents more cautiously. They sat down in the waiting-room, sparsely furnished like the rest of the place, all the chairs scuffed and an odd low sofa with hard rubber seats which left your bottom more uncomfortable than the plain chairs. His father sat uneasily on the sofa, his mother on a chair on the other side of the room.

Dr Daiches walked into the room, his glance flickering over the arrangement of the three of them. He put out a hand to Mickey's father, as the person he didn't know, and Mickey saw suddenly that his father was at least three inches smaller than Dr Daiches, and much younger.

'Mickey, I'd like to talk to your parents on their own for ten minutes. Will you stay here and I'll come and get you? Ten minutes.' He smiled reassuringly into Mickey's anxious face. 'Find him a biscuit, Angela, he's always got room.'

The receptionist laughed and passed him the tin and he sat down again, a biscuit crumbling in his hand, and the sick, anxious twitchings in his stomach. 'How's school, Mickey?' The receptionist and he were old acquaintances and it would have been rude not to reply, so he managed a response and ate a couple of biscuits, and then somehow ten minutes had passed and Dr Daiches was back, looking suddenly tired.

'Come in, Mickey.' He put a hand on his shoulder and made as if to speak, then changed his mind and propelled Mickey into the room in front of him.

His mother had been crying, he saw, heart sinking, and was still red-faced, sniffling angrily. His father, pink patches on his cheek-bones, was gazing out at a view of the car park, his chin lifted. Mickey sank into the chair set out for him, making the fourth side of a square with his parents and Dr Daiches. A leaden silence fell.

'Commander Banner?' Dr Daiches said interrogatively, and his father stirred uncomfortably and swung round from his study of the car park to face his son.

'Old boy, the thing is, well . . .' He stopped, but Dr Daiches' calm scrutiny did not alter. He took a breath. 'You know I've had difficulty in finding a good job.'

Mickey nodded, too anxious to speak, and his father leaned forward.

'I've got a job offer now – it's much better than what I've got, and it could lead on to greater things – but it's in Hong Kong. You know where that is?'

'Yes.' Any child of the Navy would know that.

'So I'll really have to take it, it's the best I can find, but it means I'll be a long way away.'

'Is Mum going with you?'

'No, old boy, no. No.' His father had turned scarlet.

'He isn't asking me to,' his mother said bitterly, ignoring Dr Daiches' quick, warning look. 'And he says we'll have to sell the house.'

'Mickey,' his father said, clenching his fists anxiously, 'the mortgage payments are four months behind, I've got debts and I can't do any more. I mean, you could get a job, Liz. It would help.'

'Why can't *she* get a job? She knew what she was doing, taking on a man with children.'

'If you mean Pamela, she can't just now.'

'Why not? Why shouldn't she?'

His father turned even redder and fidgeted. 'She's pregnant.'

Mickey felt as if he had been hit in the stomach. His mother had turned scarlet too, but it was as if she wasn't that surprised. She'd needled his father until he told her something she didn't want to hear, echoing scenes going right back into his childhood. She burst into angry tears and Dr Daiches leant forward and passed her the Kleenex, as he always did when you cried unless you found it for yourself, as Mickey had learned to do. They waited, all of them, in silence until she managed to quieten down and blow her nose.

'We didn't plan this, Dr Daiches,' his father said in appeal.

'*She* did,' his mother said, quick as a flash, and he saw that Dr Daiches agreed with her. Pamela had indeed planned this, fearing his father was trying to go back again. 'We were here first,' his mother said, the tears beginning again. 'Your children.'

'This one will be mine too.'

'How do you know?'

'Commander Banner, Mrs Banner.'

His parents fell silent, like quarrelling children, and Mickey watched them from a long way away. His father looked vulnerable and hangdog, but also ill-used, as if life had struck

107

him a peculiarly unfair blow, and his mother looked like an avenging fury, and neither of them cared about him at all. He made an inarticulate noise and got up to fumble his way to the door, ignoring Dr Daiches' raised voice, running away from all the noise to lock himself into the cloakroom and start washing his hands, endlessly, under the tap.

CHAPTER SEVEN

April 1973

'Right, that's ten chicken, twenty steak, forty chops, ten pounds mince. Make a note and put it in your pocket. Take them out, *with* the other sack, all right, but tie this one with a bit of tape.'

In the echoing, cavernous, empty kitchen, with the lights down low, Paul Seles followed his instructions meticulously, adrenaline flowing in his blood, making his heart thump, which was ridiculous, as there was no one here but him and the two commis chefs, who were involved as well. He was newly admitted to this fraternity; he had been working in the kitchen of a big West End restaurant for three weeks now, since the beginning of the school holidays, and had understood within forty-eight hours that money was being made from some fiddle by all the staff. His opportunity had come when he had put in four shifts end to end as a wash-up, and got on terms with Marco, one of the commis chefs, just a step up from the slaves, as he put it. Chef took a cut, of course, but he didn't do this part of the work which involved bagging up defined quantities of meat in a plain rubbish sack and putting it outside with the rest of the rubbish by 1 a.m. Unseen hands would pick up the sack, distinguished only from its fellows by a bit of tape, about fifteen minutes after that, and an hour later a special collection by the local council removed all the real rubbish. Paul had understood immediately that council employees were responsible for the earlier collection as well, but that was not his business as yet, it was just another piece of information about how things were done outside the class-rooms of Woolverstone Hall. His share of the take more than doubled his pay, but the real money was made on the scam operating in the bar sales. That, however, was sewn up by the two Spaniards who had been there for the last three years.

He handed Marco the slip of paper with the numbers on, showing it to the other commis chef as well. They went off to the showers, leaving him to wash the floor, the traditional final task for a wash-up. He filled the bucket, washing out the mop properly under the tap, so you weren't just pushing the dirt about, and worked fast, down one long stretch of counter, triple set of gas rings, oven, *bain-marie*, and up the other, all left clean for the morning by the chefs, then over to the pastry and sweets section, past the big chillers which held the vegetables and the freezers which held not much except ice and ice-cream. The floor was not difficult, tiled with a curve on the edge to avoid harbouring dirt, and he was finished in fifteen minutes. He headed into the showers, stripping off his sweat-stained T-shirt and jeans and hanging them in his locker – getting things washed was a constant problem for all of them, but in a slack period tomorrow someone would get out of the kitchen long enough to give the lady at the launderette a couple of malodorous sacks of work clothes, sorted into white and dark, as she had taught them. He dressed carefully in his good clothes, flares, sharp jacket, blue shirt and wide tie. He was always going to be a bit too heavy to look elegant, but he had grown another inch since his seventeenth birthday, and the sallow skin and dark hair and good teeth made him look fashionably Italianate. He ran his hand over his freshly shaven chin. It was no good him trying to get away without shaving twice a day, but the light in the tiny communal shower was poor and he had missed a bit. He hesitated and decided that Suzie would put up with that rather than have him be late. Juan and the lads at the bar would keep an eye on her for him, but if she sat unescorted at that bar for any length of time her looks would attract all sorts of undesirable attention and she would be surrounded by the time he got there. He did not want to risk her being picked up by a chef from another restaurant, a stage-hand, or an actor, or any other of the bar's late-night habitués.

He pushed through the service door and walked up to the front of the restaurant to the bar, past a couple of the trainee waiters cleaning tables, shaking out bread baskets and lining up the little individual flower vases by the kitchen hatch. The morning shift would put out fresh ones as needed, and set up the tables for lunch. He saw Suzie immediately; she was being chatted up by Juan, smiling and hiding behind her long hair, which was so fine that it clung to her neck and ears, however much she tried to make it hang thick and straight like Marianne Faithfull's. She was wearing a long, floaty skirt and a T-shirt without a bra, and Juan couldn't take his eyes off the little bumps of her nipples pushing out the material. There wasn't a lot else to see actually, as Paul knew from his explorations; she really didn't need a bra, but he was buggered if he was having Juan looking at her like that. He breathed in as Old Caldwell had taught him, then marched over with a proprietary scowl and put both arms round her in a bear-hug.

'Thanks for looking after her, Juan,' he said firmly. 'Come on, Suzie. Got a coat?' He found her long purple cardigan for her, which he had helped her to choose at Biba. She hadn't let him pay for it; she thought he was a public schoolboy earning some money to enable him to travel after he had done his A-levels.

Paul had not set out to deceive her, but when he had first seen her, at one of the clubs, he'd asked her to dance and had been very taken with her. He told her, truthfully, in answer to her question, that he was at boarding school doing his A-levels next term. He was using the voice he was beginning to adopt from Old Caldwell, who'd been at Eton, of all places; God knows what *he'd* done to end up at Woolverstone Hall. He had not dared risk telling her anything about the school; he knew she would have had a dance with anyone but was afraid that she would only go home with someone from her own, posh class, and wouldn't have wanted to mix with a lad from

Woolverstone Hall. So he had kept the fiction in place; if cornered, he was going to say that he had been at Ashford, because he knew a few names there, thanks to David Banner, but so far that had not been necessary. The A-levels, of course, he had no need to invent, and they were a creditable collection: French, German and maths, the same as any public schoolboy might be taking. He was learning Hungarian as well; Old Caldwell, unbelievably, had found a refugee in the local village who'd been a teacher in Debrecen before 1956 and was happy to teach Paul on Wednesday and Friday afternoons. They'd decided not to bother with any exams, just to race on, and his tutor now spoke only Hungarian with him. They were giving up for the three months before the A-levels, but after that he was off to Debrecen to carry messages and presents if possible to his tutor's aging parents; it was not and might never be safe for his tutor, who had been a thirty-year-old organizer in the 1956 uprising, to go back. Academically, indeed, he was doing better than Suzie, who had left her good school after a year in the Sixth Form and was attending some kind of crap course in art and design while doing what she called 'a bit of the season, just a few of the dances'.

'Where do you want to go?' he asked her, when they were outside. 'Mark's Place?'

She hesitated, tucking herself closer under his arm. 'Somewhere quiet, perhaps? I'm a bit tired.'

He cudgelled his brains. 'Franco's?'

'What about your place?'

'Well, you *could* come to my flat.' He tightened his arm round her, feeling his heart pound. He had been proceeding extremely cautiously with her, not knowing quite what these posh girls expected. Perhaps Chef was right, and they were no different from any other girl. 'The trouble is that while I'm in London I share with four blokes, all of whom will be around,' he lied. He was still quartered in the children's home in Highbury; he had a room to himself, a different one each holiday, and he had taken girls back there, sneaking them past the night staff, but he couldn't do that with Suzie.

'Well, what about my flat, then? Caroline won't be there, she's at a dance in Kent. Maggie may be, but that's all right.' Suzie lived in a flat near Kensington High Street, conveniently placed for Biba, with two other girls like herself, the lease being held by the father of one of them. She had, of course, a home somewhere in the country, but among her London friends it was assumed that everyone had a real home somewhere else. Paul had mentally allocated himself to one of the big houses in the village near Woolverstone Hall, which he was prepared to describe if necessary, but it never had been. He had discovered that the life in London was all that mattered to people of his age, sprung from confinement in boarding schools all over the country and allowed untrammelled access to music, drugs and the opposite sex.

'Have you got any hash?'

He scowled; drugs were something he didn't go in for. He had tried marijuana twice; the first time it had done nothing for him at all and the second time it had given him a headache. He had also been both amazed and infuriated by the behaviour of his associates and had decided, comprehensively, that he just did not want to float round half-pissed, talking crap about peace. 'Nah. You shouldn't need that stuff.'

'It's harmless.'

'None of those things are. Not drink, either.'

She gazed at him resentfully but adoringly, and he held her carefully. 'We need a taxi.'

The tube would have stopped running in five minutes, and in any case it was not the prelude anyone would choose if you were hoping a bird would come across. Suzie was looking tired, he thought, with an uprush of tenderness that caught him by surprise as he pushed her ahead of him into the taxi. He kept a tight hold on her, smelling her perfume and kissing her gently through a drift of the fine brown hair.

They stumbled up the stairs to the second floor and he prayed that none of her flatmates would have got back yet. The flat was dark and silent, but when Suzie snapped on the lights the living-room was pleasant, furnished with low, sagging, chintz-covered sofas and a large coffee-table. The kitchen, into which he followed her, was less attractive, a small, high, yellow room, carved grudgingly out of another space, the sink full of cups which had obviously been dumped in there out of sight.

'Maggie must have given everyone tea before they went,' Suzie said forgivingly, and ran two of the cups under the tap and put Nescafé in for both of them. Paul, used to good coffee in his place of work, set his down quietly and took her in his arms, gently, not pushing her, just stroking her.

'Suzie.' He turned her towards him and kissed her mouth carefully, his chest tight with longing. He drew back after a long minute and looked at her dumbly, hoping for a lead.

'Don't you want your coffee?' She was short of breath and the nipples were standing up under the thin T-shirt.

'Not really.' He put both hands on her breasts, rolling the nipples between his fingers, still watching her face. He summoned his vision of how an Ashford boy would behave. 'I'd really like to make love to you. In bed. Now. But I'll stop if you don't want me to.' Marina, or one of that lot, would think he'd gone cuckoo, talking like this, but he wanted this soft, thin, upper-class creature more than he'd ever wanted Marina or Christine, or any of them, and he was going to go carefully; this was going to be different. He could feel his cock pushing up; he'd had a wank the night before, but it had recovered and he was ready. She gasped and bit her lip, turning pink as he pinched her nipples more firmly and moved his right hand to push inside the waist-band of her long skirt. She reached round and undid it at the back, so that it fell round her ankles in a pile of red and gold pleated cotton, leaving her in tight little bikini pants and the T-shirt. He reached for her and pushed his hands inside her pants to cup her bottom and pull her towards him, but she pulled back.

'My bedroom's the other side of the living-room.'

He wanted to pick her up and carry her so as not to lose contact with any part of her, but he was afraid of crashing into furniture in the crowded room and just followed her, holding on to what he could, until they reached the bed and he was able to pull her pants down and feel the warm, dark patch between her legs.

'Suzie,' he said sternly, back in the Ashford mode, 'you on the Pill?'

'Yes. Yes, I am. It's all right.' She kicked off her pants and lifted her arms, so he could help her off with the T-shirt and hold her away from him to look at her, not much on top but lovely curvy hips and a tight little waist and a huge, luxuriant fuzz of brown hair. He started to pull off his clothes while she got into bed and watched him, gently lit by the bedside light, her right hand between her legs massaging herself. None of the girls he had had so far did that, and he found it both infuriating and exciting. He rolled into bed beside her, his clothes strewn everywhere, and put his hand over hers to take over what she was doing, and kept on until she came, then slid into her.

'That was lovely,' she said in his ear, as he moved sideways to shift his weight off her; naked and sweating, she was somehow more solid than when fully dressed, but she still looked frail and thin, her long legs stick-like against his strong, thick limbs. 'Can you stay?'

'Yeah. Yes, please,' he added, remembering his public school persona, and they drifted into sleep together, sweating but comfortable.

A week later, reluctantly, he was back at Woolverstone Hall. It had been the best week of his life; he had gone on working at the restaurant on the lucrative night shift but he had spent all his days with Suzie, mostly in bed. She would come and meet him at 1 a.m. from the bar, protected by the Spanish crew who ran it, so that when he emerged, showered, having put out the nightly load of meat, with money in his pocket, there she was, slight and desirable, and he would kiss her, knowing himself envied by at least half the bar. He had spent some of his money too, buying her a pair of gold earrings she had admired, and she had been thrilled but had reproached him for spending his savings. Perhaps it had been that evidence of love and concern that had given him courage when she had wanted the school's address, so she could write or telephone. He had hesitated, frightened, but not exactly unprepared, for he had known for three days that this moment must come, though he had arrived at no satisfactory strategy.

'It's not a public school exactly,' he had said to her bare shoulder.

'What is it then?' she had asked wonderingly, and he had found himself telling her all about Woolverstone Hall. She *had* been taken aback, but they were in bed and he had made love to her afterwards, and by the next morning she had adjusted herself to the idea. But he had not been able to bear to tell her about the childhood that had led him to Woolverstone, and had instead killed off Franz Vazarely – whom he had promoted to work in a bank – and Elisaveta in a plane crash, leaving himself to be taken into care. He had liked this version of his life and decided to keep it; it saved a good deal of explanation and it covered the facts from which there was no escape. And he had Suzie now, who had come to see him off at Euston on the school train, wearing flared trousers which clung to every line of her bottom and a T-shirt which showed her nipples to the unlimited envy of his contemporaries, and the gentle approval of Old Caldwell, who had been nice to her, kindly and approving, and treated them both as grown-ups.

He stood, irresolute, on the steps of the main building; A-levels were only six weeks away and he ought to have been in the library, but it was profoundly not what he wanted to do. He wanted to be in bed with Suzie, kissing her right now, and he fidgeted resentfully; he was having a wank twice a day sometimes, but it wasn't helping, nothing was. He forced himself to stand still, remembering Old Caldwell's words. 'What I do, Paul, when I've got the fidgets is just sit still and look around me; doing something makes it worse somehow.' He drew in a deep breath and opened his eyes to the familiar view of the huge, distant trees on the estate's boundary. The leaves were new and acid green and the lawn smelt of its first mowing that summer. There wasn't enough money to keep up the grounds, of course, but the park had been planted in a time when labour and young trees were cheap, and although some needed felling and there were ragged gaps in places, the bones of the estate were sound. He would miss the view and the space; even with the rash of Nissen huts there was room to move for the two hundred boys in the grounds, and the rooms, at least in the main house, had high ceilings which soaked up noise, and big windows so you could breathe and see out. He stared soberly across the lawns, watching the mower go backwards and forwards, much slower than he would have driven it, leaving the lawn in stripes behind it. He had always promised himself that he would find a house like this for himself when he got out of school, but up to now it had been not exactly a dream, more a vague conviction. He had saved several hundred pounds as a result of his restaurant activities and had picked up a brochure, left behind by a customer after his long lunch, showing a house like Woolverstone Hall, only smaller and better kept, and he had looked at it hungrily. 'Price on application', it had said, but written in pencil was '£110,000 asking'. He remembered that now, with an almost physical pain, agonized by the realization that some things he wanted were unreachable from where he was. Chef was said to be taking home £7000, and much of that was what the suppliers gave him for the orders plus his cut on what went out of the back of the kitchen. But that wasn't going to finance a house like the one in the brochure, it wouldn't pay the running-costs, never mind the interest on buying it. And yet some people were born to this, it was theirs, they had the right to a piece of space and beauty, which he was never going to have. He stood stiffly, terrified by the sense of loss; it was never going to be all right, he would always be on the outside. He heard footsteps beside him and turned sharply, ready to hit out, but it was only Sean, moving quietly. He said something, inaudibly as usual, and Paul, shaking off terror, barked at him to get his mouth open, silly bogtrotter.

'You want to go for a jar tonight? Down the pub?'

The Sixth Form, all ten of them, were allowed out once a

week, provided they were back by 11.30 p.m. Sean, in fact, went out nearly every night; he had been kept on at the school for an extra year past the official leaving-age of sixteen, because he still only read with difficulty. He could not read at all when he had arrived at fourteen, and would have been sent away again but for Old Caldwell. Woolverstone Hall was a school for boys of above-average IQ; the average boys and the ones who were a brick short of a wall went to one of three smaller establishments. Old Caldwell, however, had re-tested Sean, discovered his truly amazing mathematical abilities and insisted on keeping him. He still did not see words or letters like other people did, it all got jumbled up, but he was getting better slowly, and he was doing A-level maths a year early.

Paul thought about the invitation; he had, exceptionally, received permission to spend the forthcoming Saturday night in London, and he ought really to work all the other hours there were. 'Nah. Thanks, Sean.' He waited, expecting the little Paddy to leave as silently as he had arrived, but Sean stood his ground.

'You need a jar on your birthday, and dat's de truth.'

'It's not till tomorrow,' Paul said, amazed, 'How did you know?'

Sean ignored the question, looking away uneasily. Caldwell, Paul thought, exasperated but touched. He and Suzie were going to celebrate his eighteenth birthday in their own way on Saturday and he shuffled his feet in restless anticipation. 'Thanks, Sean, but why not tomorrow?'

'It's de concert.' And Sean was doing the lights, of course. Whatever was wrong with the wiring in his head, he was a genius with his hands.

'OK,' Paul said, warmed reluctantly. 'Thanks, mate. Usual time?'

By eight o'clock that night, Paul had forced himself to do some work which had had its usual therapeutic effect. He had also sought and gained permission for the outing, having managed to remember Old Caldwell's advice about not having battles you didn't need. He felt reasonably at peace with himself and it was a beautiful May evening, cool, with a bit of a breeze which rustled the bright green, slightly crumpled leaves on the big oak trees at the gate. The gravel crunched beneath their feet as he swung the big gate shut, noticing that the cowslips, which old Caldwell was so keen on, were just coming into flower on the bank.

'Where'd you want to live, Sean? I mean, if you could have anything.'

'One of them modern flats with a seven-foot double bed and all de gear; speakers and that. Somewhere high up, so you could see the tops of de trees, with a curtain round de bed and a bathroom. Wid a gym.'

Paul tried not to gape at him. Sean had not spoken to anyone except Old Caldwell for weeks when he had arrived three years ago, and he was still pretty uncommunicative.

'And one of them kitchens with an island in it, and a refrigerator where you get ice, know what I mean? And a bar in de lounge.'

'Have you seen a place like this?' It hardly seemed likely; Sean had come as a seven-year-old from rural County Cork to a crowded slum in West Kilburn.

'On de fillums.'

'What film?' Paul, a natural mimic, like all good linguists, narrowly avoided saying 'fillum', and listened, fascinated, while Sean explained about the James Bond epic which had featured just such a place, using his hands to demonstrate the spaces, the fingers, which were normally held slightly clenched, splayed wide in an attempt to explain his vision. 'It'd cost a bit,' he ventured carefully, wondering how much Sean understood about this fantasy.

'Yeah.' Sean's hands clenched again and he looked down at the road, as he usually did.

'You'll maybe make it off the computers,' Paul said hastily.

Sean depressed was a dangerous man, as all the Hall knew. 'De guy who started IBM made plenty.'

'*That's* true,' Paul agreed, reluctantly tasting bile from pure jealousy. Sean, inarticulate little bogtrotter though he was, was accepted as a genius with a computer; he was already programming for IBM in his spare moments and was going to a job there at the end of term. Maybe his fantasy was within his grasp.

He barged through the pub door, cheerfulness banished. The place was quiet, deserted, except for three blokes in the corner with a pint and a couple of empties each in front of them. He knew them to nod to, locals, thick as shit, probably working on a building site to judge from their dusty clothes and the strong smell of sweat. If he'd been alone he'd have gone into the saloon, but among Sean's multiple peculiarities was a hatred of anything except the public bar, and it was his shot.

'You sit down, Paul.' Sean walked over to the bar with the familiar bow-legged, hunched gait, and said something to the barman, having to repeat himself and to wait for a few minutes, while Paul gazed into space trying not to listen to the conversation from the corner table which was monotonous and boastful in the extreme. A 'pop' like a door opening caught his ear and he looked up to see Sean carrying a bottle and two glasses. 'Dom Perignon,' he said solemnly, pronouncing it phonetically. 'Yer eighteen, or yer will be, tomorrow. Grown up.'

They looked at each other and burst out laughing, and Sean, with the tight-lipped smile back in place, the upper lip pulled down to hide uneven and blackened front teeth, poured out two glasses and they solemnly toasted each other.

'Bloody delicious,' Paul said, having downed the first glass, and Sean, pleased, poured him a second. They got through the bottle in very short order, and Sean, lifting his hand against any protest, went off to get a second, which they killed more slowly.

The group in the corner were getting steadily noisier, their voices raised in argument, and the Woolverstone Hall boys, experienced with aggression, decided by mutual consent to leave. Sean, who was unnaturally tidy for a bogtrotter, got up to put back the glasses on the bar counter at the same time as one of the group in the corner lurched to his feet in search of the gents. They crossed in the middle of the floor and Paul saw it happen; the big lout trod on Sean's foot, painfully and deliberately, and Sean's knee was in his groin before Paul could get his mouth open or his bottom off the seat. The big bloke doubled up and Paul kicked his way clear of the table and was at Sean's side in seconds, but it was too late. The bloke's mates were on their feet, spoiling for a fight. One of them came in, arms flailing, and as Paul ducked to get out of the way, pain shot through his head from a blow from the third bloke who had been aiming at Sean. He heard breaking glass and felt it splinter under his feet as he went in, pain burning his mind out, to try to kill the bloke who had hit him, but he heard and saw nothing else until much, much later when for some reason Sean was trying to strangle him, twisting his tie round his neck, and the room was filled with confused shouting. He was practically blacked out but he kept his hands where they were on the big bugger's throat until he had to let go to stop himself being strangled. He fought Sean off savagely and had drawn in a huge, painful lungful, dimly understanding that blood was pouring down his own face into his eyes, and that the room was full of people.

He felt the chill of metal on one wrist, then both arms were dragged round behind his back and the other cuff clicked on; he was lying on his face in spilt beer, screaming with rage, with something large and heavy on top of him.

'He'd have killed him if you hadn't been here, George.' Paul could hear a high, over-excited voice, assuring the air above him. 'Jesus Christ, I've never seen anything like that. I knew we'd have trouble with those nutters up the road, sooner or later.'

'Call de Warden.' Sean had somehow got his mouth open. He was sitting on the floor beside Paul and cupped his hand under Paul's cheek to keep it off the floor, but Paul, beside himself still, snapped at it, and Sean just got it away in time.

'Will you look at that?' a voice said righteously.

'We didn't start it,' Sean mumbled, defeated, and the

enormity of what was happening started to penetrate the exhilarating, transforming rage that had Paul in its grip, and he banged his head on the floor in grief and misery, just like all the other times when he'd been beaten to his knees as a child with no prospect of retaliation.

'I've rung the school,' another over-excited voice reported, greeted by a rumble from the weight on top of Paul. 'You could let him up.'

Sean was crying too, he understood, and nobody had ever seen that happen before.

'In a minute.' The weight on top of Paul shifted and he cried out. There was a moment of relief as the big bloke sitting on him got up hastily, and turned him over, so he could sit up, hunched over and gasping from the pain in his ribs, hands strained painfully behind him. The door banged open and it was, thank Christ, Old Caldwell, but behind him was the Warden, looking every inch the tough screw he had once been. He had to look away; Caldwell was looking so wretched.

It was two o'clock in the morning of his birthday before the Warden had got him and Sean out of the nick and the hospital and into the Woolverstone Hall van. The four of them drove in silence, Sean sleeping like a child on Old Caldwell's shoulder in the back, he himself silent and wretched in the front seat next to the Warden, who was looking like a stone idol. The bloke he'd tried to kill was still unconscious; he had sustained a fractured skull as he went down on the floor and while unlikely to die might well be brain-damaged, as the Warden had observed several times. They were lucky, and the only reason both he and Sean were not in police custody was an absolute shortage of cell space caused by a three-week-old prison riot that had distributed the contents of the local jail to every secure space available. The consequences for Woolverstone Hall were potentially very serious, he could see. The locals periodically got their knickers in a twist about having a bunch of intermittently violent adolescents living up the road, not that they'd had any trouble for a couple of years, but this incident had everything; three local young men in hospital, substantial damage to a bar, and the whole thing blown up out of a clear sky, as the publican had sought to maintain all night to anyone who would listen.

'I'm sorry,' Paul said, forcing out the words that he had been trying to say for the last four hours.

'Bit late for that.' The Warden's mouth was set in the tight, thin line that always meant trouble. They drove on in uncomfortable, tense silence.

'Christ, you are a bloody fool,' the Warden said suddenly. 'You could have been out of here with your A-levels in six weeks' time, you idiot.' He sounded desolate rather than angry, Paul understood, chilled. 'And Kelly there; I know what'll happen, he'll forget how to read and he won't be able to work. Get the gate, please.'

Paul climbed stiffly out, very conscious of his taped ribs, and let the van through, noticing as he got back in that Caldwell, looking not just old but half-dead, was waking up, and so was Sean, fighting his way back from the depths. He stared at them. 'It's all right, my boy,' Caldwell said, between coughing his lungs out and massaging his chest, as he did when he woke from one of these little naps. 'He's still with us, just. And nobody's dead.'

Paul felt his head start to ache again unbearably as the pressure shifted behind his eyes, and then he was weeping, hugging his painful ribs as his chest heaved uncontrollably. He could not stop. It was the Warden who more or less carried him out and got them all into the big silent kitchen and put the kettle on.

'Let's see if we can find a biscuit,' he said, bustling about getting tea, while Old Caldwell threw open cupboards and Paul and Sean sat like stones at the table, not looking at each other. A stifled noise caught their attention and they both looked up wearily, just too quickly for Old Caldwell, who was clumsily trying to shut a door again. But they had all seen it by then, a large, newly iced cake with eighteen candle-holders and PAUL written on it in careful, blue, scrolled icing.

CHAPTER EIGHT

April 1973

'Banner!'

'Sir?'

'Excellent test paper. Even better than last week's. Go on like this and you could get a distinction.' The history master handed him back his paper and he took it, turning to the back page as he walked back to his place. Seventy-five per cent. A good grade, well above anything he had managed before, but modern history had gripped him in a way that the Tudors and Stuarts through which he had laboured pre-O-level had not. All those kings remained, irrevocably, characters on playing-cards, while Kerensky and Lenin were real, you could feel what they were about and see what they were trying to do. He was doing history alongside English and maths for A-level; the Army, for which he was now firmly destined, would have preferred physics or chemistry, but the Ashford masters had advised firmly against it and he had indeed barely scraped passes in both at O-level. History the Army was prepared to accept; officers, they conceded, had probably better know some of that alongside the essential English and maths. The history helped with English and European literature where he had been struggling; suddenly he found himself avidly reading Dostoevsky because he was writing about events and people who were now real to him. The head of English had wondered aloud about university, but there was no question of that. David could not face either himself or his mother having to seek more help on top of that so grudgingly given by his uncles. He had to have a paying job, straight away, such as the Army provided. He reminded himself that he was lucky to be here, away from home which would have packing-cases everywhere. He absolutely did not want to be involved in the move, carefully scheduled to take place at the beginning of the Easter holidays, but knew that his mother would never manage without him, with his father in faraway Hong Kong. He sat at his desk against the background of the rest of the second history set collecting their essays in a clatter of feet and shifting desks, and explored the sore spot that covered everything to do with his father. He missed him, the silly bugger. He understood, as his mother did not seem to, that Dad had not meant to find himself in Hong Kong, working his guts out to support two women, his three real children and this baby wished on him by a new wife. He'd meant to have a bit of fun, as he had before, and he had mismanaged it. David shivered inwardly, seeing suddenly how a piece of miscalculation, out of vanity or greed, or simply being fed-up, could mean you woke up to find yourself in real shit, with no hope of getting out of it. He put his paper aside, with a final look at the 75 per cent and the words of congratulation at the end. He was going to follow the course on which his feet were set and come out with a training and a real, paid job, leaving others to go for their degrees with no guarantee of a job afterwards.

He went on to his English class, glancing out of the window to where the buses which would take the London boys to the station were congregating in the spring sun. He was going to spend five days at home, the removal vans were coming, and he and his mother and the boys were packing up all the china and movables themselves in order to save money. He had been through the moving routine many times as a Navy child, but the Services provided you with the lot, a squad of grown men to do all the packing, so all his mother had had to do was supervise and be gracious over cups of tea. Thereafter, blessedly, he was expected for a week's training with his prospective regiment in the hills of Northumberland, so he could not be required to help at the other end. In any case there were two aunts in Edinburgh and they would help, he thought, resolutely ignoring the knot of anxiety.

Four hours later he was walking through the gate at home. Bits of kit lay all over the lawn, looking dismembered; his mother had evidently not got much done yet. The door opened and two large men came out, each carrying a television, followed at an interval by a third, carrying the family's canteen of silver – a large, heavily made elmwood box. They walked past him heavy-footed, not looking at him, and he turned to watch them push their loads into the back of a smallish van.

'Davey!' His mother came rushing down the path in a terrible fluster, and he held out his arms to her. She kissed him and clung for a minute.

'Who are these blokes?' he asked, puzzled. 'Are they moving the valuables separately, or what?'

'Oh, Davey.' She was still clinging to him but would not meet his eye. He looked up at the house for inspiration and saw Mickey and Thomas at the door. They saw him and both started to run, pushing each other off the path.

'They've taken your cups, Davey,' Thomas reported, scarlet and distressed.

'Who has?'

'Those blokes with the van. I wouldn't let them take Mum's necklace.'

He turned to run to the van but his mother held him. 'No, please, Davey. I'll explain. They're not burglars, I've told the boys they're not.'

'Then who are they? And why are they moving our stuff?' He looked at Mickey for enlightenment, but he was out of it, white with misery and doing that handwashing thing again.

'They're bailiffs, they say.' Thomas, tough little Thomas, was sounding uncertain, and he stared at his mother who would not meet his eye.

'We owe money,' she said at last, looking at her shoes, crimson to the neckline of her blouse.

'How much?'

'A bit more than fifteen hundred, I suppose, by now, with interest.' She would not look at him and he knew that if he pressed her there would be a storm of tears and rage. And there wasn't going to be, not with the little boys hanging on to him and those bastards going down the path with the big clock that had been his grandfather's, and the neighbours all hanging round in their little gardens, ears flapping.

'Look after Mum for a minute, will you, Tommy? Take her and Mickey inside and make a cup of tea.' He saw them up the path, his mother between the boys. Mickey had grown again and was nearly her height, but still so thin a wind could blow him away, skeletal inside the bulky jeans and sweatshirt. They looked, he thought suddenly, like all the pictures of refugees everywhere, trailing away to nowhere in particular, weeping in front of their shattered houses.

He stepped in front of the smallest of the three men who was leading the two heavies back to the house. 'I've just got back,' he said crisply. 'Will you tell me what's happening?'

The man looked at him warily. 'Mrs Banner – your mother, is she?'

'Yes.'

'She entered into an agreement to borrow money and has been unable to fulfil the terms of that agreement. I have a court order authorizing me to take possession of goods to the value of the debt.'

'Can I see the order, please?'

The man handed it over, and he tried to make sense of it. The debt appeared to be £1700 and the order was dated three days before. He tried again, the small man waiting like a statue, the two big chaps fidgeting on the path. A loan for £1500 seemed to have been taken out the previous July.

He had £300 in his Post Office account, and Mickey and Thomas probably had less.

'If you could wait, I can cable my father. He's in Hong Kong.'

The little man did not move. 'I'm sorry, son. I can see this comes as a shock. Yer ma would have done that, surely?'

'They're divorced . . . I mean, separated.' He stopped, hearing his words in the air. 'But he wouldn't . . . I mean . . .'

'In any case,' the little man said, having waited to see if he had any more to say, 'we've loaded the van, and we are only authorized to accept cash or a certified cheque on the spot for the full amount stated on the order.'

'Wait.' He felt suddenly competent again. 'All right, I understand. But if I can get you a cheque, can we get the goods back? Some of them are family treasures.'

The little man considered him. 'They go into a sale, see,' he said gently. 'But not for a week or so. If you was quick, you could get them back, that's what I tell everyone.'

David would have liked to smash his sympathetic face in, but he had himself in hand; if he didn't get his mother out of this mess no one else was going to. 'Thank you,' he said in his best officer tones. 'Will you leave me the name and phone number of the person I should contact?'

'My pleasure.' The man fished out a battered notebook and a biro and wrote down the required information, then collected his men and got into the van beside the driver and pulled on a seat-belt. 'Good luck with it, son,' he said and lifted a hand in farewell as the van pulled away.

David turned, teeth gritted in rage. There was mess everywhere and he kicked a rake out of his way, knocking his ankle as he did so. He banged in through the front door and saw that the house was worse; large cardboard boxes with newspaper in wild confusion on top of them and balls of paper scattered everywhere.

'Where is everybody?' he shouted, discharging rage and frustration.

'I'm here.' It was Thomas, wide-eyed, the bounce gone out of him, and David put an arm round him. 'Where's Mum?'

'In the living-room. I made tea.'

'Good lad.' He braced himself to go through the door, dreading what he would find, but she was just sitting and looking out of the window.

'What we need is lunch,' he said authoritatively, to her back.

'Then we can decide what to do, and get this place straightened up. Where's Mickey?'

'In the cloakroom.'

'Oh no, he's bloody not doing that.' He dashed into the hall and pulled Mickey away from the basin, hands dripping. 'No, you don't,' he said, scarlet with fury. 'This is *real* trouble we have here, not voices in your stupid head. Get your hands dry and come and do a day's work for a change.' He was shaking with rage and reaction and would have knocked his brother silly had he demurred in any way, but actually Mickey did none of that, just dried his hands obediently and came in to help with lunch.

They ate fried eggs and fried bread, cooked by his mother in the kitchen. The stove was filthy and the floor wet, but he ignored it, and explained, in tones brooking no argument, that Mickey and Thomas would complete the packing of all movable objects in the living-room by tea-time, then he would see what else needed to be done. After half an hour he decided he could leave the boys to finish the books and the ornaments, while he got a grip on the rest of the situation. He shut the kitchen door behind him. 'Now tell me, so I can understand.'

His mother had had time to compose herself, the floor was clean and the stove shining. They sat opposite each other at the kitchen table wrapping piles of china, so that she did not have to look at him. The story that emerged was confused and tearful, and he understood after questions aimed at clarification had been evaded, or simply not answered, that he was not going to get to the bottom of it. The general outlines were clear; his father had stopped making payments to the bank on the mortgage, obviously to put pressure on his mother to agree to the sale of the house. He had, however, continued to pay the agreed amounts directly to her, so she had not been penniless. She had, partly for Mickey's sake, but mostly, he saw sadly, for reasons having to do with her own status and her anger at his father, been absolutely determined not to sell the house. So she had sat tight, throwing away any letters from the bank or forwarding them to Hong Kong, and waiting for

129

his father to relent. After some months, a nice woman from the bank had visited her and had explained, very pleasantly it seemed, that no one wanted to take their house away and, if Mrs Banner could manage to pay some of the mortgage arrears, well, then the bank would stay its hand. His mother, assuming against all historical fact that she could manage on half the money she was getting from his father, had paid the agreed amount to the bank every month.

'Well, I *had* to, Davey. I didn't want to find us all in the street, and I hoped your father would manage to send us some more. I mean, I wrote to him.'

'What did he say?' David was suddenly consumed with rage against his absent father, living it up in Hong Kong.

'Well, he *said* he couldn't help, that his job was not working out and, of course, the bitch he went off with got ill and was in hospital. High blood pressure.'

He looked up anxiously, well aware that he was on dangerous ground. 'I forgot to ask. Is the – did the baby get born?'

'Yes.' His mother's hands clenched on the plate she was packing and she stared at them. 'A girl.'

'Oh.' He looked at her helplessly; she was sitting absolutely still, head bowed. He reached over to take her hand. 'I'm sorry, Mum.'

He thought that she was going to cry again, but she didn't, just squeezed his hand and sniffed. 'Yes. That was awful.' She sounded strained but better. 'So there was *that*, and his job not going well. I just managed as best I could, paying some of the mortgage every month, but then they said they needed more because we were falling behind and I couldn't manage to keep us even in food. So I borrowed £1000. From one of those companies that advertise. Just till I could get organized. Then I borrowed a bit more because there was this enormous electricity bill to pay.

'Why didn't you *tell* me? Or why didn't Dad?'

'I didn't want to distract you from your A-levels.' They looked at each other wryly. 'Your father said he had written to you.'

True, he acknowledged, accepting the worm of guilt that had been eating at him as he listened to this history. But his father had not made it clear what the real problem was, he had banged on about not being able to afford the mortgage, and asked him to go and reason with his mother and get her to sell the house. He had never confessed that he was dealing with the problem of an unaffordable mortgage by simply not paying it.

'We can get all the things – the ones they took – back, if we get the money together inside the next week,' he said, as neutrally as he could.

She stared at him. 'You don't think I'd have let them take anything if I could have found the money?'

'Who did you ask? Apart from Dad, I mean.'

'Well, no one.'

'All right. I've got £300 in the Post Office, Mickey's got £270. Tommy's only got £150. He bought the bike, remember, which went this morning.'

She burst into tears and he waited for her to stop, murderously angry. She had let them take Tommy's treasured bike, and they were going to get his hoarded, treasured £300, saved from two years of Christmas jobs and presents, and all she could do was weep and wail.

'I can't take your money,' she said tearfully.

'Then whose money are you going to use?'

'Don't *shout* at me.' She was drenched in hopeless, self-pitying tears. 'I can't ask James or William. They've already done a lot.'

'Granny?'

'She just asks James or William about anything to do with money.'

The door opened and Thomas put his head round, asking hopefully for tea, and got told to bugger off for half an hour. They both listened to his steps trailing down the corridor.

'I never thought it would come to this,' his mother said miserably, and he looked at her, too exhausted and angry to summon any kind of consoling response.

'Well, it has, hasn't it?' he said at last.

'And you think I've been a complete bloody fool. It's *not* my fault, Davey, it's your father who has let us all down.'

'I'll ring him.' He suddenly felt a great deal better. 'He needs to know what's happening.'

'*Could* you? He might listen to you.' She reached eagerly for the phone and he saw that she had been playing for this.

'I'll do it after tea and I want to be on my own.' She looked rebellious. 'Or I won't do it at all.'

She pouted and he remembered, as if from a hundred years ago, that he used to be frightened of her temper.

Three days later he straightened up from sorting the contents of the last box in the small loft, which had proved to contain baby clothes which had once covered Thomas, an envelope of photographs which had reduced his mother, again, to tears, and six years of his school reports which he had put into the overflowing trunk which now held all his possessions.

The Edinburgh flat had only three bedrooms and he had said firmly that one was not to be kept empty for him; when he came to stay Mickey and Thomas could double up and meanwhile one of them could share a room with his trunk. What he meant, as he was sure his mother had understood, was that he did not want to have anything to do with the Edinburgh flat or his uncles or his grandmother ever again. He had telephoned his father on the night the bailiffs had come and explained the problem tersely and angrily to the voice that had sounded pleased at hearing him. There had been a long silence and his father had then said that it was no good, old boy, he could not be sorrier but there just wasn't any money. He had £57 till next pay-day, and next month's pay was already allocated. His mother's allowance would arrive on time, but it was only £300, as David presumably knew. He had pressed, but his father had lost his temper and roundly condemned the idiocy that had made the silly witch hang on to an expensive house rather than cut clear as she'd been told to do, and then wept painfully when told about Tommy's bike. 'I'm sorry,' he had kept on repeating, uselessly, until David rang off, sick with misery and rage.

He had talked then to James, the easier of his two uncles, with whom he had always thought he got on. At first his uncle had been unable to believe that anyone could get into that degree of financial muddle and there had been a moment of rapport while David, disloyally, had agreed with his view. He had been left with the taste of betrayal in his mouth while Uncle James, an experienced and skilled negotiator, had retired to consult the rest of the family. The terms finally agreed had been just short of real humiliation; his father had managed somehow to cable £300, Granny had contributed £500, and both uncles had come up with £400, with maximum ill-grace; their sister had committed the ultimate sin of needing cash, urgently, near the beginning of a school term when every penny was needed for fees – his, as they had not hesitated to remind him, as well as their own sons'. He himself had produced the balance of £165; the uncles had taken the line that there was no point in cleaning him out, he would then only need to come to them for his officer's uniform, but he could subscribe, so that he would not fail to understand the undesirability of debt. As if anyone who had lived through the past three days could have failed to learn the lesson that for the want of comparatively small sums, you could find yourself held to ransom by an uncaring world. And treated punitively by those on whom you might have expected to rely because they were frightened of having the drowning clinging to the boat. He felt bruised all over and was desperately short-tempered by the time he got himself, three certified cheques and a wallet of cash to the head bailiff, who had wished him luck with such obvious lack of conviction. In the event that, curiously enough, had been the one comfortable part of the whole experience. The man had been both surprised and openly glad to see him and had helped him find and pack their possessions into his mother's battered car, which had already been sold, but which he had managed to hold on to for an extra day.

'I wish yer ma had come and seen us before,' he had said. 'I *hate* these companies who lend people like you cash at these interest rates. What we'd have done, see, is agree a repayment of the debt at five quid a week, something like that.'

David had stared at the man, suddenly seeing him as a person rather than part of a humiliating process. 'But the debt would have taken years to pay off.'

'So? Nothing them bastards could have done about it. You remember that, son, if you ever see trouble like this again.'

So while he wasn't going to see this trouble ever for himself, he had understood that people of the sort his mother thought common were human and even on his side, and the memory warmed him.

He looked up as Mickey crept through the door and checked, halted by his expression. He pulled himself together; old Mickey had put up an unexpectedly good show in the emergency, had packed diligently, made tea when asked to and indeed behaved so sensibly that after the first two phone calls David had explained to him what was going on, and why. And he had not fainted or wept or gone into orgies of handwashing. He had carried on being a bloody good second lieutenant, as he had told him. He had tried once, inevitably, to suggest that all this mess was his fault, but had accepted David's prompt, unequivocal, angry assurance that the whole shitty, awful balls-up had been made by their idiotic parents.

'All done,' he said now, more cheerfully than he felt. 'Tomorrow they can put the whole lot in vans.'

'And you're going to camp?'

'Day after.' He was going to give himself a treat the following evening, he most certainly was.

'You *will* come and stay with us?'

'Of course I will.' He looked at Mickey, seeing again how thin he was. 'Not these holidays, there's no time, but the next exeat weekend, I promise. You look after yourself – you can, you know. You've done brilliantly the last three days. Much better than Thomas.' And that was true, Tommy had been terrified by the catastrophe and had clung to his mother and to David when he would let him. He had received his treasured bicycle back with incredulity but not with real pleasure; he had had too much of a scare although he would get over it.

'Yes, it's all right when you're here.'

'It'll be all right without me,' David said sharply, rejecting the demands in the wide eyes and moving hands. He tried the magic again. 'Make some tea, quick, then we'll clean up here.'

The next morning he had them all out of bed at six, beds stripped, and blankets boxed, sheets in a separate bag to go into the washing-machine when they got to Edinburgh. They were going by train, leaving him to see that everything was loaded into the vans, which had been paid for in advance. The taxi arrived – he had not felt it proper that his family should leave on foot – and he shooed them into it, checking that Mickey had the £5 he had allotted for miscellaneous expenditure. He shut the passenger door and leaned through to kiss his mother goodbye, and felt an enormous grieving pain, like a stone in his chest. He reached into the back to kiss Thomas, and grinned wryly at Mickey before kissing him too.

'Ring me to let me know you're there, Mick. Before seven, remember. I'm going out.' He stepped back, hearing his voice crack, and waved the driver on, turning away so as not to have to see them wave goodbye.

The day went fast of course. Twenty minutes after his family had left, two massive vans ground up the short hill and he helped the men to back the first one up to the garage by the kitchen. They were pleased and congratulatory about the state of the house, explaining that normally these jobs where the people were doing their own packing were a nightmare, honestly, you would *not* believe. He had been pleased, even with the wry recollection that these men could have no idea what a nightmare the process had actually been, and had explained that he was destined for the Army. At that point the biggest of them disclosed that he had done four years in the Welsh Guards, as a private, start to finish. He had found it necessary to manufacture some final errand for himself to break up the coffee party, but he had retained a warm glow from their obvious admiration of a job well done. That was why he was going into the Army, because you brought order out of chaos and kept it that way, and your fellow-men looked up to you and followed you.

It was lonely once the vans had left for the London depot where they would wait overnight before the long journey to Edinburgh, leaving him and his Army issue camp-bed and sleeping-bag in the living-room, with a tin mug also out for the morning. Then Mickey rang, sounding exhausted and very far away, from Uncle James's house where the three of them were squeezed in for the night till their furniture arrived.

'Is Mum OK?'

'A bit weepy.'

'Oh, Christ. Not again,' he said, heartfelt, and heard old Mickey laugh explosively. 'She'll be better when she's got the furniture there. I'll ring her tomorrow sometime on my way to camp,' he added hastily and put the phone down before she could countermand him. He cradled the receiver in his hand and dialled a familiar number.

'It's David. Where are we going?' He felt for the remaining £10 in his wallet, and accepted, gratified, her proposal that she would raid her mother's fridge, her parents being out until dinner, and bring something round with her, confirming demurely that he would prefer that to eating with her parents.

Thirty minutes later he was welcoming Teresa Caulfield. She arrived in the Mini she shared with her mother – she had been promised one of her own if her A-level results came up to scratch. Opening the gate for her to drive through, he had a flash of self-pity; no one was going to give him any presents for decent A-levels, while the penalties for failure would be catastrophic. He thrust the thought from him and bent to kiss Teresa as she got out of the car. She clung to him but he collected her bag for her and bustled her inside; the neighbours had had enough to entertain them in the last few days.

'Goodness,' she said in awe, as they walked into the echoing, empty living-room, his camp-bed and sleeping-bag looking forlorn in the corner. She stood, clutching packages, a small girl with the same black curly hair, clear skin and long eyelashes as her Irish father, a capable developer and builder whom

David's mother thought common. 'So, where do you go now, Davey?'

'To camp. Then school.'

'But where's your home?' She had not moved her eyes from the camp-bed, and he felt an unexpected treacherous constriction in his chest.

'In Edinburgh, I suppose. I don't need one just now.'

She put her basket down and held out her arms and he clung to her, holding her head hard on to his shoulder with his left arm, so that she could not see his face. He felt her arms go round him under his sweater and he felt round her bottom with his right hand, pulling up her short skirt to get at the edge of her knickers.

'Ah,' he said, distracted. 'Hang on.' He released his left hand and pulled her skirt up. 'You're not wearing any.'

'Do you mind?'

'No, no.' He was, he discovered, a little shocked. She must have driven fifteen minutes in that short skirt riding up her legs. 'What if you'd been in an accident?'

'The ambulance men would have had a real surprise.' She was undoing the buttons of his shirt and he leant back to let her do it, basking in being slowly undressed. He waited happily, hands on her buttocks under the skirt which was up round her waist, while she reached his belt and undid the buckle. She unzipped him deftly and put a hand on his balls and he groaned with pleasure and anticipation. 'Get 'em off.'

'Hang on, you impatient woman.' He kicked off his trousers and tugged his underpants off, leaving his shirt on, shook out the sleeping-bag with one hand and pulled her down on top of him, so she was sitting on him with her skirt up and her blouse open. 'You're wet already. Christ, the ambulance men would have had a treat.'

'Let me get my skirt off.'

'No, I like it.' He pushed into the wet, welcoming place and felt it settle round him, tight and warm. She reached behind her back and undid her bra so that her breasts, large for a small girl, flopped forward, and he put his hands over them, feeling the floor hard beneath his spine. That's why people do it in beds, he thought, and then he was beyond thought, trying to hold back long enough to give Teresa a chance, his hands holding her buttocks until he came in several long spurts of pleasure, thrusting as deep as he could into her.

She lay on him when he had finished, with him still inside her, her breasts flattened on his chest and her face against his while he cried with painful, uncontrollable tears, his nose and sinuses blocking and running, so that their faces were soaked. She held him, not talking or asking him questions, letting him weep, until it somehow stopped. His penis had gone soft and he had fallen out of her, so he peeled off the condom, automatically looking to see how much there was inside, holding her tenderly.

'Sorry.'

'Oh, don't you be silly.' There were tears in her eyes as she cradled him, both of them shivering slightly now in the cold room. 'I'm only glad I was here.'

'So am I.' He had been desolate and now there was a warm girl in his arms who would feed him supper and care what happened to him. 'I love you,' he said, in gratitude, and held her as she kissed him, the tears falling.

'Supper?' he suggested cautiously, and she got up with a watery smile and did up her bra and her blouse and tugged her skirt down, so that she would be respectable if anyone were to come in, and disappeared to the upstairs bathroom. He got back into his pants and disposed of the condom and had a wash, swilling water over his face again and again, looking unsmiling but admiringly at the familiar straight nose and well-set eyes. He emerged, his footsteps very loud in the empty, uncarpeted spaces, to find Teresa in the kitchen, laying out food on the counter. He remembered he had put two decrepit garden chairs out for the dustmen and went to retrieve them temporarily so that they could sit, which was just as well. Teresa probably hadn't got much out of that performance. He said as much to her, and she blushed and said it had been lovely, although she hadn't come, and he had taken her hand, touched. But he had made certain, afterwards, on the sleeping-bag spread out on the floor, with his tongue on the little bump inside the flesh so that she had cried out, and only then when he was sure had he turned her over and gone in again. They lay entwined afterwards, her leg up over him and her face in his neck, but the room was cold and the floor dug into his spine and he started to fidget, so they got dressed, and he draped the sleeping-bag over the camp-bed to dry; there was a wet patch there that smelt of her and which would only distract him at camp.

She hesitated, looking very young in the half-light, clasping her basket. 'When will I see you?'

'Soon,' he promised. 'I've got an exeat in three weeks' time.'

'Won't they want you in Edinburgh?'

They do, of course, he thought uneasily, and he would have to go, particularly after the rescue mounted by his uncles. He looked at her ruefully, relying on her affection for him.

'And after that?'

It wasn't that he didn't want to see her, but there was A-level and, unlike her, he had his life riding on it. But she loved him, and she had looked after him, and by Christ he had needed it and would need it again. He kissed her with real affection and promised her a weekend before A-level, somehow.

'What have you forgotten, Jennifer?'

She thought, counting on her fingers. 'The parsley. But that doesn't cost *anything*.'

'Very little in the country in the summer. But in town, in the winter . . . what else did she forget?'

'The *cream*,' half the class said virtuously.

'I only used a little.' Jens said sadly.

'One and a half gills. If you add the cream and the parsley you've made a dish that you would have to charge at . . . what?'

Everyone did the sum and she gritted her teeth. William's teaching had left her much the best cook in the first year of

Fawley Technical College's catering course, but it had seriously handicapped her in one respect. William always cooked with the best ingredients and had wine, brandy and sherry at his elbow. Rich man that he was, he never gave a thought to costs, at least not cost involved in cooking food, although of course he hated eating in restaurants, maintaining with justice that he could do better at home. She sighed, discouraged, and re-did the numbers. She had been asked to produce *médaillons de veau* to a menu cost of £3.50. The first thing they had all learned six months ago was the golden rule that the raw ingredients must not cost more than 33 per cent of the menu price. Her ingredients, including the parsley, the cream, the profit and rent, cost £1.30, so the menu cost would have come out closer to £4. And the good burghers of Fawley were not going to pay £4 for *médaillons de veau* without vegetables.

'Sorry,' she said grimly. 'Back to the drawing-board.' She sat down again, not unduly discouraged. She had eight good O-levels, a very much stronger academic record than most of her colleagues in the class, and was not finding the course work intellectually difficult. She was not particularly good at getting the food out to time and to price, but this was what she had come to learn. She bent to the task, managing to get the costing right by four o'clock when the class ended, and went out to collect her bicycle for the twenty-minute ride back to the Frenches.

Seeing the familiar grey Bentley parked on the road ahead of her, she checked and pulled up alongside it, putting both feet down. When she met William on the way home, doing his rounds, they usually shoved her bicycle into the Bentley's cavernous boot and drove home together for company.

'William?' He was sitting in the driver's seat, tense, back braced, the fingers of his right hand splayed across his chest under the old tweed jacket he wore on weekdays. 'You OK?'

'Jens, old boy, bit of indigestion. Put the bike in, can you? You can drive.'

She rushed to get rid of the bicycle. William only very occasionally let her drive his car, maintaining that it was simply too big and too heavy in the hand for a teenage girl, that's why he had it, dammit, so that none of the young women with whom his household was overstocked could drive it. They had all persuaded him to let them drive with him on occasion and Jennifer had had a provisional licence for a full two months since the day she was seventeen, and was going to take the test in a few weeks. She adjusted the front seat and the mirrors and, in the best orthodox style, let in the clutch and crept into the road. She looked at William sideways for approval, but he had his eyes closed and she decided not to disturb him. He was looking a bit pink, the way he did when something had gone wrong; he would tell them at supper, no doubt.

They arrived home safely, and she woke him cautiously; his eyes opened and she could see that for a second he did not know where he was.

'We're home,' she said gently, and waited behind the wheel while he recalled himself.

'Ah, good. Sorry, did I sleep? Didn't have a good night.' He sat up properly. 'Good God, Jens, you drove all the way. Without hitting anyone?'

'You know perfectly well I have never hit a moving object,' she said with dignity. 'It has to be standing perfectly still before I can get it.' On her second expedition with William the Bentley's enormous bumper had encountered a gatepost without much damage being done to either.

'Very good. Let's find Lucy.'

They found her drinking sherry, still dressed as a Guide Commissioner, looking tired.

'Had a good day?' William asked, sitting down heavily.

'Not awfully.'

'What happened?'

'Oh, nothing, I suppose. Ali rang up. That blasted young man – the lad who came here, David Banner – took her out a couple of times before Christmas and again just after, then dropped her, apparently.'

'Ali's got dozens of men,' Jens said, jealous of the attention.

'Yes, I know, but she was rather smitten: I thought him rather a heartbreaker myself.'

Jens smiled at the old-fashioned phrase, but William was looking thoughtful.

'I thought he was under just as much strain as the kid – what was his name – Mickey. Lot of pressure on the eldest son if Dad goes off.' He thought, prowling about and pouring himself a sherry. 'I'll ring Ali, tell her to be a bit patient.' He trotted decisively, into the hall, apologizing to a yowling cat as he passed. They all listened, but he came back scowling, having failed to find Ali. Jens reached for the paper which he was removing from his briefcase.

'Give that *back*,' William said crossly. 'Do men have no rights in this female-dominated household? I haven't been through it to take out the things you're not to read. Go and give Lucy a hand to get supper on the table, there's a good girl.'

'Leaving you to do the important male patriarchal things? I've gone, I've gone!'

Lucy and she worked side by side in the big kitchen, assembling salads; Jennifer and the whole technical college ate whatever she or the other class had cooked, all of it, subjecting it to detailed criticism. William had been to a Rotary lunch and Lucy had lunched on a test meal created by a Girl Guide camp so no one was particularly hungry. William appeared and Lucy looked at him carefully.

'Did you have a tiring day?'

'Yes. I've still got a bit of bronchitis left over, that's the trouble.'

'You could see a doctor,' Jennifer suggested.

'Perish the thought. Mark my words, Jens, stay away from the medical profession.'

'You always say that,' Lucy said patiently. 'But you've had that cold and wheeze since Christmas and it's April now.'

'Thing is,' William said confidentially, 'that if you go to a doctor they feel they have to *do* something. Most of the things doctors can do are likely to lead to worse things, so it's much safer just to wait to get better.'

'William, how did you get through all those years in medical school?'

'Oh I didn't know that then,' he said cheerfully, and Jens, grinning, glanced over at Lucy, inviting her to join in, but she was looking annoyed, lips compressed. Always a little anxious for her place in this household, Jens sought to change the subject.

'I messed up costing again this afternoon.' She glanced at Lucy's bent head, but there was no response. 'I forgot to count in one and a half gills of cream and the parsley. That put the meal over the top menu price.'

'No wonder restaurant food is nothing like as good as home.' William at least could always be diverted on this subject. 'It's outrageous that we all pay three times the cost of the ingredients. That's what? . . . a 200 per cent mark-up, or was when I was at school.'

'Not so.' She was on solid ground. 'Thirty-three to thirty-five per cent on the ingredients, then the next thirty-three per cent on staff. People to cook it, wash it up, get it on to the table. The last third pays for the rent and the mortgage and the clean napkins.'

William pushed his salad plate away half eaten, and both women looked at him reproachfully.

'Not hungry, sorry, old boy.' He patted Lucy's hand, peering at her to see if she was still annoyed with him. 'Much too much to eat at lunch. And drink. Jens, you can't be trying to tell me restaurateurs don't make profits on that basis.'

'They do. But you have to watch every penny or it gets eroded. Then you can't afford new plates or pay the mortgage and you go out of business.'

'What about La Belle Hélène – you know, in Fawley?'

'A life-style operation,' Jens said severely.

'What?'

'A way of keeping old Peter and his family and the dogs in that house. His personal costs will all be mixed up with the business.'

'Is that what they teach you at college? What is the Guide Movement coming to?'

'No, I picked that up somewhere else.' She was disconcerted; she had remembered that it was Joshua, of all people, who had shown her the difference. Just after her sixteenth birthday he had taken her and her mother to dinner in an expensive French restaurant with two other couples. Jennifer had not made any effort with the people, a lawyer and a surveyor – they were being anxiously deferential to Joshua and were obviously dependent on him in some way – but she had been interested in the restaurant. It was small, seating perhaps forty, and expensive but a little shabby. The proprietor was much in evidence, doing much of the waiting himself, becoming more flushed as the evening went on.

'I never see how they make this place pay,' the lawyer had said, hoping to interest her, but Joshua didn't wait for her to answer. 'A life-style restaurant,' he said briefly. 'Man and wife team, a kid in the kitchen, whole family eats and lives off the business.'

'Not a real business,' Jennifer had said, seeing it suddenly, and for a moment there had been a flash of fellow-feeling between her and Joshua. The lawyer and the surveyor had not understood, or not in the same way. And emerging from her memories, she saw that William did not either; well, he was a paid professional and had private money and he wouldn't see it. But she wanted to create a permanent possession, a way of life, that didn't die with you if you got ill, or vanish as her father's income had done. She considered William as she finished her salad; she loved him, he was not a bad doctor, but as she now knew, *he* lived as he did by grace of a grandfather who had been in the jute business. It was he who had built something that enabled his grandchild not to work full-time and to live in a beautiful house a long way from Dundee where the money had been made.

'So you're not going to run a restaurant like that?' William was sharp and he had read the implied criticism.

'I'm not sure yet what I want,' she said carefully, and he smiled at her.

'How should you be? Lucy, I'm going to find something

mindless on the idiot box then go to bed – sorry, but I'm worn out.'

'I'm going to the cinema,' Jennifer said, in answer to Lucy's inquiring look. She stayed at the college every day until she had finished all her homework; Wanstead Abbey, if it had done nothing else, had instilled that, so she was free when she got home.

'With a man?' William asked severely.

'No way I'm going out with one of *them*,' she answered him, meaning it, and went off into the evening sun to find her bicycle.

She woke early the next morning, hearing strange noises, and lay thinking about them. She had heard Lucy, surely. It appeared only to be five o'clock, so it couldn't be breakfast. She listened for a few minutes, then turned over and went straight back to sleep, waking up dazed from a deep slumber as the alarm went at seven. She arrived at breakfast only half awake and looked round the kitchen, puzzled. Lucy got up at 6.30 and laid the breakfast table; this was an immutable piece of household routine, only it had not happened this morning. She started to lay up breakfast for the three of them, when she heard feet on the stairs. She went to the door to look but it opened in her face and there was Lucy, fully dressed, not in the housecoat in which she normally breakfasted, pale and looking quite different. She stared at Jens as if she had never seen her before.

'I set breakfast,' Jens said, for something to say.

'Yes. Thank you.' Lucy returned to herself with an enormous, visible effort. 'I don't want any. Give yourself some, please, Jens, and then get off. I've got the doctor here. William was taken ill during the night.'

'Oh, no. Is he very ill? Can't I stay and help?'

'No. There are too many people here.'

Jens stared at her, both hurt and frightened. She was a daughter of this house and Lucy was getting rid of her.

'I must go and see the doctor, Jens, Off you go.' She sounded, marginally, more like herself.

'Sure I can't help? I could ride to get a prescription. Is it the bronchitis?'

'No. Yes. No, I would rather you went off.' Lucy gulped suddenly and her face worked, and Jens, appalled and conscience-stricken about worrying Lucy, urged her to go to William; she herself would eat and go quickly and ring at lunch-time.

'That's a good idea,' Lucy said, blowing her nose, and went upstairs quickly without a backward glance while Jens got herself off as if leaving a burning house.

She worked badly that morning, miserable and self-pitying. Lucy would not have wanted Sofia out of the house. A daughter, a real daughter, was quite different from anything else, it was clear, and this crisis had demonstrated that she had no real place in the French household. Nor, of course, in her own mother's household, not with Joshua there. As the clock moved towards the end of morning lessons she found herself worrying about whether to ring as she had promised she would; it would be intolerable to be treated as a nuisance. She bent resolutely to her task and managed to concentrate.

'Jennifer Redwood?'

She looked up from her papers where she was trying to calculate the likely cost of a finger buffet for seventy people.

'Would you come and see the Principal, please?'

She rose obediently, brain still occupied with the cost of butter, and it was not until she was in the passage that the fact of the summons struck her. The secretary was hurrying ahead of her, avoiding conversation, and Jennifer started anxiously to examine her conscience for essays left undone, bicycles wrongly parked, or other nameless sins. The secretary showed her straight in. Miss Adams, Lucy's formidable friend, who ran the college and a Guide company in her spare moments, was standing with her back to her, looking out of the window, blowing her nose.

'Sit down, Jennifer, my dear.' She turned and it was clear that she had been crying; she looked small and tired.

'William,' Jennifer said in a flash of understanding, and felt blackness coming up and the room going round her, and Miss Adams's steadying hands, pushing her into the chair. 'Put your head down, Jennifer.'

The blackness went away, slowly, and she managed to get her head up with Miss Adams still holding her arms. 'He's dead?'

'I'm afraid so. A massive heart attack. Doctor Burton was actually with him, but there was nothing to be done.'

'What time this morning?'

'I don't know exactly,' Miss Adams said, surprised.

'What time did Lucy ring you?'

'Not very long ago.' Miss Adams looked at her carefully and settled her in the chair. 'It took me a few minutes to ... to ... well, to be able to send for you. I had known him for thirty years. But I am so sorry, Jennifer, he was a second father to you.'

'Yes, he was. Can I go there now?'

'Not just at the moment,' Miss Adams said gently. 'Lucy asked if I would keep you with me for the night. There will be things to do, and, of course, Sofia is coming back immediately.'

She wanted to cry but couldn't until much, much later, buried beneath cellular wool blankets which made her nose itch, in Miss Adams's tiny spare room. But she did not cry for long, it was too difficult and too painful, and she slept patchily, waking always to the knowledge that she was now, truly, on her own.

CHAPTER NINE

September 1976

'Paul Seles. I have a table for four at one o'clock.'

'That's right, Mr Seles. Nice to see you again.'

The reception at the Café de la Paix was professionally welcoming, staffed today by a young black dancer, temporarily between engagements. He offered to take his briefcase and store it securely, as they were all trained to do, but Paul refused. He would not need papers at lunch, but he never left his briefcase anywhere. He kept his expensive dark blue leather jacket on as well; he would take it off as soon as he sat down, but he carried his wallet and keys in it. He could not bring himself to adopt the continental habit of carrying a small bag; he was always checked by the vision of what the Woolverstone Hall lads would have made of a man with a handbag. He saw that the black lad was eyeing up the jacket.

'Hungarian,' he said, in acknowledgement. 'Costs a lot less there and they're famous for it.'

'*Wonderful* colour.' The receptionist reached out without coquetry to touch the sleeve. 'And soft. Is it easy to go to Hungary? I thought it was part of Russia?'

'No,' Paul said crossly, though it was a reasonable enough perception. 'No, it's an independent country. I mean, it's got its own government.' He sighed. 'It's very much influenced by the Soviets, of course.'

'Is that where that boy burnt himself to death?'

'That was Prague. In Czechoslovakia. Jan Palach.'

Curious how Palach's fundamentally pointless, painful protest, turning himself into a human bonfire in Wenceslas Square, had stuck, so that otherwise pig-ignorant Westerners knew all about it. The rising in Budapest, with the tanks two abreast grinding down the streets, crushing barriers and people, did not seem to have the same resonance here, although thousands had been killed and many, many more thousands sent to worse than death in the camps. He gave up. In the two years he had been in and out of Hungary, Czechoslovakia, Poland and the Ukraine, he had come to understand that in some fundamental sense no Brit, and no American for that matter, knew what they were talking about as far as Eastern Europe went. The Brits had not suffered invasion since, what, 1066; they had never since then had to live with an occupying power to whom you had to accommodate yourself somehow, if you didn't want to end up being systematically starved and beaten by people who enjoyed their work in some camp so remote you wouldn't even know what country you were in. Old Caldwell had once talked to him and Sean about this, just wondering aloud, as was his habit, about how the true Brits would have behaved if the Germans had succeeded in invading in 1940. It had been Sean's view, expressed with his usual difficulty, that they would have been cheerfully handing their Jewish neighbours over to be carted off to camps, along with anyone of Irish descent.

Paul looked up to see the man himself, Sean Kelly, coming through the door. He had discovered the Café de la Paix when he was looking for Sean. After the disastrous night of his eighteenth birthday most of the consequences the Warden had foretold had come to pass. The bloke he had tried to kill had not died, but had been left slightly brain-damaged – not that you could have told the difference, in Paul's view, but there it was, and this had made it all much, much worse. The Warden had fought a successful action to get the trial postponed until after he and Sean had sat their A-levels, but all his preparations had been disrupted and the exams themselves had been unusually difficult. No, perhaps they hadn't, but he had felt as if he was trying to wade through a bog all through that time, harassed by conflicting accounts from the hospital where the bloke was only intermittently conscious, by Sean's retreat into silence and by the signs of stress emanating from both the Warden and Old Caldwell. Paul knew he had done badly on the papers and he had gone into the dock with this knowledge dragging at him to find that both the other bloke's mates and another chap, who hadn't even bloody been there, had their stories pat. He and Sean had been cast as a pair of drunken psychopaths, inflamed by a rich man's drink, putting the boot into three young working men innocently drinking beer after a hard day's work. Sean had barely managed to speak, and what he managed to get out was virtually inaudible, but even if he had spoken with the tongue of angels the odds had been against them. So Paul had gone down for twelve months' Borstal training and Sean for six, with the clear implication that, had either of them been nineteen rather than all but eighteen, they would have spent a much longer sentence in a jail for adults.

He had weathered his time more easily than Sean, who had felt the whole thing was his fault, not that he had ever quite managed to say so, but if you'd known him as long as Paul had you could understand him: He'd done his best for Sean, better indeed than he'd done for himself, touched as he had been by Sean's efforts to give him a special birthday. He had managed to keep Sean going, so he got his distinction at A-level maths. And Woolverstone Hall had been dead-good there; when it turned out that IBM didn't want to know any more, Old Caldwell had picked Sean up from the Borstal gates and taken him straight to a mate of his who had a little systems consultancy firm, where he had been instantly absorbed. When Paul had got out a few months later he had been able to take off for Budapest without worrying about the closest thing to a brother he had.

He had not written more than a couple of cards in his two years away, and when he got back he found Sean had left his job and was no longer in the lodgings in which the patient men of Woolverstone Hall had installed him. He had not wanted to go back to the Hall and see the Warden or Old Caldwell, not while he was still struggling, but had been close to accepting this necessity when he had run into Daniel Scota, erstwhile captain of the Wolves, serving behind the bar in a West End pub and making a nice bit on the side out of *that*, you could see. He, it turned out, had seen Sean and thought he was doing a bit of work for a posh West End caff, so Paul had gone to the Café de la Paix on the off-chance.

For a moment he had not recognized his old mate as he stood talking to a taller man in white overalls. He had grown two inches, put on a stone and was wearing good clothes, but he still looked at the ground, or at best at the shoulder of the bloke he was talking to. Paul waited, heart thumping, until the conversation ended, then moved closer and spoke. Sean had looked up, startled, and slowly recognized him, and a smile had cracked the inexpressive, heavy Irish face right across and had made Paul embrace him as if he was one of his Hungarian or Slovak mates, totally forgetting that you couldn't touch Sean. Even that had been all right; Sean had tensed in terror, then, brick-red with embarrassment and fear, had even managed a lame, near inaudible joke about 'what de punters here would be tinking'. They had sat down then and there in the caff because Sean was installing a costing and control system for them, and talked for hours. Or rather Paul had talked while Sean listened, looking down at the table as he always used to, not meeting your eye, but throwing in the odd, hardly audible remark to show that he was with you. When they had exhausted their news they had gone through the system together, Paul explaining in loving detail where in a restaurant you could run a fiddle that extracted either cash or valuable goods, and Sean, nodding, still not looking at him, alight with pleasure, drawing symbols and boxes and lines on a pad of squared paper. If any restaurant in London had a thief-proof system, Café de la Paix was now it, they both reckoned.

Paul grinned at Sean and touched his palm in the salutation they had managed to arrive at, pleased as always by the unconcealed happiness with which he greeted him.

'Wasn't expecting to see you, was I?' Sean asked anxiously.

'Nah, I'm eating with some friends from the East. Can we have a chat after they've gone?'

'I'll be dere. I'm here to look at my system.'

'How's it going?'

'Must be good. Dey had to bung de Chef another five-tousand to keep him. And dey lost two commis the week after it went in.'

'I bet they did. And a wash-up, I expect.'

'Don't know about dat,' Sean said seriously, eyes on the floor somewhere to Paul's right, and disappeared into the small office behind the reception.

Paul turned to find a seat at the bar and wait for his guests, thinking that it might be an omen that Sean had appeared today. If this deal came off, he'd need some help, and he'd be able to afford Sean. Or he hoped he would, the little Paddy was doing himself all right, judging by the clothes. He sat where he could see the door and concentrated on the *Financial Times*, careful not to shift his attention as a familiar voice asked for him at reception. Georgy Kaplan clapped him on the shoulder and he slid off the bar stool to greet him, eyes on the smaller of his two companions.

'And here, Yussuf, is my friend Paul Seles.'

The man was younger than he had expected, probably in his thirties, dressed in Western clothes when he had been prepared for the usual robes and *keffiyeh*. They shook hands and Paul saw that Yussuf had also expected someone older. He had not been precise about his own age, but the Palestinians were careful, and someone – even if not this man – probably knew he was only twenty-one and had decided that if he was good enough for the people he was representing he was good enough for them. Not that there were any real commercial difficulties; the PLO wanted guns and the Slovaks made them, high in the Tatras Mountains. However, the Soviets, who controlled Czechoslovakia, were backing away from open confrontation in the Middle East and wanted any armour or guns to get to the PLO by an indirect route, while allowing the increasingly restive Slovakians to get the much-needed hard currency. Paul's task was simple in outline but complex in execution; he needed to convince the PLO's man that he was indeed authorized to deal on behalf of the factory and the Czechoslovak state, and that the goods would be delivered. He had worked hard for two years to get to this point, and had been lucky; he had met some of the top men in Slovakia, because four of them were of Hungarian parentage. They had been looking for Western luxuries for their wives or mistresses, plus some of the kind of sophisticated sexual aids not manufactured in the Comecon countries. He had acquired what they had asked for within twenty-four hours in Berlin, risking a lot to get them over the border.

They had been impressed by a boy who spoke four languages and could get through tightly guarded borders with so little ceremony and had used him again at regular intervals, most recently to sell for them some good nineteenth-century pictures of unexplained provenance. This latest deal, however, was a huge step up. One of his contacts in Budapest was half Turkish, and some of his customers were Arabs. No one had wanted even to discuss the deal in Budapest, so he had suggested either London or West Germany to where Arabs could travel easily. He didn't know why they had picked London and the only explanation that he had been offered was that Germany was difficult just at that moment. None of that mattered, they were here, and he knew by halfway through the main course that they were ready to do business though it was going to take a couple more meetings. These people were like that, but it was there, he could taste it, and when he had politely seen them off, sliding into a waiting black cab, he was shaking with rigidly controlled excitement. If it went according to plan he would make more than £200,000 – a fortune. And he could do it again, that much was clear. The Arab world preferred to deal with people they knew, and if he could get himself into that select band he was made. They wanted tanks next, and the sums involved were dazzling, the stuff of which fantasy was made. He stared out across St Martin's Lane on a dreary autumn day, the pavements wet under a grey sky. He saw in his mind's eye the blue skies and the wooded mountains of Slovakia with dirty brown clouds of smoke rising from the clapped-out power-stations and factories in Martin, an ugly, sprawling town with a litter of high-rise, mean flats tucked in against the hills. He'd be a hero there too; this order would keep the factories going and he would be driven round in the big limousine kept for party officials and important visitors from the Soviet Union. Not bad for a Borstal boy, he thought, drawing a deep breath and turning to greet Sean who was sidling out of the office like a horse thief in the way he still did.

A week later Paul was lunching at the caff again with the Arab, inching towards the deal, keeping himself on a tight rein; you couldn't hurry these people. If you lost face they wouldn't deal with you, you had to relax and let them come to you. He sensed that the man was not quite ready, perhaps he had another row of backers to consult, but they were doing well and had agreed to meet again in two weeks' time.

Paul saw him into the cab which was waiting for him, then he went back to the desk to pay the bill, using cash as he always did; at twenty-one with no regular employment record no one would give him a credit card, but he'd have them all when the proceeds of this deal came in. It was past three o'clock and the restaurant's pace had slackened; he nodded to Chef who was sitting at a side table, and he grinned as he thought of the commis and the wash-ups slaving to get the kitchen clear after pushing 100 to 150 covers out for the lunch session. He looked again at the Chef's table and the girl with him. She was tall, solid, with dark short hair, and pushing Chef about something, you could see. He walked past them to put a generous tip into the waiter's pocket, the way he always did, they remembered you that way.

'Thank you, Mr Seles,' the lad said in his strongly accented English – odd that the French lads never really got the accent. The girl at the table looked up sharply and stared at him, and he looked back, curious, into blue eyes. She had a slightly snub nose and wide mouth, and was good-looking, if a bit on the hefty side, and then he slowly realized that he knew her.

'Is it really Paul Seles?' She was on her feet and he saw that in heels she was almost his height and that the voice was as clear and posh as ever.

'Jens! Jens Redwood! What are you doing here?'

'I work here. I'm on the passe today.'

He knew what that was; one member of the front of the house staff, who really knew how to cook, was responsible for checking every dish that came out of the kitchen to see that it was what had been ordered, and that it looked satisfactory. Their power was absolute, they could send back any dish that did not meet their standards, provided always they were prepared to take on the Chef. Paul shook her hand, dazed, thinking about her. She was a year younger than him, that made her twenty, going on twenty-one, and, since she was on the passe, she must be good.

'I'm usually a commis chef,' she said defensively, seeing something of this in his face, 'but we're shorthanded, so I was put out here today.'

'You've grown,' he said idiotically, but she knew what he meant and laughed.

'Six inches in one year. When I was about fourteen I used to fall over getting out of bed. You look well.'

Prosperous was what she meant, from the note of faint surprise in the clear, posh voice. It sounded exactly like the vanished Suzie's voice, though she wasn't like Suzie at all, none of the fine bones and delicate features; this girl was a heavier-duty piece of work altogether. He grinned at her. 'I get by,' he said. 'You off duty? Want a coffee?'

'I'd love one, but let *us* buy.' She nodded to a barman who turned away instantly to prepare coffees, and Paul was amused and irritated, just as he had been in the old days. She'd been a bossy little shrimp then and she was the same now, only bigger.

They sat down with their coffees and looked at each other.

'I meant to write, years ago,' she said abruptly. 'I knew you were at Woolverstone Hall – you'll never guess who told me.'

'David Banner.'

'Ah. Clever. I never got round to it at the time and then . . . well, things happened . . . and by the time I remembered again you'd left Woolverstone and I couldn't get them to tell me where you were. Or perhaps they didn't know.' She looked at him inquiringly while he decided what to tell her, but she was always quick and understood when he was in difficulty.

'What is it, Paul, ten years?' she asked.

'Bit more. But except that you've grown I'd have known you anywhere.' It wasn't really like talking to a girl, he discovered, more like meeting a bloke you'd known as a kid. He sipped his coffee uneasily, torn between not wanting to be back in those far-off days and wanting to stay and talk to her. 'Your father died.'

'Yes.' She looked down into her coffee. 'Remember the night we all ended up in the police station and he fetched me? He was taken into hospital next morning, while I was at school.' She stopped abruptly, and he watched her under his eyelashes; her eyes were wide as if she'd just remembered something else. She swallowed. 'He never came back again, and he died a few days afterwards.'

'Sorry. Cancer, wasn't it?'

'Yes. Yes, it was, it's just I never quite knew what it was then, Mum didn't want it named, I suppose.'

A silence fell which he did not want to break.

'Paul, what about you? Your stepfather, I mean your cousin's husband . . .' Her voice trailed away and she turned slowly scarlet.

'What is it?'

'I was remembering, sorry. Dad was going to have a word with someone about . . . about you and him . . . only he didn't. I mean, he died, and I . . . didn't think about it.'

'I got a beating that night.' It was somehow possible to say that to Jens Redwood. 'But that was almost the last. Someone from the Social came round – oh, three weeks later at school.

Well, I'd missed the school medical, he'd beaten me up again and wouldn't let me go because he knew they'd see the marks, you see, but the next day someone came.'

He remembered that day very well; he was back at school, walking stiffly, trying to walk straight, although the cuts from the belt buckle were still seeping, when a large, unexplained lady had arrived and just took him out of school with the headmaster and straight to a clinic where he had been made, shamingly, to take off his trousers and shirt and show the world what had been happening. He'd not been able to stop crying all through the process, tears pouring messily down his face as he tried to clutch his clothes around him, away from the gentle, firm hands stripping them off. He had never gone home again, nor seen Franz Vazarely, except that once in the dock when the Bastard was lying his head off about how he'd tried to do his best for his wife's cousin's boy. Six months, he'd got.

'I was taken into care, see,' he said to Jens Redwood's horrified face, the eyes very wide, tears in the corners. 'Then I was OK.' He looked at her, seeing the fierce child he had once known. 'Your dad fixed it.'

'He couldn't have, or I don't think so.' Jennifer fished blindly for one of the restaurant's thick paper napkins and blew her nose on it. 'He meant to, but when we got home he fainted. The policeman – the driver – carried him upstairs, because Mum said, no, don't take him to hospital.' She looked at Paul, not seeing him. 'He carried him, I mean quite easily, up the stairs, I'd not remembered that, he was so thin.'

Paul reached across the table and took both her hands, loosening his grip as she flinched away.

'Paul, sorry. Don't go away, please.'

'I've upset you.'

'Yes. I mean, no. It's not you, I need . . . I need some air. Have you time?'

'Come on, we'll have a walk.' He waited while she gathered herself, bewildered, careful not to touch her, having understood instantly that somehow she had become like Sean.

'My mum remarried, so I have a stepfather,' she said when they were in Trafalgar Square, clear of crowds.

'He beat you?' Paul asked, chilled.

'No. I suppose it wasn't as bad.' She was scarlet and looked at the ground.

'He fucked you?' For Paul, brought up in a children's home, this was familiar territory, and his inquiry was entirely matter-of-fact. The kids knew you couldn't get adults to believe it usually, but the kids could tell each other and gain some comfort from that.

She gulped and looked down, scarlet to the ears. 'Not even as bad as that,' she said slowly. 'He only tried. He frightened me, though.'

He considered her, a vision of her as a little seven-year-old, fighting her corner in a playground against bigger children, totally obscuring the grown woman in front of him. 'It put you off men?'

'How did you know?' She had always been a bit innocent, he remembered, in the way posh kids were.

'You jumped a mile when I touched you.'

'I'm sorry, Paul. How very rude of me.' She was utterly chagrined, gazing at a space past his shoulder, as Sean did. 'I was taken by surprise.' She was shivering in the cold wind, her hands dug deep into her pockets. She looked at him. 'I truly, truly am glad to see you.'

'Give us a kiss then,' he suggested, in the exact phrasing of their childhood, and she laughed, embarrassed, but took both hands out of her pocket and on to his shoulders and managed to kiss him, chastely, on the cheek. Gently, patiently he put his arms round her and gave her a good old hug, so that they ended up wrapped together, his cheek against hers, the top button of her coat digging into his throat. It was utterly comfortable and totally unsexy and he revelled in it for a long minute.

'Oh, Paul.' She disentangled herself and grinned at him, and he saw that she felt exactly the same. 'It *is* good to see you. I haven't got anyone left from those days.'

'Me neither.' He hooked an arm round her shoulders and they walked, kicking the mendicant pigeons away, boasting to each other about the years between. She was so gratifyingly impressed by his languages that he found himself able to tell her the whole sorry story of his last term at school and Suzie's inevitable defection, his poor A-levels and the rotten year in Borstal. And she told him about the Frenches, and the awful second year of technical college during which she had lived with the pale, grieving ghost of Lucy, unable to cheer her and dreadfully conscious that with William's death the household could no longer easily afford an extra mouth to feed. She had fled to a job in London and a flat shared with Ali, whose deplorable father had finally died of drink, leaving just enough money to put a roof over Ali's head.

'What will you do next, Jens?' They had all called her Jens, as her father did.

'I need a chef's job for at least two years. Then I'm going to set up my own restaurant. If I can find the money. But I can't take anything from Joshua.'

'Does he still try it on?' Paul watched her fidget.

'No. No, he doesn't,' she said reluctantly. 'Well, he hasn't dared since William French offered to have lunch with him.' She looked soft and young as she talked about this other chap who had died, and he found himself wondering about him.

'Good-looking bloke, was he? This William.'

'Oh, no. No, not at all. He looked like a grizzly bear.' She was laughing, and he watched her profile, interested. 'My dad was, of course. Good-looking, I mean.'

'Yeah,' Paul agreed tactfully, visited by a memory of old Redwood the last time he had seen him, the eyes sunk back and great hollows under the cheek-bones. 'I'll put some cash up for you,' he said on impulse.

'That's very kind.' She didn't for one moment believe he had any, he could see, and he opened his mouth to tell her how wrong she was, then closed it again, superstitiously. If he talked about this deal, it could vanish.

'I have to go to Prague tomorrow,' he said instead, and saw

that he had impressed her. 'You could come,' he said on impulse, and watched her eyes widen.

'Paul, I'd love to, but I can't. I've got two shifts to do. And I can't afford it.'

'I'll take you next time. No strings, don't worry. I want to take another mate as well. Sean Kelly.'

'*Our* Sean? The one doing the new systems?'

'Yeah. We were at the Hall and at Borstal together. What's so funny?'

She buried her face in his shoulder, easily, like a sister, heaving with laughter. 'You sound just like some of the thickoes Ali brings home – my friend Alison, you must meet her – only they mean they were at Eton and Oxford, doing nothing. Oh, Paul, look, I'll pay my fare, you can't afford us all.'

He grinned down at her. 'Relax, girl, this one's on me.'

In the end it was six months before they were able to go away together, and then it was Budapest not Prague. He had slightly misjudged his Arabs, or rather Georgy's Arabs; they had wanted to move faster than he had thought and he had been whisked away into a maelstrom of negotiations in three countries. And he had made a lot less money than he had hoped; there had been too many people to look after in Martin, and Prague and Budapest, and more had stuck to Georgy's stubby fingers than the original arrangements had provided. But another deal had followed on the heels of that one and he had over £150,000 stowed safely in four different accounts in the UK, and two in Germany as well as an account in Budapest, just to store any of the useless forints that you couldn't get out of the country. And through all of this he had spent time with Jens, ringing her up whenever he was in the country, picking her up at the end of her shift and just going round with her, accepted as a regular by her sexy friend Ali who had made a pass at him. He'd been indignant on Jens's behalf, but she had just sighed when he told her and made it unflatteringly clear that Ali did that to everyone. He had no sisters and Jens had no brothers, but he knew now what it must be like, that affectionate, occasionally exasperated closeness.

He was going to use up a bit of his Hungarian forints for this outing, however, he reflected, as he walked into Gundels with Jens on his arm and Sean following them like a shadow. The huge main dining-room of Budapest's best restaurant was not yet full, the lights yellow against the warm evening. Jens, wide-eyed, wearing one of the severe dark suits that made her look like an air-hostess, was gazing about her. There were a few Westerners here, but not that many; travel in Hungary was difficult and the hotels and food in general fell woefully short of tourist expectations. And the Americans, of course, expecting the place to be full of glum-faced soldiers with machine-guns and nothing to eat, didn't come.

Paul nodded to one or two people he knew, Members of Parliament, and he stiffened as he saw the First Secretary from the Soviet embassy and a couple of their military people. Georgy had handled most of the dealings with the Soviets without whose consent no arms could have been sold, but he had been taken to a couple of meetings. The Soviets would not, of course, acknowledge him here, at Gundels, where the governing classes met, but he kept an eye on them as he studied the menu.

They agreed to go for the chef's recommendation, all four courses of it, because Jens had observed that on a Saturday night with something like 150 covers to turn out, they'd do better with that. Paul, mildly nettled, since he ate here every time he was in Budapest, had agreed, but had taken over the wine, ordering an Azul Tokay to start off and one of the heavy red wines from near Debrecen to go on with. The aged wine waiter took the order gravely, but checked as he turned to go; Jens had turned over the heavy plate in front of her and was peering at the manufacturer's make, completely oblivious of her surroundings. She did the same with the cutlery, then held her napkin to the light to admire the monogram. Paul opened his mouth to remonstrate, then saw the wine waiter was watching her with interest. She looked up and saw the man and asked him, in French, where they got their glass from, and the waiter settled down to tell her, pausing only to hand their orders to a very young minion, hovering at his side, charmed by the pressure of her interest. He lingered till the soup arrived, then left them with a '*Bon appétit*'. Paul and Sean fell on it with real hunger, while Jennifer ate carefully, savouring every scrap.

'Beautiful,' she said reverently, as a tall young waiter took their plates. He inclined his head majestically and Paul remembered that this was a scion, a nephew or something of the house, not much older than they were. He refilled all their glasses, just indicating to Paul that the bottle of Tokay was exhausted, so that Paul, with equal economy, could indicate that another of the same should be brought. He bowed slightly, no more than an inclination of the dark, neat head, and said in Hungarian that it was pleasant to see Mr Seles again. It was not in the slightest bit obsequious, but a power speaking to an acknowledged equal, and Paul sat back, glowing. The Tokay and the fish course, Lake Balaton perch, arrived simultaneously, the waiter standing back to let the other waiters get the plates down in front of the three of them and the heavy silver covers whipped off, before he filled their glasses. Paul and Sean both dug in, but Jennifer sat examining every detail of the food and the garnish, turning the plate slightly to get a better look, while the three waiters watched her indulgently. She picked up a small forkful and ate it, eyes unfocused, then had a second forkful and looked up to find herself with an audience.

'*Fenouil*,' she said definitively.

'*Oui*.' The waiter watched her as she took her third fork.

'*Trop?*'

'*Non, non, non*,' she said, shaking her head. '*Parfait.*'

He bowed and so did both the other waiters, then they withdrew and Jennifer serenely and slowly ate every scrap on the plate. Paul was both amused and disconcerted to find that the scene repeated itself on the next two courses, reinforced for the main course by the *patron* himself, with whom she discussed the exact components of the sauce on the venison steak. As they finally laid down their spoons and forks, exhausted and replete after a wafer-thin pancake on a pool of chocolate, the nephew appeared and bent deferentially at Paul's side, with a murmured invitation for Mademoiselle, if she so wished, to visit the kitchen.

'In the middle of the service?' Mademoiselle inquired when this was relayed to her, so incredulously that Paul had to scowl at her slitty-eyed. She blushed and said, stumbling slightly in French, that this would be of the greatest possible pleasure provided all were quite sure it would not discommode Chef.

Chef was not only not discommoded but totally enraptured. Paul found himself standing with the nephew and Sean under the harsh lights, backed against a row of ancient refrigerators trying to keep out of the way of the general bustle.

'She is your fiancée, Mr Seles?' the man asked.

'No, no,' he said, startled.

'I thought perhaps not your sister.'

'No. Though she is *as* my sister,' he added sternly, deciding it would be as well to put this on record.

She was engrossed, tasting, looking and asking, and Chef and his minions were talking nineteen to the dozen in villainous French, with the occasional Russian word thrown in. She wasn't much good at languages, Jens, not a particularly good ear, but all good cooking is done in French and they had an enormous common vocabulary. Paul fidgeted, torn between pride in her and a hatred of being left on the sidelines, but a big party had just come in and the kitchen was gearing itself to deal with it, and Jens was extracting herself from the line, shaking hands all the way down. She walked out ahead of him, like a queen, flushed with drink and pleasure, a smudge of flour on her cheek and a drop of tomato coulis on her right sleeve, chatting to the nephew.

'We shall perhaps have the honour of seeing you again?' The *patron* himself had come to say goodbye, as Paul paid the bill, enormous by Hungarian standards and about a third of what he would have paid in any Western capital. 'You are at the International, Mr Seles?' He was speaking French in deference to Jens, and Paul confirmed it before noticing the gleam, instantly suppressed, in the nephew's steady regard.

It was an hour and a half before they returned to their hotel, a huge, gleaming new glass and concrete palace on the Pest side of the river. This showcase of the regime was badly built, with rooms too small and spectacularly ugly furnishings and uncomfortable beds. But the views of the river and the castle and the Matthias church high on the opposite bank were beautiful. The place was said to be bugged throughout, and Paul never spoke of business anywhere under its roof, but he had thought it the best option for a holiday weekend.

Sean, still strung up by the excitement of being abroad with his friend and mentor, had insisted on a walk, so they had gone over to the Buda side and walked round the Matthias church and the castle, slowly sobering up and letting the enormous meal they had consumed work its way down, as Jens had inelegantly put it. She was between them as they arrived at the hotel, holding both their hands; she and Paul always had from the day they had met each other again, and Sean had overcome enough of his anxieties about being touched. It was interesting, Paul reflected, as he ordered large glasses of water and lemon tea, preparatory to going to bed, that he had never thought of her as a girl, as someone to take to bed; she had indeed become a sister to him. She was looking tired now, the glow with which she had left the restaurant fading, and when they had finished their drinks she went to the desk for her key and got a note, which she opened and read, and showed him, blushing.

'I could see he fancied you,' Paul said judiciously. 'Bit quick off the mark, though. I suppose lunch is all right.'

'Can I possibly not go?' She was sounding miserable and he looked at her, puzzled.

'He's all right, Jens. I mean, this Ferenc, I'd forgotten his name, he's a nephew of the house. Good-looking bloke too, isn't he?'

She bit her lip, and he realized that she was on the edge of tears.

'I'll see you, Paul.' Sean, ever averse to displays of emotion, was on his way to the lift, and Paul followed with Jens. He unlocked her room for her and followed her in.

'I must have a pee.' She pulled off the jacket of the prissy navy suit and headed for the bathroom while he opened the extra bottle of mineral water he had bought downstairs and poured it into glasses. She came out looking flushed and tearful and very young in the tidy schoolgirl white blouse.

'What's the matter, then?' he asked kindly, handing her a glass and putting an arm round her. 'Didn't you like him?'

'Yes, I did. But I'm frightened of him.'

'He won't do anything – I mean . . .' He realized he was floundering.

'I'm still frightened.'

'Because of Joshua?' He had met her stepfather by chance one day and had observed with rage and pity how Jens in his presence tried to shrink her solid five foot eight inches into a corner, well away from him.

'If he fancies me he'll want to . . . to . . .'

'To kiss you? Probably.' He tightened his grip on her shoulders. 'But we kiss, Jens.'

'That's different. You don't want to grope me.'

'And if I did?'

Jens must have had more to drink than he had realized, well, they all had, hadn't they? She took his free hand and placed it deliberately on her breast, so that he felt the firm weight of her through the thin blouse. They both looked at his hand, unsmiling.

'That all right?'

'Yes.' She sounded surprised and he wondered what to do next. She reached for her drink, her breast moving against his hand.

'Paul.'

'Yes.'

She stared into her glass. 'Do you . . . I mean, would you . . . ?'

'Would I what?'

'Go to bed with me,' she said in a rush, both hands clenched round her glass.

'What, now?'

'Well . . . yes. While I'm feeling brave.'

Paul disentangled himself, reached for his glass of water, then poured them both another one, which she drank in two gulps.

'Come here.' He took her glass away and settled her on the bed, propped up by pillows, and lay down carefully beside her, switching off the light, so that the room was illuminated only by the faint light coming off the river. She looked at him trustingly, and he propped himself on his elbow to kiss her on the lips. It was nice, he thought, pleasant, and he started leisurely to undo the buttons of her blouse, then reached round to unhook her bra, feeling he had been thrust back into his teenage years. These days his girls either undressed themselves or let him do it, slowly, with them standing up. He felt expertly for the nipple on her right breast and stroked it until it stood up, hard. He pulled back from kissing her and looked down at her face.

'Jens,' he said reproachfully. 'This is not going to work.' He moved his hand from her breast and cupped her jaw; it was rigid, teeth gritted with strain. She looked at him, tears in her eyes, and he kissed them, overcome with tenderness.

'It doesn't work like this, love,' he said, suddenly seeing everything very clearly, the ugly modern room and the weeping girl on the hard pillows. 'It isn't just because of your stepfather – girls get over that, you'll find someone you really want and it'll be OK.' He fought for words to explain. 'It's like you're my sister. If we do it, you won't be, it'll be different. You'd be – well, you'd be a girlfriend.' He stopped, unable to get to what he was trying to say, and did up a couple of her buttons, angrily.

'You mean we'd lose each other,' she said slowly, and mercifully unoffended, watching him make a mess of the buttons.

'That's right,' he said with relief. 'If you fuck someone it changes things, you have to go on doing it and marry, I suppose, or you get fed up and stop.'

'And you don't get fed up with a sister?'

'No. And I don't want you getting fed up with me. Not ever.'

She sat up and tried to do up her bra, encumbered by the blouse, so he did it for her, expertly.

'You out wit' me?' he asked, anxiously, in Sean's words.

'No. It's just that I hoped – because it was you – that I could get over this. I mean, I feel if I manage it once it'll be OK.' She wrapped a blanket round herself. 'I thought it was easy for men,' she said accusingly, and he started to laugh, acknowledging the other truth, that he had not been going to be able to get it up, not with her, not with his sister.

'Only sometimes.'

She was scowling as she had done as a fierce child. 'You mean love and sex may not go together.'

He thought ruefully of the girls he had wanted most. 'Only sometimes.'

'I love you.' She said it in the matter-of-fact way she used for sorting out the ingredients of a sauce, but he knew her well enough by now and felt the room grow warm.

'And I love you.' He hadn't said that often, and not since Suzie had he meant it. 'You get some sleep, and you have a nice lunch with Ferenc. He's not going to leap on you. He wouldn't dare, anyway, you're a Westerner and he can't offend the people here. You just be you, and talk restaurants, OK?' He rolled off the bed and bent to kiss her, looking at her anxiously to see if she was all right.

'Ferenc will probably turn me down too.'

He understood he was being teased, pulled her hair, and went grinning back to his room.

CHAPTER TEN

September 1977

Dr Robert Daiches, BSc, PhD, consultant psychiatrist at the Halliwell Hospital, finished the day's 'to do' list, observing that the things which loomed largest were not in any objective sense the most important. They were probably on the list as a way of avoiding doing the most vital things. Indeed, he realized irritably, the most difficult task was not on the list at all. He sighed for human frailty, against which being a consultant psychiatrist insulated no one, wrote firmly 'Michael Banner?' and swung his chair so that he could get up and walk to the window and stare out into the dazzling September day. The sun, already much lower now in the sky even than a month ago, was slowly burning off the mist through which the tops of the trees were poking, the wide green lawns glistening with dew. He was a good psychiatrist, allying unusual skills of empathy and intuition with an absolutely disciplined approach, and he was not satisfied that he was doing right by Mickey Banner. He should have transferred him to a colleague in Edinburgh when the family had moved there four years before; a vulnerable adolescent with Mickey's history ought to have professional help close at hand, so that he could see someone regularly. But somehow four years had elapsed and the boy was still rushing down from Edinburgh in the school holidays, having to be fitted into a crowded diary, displacing equally needy, local patients. It was inappropriate and a failure in his treatment of a patient to have allowed it to continue.

The boy was sitting huddled in a chair in the waiting-room,

with an old copy of *Country Life*, felt by the administration to be suitably unexciting for the disturbed. Mickey shot to his feet, dropping the magazine and a small bag, his face alight with pleasure. He had grown again in the four months since he had been here last, and he was now probably just over six feet, still very thin. His face had changed and lengthened under the dark blond hair falling into his eyes; a good-looking lad, but his mother's boy, nothing of the bounce of his father or elder brother. Odd that he should be able to remember the family so clearly over the intervening years.

'So how are you, Mickey? What's happening in your life?'

'I wrote to you,' the boy said accusingly.

So he had: to say that he had done very well in the Scottish Higher Certificate, particularly in languages and maths, and had a place at St Andrews University. 'You did indeed; I'm sorry Mickey, I've had a longer than usual break and I've not quite caught up with myself.'

'You're not ill?' The boy had turned pale.

'No, no. I needed to go to a conference in San Francisco. So I took the opportunity to come back slowly.'

'Where did you go?'

'All over America,' he said dismissively, since he was, after all, not here for social purposes. 'How are the rest of the family?' With this boy it had always been critical to hear how his mother was behaving, but he did not want to ask directly. There was a pause, and he looked carefully at his patient.

'She's got this man,' Mickey said reluctantly. 'He's a lawyer. Much older than her. A widower.'

Daiches waited patiently. It saved time to let the patient tell the story in his own way.

'He wants to marry her.'

'I see. How do you feel about that?'

'I don't like him.'

'Do you feel that he would not look after your mother?' He watched, unsurprised, as Mickey's hands twisted together in his lap.

'No.' It was late and reluctant. 'But he's so dull. And so old.

Mum's very pretty. It looks . . . well . . . ridiculous. She looks like his *daughter*.'

'How old is he?'

'Old. Nearly sixty. Mum's only forty-four.'

'How does your mother feel, do you think?'

'She wants him because he makes her feel safe. I heard her telling Davey. My brother.'

'I remember. Has she talked to you about him?'

'No. She knows I don't like him. He's pompous. He doesn't like me, he doesn't understand about my being . . . my being ill, and he thinks I'm a loony.'

'Does your mother seem happy?' This boy, for all his difficulties, was a shrewd observer.

'Not entirely. She'd give him up and try and find someone more exciting if Davey told her to. But he doesn't care, he just wants her – all of us – tidied away, off his back.'

'Tell me about Davey.'

'He's in Germany with his regiment, in Münster, in North Germany. He hardly ever comes back. He's doing very well.'

'Ah, yes.' He thought of that restless, driving young man and wondered how he liked the BAOR.

'He's been very busy, he says, learning German.'

Daiches assumed that all the BAOR learned German, but it was clear from Mickey's tone that his brother was unusual in this. 'But he's enjoying himself?'

'Davey always enjoys himself. Nothing seems to worry him, he's so strong.'

The psychiatrist considered Mickey carefully, deciding that this element of jealous self-pity was a little more than normal teenage behaviour and should not be totally ignored. 'You remember I told you that eldest children had certain built-in advantages?' he said bracingly. 'All that heavy-duty parental attention in their early years and no competition for it. Gives them a head-start, unlike the wretched middle child.'

Mickey gave him a careful look and managed a smile. 'I do remember. Well, that's Davey, making the most of it.'

'And you yourself?'

'Well.' The boy's hands twisted. 'I found the exams a strain – I mean, I thought I was going to crack up. I tried to ring you.'

'But you didn't get through?'

'No. I thought you might not want to talk to me on the phone.' The self-pity was very clear now but he was too experienced to react fast.

'It's never very satisfactory trying to deal with a patient over the phone,' he said neutrally. 'And anyway you did very well. You've come a long way, Michael.'

'You've always called me Mickey.' He sounded both accusing and panicky.

'Well, you're seventeen now. I thought you might be putting aside childhood nicknames.'

'No, I haven't. I'm not.' He pushed his hair distractedly out of his face and looked at Dr Daiches pleadingly, eyes huge in the pale face. 'I came – I mean, I asked to see you – because I'm feeling worried. About myself.'

The note of whining resentment was very like the old Mickey, he thought soberly. It must not be allowed to degenerate into miserable collapse, which was the only way Mickey allowed himself to express the boiling anger threatening him.

'Are you angry with your mother?'

'No, of course not . . . yes, yes, I am. A bit,' Mickey said finally.

'Quite a lot, I think?'

'Why can't she wait?'

'Your father has been gone . . . how long?'

'Nearly five years,' the boy admitted reluctantly.

'And he has two more children. How do you think your mother feels about that?'

The crushed expression was succeeded by sheer horror. 'She can't want more children?'

'My point is, there is a lot of life left at forty-four. She wants to get started again. And she had a bad shock when she was left without money or protection by your father. Remember, Mickey,' he used the diminutive deliberately, 'I told you long ago, people do things for reasons that don't have much to do with you. She isn't deserting you. She isn't angry with you. She just wants to get on with her life.'

'But what about me . . . and Thomas? He's got Highers next year.'

'Shall we let Thomas worry about himself?' Mickey looked like a trapped rabbit, a good deal younger than his years, mouth turned down dramatically, and Dr Daiches felt a most unpsychiatrist-like urge to clout him. He summoned patience and technique. 'I expect lots of people will be sympathetic to you, getting a stepfather you don't like, but I'd like you to think about something. If everything in your home were always comfortable and as you would want it to be, then you would never leave or grow up. You need to be a bit uncomfortable and unhappy, so that you can leave and take the next step.'

Tears filled the boy's eyes and Dr Daiches waited, patiently, then pushed the box of Kleenex silently towards him. The quiet room filled with miserable sobbing as it often had before and would do again, as people fought with themselves. They were always better for it; the patients who wept, which was most of them, often managed to move on, as if the tears dissolved some obstruction.

'And I was worried about you.' The boy took an enormous gulp of air and blew his nose hard, chucked away the Kleenex and found another and started to shred it in his hands. 'I thought when it was so difficult to get in to see you that you were going to leave me too.'

The doctor opened his mouth and closed it, deciding that now was not the moment to try to wean this anxious, dependent adolescent. He looked at him reflectively and was disconcerted to see that the hands had stopped moving and that Mickey was watching him like a hawk. He hesitated, chilled, then pulled himself back; this was a distressed teenager and inevitably manipulative. Kind but firm handling was always needed with these cases. 'I won't be here for ever, you know,' he said, hearing but not able to retract the implied commitment, but the boy had relaxed and mopped his face, saying how much better he felt, and chattered about his own, relatively normal teenage preoccupations. But after he had seen Mickey off, he stood watching the long figure walk briskly down the drive, and decided that he must sink his pride and talk to a trusted colleague.

And, mercifully, one was to hand: a specialist in children and adolescents. Ruth was particularly useful: a lay analyst, not medically qualified, but the truth was, a lot of the lay people were better than those who, like him, had come down the medical route. It was simply easier being medically qualified; people – parents, hospitals, general practitioners – were more comfortable referring patients to someone with MD after their name. He pursued her to her office and gratefully accepted coffee while telling her about Mickey and his family.

'Well, for a start, Robert, you have little with which to reproach yourself.' Ruth was ten years his senior, an Australian who disliked her native country and had fallen, thankfully, into England and precise, careful English usage. 'The boy could have been dead, or in a long-stay hospital without you, and here he is, living with his family, getting good exam results and going on to university.'

Daiches drank his coffee, calmed by the judicious praise. 'I haven't managed to stand him on his own feet.'

'No.' Ruth never failed to acknowledge a problem, and he waited, hopefully, for her to suggest a solution. 'It is difficult for boys whose mothers reject them as you tell me this mother has. And then his father left. It is not easy, and he may always need to find a mother.'

'Why is it, Ruth, that some of the children we see can take and use really awful childhood experiences far worse than this boy's, and indeed in some sense benefit from them. And others, well . . .'

'And others are like your Mickey. I have one too at the moment. I don't know. Why are some tempered in the fire of a bad experience and some destroyed? Of course, if we knew *that* we would not be here.'

'They're all changed and distorted by bad childhood experiences of course,' he said irritably. 'I mean, we've always known these kids aren't going to grow up as sunny, happy, placid, salt-of-the-earth people. Mickey's elder brother is an ambitious, capable creature, but driven by demons – I've seen him twice and it's very clear – but he isn't . . . well, worryingly dependent like Mickey.'

'Your boy – Mickey – and perhaps the older brother too will need to find a woman to lean on, heavily, who will take the weight because she very much needs someone to mother,' Ruth reflected calmly, gazing out of the window. 'I think you should keep him for the moment, but set him a time-table.'

He finished his coffee, feeling much better. 'Perhaps I should soldier on. He is much better.' He smiled at Ruth, but when he got back to his own room, all he could see was Mickey's wide eyes watching him coldly above a wodge of Kleenex, the long hands stilled.

David saw her at once, as she came off the aeroplane, an RAF special loaded with women being flown out to see sons and brothers and boyfriends in the BAOR. She was a small girl with a determined chin and a square jaw, and he started to smile as he saw her, so that he was one big grin by the time he bent to kiss her. He was wearing his working uniform of khaki shirt and trousers, with a second lieutenant's flashes on the shoulders, because he was technically on duty, accompanying a major's wife and three drivers to meet the young women who had come out for the regimental ball the following night. Several female heads turned to look enviously; on Army rations and Army exercise he had grown an inch even since he was eighteen and was now at twenty-two just over six foot, fair hair bleached and skin browned by the hot sun of the North German summer. In the languid, humid heat of the afternoon he was bouncing with energy and a sight to fill the eye.

'Ann!'

She was grinning too, openly overjoyed to see him, and he turned to present her to his major's wife. He had not enjoyed the ride to the airport at all. He had had a desultory affair with Mary Phillips for a few months, largely because she had asked him. He had assumed that her husband, a major, attached to the regiment as an adviser on his way through to greater things, would be posted on before this indiscretion had serious consequences. The wheels of Army life had stuck somewhere; the man was still with them, and Mary Phillips had wanted to keep on with the affair while he had cooled. She had accepted his awkwardly expressed excuses with poor grace; she had too much pride to allow herself to be the subject of scandal, but he was uncomfortable with her and had tried to see her only in large groups. Ann disarmed her somewhat by being her own straightforward self, a small, brown, Yorkshire girl, pretty without being anywhere near a beauty. Mary Phillips went off to round up her other charges, giving him a chance for a moment with Ann before he had to organize the sergeant who had been driving the other minibus, to get the luggage into the bus.

'Dad and Mum send their regards,' she said conscientiously, and he nodded, warmed by the implicit claim. He had liked her parents on sight; Mrs Hardiman had treated him unself-consciously as a son, while Mr Hardiman, after taking his time to consider, had received him with real kindness, taking him for long walks with the dogs, telling him about the politics of the local council on which he sat as a Labour member. Ann was the youngest; her elder brothers were safely married, solid professional men, disposed to look indulgently on a young man with a steady progressive career. They had met some months ago in the most conventional way; she had been staying in Edinburgh with Uncle James's second daughter, who had been sent south to be a boarder at the Mount School, York, where Ann had been a day girl. David, fretting on one of his precious leave weekends, had gone sulkily to lunch with his Uncle James as a poor alternative to ringing up a girl with whom he had had a brief walkout on a previous visit. He had smiled automatically at Ann's pretty face and she had smiled back, blushing, but thereafter had treated him matter-of-factly. He had been showing off, in a carefully concealed way, to his aunt, recounting his experiences with his platoon on a NATO exercise, when he had glanced towards Ann and got a shock. She was watching him, not critically exactly, but thoughtfully, hands clasped in front of her on the table, self-contained and absolutely at ease with herself, not doing any of the things girls usually did with him, like exclaiming or urging him to go on, or talking vivaciously about experiences of their own. He finished the story rather abruptly and she smiled at him and said what fun it must have been, and gently brought his cousins back into the conversation. He sat, uncharacteristically quiet, noticing the square jaw, with the cleft in the chin, and the snub nose, liking the way the brown hair curled in at the nape of her neck, and at the end of lunch he asked her out, under cover of the general conversation. She took it for granted that his cousins were included in the invitation, since she was staying in their house, and he had agreed hastily, both slightly chagrined and in some fundamental way reassured by her certainty about what was proper.

He had not as much as held her hand that evening, but he had felt her shoulder against his own, comfortingly, all evening and he had been able to kiss her cheek when he kissed his cousins goodnight. He offered to take her for a walk on the Sunday morning but, unreproachfully, she made it clear that his mother's and brother's claims on him must come first. So they had gone for a walk *en famille* and she had listened, restfully, to his mother, who had told her far more than she had told him about her relationship with the boring lawyer, fifteen years her senior, who had been carefully introduced to him the day before. He had not particularly liked the man, but he had been deeply, fundamentally relieved by his presence. He was senior partner in his own firm, delighted to have found a pretty woman to cherish and obviously well able to do so. David had felt a burden shift, and became increasingly cheerful as the weekend progressed, resolutely ignoring Mickey's unhappiness. Not that Mickey had dared to express it openly; he had walked with him that Sunday morning, listening to a feverish description of his school, hoping, wearily, that the Highers was not going to be too much for him. Then he had kicked a football endlessly with Thomas until, to his frustration, Ann had gone back to lunch – to which he was not invited – with his cousins. He had got himself over there for tea and had sat on the floor at her feet for a couple of hours. And on the Monday, he found, she was on the same train as he, only she was getting off at York while he was going on to London preparatory to embarking for Germany and the BAOR. He had talked non-stop for half an hour and she had listened, and when he had wound down she had poured coffee for them both from a Thermos and provided him with biscuits. He had missed breakfast and was ravenous, and fell on the provisions gratefully.

'Do you always travel with a Thermos?' he asked, feeling better.

'My mother says you never know when the train will be delayed for hours.'

It was an answer to his question, he realized, with a sense of great peace and comfort. She had seen someone who needed a bit of mothering and done that, automatically. And she always would, confident in her sense of what was right and appropriate.

'I've got home leave again in a month. I could fly back. Can I see you?' he had asked urgently.

'I'd like that,' she said, and blushed, melting his heart. 'But it's a bit hard on Susan if I ask to stay with her again.'

'We could meet in London. I've got friends I can stay with.'

She had considered this, still pink, but taking her time. 'Or you could come and stay with us if you liked, after you have seen your family. It's a big house and my parents like to have people.'

He accepted, understanding that she was setting the pace she wanted, and took her hands, small, square and capable like herself. She met his eye steadily but her hands were trembling and he wanted her very much.

He had not got into her bed that next time, nor indeed the hurried leave after that, which was in itself a new experience for him, but one which did not dent his confidence since it was clear that she wanted him as much as he wanted her. But she also wanted, as he understood, a serious relationship, one where she knew who he was and what she would be getting, and he was both charmed and reassured. He took his own success with women for granted and mostly enjoyed it, uncritically, but had seen that many of them, like Mary Phillips, did not feel the need to know very much about him, or do much for him, except in bed. Ann studied him, as they said in her part of the country, and looked after him and teased him gently when she thought he was showing off, and deflated him with kindness when he took off on a fantasy about his future.

At the end of July, however, she had agreed that during this leave he need not spend time with his family, and had met him in London where he had borrowed a tiny flat belonging to a brother officer. He had not wanted to rush her, although he was nervous himself and would have liked to try quickly. She had let him know he would not be the first; there had been a man a year ago, but he was no longer around. He did not feel threatened by a rival, accustomed as he was to success, but he had not quite dared to ask what had happened to that previous lover for fear of finding that he had been discarded as not up to the solid standards Ann had inherited from her family.

He met her at King's Cross and whisked her away to the small Kensington flat in a taxi. She hung up her coat, looked appraisingly round the flat which he had polished and cleaned to the point where it would have passed any senior officer's inspection, unpacked her small case and made them both a cup of tea which they had drunk sedately in the tiny living-room. Then she had washed up and reached up to kiss him as he dried the second cup. He kissed her back gently until standing up had become uncomfortable and she had then taken his hand and led him through to the bedroom. He had only just managed not to make a nonsense of the whole thing, despite his experience; the first condom had slipped from his hands and he could not get the second one out of the pack, but she had kissed him easily, and helped, and it had been marvellous if rather too quick for both of them. But he had put that right, as obviously the first chap had not known how to, judging from her reaction, and the rest of the weekend had been fantastic. She had had to confess to being a bit sore by the Sunday and he had been appalled and miserable for her, but they had even weathered that; she had thought with her customary care and said she would go and see her doctor about a diaphragm since the condoms didn't suit either of them that well. He had suggested the Pill, cautiously, but had understood from her reaction that sex was for her a considered choice, not something you were ready to do at any time, a view which he found mildly annoying but fundamentally comforting at the same time. She was old-fashioned by the standards of the times, careful with money, his as well as hers, having after the first meal out insisted on cooking for them in the flat. He had gone shopping with her, watching with admiration as she chose carefully in the butcher's, tight-lipped about London prices, and in bed on Sunday morning he had found himself telling her how the family had come to leave London. She had listened, shocked but uncensorious.

'How old were you, Davey?' She had taken to calling him by the family diminutive.

'Eighteen. No, seventeen.'

'How terrible for you.'

He opened his mouth to deny that he had not been more than capable of dealing with this or any similar crisis at any age, but found himself unable to go on and had wept, for that awful time, and his own terror in the face of his parents' total collapse. She had held him and cried with him, for them all not just for him, and then climbed out of bed and brought him tea with far too much sugar and milk, just as he liked it.

And here she was, two months later, and he was desperate to be alone with her in his own tiny bachelor officer's quarters which he had smartened up as best he could, without being able to do much about the desolate institutional feel of the two small rooms. But this was the Army and his regiment did not want their officers to marry until they were at least twenty-five. The girls, chaperoned, were to be taken to their hotel so that the proprieties would be observed. He got behind the wheel of the minibus, Mrs Major Phillips a jealous shadow behind him, and Ann at his side where he could see her when he could spare any attention away from the road.

He saw the girls into the hotel; a mixed bag, he noticed, some very young and on an excursion from the Season, with loud voices and very short skirts, some a bit older and quieter like his Ann. One of the noisiest and shortest-skirted was Camilla, more correctly the nineteen-year-old Lady Camilla Huntingdon, who was Peter's girlfriend. And Peter Fountain was the brother officer who had lent him and Ann the flat, so it was with Peter and this Camilla that they were dining tonight. They were going to a restaurant outside Münster and it was going to cost a fortune, but he had not felt able to do anything else, given what he and Ann owed to Peter's small double bed.

'I'd like to pick you up at five-thirty,' he said to her firmly, depending on her willingness to let him lead and make arrangements, and getting a small flicker of a smile in acknowledgement. That would give them two hours before they needed to meet for drinks, and they needed the time.

In the event he picked up Camilla too and delivered her to Peter, the two of them being obviously of the same mind as he and Ann. Lady Camilla, indeed, who had been eyeing him, looked to be well capable of proposing an instant foursome, and he whisked Ann away hastily and, letting out a long breath of relief, closed the door behind them and took her in his arms. They made love on his uncomfortable single bed and lay cosily entwined. She wasn't experienced, of course, although physically a little like Teresa, who had married last year and produced a daughter rather soon thereafter; Ann had none of Teresa's relish or inventiveness, but then she had none of her wildness or extravagance either. They got up and dressed to join Peter and Camilla, who were obviously at odds; she was in a sulk and he was looking anxious, but both brightened up as the other two arrived, and got the champagne open. It was always champagne with Peter; like many of the regiment's officers he had a substantial allowance on top of his pay, but he was a generous young man and shared his good fortune. David, responding to the toast, caught Camilla's eye; she was watching him, tongue just caught between her teeth and her long, thick, blonde hair all over her face. She crossed her legs, giving him a quick view all the way up; she was either wearing no underwear at all or something of the order of a G-string, and he looked away hastily.

He had had more champagne than was wholly wise, he realized, as they got into Peter's sports car, he and Ann squashed in the back with Camilla in the front, skirt high on her thighs. Peter, mercifully, was as steady as he was kindly and they arrived at the newly converted Schloss Wilkinghege and shot across the surrounding ditch into the courtyard. It was one of the moated houses, built like castles in the eighteenth century, which were common in the flat, wet Münster plains, and this one had been made into a small hotel and restaurant, its huge, high-ceilinged main drawing-room now serving as the dining-room.

It was quiet and refreshing after the barracks and David looked up at the great chandelier with real pleasure, just noticing that Peter and Camilla hardly glanced at their surroundings, except to observe that it was a bit like Freddie's place in Gloucestershire really. He was always being taken aback by the layers of privilege and wealth there were, well beyond the imaginings of a middle-class Service family, and the realization always depressed him. He looked to Ann for comfort and found it. She was examining her surroundings carefully, with an entirely friendly interest, and she smiled serenely at the smooth German type who came up to explain the menu to them. Peter and Camilla were openly impatient of this, preferring to giggle together over the German on the menu, and he had not needed to listen. He had applied himself to the strictly voluntary language classes from the moment he had known that they were going to Germany, putting a solid layer of vocabulary and idiom on top of his schoolboy German. He spoke German whenever he could, with local clericals or in the shops, and was becoming fluent. He admired the hard-working local people and the huge university of Münster with the big, well-dressed Westphalian students, but knew that outside the Intelligence Corps his interests were unusual. Most of the BAOR treated Germany as a transplanted Caterham.

Camilla, seeing him quietly going through the menu with Ann, decided to appeal for his help and monopolized him for the next ten minutes, noisy from too much champagne and basking in the admiring looks from all the men in the room. The women, of course, all disapproved; Camilla's skirt was at least eighteen inches shorter than anyone else's, and German women, however much they ruled the roost at home, sat demure and quiet in public while the men talked. If the dream of a United Europe was ever going to come about, some pretty massive adjustments were going to have to be made, he observed quietly to Peter, who looked at him blankly before observing that it was only going to be a business thing, wasn't it, not that the Krauts weren't doing a bloody sight better than we were, presumably because they didn't have the trades unions to contend with.

'They do have unions, of course,' Ann said, looking up from the pâté which she had been eating with relish. 'They have worker representatives on the boards of all their companies.'

Peter and Camilla gazed at her doubtfully, and it occurred to David that he had never quite explained Ann to his brother officers. Mr Hardiman, Ann's father, son of a Quaker wool merchant, had been brought up as a Liberal, but had moved over to the Labour Party and sat on the council in the Labour interest. He had once explained to David that had his father been around after the war he too would have joined the Labour Party because they were the only ones who were both interested in using everyone's talents to the full, and had any prospect of power. He had been impressed by the argument; he had voted in 1974 just after his eighteenth birthday and had opted for the Conservatives, but come the next election he was not going to make that mistake again

'How odd,' Camilla said, draining her glass and looking expectantly for someone to fill it.

'No,' David said, out of a need to support Ann, 'not odd at all. It's probably why they're so successful. They educate and train all their people in a way we don't.' He swallowed a gulp of his wine, suddenly seeing things fall into place. 'Peter, your men are like mine, aren't they? Go anywhere, do anything, much better than we are at making themselves comfortable. But half of them can't actually read and write fluently, that's why they all read those awful comics if they read anything at all.' He felt for the words. 'It's a waste. Look at them. They could do a lot more if they were ... well ... properly educated.'

'Our gardener couldn't read,' Camilla put in helpfully. 'We only found out one day when Pa left him a note saying "Leave the roses after all" and when he came back they were all gone. Evans swore blind he'd never seen the note, but Jennifer – that's the girl who lives in – told me he couldn't read.

'Well, that's awful,' Ann said, pink and abrupt. 'He must have felt terrible. Your gardener, I mean.'

'Oh, he did. And Pa felt awful too; he'd kept saying to him, "Can't you read?" And, of course, he couldn't.'

'What happened in the end?' David was suddenly sure he knew the answer to this question.

'Well, it was awfully sad in a way. He left. He couldn't bear us all knowing.' Camilla was wide-eyed.

'Silly chap,' Peter said robustly, 'wouldn't have made the slightest difference. I mean, I have to read everything my lancejack gets, but that doesn't matter.'

'Oh yes, it does,' David and Ann spoke together and looked at each other sideways in wonder, while Peter and Camilla looked back, united on this issue at least.

Ann had managed to change the subject of course, bless her, by asking Camilla where she had got her necklace, so that the girls had disappeared into clothes gossip while he and Peter had talked shop, which they could always do. For all his limitations, Peter was a good officer, shrewd and careful, even if as David understood for the first time, all this was based on a deeply feudal view of human relationships. They finished the beautiful dinner, and he and Peter split the bill and they had managed to part on good terms, with Camilla bending to embrace Ann, then giving him, with a warm hug and feel of her breasts, a kiss much too close to his lips.

The next day they toured the barracks, then drove through the country for lunch before having a rest. The regiment had put its best foot forward for the ball; traditionally generous in hospitality, it had striven to please and the arrangements were both lavish and efficient. It was still very warm at the end of September, the night sky white with stars and the wooded enclave in which the barracks had been placed full of bright uniforms which outshone any dress the women could manage. Camilla, whose family were Army, wore white. Ann – whom David had not dared to advise – wore a clear, pale green silk dress which worked with all the uniforms. He took her out to look at the dance-floor lit up under the moon, with its frieze of couples and backdrop of straight-faced mess servants, and co-opted men from the regiment all of whom he knew would be observing every detail. Well, Ann did him credit there; they might all stare at Camilla but Ann had talked easily with all comers, whether it was the Brigadier Major or his own lance-jack, who was parking cars in military straight lines.

She tucked her arm into his, holding up her skirt to keep it clear of the ground, damp and slightly muddy as it always seemed to be on this flat, wet plain. 'That Camilla. She's had a little too much, of course, but she was telling everyone in the Ladies that I'd got the best-looking one of the lot.' She grinned up at him. 'And so I have. Not that looks count for everything, mind.'

He burst out laughing, pleased but unembarrassed. 'I've done pretty well too.' He bent to kiss her; she tasted of champagne and her cheek was warm to his touch.

'Yes, I've had quite enough to drink myself,' she said peacefully. 'But it's been lovely, and I'm not surprised you like the Army. I just wish you weren't here while I'm in England.'

'We'll be home in a year,' he said automatically, and it came to him that he had no home that was not the regiment. There was no room for him in Edinburgh and if he was being honest he wouldn't have wanted it if there had been; it tasted of defeat and anxiety there and he hated it. And Ann lived with her parents, and although he was fond of them it wasn't easy to stay there and make love to her as he wanted to. They liked him but he knew they thought he was too young to accept him as a serious suitor. He looked down at Ann and felt a wave of desolation at the prospect of losing this small, calm, warm oasis in his life.

'I haven't got a home. I couldn't even offer you married quarters,' he said. He looked down at her startled face anxiously.

She stood on her toes to kiss him. 'Davey, I wouldn't want you to be tied down like that. I tell you what, if you . . . if that's what you want . . . I could get a job over here somewhere, I mean with the Army – so we could see each other more often.' She looked at him questioningly, to see if it was what he wanted, and he understood that he had what he needed here, in his arms, and held her to him, wanting to cry.

'You'll have to get a job for a bit, so that we can afford somewhere to live together . . . I mean, until I qualify for married quarters. But I want to get married.'

She returned his hug and they kissed for a long moment. Then she pulled herself back. 'And what about me? You haven't asked me.'

He looked down at her, momentarily taken aback, then, understanding she was in earnest, he placed a hand on his heart, dropped on to his knees in the mixture of mud and leaves under the high trees, and sought the honour of her hand in marriage, so that she ended up laughing and crying, holding him to her and agreeing to be his wife, just as soon as that could decently be arranged.

CHAPTER ELEVEN

February 1982

The tall, stooped, grey-haired man, with the hunch of the shoulders that comes with pensionable age, crossed St Martin's Lane in an abrupt downpour, huddling into a battered mackintosh. He arrived, dripping, at a plate-glass door, pushed through it blindly and stood on the other side, polishing the rain off his glasses with a large, grubby handkerchief.

'Sir. Mr Caldwell!'

'Paul, my boy. And Sean.' He beamed at them as they converged on him and extracted him from his raincoat. 'How wonderful to see you both. I've never been here and I hear it's very fashionable.'

Paul and Sean stood drinking in the sight of him, stooped and pale with the lined skin of the habitual heavy smoker. He was dressed in the familiar tweed jacket, the like of which, as the lads at the Hall had been wont to say, you only ever saw on television on the back of someone got up as an eccentric aristocrat. This, combined with shapeless grey trousers and grubby tie, should have made him look hopelessly out of place among the grey-suited, loud-voiced young men and women, but, as always, he looked perfectly at home.

It had been Sean who had kept in touch and who had decided to go and see his old mentor in his retirement and invited him to come to lunch when he was in London to see about his teeth. Paul, feeling a smile nearly splitting his face as he watched Old Caldwell search all his pockets for his cigarettes, wished he had made the effort as well.

'Terrible news,' he observed to both of them, and they stared at him.

'The *Falklands*.' He looked at them reproachfully, but Paul pulled himself together.

'Sorry, sir, we're not with you.'

'The Argentinians have invaded. This morning.'

'Bloody cheek,' Paul said, outraged, but saw that this was not the right reaction.

'Total failure of this government to understand what's going on. We should have made some sensible arrangement years ago, Paul, my boy. And you, Sean, you should understand all this. What do you think is going to happen now?'

Paul forced himself to consider the problem. 'We'll have to throw them out. I mean, it's a British island, isn't it?' He saw that Old Caldwell was looking at him over his glasses with just that quizzical, questioning look which had been so annoying and so challenging when he was a teenager. 'See what you mean, sir. It's twelve thousand miles away.'

'Yes. Well outside gunboat range.'

'De paratroops,' Sean supplied helpfully.

'No air-bases worth the name within range.'

Paul shifted irritably. This had been meant to be a pleasure, a long lunch on a Friday with the weekend beckoning and not a lot he had to do before Wednesday next week.

'Sorry, my boy, lead me to the food. Not much the three of us can do, as I always remind myself. The Foreign Office, of course, is not what it was. But you lads must take an interest. Parliament is going to sit tomorrow to debate all this – I can't remember when it last sat on a Saturday. Half the members must have been on their way home to their constituencies.'

They led him to the table, still feeling in all his pockets for a cigarette. They had ordered champagne and watched Old Caldwell's face light up as he saw the treat coming toward him. Thirty years at the Hall would not have left him with a large pension, of course, and Paul cast around to think what he could do. He was enjoying the meal too; Old Caldwell knew his stuff and had picked his way lovingly through the menu and the wine list, taking them at their word as they urged him to have whatever he would like. He was looking ten years younger by the time they got to the pudding. He was still the same good man they had known, coaxing Sean to talk about his new flat and teasing him gently about his peacock clothes.

'And you and Paul work together?'

'I do some for him, yeah.'

'Tell me about your work, Paul.'

Paul had been ready for this difficult moment and launched fluently into his explanation, which postulated an import/export business in heavy engineering, operating out of the Comecon states.

'Machine tools?'

He always forgot how street-smart Old Caldwell was. 'Some, yes. Mostly Polish.'

'And the Arab states buy them in preference to German?'

'They're cheaper. And, of course, there is some politics in it, they want to keep in with the Soviets and the Eastern Bloc countries.'

'Yes.' Caldwell was considering him with the bright, sideways look he remembered so well, greeting his more ingenious explanations as to why he had not been where he said he would, or done his homework. 'Does it pay well?'

'Yes,' he and Sean confirmed simultaneously, and their old teacher looked at them both thoughtfully. 'That would be important to both of you of course,' he observed, in just the way he always had done by dropping absolutely direct emotional statements into the conversation. 'What are you doing with your riches, Sean?'

'I've got de flat.'

'Very nice. What about you, Paul? Do you still want a country house?'

'Not just now. No, I want to buy a company here. And I'm going to finance a restaurant for a friend of mine.'

'Another lad? Sorry, Paul, I always forget with my old pupils, but you and Sean are . . . what? . . . twenty-seven? How time flies! I remember you both when you first came to the school.' They eyed him warily, not wanting to be reminded of those chaotic days and their family backgrounds, but he moved on smoothly. 'Someone your own age.'

'Yeah. But it's a girl.'

'Your girlfriend?'

'No. My sister – not a real sister, of course, but we were in a gang together at school when we were kids.'

'Oh, really?' Old Caldwell lit up. He had always been on at his charges to keep in touch with their families and their childhood friends whenever possible. 'Is she also of Hungarian origin?'

Paul and Sean both started to laugh, tickled by the idea. 'Nah, she's very English,' Paul said.

'Posh family,' Sean volunteered.

'Goodness me,' Old Caldwell said openly curious, and Paul looked at his watch.

'She's coming here, oh, in half an hour. If you've got time you could stay and meet her.'

'I couldn't resist it.' He beamed at them. 'And I could have some of that delicious brandy I see over there.'

They fell over themselves to order him one, watching with triumphant pleasure as he savoured it, Paul telling him about Azul Tokay, and realizing halfway through that this was familiar ground to his mentor. Even Sean was chatting away, reminiscing about the poteen run up by his grandmother in some God-forsaken Irish bog in West Cork.

They looked up with a start to see Jens striding across the restaurant, looking stern and ruffled. Old Caldwell shuffled to his feet, beaming, showering napkin, matches and cigarettes on the floor and knocking the table so that all their drinks jumped.

'You must be Jennifer,' he said, extending both hands, so that she had to stop looking cross and take them and be swept into a hug from Paul, who had found himself on his feet in imitation of his old teacher. She leant over punctiliously to kiss Sean; she and Paul had agreed that the only way to accustom him to human society was to keep on touching him, socially, and kissing him in greeting.

'Chef's looking for you, Sean. The kitchen screen's playing up. When you've time,' she added, with a sidelong look at their guest, but Sean vanished with the light of battle in his eye.

'How'd it go?' Paul asked her, knowing she had been seeing her bank manager.

'Not well. Tell you later.' She turned politely to talk to Old Caldwell, true to her posh upbringing, and he watched, both amused and annoyed, as they did the English thing of fishing for mutual acquaintance. Didn't take them long to find it either, he saw jealously, as Old Caldwell turned out to have known Jens's grandfather, for God's sake; he must be even older than he looked.

'You're very young to be starting your own restaurant,' Caldwell said with interest.

'I'm only a year younger than Paul. I'm twenty-six. I went to catering college at sixteen and I've been working in restaurant kitchens since I was eighteen.'

'Your father died young, of course,' Caldwell said gently.

'When I was eight.'

'Mm. And your mother?'

'She remarried.' Jens was looking pale and wooden and not looking at any of them. Paul shifted uneasily. Reluctantly she looked across the table to where Old Caldwell was sitting absolutely still, like a cat at a mouse-hole. 'I haven't lived at home since I was sixteen.'

'So you, too, are a child of a harsh winter.'

'What?' She blinked at him, startled.

'It's a Russian proverb.' He said it in Russian, and Paul half-recognized the words. 'That means children of a harsh winter grow up strong.' He looked at them carefully, in just the way Paul remembered, to see if they had found their way through the metaphor.

'Some do,' Jens said, interested, as Old Caldwell's pupils always had been.

'Yes,' he agreed. 'And some, of course, don't grow up at all, the harsh winter kills them.'

'And some get bent out of shape and grow up a bit odd.' Jens, intellectually tenacious, was considering the implications.

'Like you and Sean,' Paul suggested.

'Sean's not *that* odd. And he's getting much less peculiar,' Jens said scornfully, and Caldwell choked on his brandy.

'Sean is gay,' Paul explained, matter-of-factly.

'That's not necessarily a distortion,' Caldwell said mildly, patting himself on the chest to stop the cough. 'It may be a valid way of life for Sean. Some of the children of a harsh winter apparently grow up strong,' he added, thinking it through, sipping at his brandy, forgetful of his audience. 'But there's a weakness right at the core and they break under pressure.'

Paul drew breath uneasily, until he realized that Jens had not taken this personally and was fussing over Caldwell's coffee and insisting on a new, hot cup being produced. He left them to it, deciding he would go and pay the bill.

Caldwell, sobered by the fresh coffee, considered the young woman opposite him; curiously like her grandfather with his snub nose and determined jaw, but with none of his tentativeness. A self-contained creature, well in command of herself.

'It's a long time since I've seen both these young men. They've done very much better than seemed possible.' He looked at her anxiously. 'You do know their history?'

She nodded. 'Oh, yes. Paul really is nearly my brother. I've known him since I was five and it turns out it was my dad who put the Social Services on to him. I know Sean less well, but Paul's and Sean's lives make my troubles seem remarkably unimportant.'

'Ah, yes. I saw that there had been a tip-off when I looked at Paul's records. His guardian was a monster, it's clear, not just one of these hopeless men who can't cope with the demands of children. I mean a real sadist.'

'He still has scars,' she said, reaching for the brandy. 'And burn marks.' She looked up into his considering gaze. 'We're not . . . I mean, there is no question of our being lovers.'

'I did not suppose so. Does Paul still hit out when crossed?'

'Not with me or Sean.' She was horrified. 'Actually, I've never seen him do that with anyone, he's rather patient.' She laughed, the serious face illuminated by it. 'He has this series of absolutely idiotic blonde women, thick as bricks, and he doesn't get cross with *them* either.'

'Well, that's sex of course,' he observed, laughing.

'I suppose.' The vivid, snub-nosed face had gone abruptly wooden, and he eased away from difficult ground, wondering uncomfortably what had gone wrong. 'So Paul's going to finance your restaurant?' he said. 'My goodness me, isn't that rather a lot of money?'

'We need about £300,000. And Paul could do it all, don't ask how, but he isn't going to. I mean, I won't have it, I don't want to be owned.'

Not even by the closest thing in her life to a brother, he noted. 'You're not planning to marry anyone just yet, then?'

'Absolutely not. And not Paul. We agreed that.'

'I see. Well, don't leave it too late yourself.'

'I was planning to leave it out altogether,' she said, tilting her jaw.

'Ah,' he said, and smiled at her, looking over her shoulder to where Paul was coming back with Sean, pocketing credit cards, a big, powerful man now, carrying a stone or so too much weight, but good-looking and effective, and by the account of the young woman opposite him, commanding more money than he himself had amassed in sixty-two years of living. 'Well, I must leave you young things to get on. It's been a great pleasure to meet you, Jennifer and I hope you'll invite me to your restaurant.'

'I will.' She shook his hand and stood by while Paul found him the Gents and a taxi, so that his last vision was the three of them standing side by side on the pavement waving to him. They look all right, he thought, please God they'll stay that way.

'Come on then, Jens, let's hear about the bank.' Paul watched the taxi out of sight and pushed impatiently in front of her, back into the restaurant, where they were allotted a table at the back, well away from casual passers-by. Sean, annoyingly, had faded back into the kitchen with a muttered excuse.

'What'd he say?'

'Wouldn't lend me any money is the short answer,' she reported wearily. 'Said that new enterprises were always difficult, restaurants in particular, anxious work for a young woman like myself, blah, blah, blah.' She scowled furiously at the waiter bringing her tea, who, stricken, looked carefully at every detail of the tray before laying it in front of her with the air of a man poking meat through the bars of a tiger's cage. 'And it didn't help that they were all in a panic worrying about war. We *can't* be going to war with Argentina over some grotty little island in the South Atlantic, for God's sake. To hear him talk you'd think the whole banking system of the Western world was threatened.'

'I was afraid it would be like that.' Paul extracted a cigar from his jacket and lit up, sprawling luxuriantly.

'There is no point at all giving up cigarettes if you're going to smoke dozens of those things instead,' she said sharply, and he sat up with a jerk and concentrated.

'No need to take it out on me, Jens, your man's about half right. I can see you're pissed off but you really don't need the problems of borrowing money while you're trying to make the place work.'

'How would you know?'

'I may not have borrowed from a bank, but I know what it's like not being able to pay a bill. Come on, Jens.'

'Fair enough. Sorry.'

He sighed. 'I've got money, Jens. You don't have to borrow. And, of course, you get a fifteen per cent shareholding for free.'

She looked at him carefully. 'Paul, I don't want you owning eighty-five per cent. I know I've got to have shareholders, but I want lots of them, not just one.'

'If you lose the whole lot – which you won't – I can afford it,' he boasted.

'That's not the point.' She was looking harried. 'I want it to be mine, not yours. And if you have eighty-five per cent it's yours. That's why I wanted to borrow, so I could have a quarter and you could have a quarter.'

Paul coughed on his cigar, incredulous. 'And who the fuck else are you going to get in? We always said I'd do it.'

'No, we didn't. We said you'd take a share.'

'I said I'd do it.' He stared at her, feeling himself going scarlet, and pressure round his head. 'You're winding me up,' he accused, and seized her wrist painfully.

'Paul,' she said furiously. 'Paul, you're hurting. Stop.'

She was looking at him as if he'd just turned into a gorilla and he ground his teeth, struggling for words.

'Paul, I'm not trying to put you down, I'm trying to tell you what I want and I'm sorry if you think it's unkind. It may be, but it's what *I* need.' She pulled at her arm, tears starting in her eyes, and he saw, as if it was in a film or something, that the ring he wore on his right fourth finger was cutting into her wrist. 'Paul,' she said, stopping the struggle, 'where are you? It's me here.'

He looked into the familiar blue eyes, round with pain and bewilderment, tears dripping from the corners, and the noises of the restaurant around him suddenly became audible again. He let go of her wrist abruptly, then snatched it again as she pulled it away. 'Jens.' He wanted to say he was sorry but the words would not come and he looked at her in sullen appeal.

'You didn't know who I was for a minute,' she said slowly.

'Yes, I did. Only I thought . . . I thought you were getting at me. Trying to put me down.'

'Trying to humiliate you.' She had stopped trying to take her hand back and had turned it over so she was holding his, palm to palm, ignoring the trickle of blood from her wrist.

'Yes.' He reached for a napkin miserably, and dabbed at the blood. 'Sorry,' he managed. 'Sorry.'

'Paul, dearest Paul. I have to be allowed to say what I want.'

'You do,' he acknowledged wretchedly. 'But I thought I was your partner. Your brother. And you want other people.'

'I want equality. And I can't have that if you have most of the shares.'

'You can have half. For free. 'Course you can.'

'That wouldn't be fair on you.' He flexed his fingers round hers, struggling not to say that he didn't care what was fair, provided she was still his sister, but she forestalled him.

'Let me tell you who else I hope will come in.'

He nodded miserably.

'Sofia. William said to her in front of me when I was ... when he was ... when I was living with them, I must have been sixteen, that he knew I would be a successful restaurateur if that was what I wanted, and he would stake me. He told her she would have a comfortable old age that way. So she and Lucy want to put up a quarter share because he was always right about money things.'

'I thought they were poor. You always said they had problems keeping you after old man French died.'

'He was not old,' she objected, with a stab of remembered pain. 'And yes, that was true because about two-thirds of their income died with William, it was one of those trusts that goes with the male line. They're not all that well off now but they both got some when Lucy's mother died and they've had a bellyful of trustees. They'll need dividends of course but we can do that, in three years anyway, the plan says.'

She looked at him anxiously, loving and determined, and he felt some of the pain ease. Sofia and Lucy, well, they were family, not rivals, that was different.

'Who else?' His voice sounded odd in his ears, gruff and painful.

'My mother.'

'*She* doesn't have any money,' he objected, startled.

'No. It's Joshua's of course.'

'We don't want *that*?' He was so shocked that he forgot his own grief.

'Yes, we do. The shares would be registered in her name, dividends go to her and she'll be all right, even if Joshua dies or goes off with one of the girls in his office. She'll have her own money.'

'What if you lose it?' he retaliated automatically, but the band round his head was easing steadily.

'I won't and if I did she'll be no worse off. The only thing Joshua is going to give her money for is me. You're right he wants a stake in me, still, somehow. She might be safer with shares in ICI, but he won't give her them.' She waited and then looked at him carefully. 'Is that OK? Can you bear that? I do want you in. I need you, you *know* that.'

He looked down at their joined hands, burning with shame, hardly able to sit in his seat.

'Paul!' It was an appeal.

'Oh, Jens. I'm sorry. I don't know what happens to me.' He mopped her face distractedly, took the napkin back and blew his nose on it.

'Yes, you do.' She seized his glass and took a healthy gulp of his brandy. 'You see your guardian.'

He clenched his jaw against the memory, but there was something wrong with the way she described it.

'No, I see me. Curled up in a shed, bleeding, too frightened to tackle him.' He clenched his hands in agony, but she patted him, unfrightened.

'You were a baby when he started on you and you were only ten when you got away. He'd probably have killed you if you hadn't given in.'

'Yeah.' He was never, he saw, going to be able to explain the desolation, the feeling that everything was lost and that there was no way out. The bitter taste of defeat and loss would be with him always.

'There's one more I'd like to bring in.'

'Who? That bloke you've been seeing?'

'No, you cuckoo. Sean.'

'Sean wants to spend some of his good money?'

'He understands about restaurants. He thinks they're the same as pubs, and all Irishmen understand about pubs. But he didn't want to cross you. *He* said you wanted to be the only one with me and I said you couldn't possibly be that silly.'

'Yeah, all right. And I disappointed you.' He sought for a

way of getting back at his sibling. 'I'm no worse about all *that* than you are about men. My heart bleeds for that poor bloke, what's-his-name, Andrew. Or it would if he wasn't so wet.'

She had gone satisfactorily scarlet, he noticed.

'Shut up, Paul.'

'No, I won't.' This was better, he could feel the worst of the pain being soothed. 'You haven't managed it with anyone yet and you're twenty-six.'

'As a matter of fact I have, so there.'

'Liar! Who with?'

'Andrew, of course. And before you ask, it didn't do much for me – and I bet it didn't for him either – but it was all right. I mean, I wasn't frightened. And it didn't hurt.'

She was pink and ruffled, but defiant, looking so like herself at eight that the tension in his chest eased off.

'Well done, Jens.' He paused to think. 'Just the one time, was it?'

'No,' she said smugly. 'Three times now.'

'Did it – does it – get any better?'

'No. But it doesn't get any worse either, and at least I can stop worrying about it. Please pass the brandy, I'd better catch up with you.'

He moved the bottle sternly out of her reach. 'No, you don't. Come on, let's go and look at the site again and then let's see if the rest of your punters can find their cheque-books. If you want this place open before next year we ought to get a move on. Get Sean out of the office and tell him he's in. Ring up your family and we'll have a meeting tomorrow morning. For fuck's sake, Jens, you have to sign a *contract* next week, or someone else will get that site.'

'Is it here, sir?'

The driver sounded doubtful, and Joshua Logan, peering out through the rain-covered side window of the big car, understood why. The not very wide frontage to which the number he was looking for was attached appeared to be full of dusty advertisements for gas cookers, but the presence of a Conrad Ritblat 'For Sale' sign reassured him.

'Doesn't look like 16,000 square to me,' he said, 'not unless it's very deep. Which it could be.' He touched his wife's hand. 'Go on, Mary, Tom can take me to the office while you sort out your daughter. Any problems, say you have to talk to Linklaters. All right? Ring up when you want fetching.' He squeezed her waist reassuringly, kissed her on the mouth and sent her on her way blushing, observing sourly that Lucy and Sofia French were getting out of a taxi.

'That's my mother, Mrs Logan.' Jennifer was standing in the middle of the plain, empty, dusty space, beside a trestle table covered with two Café de la Paix table-cloths and set with pads, pencils, glasses and water jugs. Beside her stood her newly acquired solicitor, Charles Hazell, a thin, dark young man in heavy horn-rimmed glasses, a sports jacket and tidy grey trousers. She had got him at some trouble and expense, finding out in the process that even the most newly promoted partner in one of the top ten City solicitors was already working for a client on that Saturday morning, which was why the meeting was taking place at tea-time. They had eaten dinner together the night before and sandwiches at lunch, with Paul added to the party, and she was as well briefed on the problems of setting up a company and the shareholders' agreement as had been possible in the time. She had understood after the argument with Paul yesterday how much she had been depending on him to see her through all this and, cursing herself for not taking charge of her life, had done the best she could in the time available. She waited beside Charles, feeling slightly sick with anxiety and shortage of sleep, but knowing, wryly, that she looked calm and self-contained and confident; it was a trick she had developed when she was fighting to keep her place in the crowded, male-dominated kitchens where she had done her apprenticeship. She kissed her mother, battling down the old complex feelings of love and rage, and threw her arms round Lucy with no difficulty at all. Paul, with Sean in his shadow, was next in, greeting people punctiliously and, she was pleased to see, kissing Sofia, who fancied him in the carefully concealed way she indicated interest in any man. Paul, exclusively interested in blondes, was alarmed by her and jealous of her relationship with Jens, but had managed to get to the point of treating her as a woman friend. It would have to do.

She introduced Charles to everyone, explaining that he had helped her with the thinking and must, in this context, be regarded as her adviser. It was expected, she said as calmly as she was able, that once the shareholders' agreement was in place, he and his firm would act for the company. She considered her audience: Sofia and Lucy were listening carefully, Sean probably was too, but as usual his eyes were fixed sternly on the blotter in front of him. Her mother was anxiously consulting a typewritten piece of paper which she had produced from her handbag, and Paul was looking ostentatiously bored.

'We need something to talk about, as it were, so Charles has produced the skeleton of an agreement, a list of the points we have to sort out before he can produce a document. I have talked to everyone, and I hope that inasmuch as any bits are filled in they are what we agreed.' Jennifer handed round the two sheets on which she felt as if blood had been expended, and looked down at her wrist, realizing that she had covered the small, deep cut made by Paul's ring with the bright blue elastoplast which is always used in good kitchens, being instantly visible if it falls off into anything. She shuffled it under her cuff, self-consciously.

The prospective shareholdings were set out: Paul Seles to subscribe £75,000 for a 25 per cent shareholding; Mary Logan to do the same; Sofia and Lucy to subscribe for 12½ per cent each; Sean Kelly for 5 per cent. The remaining 20 per cent was hers at a price of £30,000, half what the others were paying. As of last night she had £15,000 from her grandparents' estate, hoarded for five years without even drawing the interest. One of the things she had done in the intervening twenty-four hours had been to find a mortgage broker who had assured her that he could find someone to lend her the other £15,000 on the security of the flat she had bought four years earlier – just. She was still shaking from this. She of all people ought to have known never to depend financially on a man, but she had been, albeit unconsciously, doing just that, and had very nearly been trapped.

She looked at her mother, whose lips were moving over the piece of paper she was carrying.

'Questions?' she said coolly.

'Darling.' Surprisingly, it was Lucy French, brow furrowed. 'Can I just check? We all have to take our shares in our own name, is that right? I mean, as you know a lot of Sofia's and my money is in trust. But you won't let the trustees invest.'

'That's right,' Jennifer said, grateful to have this point on the table, then saw from Lucy's nod that she had understood it perfectly well and was being helpful. 'Is everyone clear on that?'

Paul had not wanted the shares in his name either, but in the name of a company in Guernsey. She had let Charles take him through the reasons against that, listening terrified but admiring. She had understood, for the first time, something of the nature of Paul's affairs. He had, from the first, arrived as if in a shower of gold, taking her out, taking her away with him, buying her clothes, casually generous and usually paying cash. She had been long enough in a cash business to know that not all of this had been come by honestly, but she had managed not to think about it. But what she had not understood was the world of international trading. She knew commissions were paid and in huge amounts; she had never asked herself what Paul did with those commissions, and it became crystal-clear that he took enormous trouble to conceal his pile from any authority that might tax it.

'But Charles,' she had said, somewhere late the night before, watching Paul's square back, every line eloquent of frustrated rage, as he went to fetch more coffee. 'why can't Off-shore Tax Evasion Funds Ltd, or whatever Paul's company is called, be the shareholder? I mean, *I* know it's Paul.'

'No, you don't,' Charles had said grittily, across Paul, who had slopped a cup down in front of him. 'You have no idea. And Paul can't reassure you – or us – without risking trouble with the tax authorities. And even if it is a company wholly controlled by Paul now, who knows what happens in the future?'

'I could end up with the Mafia as a shareholder,' she had asked, resolutely ignoring Paul's furious scowl.

'That's right,' Charles had confirmed. 'That's why you want everyone's shares in their own name.'

'And what if people don't want to subscribe on that basis?' Paul had asked, fingers clenched round the cup, and the lawyer had looked at her to answer.

'Then I miss this site, and I have to collect a set of people who can invest in their own names,' she had said stolidly, having gone through this with Charles, grieving for the loss but ready for it. And she had managed to sit, letting the silence speak, drinking coffee.

'It'll cost me a fucking fortune to come in,' Paul had said finally, and she had known she had won, and slowly relaxed the breath she had been holding.

'Because you will have to repatriate some profits,' Charles had said, perking up. 'We could perhaps help there with some advice. One of my partners is a specialist in these schemes.'

So Paul was sitting opposite her today, having bitten that bullet, and she did not even have to glance his way to bring him in with his confirmation that his shareholding would be in his own personal name. Sean told the table that he would not dream of putting any other bugger's name on his fifteen-tousand, so that left only Mary Logan, still anxiously re-reading her list.

'Joshua . . . that is, both of us, wanted my shares to be in a company name.' She looked up. 'For tax reasons,' she said, hopefully.

Jennifer felt every muscle tighten and saw Paul's mouth twitch. He had warned her, he had indeed, his own need to control giving him a very clear view of how Joshua would operate. 'I'm sorry, Mum,' she said, as smoothly as she could.

'Them's the rules. Only named individuals can be shareholders.' Her mother paled and looked hopefully down at her piece of paper.

'Jens, what is to stop any of us transferring our shares to a trust or something at a later stage?' It was Sofia, whose sound academic mind worked in whatever field she was, and Jennifer felt as if she had been stabbed in the back.

'Provision is always made in a private company that all shareholders must approve any transfer,' Charles said promptly, and she understood, as she should have known, that Sofia meant only to help. 'I mean, a shareholder can execute a transfer, but the other shareholders can agree that the transfer would not be registered in the company's books.'

'Making the shares worth not a lot,' Sofia observed.

'That's right.'

Jens looked towards her mother, ready to suggest she went back to Joshua and told him to keep his money, but Paul got in first.

'Mrs Logan, why don't we ask your husband to join the meeting just so that we can sort out here and now whether you are a shareholder or not?'

Jens felt the darkness rising to fell her, but she sat still and it receded.

'Where is he?' Paul persisted.

'At the office.' Her mother, who had always disliked Paul, looked at her frantically.

'Good idea,' she said stoically. 'Because if you aren't in, Mum, then I need to make other arrangements quickly. Ring him up. We'll have a break and get some tea.'

Joshua turned up inside ten minutes, but refused to join the meeting, saying he wanted to talk to Jennifer first. She refused to discuss money without her lawyer present and introduced Charles, not offering a chair to anyone so that the three of them had had to stand in a little group by the dusty fireplace. Joshua understood immediately, she saw.

'What are you going to do if I can't agree?'

'Paul will lend the other £75,000 to the company until we can take in other shareholders.'

'In his own name?'

'That's the deal. He grumbles, of course, saying it costs him dearly bringing that amount into the country, but he is none the less willing.' She deliberately turned and smiled across the room at Paul, who was watching her while apparently considering a defective plug socket. She turned back to Joshua, who was considering her openly, and let him do that, preserving a courteous, interested expression.

'Well, Joshua,' she said, deciding she could afford to be the one who broke the silence. 'Is Mum in or out?'

He had gone on being silent, but she had not moved. 'In,' he said, when it seemed as if the walls must close in.

'In her own name?'

'Subject to the shareholders' agreement not being a dog's breakfast.'

'I expect Mercer Hall can manage that, can't you, Charles? Where do you want it sent?'

He told her, looking around him. 'Lot of work to do.'

'Yes, Mum's got the draft plans.'

'I could help, you know. I am in the construction business.'

She considered him, understanding suddenly that in this at least he was sincere; his fingers itched as hers did when he saw a job to be done. 'Thank you, Joshua. I'll bear that in mind.' It was the best she could do across the familiar tension in her stomach, but he took it, she saw, as enough of a concession to enable him to agree to the deal, and to sit in, at her invitation, while they polished off the other main headings of the agreement. She even managed to kiss his cheek lightly in farewell; to do otherwise would have been conspicuous since she seemed to have kissed everyone else, including Charles.

Left in the huge, echoing, dusty room she felt a slow joy overwhelm her. She had got her restaurant, on her terms, she had understood how to do it and she had manoeuvred her way to get there. Better than sex, she thought jubilantly, better than *anything*; if I can do this, I can do anything I want.

'Paul.' He was crossly switching off lights, withdrawn from her, and she contemplated him with affection; the cunning, loving brother, who had swallowed his own defeat and forced her to take on Joshua as she could not have done if she had had warning. And given her the means to win that war. 'Would you like me to come and help murder your guardian? We've just got time before supper.'

He turned, like an animal at bay, saw her huge smile and came to hug her. 'Come on,' he said, rocking her in his arms, 'you've got your restaurant, you'll be barefoot in a kitchen for the next year, but tonight we'll live it up.'

They stopped to lock the place up and she heard him exclaim and leave her side to come back with an evening paper.

'Bugger me. They did it. We're going to chuck the Argentinians out.'

She craned over his shoulder to look. 'Dear God, it's twelve thousand miles away.'

'We'll do it,' he said confidently, and led her off to celebrate.

CHAPTER TWELVE

October 1982

'Eyes . . . right.' David's head snapped round, his right hand rising stiffly to the salute as he passed the chair by the Guild-hall, seeing a quick glimpse of scarlet, fur and gold chain and next to that a flash of bright blue. The Prime Minister, taking the salute with the Lord Mayor of London, presumably because she was on his territory. He didn't grudge her this tribute; if you had to rush 12,000 miles to defend a set of God-forsaken islands, you could not have wished for more resolute political support. Three companies, including his own, had been plucked out of Caterham, where they had been waiting to go to Northern Ireland, placed under the charge of a major and regrouped with several other lots, and two weeks later at the end of March had been stuffed into the MS *Canberra* with the minimum conversion necessary to enable several hundred men to get enough exercise to keep them fit for battle. Even the most unimaginative and least critical of the officers were openly censorious of the way the UK had apparently been totally wrong-footed by the Argentinians. You would have had to be stupid not to see that someone had massively blundered, and the presence of a royal prince with his helicopter squadron had not convinced anyone that this was other than a shambles. It was also, partly because the crisis was so sudden and so far away, excessively difficult to focus and to take seriously. They had been briefed to be ready when and as they got there for instant action of almost any sort, yet the newspapers were full of reports of peace initiatives. He and Peter Fountain, also here with his company, had agreed that by far the most likely outcome was that they would get as far as the middle of the South Atlantic, with a third of their men still seasick – 'This boat doesn't usually go where we're going,' as Peter had observed – and would then be told to turn back, so the chaps could be sick all the way home. But none of these doubts had been allowed to show; the whole authority structure had had to behave for the full six weeks of the trip as if they would be going straight into action the day they arrived, and train accordingly. And so, in the event, they had. The PM had spared them the worst horror, which would have been idiotic politicians getting the Army into an intolerable situation, then not supporting you properly. But they should not have been there at all, he thought sombrely, remembering the appallingly burnt casualties from HMS *Sheffield*; a kindness to have left some of them in the water, it would have been. He frowned, puzzled, as the ranks ahead of him hesitated, and shortened his stride automatically while his ears caught up with his instincts. The huge crowd gathered on this bright October day were roaring in song with the band, dragging behind the beat as a crowd always would. 'Rule Britannia,' the mob roared, flags waving, 'Britannia rules the waves / Britons never, never, never shall be slaves,' as the drummers strained to keep up the beat. The crowd sang it all over again as he swung his men past, counting under his breath to keep the pace; the spectators naturally did not know the words of the second and third verses, so they just repeated the first verse again and again. He was heartily sick of the sound by the time he reached the point where he was to fall his company out and join his lieutenant colonel – a colonel now, in the rush of promotions that had followed the brief Falklands action – at the lunch in the Guildhall.

He fell in automatically beside Peter Fountain, who always knew where he was going and appeared to know most of the senior officers present. Peter's father had been a much-decorated serving officer in the Korean war, begetting Peter and his brothers between long patches of service, and had retired as a brigadier in the late seventies. Peter had once let drop that his father was opposed to the use of the Army as police-men in Northern Ireland, on the basis that the whole thing was a total political nonsense, and the Army ought not to be there at all, as sticking-plaster on a gaping political haemorrhage. It was a particular irony that Peter himself had been saved from service in Belfast only by being dispatched on an expedition which his father would have categorized as a similar fool's errand, had he been alive to see it.

They both snapped to attention as a familiar bemedalled brigadier stopped by them. He acknowledged the salute, and inspected, carefully, the ribbons they both wore. 'You both got that one,' he observed. 'Well done.'

'Thank you, sir,' David said, and added hesitantly, 'And congratulations on . . . on . . .'

'On my elevation? Thank you. Temporary, acting, and I don't expect it to be permanent.'

'Sir?'

'I said when I got down there that I'd win the war for these buggers, then I'd go. And I meant it, as it turns out.'

David gaped at him, but Peter, who had known the man from childhood, glanced round warningly.

'Couldn't matter now, my boy. We won, no one will worry. Doesn't matter that they had half-grown recruits up against us, no one will know. Were you at the St Paul's service?'

'No, sir.'

'Much more, well, *appropriate* than all this. Still, bread and circuses, as we used to say at school. Good luck to you both.'

He nodded and was gone, leaving them both staring after him. David took a deep breath, excited and alarmed by hearing said aloud what he had only half thought in the chaos of the invasion. It had been real, while the well-trained Argentine pilots had been screaming through the skies in their superior pricey jets, and while they all lived in fear of being knocked out by an Exocet and burnt alive like those on the HMS *Sheffield*. Then they had all found themselves wondering what they were doing 12,000 miles from British waters, risking a horrible death, for the sake of some scattered, half-deserted islands. But, curiously, he had felt even worse when, with the Argentine Air Force neutralized, they had poured men on to the islands to find their adversaries were half-trained, hungry conscripts whom he would not have trusted to look after a cookhouse in the middle of Dartmoor. You could only conclude that this was strictly a politicians' outing and that, as one of his lancejacks had observed, next time you ought to issue Mrs Thatcher and her Cabinet and Galtieri and his with a set of superannuated revolvers each and let *them* fight it out.

But these views seemed churlish and unreasonable in the warmth of the Guildhall, the whole organized with military neatness and smiling, pleased faces everywhere. All the Services had had a good war; the Navy perhaps the best of all, because it would take a brave politician to try to cut the fleet as they had in 1981. But most of the Services had had the time of their lives; gone were the peace-time stringent controls on expenditure which meant you only got to fire a live rocket about twice a year. Every piece of kit had been used and tested and in many cases quietly and thankfully discarded. Better yet, some of the Services' elite, the dress soldiers, the Guards, had been somewhat less than effective in a real war, as all other infantry and armoured regiments had always known they would be. And one group of the death or glory boys, the SBS, had come ignominiously unstuck; dropped on an ice-floe on the usual assumption that they would succeed in overpowering the entire Argie occupying force, using only teeth and their bare hands, they had failed to get anywhere at all, and had had to be picked up, two weeks later, suffering from frostbite and acute hunger, having progressed about half a mile. Nothing in the whole short war had given as much pleasure to the regular Navy or for that matter to the detachments from the real Army regiments. Not that anyone had told the general public about that particular shambles, and there was a senior SBS officer sitting at the next table but three.

It was a good lunch and he enjoyed it until it came to the Prime Minister's speech, a paeon of triumphalism and mutual congratulation. She had, according to Service lore, spat feathers after the St Paul's service where the Archbishop of Canterbury had insisted in his sermon on speaking of the grief of the mourners on both sides, and where he had apparently vetoed 'Onward Christian Soldiers' as a hymn. Quite right too, David thought suddenly, this had not been a Christian war, if indeed there was such a thing. And the Archbishop had not started it either, it had not been he who had so signally failed to comprehend what Galtieri was saying or doing. He joined in the applause, in a competent soldierly fashion, but the day seemed to have got darker and the food sat heavily on his stomach.

He walked with Peter into the littered street, still crowded with people wandering about, and both of them made disapproving comments in the manner of men thirty years their senior about the indiscipline of the average civilian who dropped his ice-cream wrappers where he stood.

'You for home, David?'

'Yes, I suppose so. It'll take me an hour and a half to Winchester. What about you?'

'My ma's expecting me, so I'd better get out of this lot. I told her I might be late, thinking, you know, there might be enough at lunch to get mildly pissed. Should have known better.'

'They didn't want us destroying civilian morale by falling about in the streets, I expect,' David said, with a cold eye on two neatly dressed middle-aged men, scarlet and cheerful, sitting side by side in a doorway, brandishing a bottle. He was not particularly interested in going home to Ann. She was seven and a half months pregnant with the baby they had started when he knew he would be going to the Falklands. He would himself rather have waited a little longer for his second child, but he owed Ann a great deal and it had seemed churlish to deny her a baby when he was off on such an uncertain mission. Their first, Francis, had been born in Hong Kong, when he had finally qualified for married quarters, and was only just two. He had found himself gently, imperceptibly bored with marriage to Ann, while knowing absolutely that it was what he needed, and had continued, discreetly, to have other women, most notably over the later stages of her pregnancy with Francis. That had been a mistake from which he had only been rescued by the Army posting his lover back to London, whether deliberately or not he had never tried to establish. And just as well; Ann was his life and his base, and without her he knew he would not manage. She had healed a lot of wounds for him; when they were in Hong Kong she had reunited him, gently, with his father and half-sisters, not all that much older than his own child. His father was not making an enormous success; he saw with adult eyes that he was difficult to work with, touchy and not nearly as good as he thought he was, but he was happy with his Pamela and his new family and his new home.

And Ann had done well by the rest of his family too; seeing he wanted it, she had encouraged his mother to remarry and supported her in that marriage and kept them in touch. She had been more than good to Mickey, having him to stay and indeed seeing him through these bloody infuriating self-indulgent patches when he could only weep and wring his hands, while David had been in the Falklands. As if Ann didn't have enough with one little one and another on the way, he thought, righteously annoyed. Mickey had descended on Ann more or less as soon as he had left on the *Canberra* and proceeded to have a breakdown in the small room into which the baby would go when it arrived. Ann, bless her, had got him to see her doctor and regrouped him so that he had actually managed to sit his finals in June and get a decent degree. He had moved out just before David had arrived home, but was still there for meals whenever he could persuade Ann to invite him. David could not really take Mickey in this mood and was fed up with finding him in the tiny house near Winchester which the Army considered adequate for a couple with two children. He was so depressed and so threatening; he seemed to be everywhere at once, rushing to open doors and carrying things for Ann, whom he loved, and clinging with the desperation of the drowning to his place, hinting intolerably at the loneliness of his life. It would sort itself out of course when Ann had the baby; there would be no room for anyone else in her world, not even him for a bit, but he could stand that. Mickey would be right out in the cold, whether he knew it or not.

'Excuse me, but were you at the lunch? Has Mrs Thatcher gone?'

It was a very pretty girl with long, dark hair, and her blonde friend was just as good-looking. He smiled down at them both, pleased with their open admiration.

'About twenty minutes ago, I'm afraid.'

'Was it a good lunch?' the dark girl asked, smiling up at him.

'Well, you know. Yes.' He was smiling back into her eyes, which usually worked.

'Sally.' It was an irritated male voice, and he glanced over her shoulder at the large, dark man, not as tall but a good deal broader than himself, and blinked. The man looked momentarily surprised, then amused. 'Trust Sally. Hello, David Banner.'

'Paul Seles! Good God. How *are* you?' They shook hands guardedly, sizing each other up, and David saw that it was the blonde girl who was attached to Paul. And that, somehow, he had prospered; he seemed to have grown, and the clothes and the gold watch shouted of money.

'You were there?' Paul sounded openly envious.

'Yes,' David said, deciding that it must be ten years since they had met. 'Not that we did much more than sail down and sail back again.'

'Pushed a few troops off the islands, as I read it,' Seles said drily. 'We've had lunch too, but we thought we'd just go on drinking. Any chance of you joining us? I've got a flat in Kensington with a fridge full of champagne.'

'Do come,' Sally urged boldly.

'I can't in these clothes,' he temporized, taken aback.

'Oh, *why*? They suit you.'

'All sorts of boring rules about men in uniform stamping

about the streets, I'm afraid.' He spoke as if to her alone, another infallible trick which he only half knew he used.

'And quite right too, Sal, you wouldn't want that, not if you'd seen Budapest,' Paul Seles said firmly. 'David, do come if you can. It's your day, isn't it, and we'd be honoured. Here's my card – no, damn, not that one, that's the head of the Air Force in Hungary. This one. We're making our way there now. We'll collect a few more people, and I'll organize some food for later.'

It sounded all right, in fact it sounded better than all right with pretty Sally openly unwilling to leave him, even while he nipped back to the central barracks to change his kit. And it wasn't going to cost him either – Paul Seles had made that casually clear – and he liked the idea of being able to do a little gentle boasting to an audience that had neither been there nor heard all about it already. Ann would not mind his having a bit of a treat.

And it was a good place to be; he saw that the moment he arrived at the big mansion flat in Campden Hill. There was a white-jacketed waiter behind an improvised bar and lots of food in the kitchen; lots of pretty girls, some of whom had made tea, and people kept arriving as the day wore on. After a couple of hours he guiltily asked Paul for a phone and was shown into a big room, fitted out as an office with a computer and a telefax and all the latest electronic gadgets.

'Looks like the command centre in Stanmore,' he said, awed.

'I need this lot. You can't get anyone on the phone in the East, and it's pretty difficult with a telex, but at least that goes ultimately – I mean, the girl doesn't have to stand over it.'

'What is your business exactly, Paul?'

He got a long, thoughtful look in return and a pause. 'I sell machine tools mostly.'

David had only a hazy idea what these were, except that they were involved in the manufacture of just about anything, so he nodded wisely, accepted instructions on how to use the phone, and called Ann to explain that he and some of the chaps had decided to go and celebrate a bit.

'Oh,' she said, sounding weary. 'Well, that'll be nice for you. Come back when you're ready. I'll ask Mickey to stay to supper.'

'Very nice. Give him my love,' he said and put the phone down, relieved of care. There was no way he was going home before midnight, when Mickey would have taken his unhappy face away. The rest of the day was his.

The door opened and his host came back through it side-ways, carrying a bottle and two glasses. 'Thought you'd like one.' Paul was pretty much sober, he noticed, and wondered if he himself had been going a bit too fast. Then Maddy and Sally came in with several other people and a lot of champagne, and they had some of *that* before going off for a riotous late dinner at a place where Paul was a good enough customer to be allowed to do what he wanted.

David woke the next morning in an unfamiliar place and lay tense while the memory of who and where he was came back. The bed was warm and smelled of sex; he turned his head cautiously to see the back of a dark head on the pillow beside his own. He slid quietly out of bed, naked and urgently needing a pee, his head aching ferociously as he stood up hunting for his trousers. He pulled them on, zipping them gingerly, and pulled open the first door he saw which, thank Christ, was a bathroom. He had to wait a bit; he'd woken up with an erection, as he often did, and it had to go down a bit before anything would happen. The enforced pause gave him time to reflect as he cradled his aching head. He had managed to phone Ann again last night; she had agreed resignedly with his view that he was better to spend the night where he was than to drive home. Apparently Mickey had volunteered to stay and keep her company, so he had hardened his heart against feeling guilty. He had, oh God, told an entire London restaurant about his plans to enter politics in the Labour interest. And most certainly he had had Sally twice if not three times, once before anyone went out to supper, once when they had all arrived back, and, he rather thought, once again in the middle of the night, unless that had been a dream.

He managed finally to pee and get into a shower, where he stood for ten minutes, finishing off with cold water. He bounced out, feeling much better, and tucked a towel round his waist, then found a neat little package with toothbrush, toothpaste and razor, courtesy of MA. Interesting that they had such refinements in socialist Hungary. He thought, through his headache, about the flat; if he really was going to jack the Army in, he needed a job, and Paul Seles was plainly rich enough to have at least one of those in his gift. He did his teeth, considering himself narrowly in the mirror; he didn't look too bad, but then the sunburn hid the worst, and his hair, cut ruthlessly short in military style, curled neatly on his skull whatever he did to it. He could sell things, whatever it was Paul had to sell, of course he could, and his German was still good. He gave the even white teeth a further scrub, liking the vision of himself in a good suit flying first-class into unknown glamorous places.

'Davey?' Sally appeared in the doorway, yawning, wrapped in a sheet, and he felt a pressure against the towel he was wearing. Nothing like alcohol in the blood and a cold shower to bring you up nicely, as he had long observed.

'I want to have a shower too,' she protested, pushing him off, so he let her go and padded out to the kitchen to find them both some orange juice. He was spiking it with a half-empty bottle of champagne, when Paul walked in, fully dressed and carrying the day's papers.

'No, you carry on, Davey, don't let me interrupt.' He was looking particularly prosperous this morning. 'Do you want to borrow a pair of pants? They'll be a bit big.'

'Don't you believe it.'

'Like that, is it? Sally OK?'

'I certainly hope so. Thanks for letting me stay.'

'You're most welcome. Look, I have to go out, but why don't you come? Jens — Jennifer Redwood — is with the lads at our restaurant. It opens in a week, Christ knows how, and she's more or less living on site. I promised to go and see her, give her a hand. No, no, I'm useless with my hands, but I know where to find people.'

David hesitated and Paul swallowed coffee. 'You can come back and do that, it'll wait. Or bring her. Maddy's coming, aren't you, Maddy? No? I'll be back.' He patted the pretty blonde on her bottom and picked up a briefcase. 'You got five minutes, Davey, I have to make one call.'

In the event Sally decided not to come with them and it took longer than five minutes to get going. By the time they arrived, twenty-five minutes later, his head was aching painfully and he was wishing he had either stayed in bed with pretty Sally or started back to Ann. He trailed sulkily behind Paul and started involuntarily to cough as he came through the door. A drill was screaming close at hand and the dust was dancing thick in the bright October sun, further obscuring the filthy plate-glass windows with stickers and crosses all over them.

'Go away.' Two boiler-suited figures emerged from the dust, one of whom he would have known anywhere, spiky dark hair standing away from her face, wide blue eyes, snub nose and jaw tensed.

'It's me,' Paul said, reaching to kiss her.

'Oh, all right.' She waved angrily at the man with the drill, who nodded and stopped. David considered her with respect while he was formally re-introduced. She inspected him, to his carefully concealed pique, without a flicker of sexual interest and with some hostility, which he did not feel he deserved.

'Jens, come out with us,' Paul coaxed hopefully, 'let them get on here, I'm sure they don't need you for an hour or so and you're looking worn out.'

'They always need me,' she said crossly. 'And Jeremy is picking me up here in ten minutes anyway. *You* look terrible. What have you been doing?'

'Celebrating the Falklands march. With David here.'

'Why? Jim, wait a minute, will you, I just want to see that before you glue it in.'

'Well, David here was in it. The march and the war.'

'That means you've both got hangovers, I expect.' They had followed in her wake to what was recognizably a kitchen, and she was considering, slit-eyed, a detail of the counter. She stood square in front of it, absolutely concentrated and totally unself-conscious, the unbecoming boiler-suit creased and grubby, as the five men in her immediate surroundings watched her carefully. She fished a huge pan off a counter and experimented, shifting the pan from the gas. 'The whole thing's too high. About an inch.'

'Your chefs are going to be men, aren't they, darling?' Paul said. 'Try it on me, or Davey.'

'Neither of you know what you're doing. I'm five foot eight and I can aim off for men. They're mostly not that much taller, if at all.' She returned to her scrutiny, and David realized with amusement that both Paul and he had pulled themselves up to their full height. 'OK, off an inch. Sorry.'

The group around her converged resignedly on the counter. Paul put his arm round her with the easy possessiveness of a brother. 'You are going where with Jeremy in that boiler-suit?'

She blushed. 'To his flat, since you ask.'

'You've got that far with him?' He might as well not have been present, David thought, fascinated.

'Yes, thank you. And it's perfectly all right.'

'Oh, that's *good*.' He embraced her warmly, leaving David to hope fervently that Sally for example would be returning some more enthusiastic verdict.

'There's someone trying to get in,' he volunteered.

'Jeremy.' She disengaged herself and rushed to the front of the shop, with him and Paul following more slowly, so that he got a clear view of Jeremy Lathen, taller than either of them, fair-haired and a very good-looking man, no arguing with that. Jennifer introduced them while he fidgeted, wanting to get back to Sally, or to ring Ann, or do something sensible with his day, but interested despite himself in the group. This Jeremy was being actually rude to Paul in a very smooth style, apparently without Jennifer noticing a thing. And she looked quite different, pink, and more tentative, no longer on home ground.

'Is it really going to be ready next week, Jenny?' Jeremy was asking in patronizing tones to the concealed fury of the workmen around him.

'It will have to be,' she said, in a brief return to her previous form, and he felt a ridiculous urge to join in to support her, but Jeremy had turned his attention to him.

'Were you in the show yesterday?'

'Yes, I was.'

'Mm. Which is your lot?'

David told him and was unsurprised to hear in return that this elegant creature was a director of a merchant bank.

'I know Argentina a bit,' he said. 'We used to have interests there. Still do, indeed.'

'Ah.' Yes, of course, whatever the poor bloody infantry was doing, the bankers would still be keeping up their contacts, weaving a web of money. He had the look of a rich man, come to think of it, smooth and sharp and polished. He looked doubtfully at Jens Redwood, who was unself-consciously stripping off her boiler-suit to reveal well-fitting jeans and a shirt underneath. She looked solid and workaday and serious beside Jeremy's greyhound elegance. She dropped the suit behind the bar and came back to kiss Paul, easily, and to say something to him privately that made him laugh.

'Nice to have seen you, David,' she said punctiliously. 'You must come when we get this place open.' Then she was gone, slipping her arm in Jeremy Lathen's, and making for the sports car parked with two wheels on the pavement.

'She wasn't all that pleased to see you,' Paul said, just a little smugly. 'What did you do?'

'Nothing to her, I don't think. Ah.' He remembered the beautiful Ali whom he had dropped and never picked up again when they had finally had to leave the house, and offered Paul an edited version.

'She's married now. Ali, I mean.' Paul was casually amused. 'Jens'll forgive you. Come on, let's go back and collect the girls and have a bite to eat.'

They both looked up as a yellow sports car, badly driven, pulled up close to them.

'David, we've had a call from your brother.' It was Maddy, blonde hair flying, ravishingly beautiful, even without benefit of make-up and with her eyes puffy from a long night. 'It's an emergency, I'm afraid. Your wife's been taken ill.'

He felt his heart pound with panic and he rushed to squat by the car window. 'How? When?'

'He didn't say.' Maddy was tight-lipped but he did not care; they'd known he was married, ten minutes after he arrived at the party, they were grown-up women and in any case nothing and no one mattered besides Ann.

'We couldn't make anyone hear on the phone there. Get in, I'll take you back. He was calling from a hospital but I've got the number.'

They gave him Paul's study and he pushed buttons with fingers gone stiff with anxiety. Mickey was there, thank God, waiting by the call-box and sounding anxious but in control. 'She had a very uneasy night, apparently,' he reported against a background of clinking cups and other people's conversations, so that David, alone in the quiet study, pressed his free hand to his ear the better to hear him.

'Then she was sick at breakfast and she started to have these pains. So I got an ambulance.'

'Why didn't you drive her?'

'I thought the ambulance was safer. She could lie flat.'

'Christ. Yes. Well done, Mick. Sorry. How is she?'

'Well, they said they need to get the baby out. They wanted you to sign an authority or something.'

'I can't, I'm here.' He felt as if he were going mad.

'I signed it. They said that was OK. Thank God I'm over twenty-one. She's in theatre now and they say she's all right.'

'And the baby?' He did care, a bit, but nothing mattered if Ann were not going to die.

'I dunno, Davey. It'll be a bit early but not that early. Come as soon as you can. Davey, wait . . . listen. *Don't* drive yourself if you were up late, we need you.'

Mickey sounded like *his* elder brother, he thought, dazed but unresentful. He was always good in a crisis, come to think of it, it took him out of himself. 'Right, right,' he said, brain racing. 'Give her my love and tell her . . . tell her I'll be there soonest. And tell her I'm sorry I didn't get home.' And what use was *that*? he thought savagely, raging at himself, what she had needed was him, there. Thank Christ Mickey had been there, what if he had not? Well, there would have been neighbours, of sorts, Annie always made good friends wherever she was. But she had needed him and where had he been? In bed with some indifferent woman, as usual. The door opened a crack and Sally's pretty, anxious face looked in, and he looked back, hating her. She vanished, to be replaced by Paul Seles who sat stolidly while he paced and raved and worried about the trains.

'Forget it, Davey. I'll drive you. My man's sleeping it off, he was at the party, but I'm off the sauce just at the moment.' He rose, formidable and fresh as a daisy, and David did not seek to argue but followed him, stopping only to say a constrained, awkward farewell to Maddy and to pretty Sally, with a peck on the cheek each.

'Sorry we seduced you from the paths of virtue,' Paul Seles said drily, when they were speeding out on Western Avenue and David had managed to relax enough to hunt up the best route to the hospital.

'I feel fucking awful. But it's strictly my fault, not anyone else's.' He felt absolutely no better for this unequivocal acceptance of responsibility, and his stomach lurched as Paul cornered. He drove well, at one with the big, opulent Jaguar, but nothing was helping, and David settled down wretchedly to endure.

'Coffee in the flasks in the back. You could give me one.'

He leaned over gingerly and found coffee for them both. It did help a bit, anything to ease the gnawing anxiety and guilt.

'Thanks.'

'Wonderful show the Falklands. I was proud to be British.'

David coughed on his drink and considered his driver. 'Were you born here?' he asked, remembering that he had not been.

'No. In Hungary. And if you saw Hungary today, or most places in the East, you'd know why it's good to live here. You don't have to wonder if your neighbour's telling the NKVD everything about you. And your kids can get an education.'

'Well, only some of them.' Despite his misery, he was not going to let this one pass unchallenged. 'Half my lot – my company, I mean – can't even read and write properly.'

Seles looked distinctly taken aback. 'Are you sure? Even at my school we all got O-levels.'

'Yours was a school for the clever ones, wasn't it? I remember the Head told us that when we were playing you.'

'That's true. Woolverstone wouldn't take you below a 120 IQ. I remember the lady in the Social telling me that, not that I could have cared at the time.' He was looking into some far country, and David, experienced with all sorts of men, sat tight. 'Well, there's an example,' Paul said, coming back from where he had been. 'I mean, in Hungary, I guess, he'd have been allowed to go on, my guardian, I mean, until one of us killed the other. Here, there were people to help in the end.'

'That's why you were at that school?' Against the disaster possibly facing him, nothing seemed to matter, he could say anything.

'Yeah. Lot of us in the same boat.' Paul swallowed the rest of his coffee and David poured another. 'But we got a decent education.'

'Whereas a lot of mine don't seem to have.'

'But they fought bloody hard.'

'No, they didn't,' David said crossly.

'What?'

'They didn't have to, because we were up against a rabble, I mean, no proper officers, no proper kit, just conscripts, stuck there.' He looked at his cup, he had not until now seen all this quite so clearly. 'I mean, we got there, I suppose that's to be said for us, but their Air Force bloody nearly knocked us out. And we *should* have won on the ground. I mean, we're professionals, they were just farm boys.'

'Like the Budapesters or the people in Prague, trying to deal with the Russians.'

'Not quite. The Argies had better weapons. And it's not tank country. A lot of the fighting was infantry hand to hand. Well, a lot of what there was of it.' He finished his coffee and put his and Paul's cups tidily away in the back. 'I'm for out of the Army,' he said suddenly. 'We're in the UK for about ten minutes now, and then probably Northern Ireland, which is where we would have been but for this outing. My best mate in the regiment, Peter Fountain, his father was there and he says both sides hate you, and they both try and kill you and you're not allowed to shoot first. And what for? I mean, it's another political fuck-up, isn't it, and it's been going on for years. I mean, does *that* make you proud to be British, Paul?'

Paul Seles frowned at the windscreen. 'No,' he said reluctantly, 'it isn't even sensible. I had this teacher at the Hall – Roger Caldwell. He made us read the papers and he asked the Sixth Form one day to say what they thought was going to happen there. Sean Kelly, my mate, he's a Paddy, he reckoned they should all be allowed to kill each other, and Old Caldwell said that wasn't the question he'd asked, what he wanted to know was what would *happen*. So we all thought about it, and this is . . . what . . . nine years ago . . . and we decided it would go on in the same way, with people being killed at about the same rate. Well, it has, hasn't it? And what's to stop it? We decided in the end that the whole of the leadership would have to die. I mean, Haughey and Paisley and all of them. Old Caldwell said that that was often the answer, a whole generation had to change, and *that* was why assassination didn't work. You only got one man, not the lot.'

'That's right,' David agreed slowly. 'And meanwhile my blokes get killed. And civilians. It's like what I've just been doing.'

'Maybe we should go into politics. Both of us.'

'What as? Sorry, Paul, I mean, what side would you be on?'

'Labour, I suppose. It was them that rescued me, there was this Councillor Redwood, Jen's father. Posh family but Labour. She was at school with me, because he believed the country would never come right unless everybody got the same, good education in the same school. He thought everyone was equal. Well, this lot don't, do they?'

'It's not that, exactly.' David fidgeted in his seat, feeling the need to move about under the pressure of the idea that was driving him. 'They don't really *know*. They don't know half my lot can't read properly and they'd probably think they were stupid if they did. They think if you're not making a success somewhere you've had it, you're just a dead loss. But some people have a rotten start and some have bad times.' He saw Paul looking at him quizzically. 'Well, all right, nothing like you had, but my father left us and we went bankrupt and the bailiffs took all our things. And no one gave a fuck except this chap in the bailiff's office.' He told Paul about all that, as he had no one else but Ann, and got in return the story of Paul's time in Borstal, after which they sat in companionable, reflective silence.

'Get the map out, we'll be at the junction in five minutes,' Paul said suddenly. Unbelievably, an hour seemed to have passed in discussion, and David managed to thank him.

'Forget it,' Paul advised as they drew into the car park. 'Look, I'll stay here till you know what's going on, in case I can be useful. Might as well.'

David ran, knowing he was too late to be useful, and skidded into Casualty where he saw Mickey, looking calm and patient, reading a paper.

'She's OK,' his brother called across the room. 'She's all right.' They met in the middle, David shaking with reaction, and his young brother took him firmly in his arms. 'The baby's fine too. She's in an incubator and on a ventilation machine but they say she's doing all right.'

'Annie.' It was all he could manage, but Mickey was leading him firmly down a corridor and stopping to speak to Sister, and he gathered himself to charm. But none of it was necessary and he found himself shown into a room where his wife lay, asleep but blessedly, praise God, alive. He tiptoed over to her, desperately wanting her to wake, and her eyelids flickered as he arrived at her side.

'Annie.' He sank into the chair and stared at her quiet face as the eyes opened slowly.

'Davey?' She smiled, just a twitch of the lips. 'The baby?'

'I haven't seen her yet but she's OK. Really.'

'Go and see her. Now. I need to know.'

He went, fighting back tears, and found the nurses. After a maddening delay while he was gowned and masked, painfully conscious in this sterile atmosphere of the smell of drink and cigarettes that seemed to cling to him, he stood by the machine that contained his daughter. She was smaller than he would have believed possible, half the size of a normal baby, yellow and silent, with tiny, froglike limbs, and he could not stop looking at her.

'Breathing difficulties are standard at thirty weeks,' the Sister said quietly. 'But she's a strong little girl. She's got a good chance.'

He went blindly back to find Ann and tell her the baby was doing all right, then he just put his head down on her shoulder. 'I should have been there. I'm sorry.'

'Oh, Davey. It would still have happened. Something went wrong. And Mickey was wonderful.'

'It was a party and I got carried away.'

'You got here quickly, though, when Mickey called.'

'Ah. An old friend drove me,' he told her, holding her hands, anxiously watching her to see if she was going to forgive him, until her eyes closed again in exhaustion and reaction from the anaesthetic, and the nurses took him away and delivered him to Paul and Mickey, who seemed to have become fast friends in the intervening two hours. So Paul took him back to the small house that the Army had allotted them and they collected the car, and Paul bought Ann a mountain of flowers. When David got back to the hospital two hours later his daughter was breathing by herself and his wife was sleeping easily, and he understood that he had been lucky once again, more than he deserved, and his life was shaken but intact.

CHAPTER THIRTEEN
May 1983

Jennifer Redwood stood shivering on the street with two gloomy men, gazing up at the elegantly scrolled sign above the canopy. The 'E' of REDWOOD'S had gone again, for the fourth time in the six months since the restaurant had opened last November.

'Got to be a short,' one of the men volunteered, and she resisted the urge to scream that of course it was a short, that was what he was here to fix. No good could come of losing her temper; permanently tired though she was, the whole of this enterprise was founded on her and her ability to keep her head while all around were behaving atrociously.

'Whatever,' she said dismissively, in a compromise between civility and a desire to murder him. 'But can you fix it this time? If not, I am looking at having to replace you, which would mean your firm would never get paid the agreed retention.'

The man sucked his teeth mutinously, but she ignored that, she needed the job done before any more of the lunch-time clientele told her that the 'E' was failing to light. The whole of the business of running a restaurant was in the detail, it all had to be right and immaculate, or the customer felt unsettled without quite knowing why. There was quite enough choice in the West End for them not to eat anywhere that did not make them feel instantly happy. Not at home exactly, as Paul had observed, given what was in most people's homes, but comfortable. And something had worked; they had overspent on the conversion, just as everyone had warned her, but it hadn't, in the event, mattered at all. Redwood's had beaten its turnover projections from the first week, and six months into full operation had settled down to having its two hundred seats mostly occupied every lunch-time, building to a peak at Friday lunch, reasonably well taken up in the evenings and absolutely, totally booked from ten o'clock onwards, when the theatres closed. That made staffing a nightmare. In a restaurant which operated till 2 a.m. you could not realistically hope to employ staff on the traditional split shift hours, in which they worked lunch, then had three hours off, then came back to do the evening shift. Two full shifts had to be operated, and the first thing a manager coming on shift did was to count heads and make increasingly frenzied phone calls until he had something approaching a full staff. But these were problems of success and with them had also come the ability to pay off contractors and suppliers who had to wait an extra couple of months for the money.

She nodded to a couple of people who looked familiar as they came in; they were probably artists and mates of Jean, the elegant Moroccan on reception.

'Jens!' The imperative call from behind her could only come from Paul, but she twitched a napkin into line before responding; first things first. She considered him warily; he was in one of his hyped-up states, crackling with energy, chatting feverishly to Jean, smoking and finishing a newspaper at the same time. He was extremely difficult to deal with in this state and she was already tired. 'How is Maddy?' she asked, when she had got him sat down right at the back of the restaurant with his habitual Perrier. He assured her that his wife of three months' standing was well, and probably still in bed following a party the night before. 'She sends her love,' he added, both of them knowing that he lied. Pretty, blonde Maddy, three years Jennifer's junior, was alarmed by her and jealous of her relationship with Paul, and nothing was going to change any of that. And she hadn't been very nice to Maddy either, fearing that she would take Paul away, though this had not happened so far.

'It's nice being married,' he said complacently, stubbing out a half-smoked cigarette and reaching for a small cigar, ignoring her scowl. 'You should try it.'

'I hope I'm going to.'

'With Jeremy?'

'Well, for Christ's sake, Paul, who else?' It was a relief to lash out at Paul. He was jealous of Jeremy, of course, she reminded herself comfortably, watching him under her eyelashes. There was no point in talking to him about it. As she uneasily acknowledged, when she thought about it, Jeremy, unlike Maddy, would not allow her and Paul to go on in the way they always had, in a relationship closer than most brothers and sisters. But she had to have Jeremy. She had met him at a banker's party to which she had gone in the hope of finding funding for the restaurant, and noticed him at first only as a very good-looking man. He had been openly interested in her, so that she had looked at him properly and been disappointed when she had had to refuse his invitation to dinner because she was dining with Lucy and Sofia. That had done her no harm with Jeremy; unbelievably, he had been attracted to her to the point of ditching, within three weeks, the well-connected young woman to whom he was informally engaged. For her part she had felt then, and continued to feel secretly, that the star on the Christmas tree had against all precedent been allotted to her. It seemed as if all the struggles and tension of her life had been redeemed and rewarded by finding that she loved and was loved by a staggeringly attractive man, whom every other girl wanted on sight. That she would get the instant security, socially and financially, that would accrue from marrying into a rich, well-connected banking family, was an attractive bonus, but it was just the icing on the cake. The cake itself was Jeremy, two years older than herself, already a director of a merchant bank, charming and blessed with looks that turned all female heads. It was no good trying to tell Paul any of this however, so she sought a change of subject.

'How's your deal coming on?' she asked, being sceptical about Paul's idea of buying into a small quoted engineering company which no one outside a small and technical audience had ever heard of.

'I knew you didn't really understand it,' he said indulgently, to annoy her. 'But it's done, since you ask, the shares were being suspended half an hour ago and tomorrow I'll be in charge.'

'Of three companies making things like motor-bikes?'

'And two little jobbing engineers in Yorkshire and a marine engineering consultant in Tiverton,' he agreed, unruffled. 'But it's quoted on the stock market, I'm putting up a lot of cash, and you watch, we'll start buying things.'

'You and Sean?'

'Oh, he's essential. By the time you've had Sean over the figures you really know what's what. And I want you on the board too.'

'Why? What I know about motor-bicycles could be written under the proverbial stamp.'

'It's not what you know, Jens, as I've always told you, it's who you know. You had a good press: "Girl wonder starts new London restaurant". You'd make us a bit flash and people would want to follow the shares.'

She looked up to indicate to the waiter that he might approach and take their order; neither of them had consulted the menu, because they both always had the same. Paul had steak and *pommes frites* and she the warm salad with either chicken or fish as the centre. Paul was going towards fifteen stone, but didn't care; she was trying to stay under eleven stone and cared very much. She told the waiter what they wanted and watched beadily as he changed Paul's ashtray.

'Why are you buying a company at all?' she asked. 'I mean, you've always been perfectly happy keeping your money in a bank. Or a lot of banks. What's happened?'

'Nothing.' He sounded irritable and she waited patiently. 'Yes, all right, I want to live here, in England. I wasn't sure I did before, but I do now. So I want to have a business here.'

'And pay taxes here?' She had not forgotten his cries of outrage at the tax demands made on the cash he had brought over last year to buy his shares in Redwood's.

'Oh, that's all right. Most of my shares are held by an offshore trust.'

'Ah, not in your own name.'

'Some are, but it's only nutters like you who insist on that sort of thing, Jens.'

'I bet there are people like me among those you want to follow your shares.'

'They won't understand it,' he said crossly, his neck going scarlet, and she understood that she had touched a sore spot. She also realized in her bones that she would be better not to be on any board run by Paul, love him as she did.

'What sort of things are you going to buy, Paul?' she asked, interested.

He waited till the waiter had left their food and gone before telling her in a conspiratorial whisper that he wanted to build up a big engineering company. 'I can buy abroad, you see, in Hungary and in Czechoslovakia. It's difficult but we'll make a fortune, and get a lot of publicity.'

'You want your name in the papers too,' she said, suddenly seeing it.

'Why not? Hasn't done you any harm, has it?'

No, it hadn't, she acknowledged privately, and she wasn't doing it just because it helped the restaurant. It gave her a boost when she was feeling low to see her face in the papers. And Jeremy liked it too, he liked her being fashionable. She considered this perception uneasily. Jeremy might like having a clever wife who ran a restaurant, but she was not at all sure he was going to be willing to put up with the totally unfashionable hard work and long hours that his wife would have to go on putting in. She was afraid that he thought she could do everything necessary to enable a very large, new West End restaurant to prosper by appearing for a few hours during the day, in between cooking him breakfast and meeting him at 7 p.m., bathed, dressed and rested, ready for a dinner party with one of his clients, or the opera, or an intimate, immaculately prepared dinner with him. The reality of her life was that she started at eight o'clock in the morning and did not stop unless she was seeing Jeremy, in which case she usually nipped into one of the staff shower-rooms to get some of the kitchen smells off before changing in a corner of her office and arriving, breathless and exhausted but hopefully clean, at whatever entertainment he had devised for them. And any quiet evening with Jeremy tended to be punctuated by phone calls from the restaurant, sometimes with truly disastrous timing. Going to bed with Jeremy was a ceremonial process; to her relief it had been both easy and pleasant the first time and thereafter, because he treated her with great care as if she were fragile, so that she was never reminded of Joshua's avid grasping hands. On the other hand, it contained none of the ecstasies and passion she had read about and she never came near reaching orgasm. And she knew herself capable of *that*; determined to overcome this problem, she had read a book and practised until she could bring herself to a climax in about four minutes. But this private ability did not seem to help her with Jeremy; she seemed not able to explain to him what she needed and indeed felt guilty about having to ask. She had put the whole issue firmly into the category of things she would get round to sometime later.

'So, how's the sex with Jeremy, then?' Paul had always been able to guess what was going on in her head, curse him. And he was cross with her, that too you could always tell.

'It's OK.' No matter how much he annoyed her, she did not dissimulate with Paul; he could smell a lie.

'Not better than that?'

'I'm so tired all the time.' She could hear the whine in her voice and tried for optimism. 'I'm sure it'll be all right when we're married.'

Paul put down his fork and put a heavy hand on her wrist, so that she reluctantly had to meet his eyes. 'You shouldn't marry him, Jens. It's not just the sex, he's wrong for you. He wants you to give this up, doesn't he?' A jerk of his head encompassed the carefully detailed, beautifully arranged dining-room.

'He just wants me not to work so hard, so he can have more of my time,' she said defensively.

'Hardly. He's got other women to fill that up.'

'How do you know?' She was outraged, stiff with anger.

'Maddy. I wasn't going to tell you, but one of her mates is having a walk-out with him. Casual, nothing serious, but you won't be able to cope with that.'

'You're jealous.' She rose to leave, but his grip on her wrist tightened.

'Jens. You think he'll look after you, don't you? Well, he won't. Look at him, divorced parents, dragged up between them. He's looking for someone to look after him and put up with his girls and just be nice about it. He's a prick.'

'Get the fuck out of here, Paul.' She twisted her wrist away, white with rage. 'Maddy's so stupid and so jealous of me you can't trust anything she says. I'll never understand why you needed to marry anyone that thick, but *I* don't say it. Or I wouldn't have, if you hadn't started on Jeremy.'

'I'm going.' He was as angry as her, sorting credit cards with his thick fingers trembling. 'But don't reckon on me at the wedding. Not that there'd be room with all the girlies!'

It was on mornings like this that he missed the Army most, David thought, as he took the stairs to his office two at a time, sweating lightly. He ran the four miles to work on those days when he knew he would not need the car, and never used the lift, but it was still difficult to get the exercise he needed. The regiment had always insisted that even its most senior officers kept fit, because otherwise their brains did not work, and he was quite sure they had been right. The men in civilian life who sat rotting behind a desk or the wheel of a car were getting old before their time, and losing their edge.

His office looked out over green fields ending in one of the sudden sharp escarpments common in this part of Yorkshire. It was good for the legs; a lot of demanding up-and-down work was necessary even in the four miles from home. He picked up a clean shirt from his desk drawer and the suit hanging on the door and headed for the Men's to wash and change; he was working on the costings to get a shower put in, there was plenty of space, and one or two other men had started to run during lunch-hours in emulation of him. The difficulty was that life was more leisurely here; if you were going out in the evening you went home first, like gentlemen, to wash and change, so a shower in the office could not be claimed as a necessity.

'Morning, Davey.'

It was Hammond's, his boss's, secretary, small, rounded and pretty, perhaps five years older than himself, and she was looking at him with open admiration.

'Susan. You're looking very beautiful today.'

'Get over.' She was pleased, though; she had made it discreetly clear that she would welcome any attention he felt like bestowing. He liked her, and would have responded in any other circumstances, but his affair with Mrs Major Phillips had taught him to avoid his own doorstep. He made for his own office and rang Ann, as he always did when he arrived, to assure himself that his base was secure and his home the same warm, comforting place he had left an hour earlier. He listened with mixed pleasure and impatience to her description of the small events of her morning. Caroline was almost a year and was into everything, while Francis was a sober three-year-old now, jealous of his mother's attention. Together they constituted a major job, and he was sneakingly, heartfeltly relieved that he didn't have to do it all day but could arrive home after they had gone to bed and have Ann to himself.

She was going round to a neighbour or entertaining one, he didn't listen properly, but neighbours in the small isolated East Yorkshire village were all-important, and Ann had promptly made friends. They had bought there because it was cheap, and the countryside was beautiful, but it was a very small house, a cottage indeed, with just three bedrooms and one bathroom for the four of them. He had resisted, absolutely, taking on more than the smallest mortgage that enabled them to buy anything at all. Being careful with money – well, mean, you could say – was right in his bones, and Ann understood that and agreed with it. He had let her father help with a small amount, because he and that careful man saw eye to eye in this. Neither of them wanted Ann to have to work and both of them understood the importance, in politics, of being in debt to no man.

He had got this job as a personnel man in a rapidly expanding grocery chain for himself, without his father-in-law's promptly offered help. It had not hurt, of course, being married into the Hardiman family, but he had seen the advertisement, applied and been offered the job before he had told his employer where he was married. Ann knew where he was applying, he told her everything of that sort, but she believed in an old-fashioned and comforting way that men took the decisions about work and how they did it. She had been surprised when he told her that he had decided to leave the Army, but instantly supportive both of that and of his decision to make a go of entering local politics, as a stepping-stone to higher things. Knowing himself to be a fortunate man, he, in his turn, had agreed when she had suggested they settle in Yorkshire; she would have the support with the children she had done without so far and he could use her father's well-established Labour connections.

'Davey.' It was his employer, a small, square Yorkshireman, twenty years his senior, and David stood up automatically. 'Sit down, lad, you're not in the Army now.' He beamed benevolently from the door. 'Pam wants you and Ann for dinner, Thursday week. Is that all right?'

'Mr Hammond ... Ken ... I've got, well we've got, Ann and I, a selection meeting.'

'Oh, aye?'

'I'm on the list to take Paul Waite's place. He's giving up and the ward is trying to put someone in place well before the council elections next May.'

'Well, you have to do that, I suppose.' His employer did not share his politics; he had never voted other than Conservative, but the council was Labour-controlled in this his headquarters and in several places where they had stores, and the local council's planning department was of key importance. David

232

had disclosed his political ambitions at the second interview which had been conducted by Hammond himself, and understood his employer's calculations. 'I'll tell Pam and we'll find another date. Better do that quickly if you're going to be a councillor.'

'I have to get the nomination still. It may take a bit longer, I mean, I've only been here a few months.' It did not do to take your welcome for granted in Yorkshire; he liked the people here but it was a very settled society by comparison with the restless, fast-shifting South.

'You ought to get it. That trades union bugger's made enemies amongst his own lot. And once you've got the nomination you're in, in that ward.'

Hammond would know the details of a contest even in a party of which he was not a member, it was that kind of close-knit society, and he would have to get used to it. He saw, in a small flash of revelation, that Hammond had known exactly who he was when he interviewed him; so much for his determination to get a job on his own.

'That's true,' he said, adjusting instantly as was his gift. 'Put up a monkey in that ward and he'll get in.'

'Only if he's a Labour monkey.' Hammond was grinning, a sight rare enough to be unnerving. 'Good luck with it, Davey. My regards to Ann and we'll get you round soon.'

David turned his attention to the pile on his desk; he needed to go and jolly up a training course for cashiers in an hour, but he had time to clear the in-tray if he worked fast. He disliked disorder; the Army had made him obsessively efficient and he never let paperwork pile up. The phone rang sharply and he picked it up. He had a share in the typing-pool but no secretary yet.

'Paul Seles here.'

'How are you?' He was, to his surprise, delighted by the call. He had had an uncomfortable and uneasy three months after the victory march last year while he got himself round to leaving the regiment, refusing to sign on for the next six years as they had wanted him to, and had suffered serious and unexpected anxieties despite Ann's support. Peter Fountain had also been unexpectedly helpful; he had urged him to go, while he could, and before he got trapped in the Army habit like the Fountain family. But even so, he had been torn by anxiety and much comforted by Paul who had understood his worries and had been more than helpful about providing distractions. And, of course, he would be forever grateful to him for his help on the day Caroline was born, and the absolute discretion he had maintained, then and thereafter.

'How's business?'

'Great. Just bought a company. How's politics?'

'I may be selected to stand for a council seat.'

'Wow! Gee whiz! Not *really*?'

'All very well for you tycoons. It's slow stuff in politics at the start.'

'I depend on you, Davey. I need you in charge of the Department of bloody Trade and Industry. Or better yet, Prime Minister.'

'I'm trying, I'm trying. And so is my leader, and he's a lot more use than Foot ever was. What is it, this company?'

'Seven little businesses in different places. Shit, that's the other phone, take it, will you, Dolly, yes? No, no, tell him five minutes.'

David listened with familiar exasperation as the man noisily sorted out his affairs. Paul had offered him a job immediately when he had confided his plans to leave the Army, and he had been tempted; the money would have been much better. He had spent a day in Paul's office at the end of which he had known, regretfully, that he could not work with or for a man who habitually talked into two telephones at once and shouted at whoever was there when he wanted something done. But he was, improbably, a good friend and he missed him in the sedate fastnesses of Yorkshire.

'Saw Sally the other day. She says hello.'

'Ah, nice of her. How's she doing?'

'Got a bloke, he's OK.'

He felt a pang of jealously heavily mixed with relief. He had picked up his affair with pretty Sally where he had had to leave off as a distraction from the anxieties attendant on leaving the regiment, and there had been violent scenes when he had gone off to Yorkshire with Ann. He had carefully not contacted Sal on any of his subsequent visits to London and it sounded as if she had got the message. She had got very involved, he recollected guiltily, and wanted him to fuck her without benefit of the condoms he always, always used, but he knew where that could lead and had steadfastly refused. Fun was fun but you didn't risk hostages.

'Can I do anything, Paul?'

'Nah. Just ringing you to see if we could get you to London. And Ann, of course. No? In the New Year maybe? *Ciao.*' He rang off abruptly, phones shrilling in the background, leaving David feeling lonely.

'Michael.' The thin man in his mid-thirties was being patient, but he was getting fed up. 'You need to tell me what's going on. This is an examined graduate degree and you should have produced three papers as part of the course by the 1st of June. So far I've had one. Which is good, well up to standard. It is now nearly the end of May; at what stage are you with the other two?'

Mickey looked at him with hate, trying not to scream. 'I've done a lot on both,' he lied, as steadily as he could. 'I'm very sorry I'm late, I've just been in a muddle. If you can give me till the beginning of July they'll both be finished.'

His supervisor sighed. 'There's no point in my just giving you more time. June 1st is the deadline for a second paper, after that it's all over and you go back a year. I am here to help, let me see what you've got and we'll see how best it can be finished.'

He was right, of course, Mickey thought bitterly, indeed he was one of the best supervisors in the faculty; if you got stuck you often could get going again with a bit of skilled help. But there was no way he could ask for help; it wasn't that he hadn't worked, he did, all the time, and his room was full of files, he just couldn't make any of it into a term paper, never mind two papers. It was hopeless and he was going to fail. He felt the old resentful panic building up.

'Can we do that, Michael? However rough it is, let me have the one paper that is in best shape by the end of the week and we'll see what can be done. Then you tackle the other.'

He agreed, of course he agreed, anything to get out of the large room, with its well-ordered shelves and tidy desk with papers neatly piled in labelled trays, in miserable contrast to his own cluttered, paper-strewn study bedroom, with the dust thick on some of the piles. He spent hours in that room every day, drinking coffee and reading, but he never got closer to writing either of his papers and now he was frightened. He changed course, with sudden hope, feeling in his pocket for change, and rang the familiar number. Ann didn't understand his work at all, of course, but she made him feel calm and in control, and perhaps if he could spend an evening with her and Davey he would be able to work. It would be worth the taxi there and back.

'I'm sorry, Mickey, but it's Davey's selection meeting. No, I have to be there too.'

He felt a pang of murderous jealousy of his confident brother, who seemed to be able to make his way effortlessly through the world and had Ann as well. No, that wasn't fair, he worked hard enough, did Davey, but he never seemed to worry or agonize about what he was doing and he always got by.

'Come tomorrow – oh no, I'm sorry, my mother and father are taking us to the opera. The weekend? Davey'll be pleased to see you then, don't be daft.'

He trailed miserably back to his room, his heart sinking at the unmade bed, the unwashed cups, and everywhere the piles of papers. He rinsed a cup and made himself a Nescafé, wallowing in a sense of injustice. How could he possibly produce anything out of this by Friday? It was unreasonable of his supervisor to ask, and if he only had till the New Year he could produce something really good. He drank his coffee, alternating between rage and panic, until he was unable to stay in the room any longer. He walked out, feeling desperate. 'I'll break down again,' he warned the air silently. 'I can't take this, it's not fair.'

'Hi, Mickey!'

'Martin!' It was a very competent fellow-student who had greeted him, a chap of his own age who reminded him a little of Davey, much more academic of course, but with the same energy, not troubled by doubts. He looked at him hungrily. 'Martin, I need some advice. Have you ten minutes?' People usually conceded ten minutes, he found.

'Sure. Want some coffee?'

He had sat gratefully in Martin's tidy room and offered him a heavily edited version of the problem which implied a term paper at least half done, and stuck only on a difficult point of how to handle a corner of economic history.

'One of my papers is right in that area.'

'Yes, I know.' Mickey watched hopefully while the other young man thought.

'Well, shit, Mickey, we've got different supervisors. Would you like to borrow my paper? It'll cut a few corners for you. Careful, though.'

'Oh, I will be,' Mickey said, meaning it. 'Thank you. I'll give it back by the weekend, truly.'

He was packing up for the end of term, looking forward to seeing his mother, when the blow fell. He had felt the clouds of depression lift from the moment he had actually handed in a script only twelve hours late to his supervisor, who had been both surprised and pleased. He was piling papers on to shelves, mildly chagrined by how dirty they seemed to be, when he heard the knock on the door and opened it to his supervisor.

'I won't come in, thank you. Michael, we need to talk. Now. I'd like you in my office in five minutes, please.'

The man had gone before he could protest, leaving him sick with fright, literally unable to stand up. He sat heavily at his desk, still covered with debris and cups, staring out of the window, then dragged himself up.

It was worse even than he had feared. His supervisor motioned him in, grim-faced, and made him sit at the big table rather than in an armchair, and with the speed and clarity of terror he saw on the man's side of the table a copy of Martin's paper, laid beside his own. He sat staring at them, unable to look away.

'Why did you do it?'

'I don't know,' he said. 'Yes, I do. I was frightened.' He managed to look at the man, expecting if not sympathy then help, as Dr Daiches always gave him.

'Well, there's not a lot to say, but I'll say it just the same. I thought it was a good paper, if hastily written, but then I knew *that* would happen. I was going to get you to tidy it up a bit, do yourself justice, but I thought I would show it to Roger Lilley, just to get his view before you spent the holidays on it. It's more his speciality than mine.' Mickey sat watching his face, hypnotized. 'Well, he recognized most of it straight away.' The man was staring at him, as if he were mad or something. 'It was more or less verbatim, I mean, what did you do, copy it out?'

'Martin lent it to me.'

'I know he did. Roger Lilley's already had a word with him. He didn't expect you to use it like that.'

'No.' Terrible burning shame overwhelmed Mickey, then the familiar, more comfortable misery and self-pity. 'I got into a mess. And you wouldn't give me time. It was all I could do in three days.'

'Why the bloody hell didn't you just turn up with whatever you had and let me *help*?'

He saw, with just a tiny glimmer of hope, that he had got through, that the man was feeling guilty. 'I didn't dare. You'd told me I'd get thrown out.'

He had shaken the man, he was looking winded. 'Yes, I did,' the supervisor acknowledged angrily. He sighed. 'And now you will be. Roger Lilley and I felt we had to tell Michaelson and he is taking a quite uncompromising view.'

'You aren't giving me a chance.' Mickey could hear himself

whining but he could not stop, the oncoming reality was too terrible.

'This is a university, Michael. We aren't in the business of giving people who copy other people's work a second chance.'

'I've not been well.'

'In that case you should have told us and we could have made special arrangements.' He stood up. 'I'm sorry, but there is no way back. There isn't going to be a great fuss, you just don't come back next term.' Mickey stared at him, paralysed, and he sighed again. 'I know you've had problems in the past, and if you're still prepared to listen to my view, I don't think academic life was ever going to be right for you. Too competitive, and it really isn't given to everyone to be able to work for weeks on their own. You need a job, with other people.'

'But how can I ever get one, after this?'

'Oh, we will just say you left without completing your MPhil. Happens all the time with graduate degrees. Unless, of course, you want to go on somewhere else when we'd have to tell them what happened, but we'd put it that you got yourself into a mess, which is true, isn't it?'

'I can't quite believe this is happening,' Mickey said pathetically, and realized it was a mistake as the man's face hardened.

'Well, it has, it did and you did it. There's an appeal procedure, of course, and you can use it if you want to, but I have to say that I believe it will only prolong the agony. You'd be better off making a fresh start somewhere quickly.'

He had crept away, crushed by the extent of the disaster, and was packing numbly when Martin appeared in his room.

'I'll help,' he had said briefly and did so, to some purpose, finding him extra boxes and packing his papers neatly.

'Did you get into trouble because of me?' Mickey asked, both hoping that he had and worried for him.

'No. They accepted that I was an innocent bystander, Mickey.' He stopped in mid-box. 'I would have helped *earlier* if you'd asked.'

'I got in a mess,' Mickey said miserably, feeling as if he had been saying it for weeks.

'Where are you going now?'

'I was going home. To my mother. But I can't with all this stuff.' He gestured hopelessly at the trunk and eight boxes now neatly ordered, filling half the room.

'You've got a brother working near here, haven't you?'

'Yes, but I can't tell *him*.' He understood resentfully that Martin was trying to pass on the responsibility.

'You've been very kind, Martin,' he said with a mighty effort. 'I'm glad I didn't get you into trouble. I'll go and get myself some lunch while I work out what to do, then I'll organize some transport.'

'Is that OK? It's just that I'm playing football this afternoon.'

'Yes, really.'

'I'll look in afterwards, about six.'

'Thanks.'

Left to himself, he sat staring across the hilly field to the next row of plain, four-storey buildings, with the sun slanting towards him. There was, he thought furiously, no way to turn, no one to help him. He could do nothing right, he'd messed up his academic career, having been lucky to get here at all on his rather ordinary undergraduate work and he would probably go on messing things up. He banged his head against the edge of the window in rage and misery and depression. He would *not* ring his mother or Davey and explain that yet again he was in trouble, he had had enough and they wouldn't help, anyway. He wept angrily for a bit then calmed, soothed by a dawning realization that he didn't have to go on, he could just stop, just opt out. He made himself coffee, choked, threw it out and started again with plain water, rescued his duvet and pillow from the top of his trunk and put himself to bed, arranging the bottle of sleeping pills the doctor had given him over a year ago, and took them slowly, crying luxuriously, in sets of three until he had reached the end of the bottle, then closed his eyes in sleep.

*

'Can you move up a bit and I'll adjust your pillow?'

There were lights and he screwed his eyes against them and moved obediently, so that the pain in his shoulder eased, wedged now against a pillow.

'That's all right,' the same brisk voice said, as he slipped back into sleep. 'Responding, you see.'

The next time he woke he was in bed, too hot, huddled underneath blankets and desperately thirsty. He wasn't in his own room, though, and he didn't know how he'd got here. Through slitted eyes he could see a familiar figure sitting reading the paper, irritation and restlessness in every part of his body. He closed his eyes again quickly.

'Mickey, wake up!'

Davey was angry with him but he shouldn't be, he was so miserable and he'd taken all those pills. He felt Davey lean over him and opened one eye reluctantly.

'What the fuck were you playing at?'

'I wasn't playing,' he mumbled, tears starting to his eyes.

'What you took never came near killing you. They didn't even bother to pump you out. Said you'd sleep it off. And the lad who found you – poor bugger – said you knew he'd be back at six p.m. He said you've been chucked out.'

Mickey pulled the blanket over his head, furiously angry, determined to escape, but heard light footsteps.

'Davey, will you take the children for a while?'

'If I must. Don't waste your time, Ann, he's playing for attention.'

'I won't be long.' He waited while Davey banged out of the room, and groaned.

'I've rung your mother. She'll be down tomorrow.'

'Oh, God,' he moaned. 'I'm sorry, I'm sorry, I've been such a nuisance.'

'You have.'

He peered at her from the bedclothes, wounded.

'The best apology you can make, Michael, is to pull yourself together and get a job.'

He was horrified. If kind Ann was going to behave like this, where could he turn? 'Is Mum taking me back to Edinburgh?' he asked hopefully.

'Not yet. Davey's talked to the doctor and they want to send you to . . . to a nursing home for a week.'

'I bet he did. He wants to get rid of me.'

'He wants you to get help.' She'd been crying, he saw, and felt better. At least she'd had a row with Davey about him. She patted his hand. 'I'll be back tomorrow.'

The door swung open and Davey, looking like a thundercloud, walked in, carrying Caroline, Francis clinging to the edge of his jacket. He put his arm around Ann, and Mickey had to close his eyes, feeling utterly small and helpless in the face of their united strength and competence.

CHAPTER FOURTEEN

November 1984

'Jens, keep still, will you? I want you and Hugh, and the parents ... that's right ... come on, Joshua and Mary. And you, please ... yes, that's right, Lady Winterton and Sir Henry. Just a couple more.' Paul Seles, behind a camera the size of a tank-gun, was in his element, and the members of the wedding lined up obediently, shivering in the chill November wind. Five minutes later, seeing him prepared apparently to go on snapping forever, Jens opened her mouth to yell at him but closed it obediently in deference to her new husband, who indicated economically that there were two press photographers to the side of Paul.

'I'm sorry this is a bit tedious,' she said instead to her new parents-in-law, who were looking glazed. Henry Winterton had retired as the First Commissioner of the Building Societies Commission and nothing in his career had prepared him for a daughter-in-law who owned and operated a fashionable restaurant or for her associates. She glanced to her left where Joshua was openly enjoying himself, favouring the press with what she thought of as his bluff King Hal look. At least half his attention was on Maddy, looking dazzling despite pink and brown eye-shadow for the photographs and the attentions of Stephen, aged ten months, ravishing, blond, cuddly and demanding. 'Have you enough, Paul?' she asked finally, and Paul gave her a thumbs-up sign and handed his kit to Sean, who took it away to stow in the waiting chauffeur-driven car, freeing Paul to seize his son from his wife and carry him off.

'I hope you've brought your nanny, darling,' she said maliciously to Maddy. 'You two are going to get awfully tired of Stephen.'

'I'd have left him with her, Jens, you know I would. It's Paul, he wants to show him off. Oh shit, now he's crying. I'll drop him off. I can't face lunch with him.'

Jens turned her attention to guiding the Wintertons into a car and found herself face to face with Joshua.

'Do I get a kiss today?'

'Of course,' she said, fighting down the old involuntary terror and kissing him lightly on the cheek. She cast around automatically for something to distract him and found Lady Winterton dithering. 'Joshua, could you be very kind . . . ?'

'Absolutely.' He strode off and she let out the breath she had been holding. Hugh, her husband as of half an hour ago, was reliably putting Lucy French into a car, and she looked at his back with affection; it would always be he who noticed if anyone was getting left out, or was being made to wait on a cold day, as women in their late sixties like Lucy should not have to do. She turned to watch her friend Sofia, who had quietly collected the screaming Stephen from his father's arms.

'Thanks, Sofe.'

'He's a lovely baby,' Sofia said regretfully, and Jennifer considered her. Her good friend had so far not found anyone to suit her, having spent two years in an unsuitable relationship with a married academic who was all too clearly not going to leave his wife. She was openly, ungrudgingly wistful about Hugh, who represented most things she would have liked, being large, kindly, pleasant-looking and academically talented, making very rapid progress in the Treasury. Jens was hoping to find some better husband material for her among Hugh's colleagues, but on this cold November day her friend was looking sad and stoic. Paul, by contrast, clad in his wedding finery of immaculate conventional Savile Row tailoring which slimmed his powerful shoulders and torso to something nearing elegance, looked happy. His dark hair was carefully cut, he was shaved and manicured, he was wearing a subdued Gucci tie and altogether he had done her proud.

'You're a good lad,' she said proprietorially, and he hugged her.

'So's your Hugh. You've done well. So much better than that Jeremy.'

Only Paul, she thought, feeling a stab of pure pain, would have chosen this morning to have reminded her of Jeremy. This time last year, near enough, she had expected to marry him, with the usual reception at the Savoy firmly ignoring twinges of doubt and anxiety, putting them down to exhaustion and not getting the restaurant open on time. Sofia closed up beside her and she felt rather than saw her frown at Paul.

'See you at the caff,' he said, abashed, and kissed her, watching her anxiously to see if she was angry.

'Yes,' she said steadily. 'You go on.' She stood, breathing in against the pain, not minding Sofia who was so familiar as to be effectively part of her.

'Tactless,' Sofia said crossly.

'He thinks I am greatly blessed to have found Hugh and that I need reminding of it. Which I don't.'

It had been Sofia who had put an end to any chance of her marrying Jeremy, and she was probably the only other person in the world whom she could have forgiven. Just a year ago Sofia had insisted, uncharacteristically, on her coming to lunch at the pleasant flat in Kensington which she now shared with Lucy. Jennifer had gone, expecting to console her self-contained friend for some disaster of hers. Sofia had given her a stiff drink and a delicious warm salad and told her that her Jeremy was conducting an open and serious affair in Shropshire with a girl five years her junior.

'Her father is Lord Lieutenant. I'm very sorry, Jens, and I'm very sorry it's me who has to tell you, but I thought I must. Everyone there knows.'

'And who is everyone?' she had asked, furiously fighting down the cold chill of recognition and fear.

'Her aunt told Mum. She's the Commissioner for the county.'

'It would be the bloody Girl Guides,' she had said through

stiff lips, and had gone and been terribly sick in the eccentrically furnished bathroom, with Sofia, as always, waiting patiently for her to be better, not hanging round her.

'Jens,' she had said afterwards, pouring her lemon tea, 'you have to talk to him. It may just be a last-minute thing.' She had not sounded either convinced or convincing, and the two of them had sat and looked at each other soberly.

'Mum would say that if you really love him it will come right.'

'But I don't. Not if he's doing that,' she had said, in momentary blessed relief at recognizing a real truth, which was overtaken almost immediately by terrible, painful regret for the loss of the Jeremy she had once had, who wanted her as much as she wanted him and with whom she was going to live happily ever after, just like it said in the fairy tales. She had felt dully through the grief that she had known, really, that these things did not happen; the star off the Christmas tree faded and fell apart, and she had been silly even to think otherwise . . . miracles did not happen. The old buried fears, that women like her, damaged goods, did not deserve the wonderful, good-looking, driving men had undermined her. She had had a terrible four months, fighting depression, grief and loss. And worse, a sense of sexual failure; why should Jeremy not have preferred after all some lovely blonde who really liked going to bed with him and doubtless reached orgasm easily besides thinking of all sorts of unmentionably exciting things to do for him. If only there were a good college, she had thought suddenly, while considering a *caneton à l'orange* with the whole kitchen waiting upon her verdict, where they taught you how to do sex, as patiently as she had been taught to cook, then she could perhaps have managed. She had always been able to learn, and she was thorough and conscientious, she'd probably have been good at it. She had tried the idea on Paul who had said, sadly, he didn't think it worked like that, and cautiously suggested a therapist, but in the end she had worked her way through the black depression, just as she usually did. And one real advantage of a hard childhood was that she knew how to endure and try to find happiness another way when the easy, joyful route was blocked. Nor had she in practice taken very long to readjust; she had met Hugh six months after the final awful scene with Jeremy and recognized instantly his quality, his confidence in himself, his unusual intuitive sympathy with other people and his rocklike steadiness. She had seen him across a room, dark and solid, standing wedged in a corner by a taller, thinner man, every line of whose hunched shoulders and jabbing hands spoke of obsession and tension. She watched, interested, Hugh's calm, serious face and saw the tension ease in the other man, so that after a bit he turned towards the party, smiling, and moved away, leaving Hugh to take a long drink. She had found her liking for the look of him confirmed; he had been openly admiring, and asked her out, and they had started sleeping together within a couple of weeks. She had been able to tell him about Jeremy and he had understood instantly, explaining to her apologetically that he was not long escaped from a totally obsessive relationship where he had been unable to leave a girl who did not suit him and infuriated him and who had herself ultimately ended the whole dragging, boring, painful affair by going off, resolutely, with the other man.

'I'd have to say I was grateful to her,' he had confided in bed. 'I think I would have managed to stop being such an idiot some time, but it would probably have taken another year. Or more.'

She had kissed him warmly, charmed by his ease and lack of masculine posturing, just understanding that with Joshua, Paul, Sean and Jeremy as her principal masculine exemplars she had no idea what Reasonable Man looked like until she had found Hugh. He *was* reasonable, one could talk to him, and they had made adult, rational, mutually supportive plans; he would go on in the Treasury where he was rising fast, while she opened the next restaurant for which the site was already identified. He did not want her to stop work, he was proud of her and prepared not to be cherished and fussed over as his father was.

They would start trying to have children straight away because Jens was, after all, twenty-eight, and if there were to be any difficulties then the sooner they were found the better. Paul would of course be godfather to the first child, regardless of sex. It might not be the wild romance that marrying Jeremy would have been, but she would be safe, as she knew she could not have been with Jeremy, and it had all the ingredients for stable happiness.

She smiled benevolently at David and Ann Banner. She did not see Ann often because she lived in Yorkshire, but she had invited them because she knew Paul was fond of David and valued his company. And Paul did not have that many friends, apart from Sean, so she encouraged the ones he did have. They had brought their children, a delightful four-year-old who looked exactly like his mother, and a pretty small girl of two with David's bright fair colouring. She watched, amused, as David handed the little girl to Ann and attached his son to a slightly older child, freeing himself to embrace Maddy and then come over and give her a hug. She hugged him back, liking the feel of the hard muscle in his shoulders, but wondering if they were quite on those terms. He looks a bit like Jeremy, she thought suddenly, and drew back, a shadow coming over the day.

'How's politics?' she asked hastily, and understood immediately that she had clouded *his* day.

'Oh, slow. It's uphill work.'

She tried to remember what Paul had said to her, eager to spread goodwill. 'But you're in the running for a seat?'

'Up to a point. Yes. Yes, of course I am.'

She considered him, a big chap, extremely good-looking but with the bouncing energy that was so much part of his charm suddenly gone, so that he looked older.

'It's just a long haul,' he said, recovering himself. 'I tell myself it's like waiting under a fruit tree. You just have to be there with your hands out at the right moment.'

'*That* must be difficult for you.'

'Oh, it is. Look, never mind me. I came to say you look

absolutely beautiful and to thank you for inviting us. It's tremendous fun. I love your restaurant as well.'

She beamed at him, genuinely pleased, and saw him off towards a car, watching him with admiration and noticing how female heads turned for him.

Sean arrived at her side, manfully steadying himself to kiss her and to indicate, without moving his lips more than fractionally, that he was waiting to put Sofia into a car. He had his schoolmaster with him, Old Caldwell, as they all called him, and she kissed him too. He had got smaller, she noticed anxiously, and bonier, but the eyes were as bright and observing as ever.

'A good man, Jens. The one you are marrying, I mean.'

'As opposed to which of the company here present?' Sofia asked briskly, and drew the full force of that bright look, as Sean left them to get the car.

'As opposed to the ones she didn't marry, of course. And a good man in the sense that he is a solid citizen, secure in himself, which makes for a good husband.'

'Unlike Paul?' Sofia asked, interested.

'Paul is probably not an easy husband.'

'Perhaps none of your chicks would be,' Jens said, realizing that both she and Sofia treated Roger Caldwell much as they had treated William French, as an absolutely reliable grown-up man, who could be asked anything you needed to know, and be relied on to answer truthfully and to the best of his ability.

'Well, no. Some of my old boys are doing very well with women who provide the mothering they never had. The ones from violent backgrounds do less well, it's difficult not to import all that into a close relationship.'

'Particularly when children are involved,' Jennifer said, uneasily recalling a spectacular shouting match between Paul and Maddy, with Stephen screaming in his cot.

'Yes. That puts on a lot of pressure. But come, my dear, it is your wedding day, let joy be unconfined. Is there champagne?'

'Sir.' Sean stood by the car with the door open, an anxious eye on his old teacher. 'Of course dere is.'

'Flowing from the taps,' Jennifer assured him, laughing, cheered by his open innocent expectation of pleasure, and waved them off, confident that Redwood's would see champagne into all hands whether she was there or not.

'Hugh,' she called, and saw him turn to collect her, beaming. She grinned back, on top of her world, with 150 guests waiting for her at her own successful restaurant. 'Time we got there.'

'It's very good of you to see me on a Saturday.'

It was indeed, Dr Daiches thought irritably. Mickey's arrival on this dull November weekend had seriously disrupted his train of thought. He was in his office only because he needed to finish a long article for a Sunday paper; this visit was a nuisance and he should not have allowed it. Nor was it clear quite why Mickey had pleaded to come, he was looking much better than the hangdog creature who had been in his charge for most of last year, bigger, fatter and calmer, but his hands were clenched together in his lap.

'Well, how are you, Mickey? It's five months since you were here, isn't it?'

'Yes. I'm well.' The boy – no, he wasn't a boy, he was a young man of twenty-four now – looked at him anxiously. 'But I needed to see you. I'm getting . . . I'm thinking of getting married.'

Six months ago this young man had managed to get back into normal life after a failed suicide attempt. Marriage did not *prima facie* sound like a good idea.

'How's the job going?'

'Not very well. I mean, it's very boring.'

That was, of course, the reason he had urged Mickey to take it; an undemanding, not much better than clerical job, in a local authority's housing department had seemed like a sensible first placing for an unstable ex-graduate student of history with no particular vocational bent.

'But you are managing?'

'That's not what I came to talk about. It's Jean.'

'Tell me about her.'

'We want to get married,' Mickey said defiantly. 'She's older than me. And she's got children. Three and four.'

'A divorcee?'

'No, a widow. He was killed in a car crash.'

'How long ago? I mean, how long has she been a widow?'

'Seven and a half months.'

'Mm. Not very long.' No time at all in psychic terms, no time to grieve fully or to reflect, or to adjust herself to living. 'And you have known her . . . how long?'

'Four months.'

'It's too soon, Mickey. For her.' He was blunter than he would usually have allowed himself to be, but he had been seeing this patient for ten years and reckoned he could afford to cut a corner.

Mickey looked agonized. 'But I want to.'

'Then why have you come to talk about it? If you know you want to do it anyway?' He was relieved to see a flash of pure rage; this lad still had the greatest difficulty in expressing anger or frustration.

'I'm frightened.'

'Quite rightly.'

'Why?' It was Mickey's most aggravating whine.

'Would you want to marry someone on the rebound from an affair with another man?'

'Well . . . no. I mean, I suppose not.'

'She is essentially in that position. The man is dead, that's the only difference.' The lad's face twisted in agony and he realized he had made the mistake of talking to the highly intelligent man, rather than to the distressed child under the façade. He tried again. 'How does she feel about it? I mean, does she think it sensible to marry again so quickly?' Mickey sat silent. 'Which of you is pushing this, Mickey? Her or you?'

'Both of us,' he said swiftly, looking sincerely straight at him in a way that always meant that he was clinging to a lie.

'Mm.' He let a silence fall and listened, unsurprised, while Mickey, eyes slightly crossed in his desire to convince, explained to him the advantages of marriage and how much easier his life would be with someone who was there for him.

'Like Ann is for David,' he said, obviously feeling he had scored a winning point.

'Ann is your brother's wife? And how is he getting on?'

'Very well, as always. Shooting ahead in his job, apparently. Chair of the Housing Policy Committee or something like that on his local council.' Mickey, nobody's fool, had understood that he had not succeeded in selling the idea of this marriage and was sounding resentful and depressed.

'And you believe that his wife has a lot to do with his success?'

'Of *course* she does. She makes a home for him, she looks after him, she does everything he wants. She isn't a doormat, though, *he* didn't want me around after . . . after, well, when I was so depressed, but she made him have me to stay when I came out of the place and couldn't stand Edinburgh any more. You remember . . .'

'I do.'

'Not that Davey was there much – I mean, when I was there he seemed to be out every night. He said it was council business, but someone told me it was another woman. Someone in the council offices, they said.'

'Is it possible, Mickey, that you want to marry to be upsides with David? Because, very reasonably, you envy him his marriage?'

'No. Yes. Well, why not?'

This was better, this was the real person talking, not trying to trade off some unsaleable bill of goods. 'Why not indeed? A happy marriage is a good aim, and you're lucky to have your brother as an example. But I still don't understand why you have to rush. Will she not wait?'

Mickey's sudden look of desolation told him the answer. Fear of loss, of course, it motivated this lad's every action, he must not forget. 'Are you afraid that she will find someone else? If she is *that* easily distracted, Mickey, you have the wrong girl.'

Mickey looked down, shamefaced. 'No, I don't think that, I really don't. I mean, she says she loves me.' He looked out of the window; a sharp hoar frost was melting only slowly and the distant trees were exquisitely outlined in white against a clear pale blue sky, '. . . and I like the children, and she says I'm very good with them. They like me too.'

'All that's fine, but why rush?'

'I want to get *settled*,' Mickey said with passion. 'I want to have a proper home and a proper job and to get going.'

'And she has the home.'

Mickey looked at him, wounded. 'Yes, well, I mean, it was half hers.'

'I'm not being critical, Mickey. Marrying into a ready-made set-up has great advantages. I'm just trying to find out why you are in such a hurry. And indeed why you came to see me.'

When the session ended, twenty minutes later, he was ruffled. He had not managed to get an answer, which meant that he, for all his experience, had failed, that Mickey himself had not been helped; he had neither been persuaded to wait until he felt more confident about this marriage, nor to isolate the source of his discomfort. He paced round his desk, trying to discharge enough emotion to get started again.

'Robert? I do apologize, but you have my calculator.' It was his good colleague Ruth, and he greeted her with relief.

'I've had my boy Mickey again.'

'Robert! The one you were going to transfer?'

'Every year since 1979. I know. He had an attempted suicide last year – one of those slow breakdowns in graduate school that no one ever recognizes until it's too late, and then got desperate and got slung out for cheating. So I kept him.'

'Now what? No, wait a minute, let me guess. He is in his twenties now.' She considered for a minute. 'He is marrying and has got alarmed.'

'Very good,' he said grudgingly, and told her about it.

'It may work,' she said thoughtfully. 'If they both need each other enough. Which is why they are both rushing into it, of course.'

'Yes. He is frightened to go in, and terrified to stay out.'

'They have a bad time, these children of a harsh winter.

This is the boy who lost his mother, effectively, to a younger child?'

'Yes, that's right. She rejected him and she's still doing it.' Ruth had a phenomenal memory, but he must have talked more with colleagues about Mickey than he had realized. He sighed. 'And Father went when he was twelve, and Mum remarried, and the elder brother's got fed up. As successful siblings do.'

'They feel threatened, of course. The older brother will be suffering some of the same problems, it's the same family after all, and it *is* frightening to see a sibling collapse. Did you try family therapy?'

'Briefly. Damn. I'm not going to finish this article.'

Ruth considered him kindly but sternly. 'In one hour precisely, I will come and take you to lunch. Until then, do what you can.'

'Yes, Ma'am.'

She laughed but left him comforted and with a defined space of time within which to do a clear task, with the prospect of a treat at the end of it. What all we humanoid apes need, he thought wryly, and turned back to his typewriter.

David Banner shook hands punctiliously with all his hosts; he had been in the grim building that housed the nerve centre of the party in Walworth Road for the last hour and was being careful not to outstay his welcome, so he had invented another appointment. He picked up the old navy quilted jacket, which he wore for preference, noticing with amusement that it hung next to several others of much the same design and vintage. He ran down the shallow steps that led into the undistinguished South London street, blocked with cars. It was a rotten day, rain pouring down, but he needed to buy Ann's Christmas present and it needed to be a good one, so he would have to make for the West End. In any case he was still excited by the meeting he had had; what he wanted was lunch with someone who would understand it. He found the tube and a telephone, talked briefly to Ann – who had waited in patiently until she heard from him – and then to one of Paul Seles' secretaries. He got impatient after two minutes; he liked Paul but he was not prepared to wait around on the phone for anyone, and he left a message that he was in London and would eat a snack at Redwood's.

He arrived just after one o'clock. The restaurant was filling up and there was a small queue by the reception desk, which combined the office and cloakroom. He stood in the queue, admiring the place. It was a dark, wet day outside, but in here everything was light and shining and warm, huge mirrors and superbly polished brass everywhere against immaculate white table-cloths, rather like an officers' mess. He had forgotten how large it was. It was all done in the same style but, unlike an officers' mess, you could eat anything from a four-course meal with beautiful wine to a one-course snack at any table. And anything went in the line of clothes; his own battered jacket fell somewhere in a range between the sharp-suited businessmen and the bejeaned actors. It had the unmistakable buzz of the successful operation and he was impressed, reluctantly contrasting it with the sullen air of defeat and not enough money that still hung round Walworth Road. Well, some of his colleagues might disapprove, but this place was no palace to greed, the prices were fair and it was deservedly popular. He smiled at a pretty waitress, ridiculously clad in a very short black skirt and a very long white apron, which made her look like a nun from the front, while leaving not a lot to the imagination from the back.

'David?'

He turned and looked into amused blue eyes above a snub nose. 'Jens. Sorry, didn't see you.'

'I can see why not. That lovely girl is an experiment, we have stuck to boys on the floor so far. She'll need to wear trousers.'

'Oh, no, why?'

'Well, we're not running a cabaret here. We want the service fast and unobtrusive and that isn't it.'

A hovering floor manager, a man older than she, had arrived

at her side and waited for orders, and she stepped aside to give them. David watched, interested, as the girl left with the manager. 'Like the Army,' he said nostalgically.

'Yes,' she agreed, following his line of thought. 'Do it now. I have a message delivered via various radio telephones. Paul will be here by one-fifteen . . . well, he won't probably, but he wants to buy you lunch. Would you like to wait at the bar or the table? Fine, give me your coat.' She passed it on to a hovering waiter and took him personally to a big corner table and organized him a drink, leaving him, without fuss, to deal with a message from the kitchen.

He watched her go, momentarily jealous. She was a year younger than him, not thirty yet, and she commanded – and owned – a large amount of this substantial enterprise. He waited twenty minutes, at first content to watch the tables fill up, then irritated; restless and given to packing his day full, he hated to sit still with nothing to do.

An evening paper arrived, proffered by a passing waiter, and he looked up gratefully to wave at Jens, who was greeting a familiar actorish face and settling him and his party at a centre table. He was reading the political section when Paul Seles arrived, unapologetic and beaming. He rose to greet him and was swept into a fraternal embrace.

'Paul,' Jens said, appearing at his side, 'give that here, you know we don't allow them on the floor.'

'Jens, I'm expecting a call.' Paul clutched a mobile telephone to him and lowered his voice theatrically. 'From a Defence Secretary in Moscow.'

'I do not give a monkey's if HM The Queen is urgently seeking you. A message will be conveyed forthwith. Give it to me, now. Is this the only one?'

'Cor, bloody hell, it's like eating with the KGB.'

'I wouldn't know. David here has been waiting for at least half an hour and I expect he is starving. I'll send Gerard to you, but *order*, right?' She nodded impartially to them both and swept off carrying the telephone and Paul's briefcase.

'No special treatment for shareholders?' David asked, grinning.

'I have to *pay* as well. She won't even give me a discount.'

'That's capitalism for you.'

'On the other hand, I can get served here, or rather anyone can. In Moscow, if you're an ordinary bloke, you wait an hour and get whatever they have. So how was the South London Kremlin then? What were you doing there?'

'Renewing acquaintance.' Champagne had appeared by the table, magically, a waiter was easing the wires, and Paul was ordering soup followed by steaks and *frites* for both of them, ignoring utterly any *specialités du jour*.

'You have to do that, do you?' Paul asked.

'Yes.' He waited until both waiters had left. 'The chap who has the seat's had a heart attack and has to take it a bit easy.'

'What, you mean there'll be a by-election?'

'He doesn't want to give up, and I don't want him to give up either, not yet. It's a year or so too early – I've only been there just under two years. I think one of the union people would get the nomination if it came up now.'

'So you were showing your face at HQ?'

'That's it. They need new people and they know it. Well, they should, after last year.'

'That was because of old Foot, though, wasn't it? I mean, even Jens, whose family has been in your lot since it started, said no one could possibly have thought Michael Foot would make a Prime Minister. Or not in the last quarter of the twentieth century.'

David nodded in heartfelt agreement, still raw from the memory of the leader of his party at the Cenotaph the year before the election. Lank, greasy locks above an ancient duffle coat. It had been, well, an insult, and had shaken his faith in the whole idea of the Labour Party. The morning at Walworth Road, by contrast, had cheered him up; the man he had met was wearing a proper suit and had been briskly businesslike, polite but absolutely direct, exposing any weaknesses in his own position and showing an impressive knowledge of the internal politics of his prospective constituency. He had been drawn to him, impressed by the ease with which he broke across formality to make him welcome, directly asking, as everyone else had not, quite, what had brought an Army officer into the Labour Party. He had found himself explaining his growing sense of injustice, his feeling that most of the citizens of the UK were not being offered the chances that ought to be available to everyone in a Western country with a developed economy. And that the Conservative Party, whatever they might say publicly, were not interested in making sure these chances were available; their view was that if you were strong enough to grab, that was fine, but they were not, ever, going to force through the system the changes that would ensure that those less able or inclined to grab got what they needed. In conclusion, the man had offered some shrewd advice on dealing with a particularly difficult member of the local party, and left him feeling much, much better about the course he was taking. He had also, fairly, warned him that the party was still split down the middle. It looked, David had thought, as if the rift in the constituency party between those like him who wanted to draw new voters in and the hard-core trades union people who appeared to want to put them off was echoed exactly here at HQ. You would think that the débâcles of 1979 and 1983 had never happened.

He told Paul most of this, drinking his share of the champagne, relaxing in the cheerful buzz of people enjoying themselves; somehow Jens, who ran the place like a well-conducted army camp, had also managed to make people feel they were, for an hour or so, on holiday, and at 2.15 p.m. no one was showing any signs of going back to their places of work.

'Like the East European parties,' Paul said promptly. 'Hungary is just the same, there's the people who want to open the economy up and the others, the stupid buggers who can't see a day ahead, who want to keep it all tight with themselves in control, and nothing to buy and nowhere to eat, except Gundels which no one can afford. Same thing.'

'No, it's different, Paul. Or rather, it's the same behaviour, you're right, but it makes *sense* for the old guard to behave like that in the East. I mean, they're in charge there, they get the best of what's going, don't they? But here, that behaviour has lost us two elections, and the other side is well and truly in charge. The unions are losing jobs – and members – and having no success at all in preventing that. And it'll get worse.'

Paul looked at him sideways, a forkful of *pommes frites*, dripping sauce, poised to go into his mouth. 'You don't reckon the miners' strike is going to overthrow this Government?'

'More likely to put *us* back ten years.'

'You've got miners in your area, haven't you?'

'Some, and *that's* been difficult. I never supported the strike, from Day One, and that tells against me with several people. But it was truly madness in the full sense of the word. There is enough coal stock-piled to run the power-stations for a year. Then Scargill calls a strike in March, so people have to do without pay all summer when no one cares whether they work or not. I tell you, Paul, and I wouldn't say it to everyone, that starting the strike was far worse than the Government taking us into war over the Falklands.'

'Why don't you change sides if you think that?'

'Because the party of which I have the honour to be a member is against Scargill. They can't say so but they are. And once we get rid of him we can move on. A lot of the trades union dinosaurs go with him.' He looked at his plate, amazed; he seemed to have got through the whole bowl of fries as well as the steak, and Paul, grinning, pushed his own bowl over.

'Or we'll get some more if you want. Here, hang on. There's Hugh. Over there.' David looked and saw the amused square face above broad shoulders, cracked in laughter over something his companion, an older man with a familiar face, had said.

'He's with Dawson. Chief Economic Adviser to the Treasury. I want to meet him. Come with me.' Paul was looking across hungrily, poised to go over. As the Treasury pair rose, he sped over to intercept them, pulling David, who had decided that embarrassment should not stand in his way. Hugh turned, revealing a bald spot at the back of his head and causing David to think complacently of his own thick hair. Jens, arriving from nowhere, kissed her husband warmly and put a restraining hand on Paul so that the Treasury team could escape if they wanted, but Dawson was exerting himself to be civil and David understood with a pang that he was interested in Paul Seles as an up-and-coming business star but not at all in an obscure personnel manager from an unfashionable part of the country. He waited politely, feeling small and depressed until the Treasury pair left, then trailed back to the table.

'What I've never understood,' Paul said, sliding into his seat, 'is why you didn't join the SDP. More your sort of middle-class dissident, I would have thought.'

'There's something in that,' he acknowledged, pulling himself together. 'Two reasons: first, I don't think they're for real, too undisciplined, no real background. Politics is hard grind, you know, on the knocker, in the constituency. They don't have people to do that, we do. And in any case, where we live, I'd have been as well off joining the Brownies.'

Paul burst out laughing, spraying coffee. 'Sorry. 'Course you would. The SDP's south and south-western, aren't they? Bit airy-fairy for where you are.'

'That's right.'

'How's Ann?'

'She's fine.' He fidgeted. He didn't want to talk about Ann. 'How's Maddy?'

'Also fine. Look, I need to talk to Jens quickly, but there's this club I know. You want to come?'

'Yes. Oh, shit.'

'What?'

'Before we do any of that, I have a favour to ask.' He was embarrassed, but knew he could not go home without discharging this commission; Ann had reminded him this morning. 'You know my brother Mickey? Michael? He's getting married to this nice girl. Older than him, couple of kids, widow. It's a good idea, she'll look after him, get him off Ann's hands.'

'So he needs what?'

'A job. They want to be near Leeds, her people are there. You've got a couple of businesses there. Would your people see him?'

'Sure. We can always use another pair of hands, and he's your brother. We'll fit him in somewhere.'

David let out a long breath of mingled relief and resentment; he had not realized how important it was to him that Mickey should be securely slotted into his marriage, and prevented from being a burden on him and Ann. 'Thanks, Paul, I appreciate that. I'll give your office the details.'

'Hang on for me.'

He watched Paul trap Jens neatly by the reception desk and lead her to an empty table. They looked like twins, he thought, interested and jealous, the dark heads together, but at that moment the pretty waitress, long legs decently clothed in very tight jeans, came past and smiled at him. He brightened, the anxieties of the morning temporarily banished, as always, by the company of an admiring young woman.

'That David is distracting my staff,' Jens said crossly.

'I'll take him away in a minute, but concentrate, Jens. There's this site, the chap who had it paid way over the odds and has gone bust in the middle of the conversion. We can get it for a hundred and ten thousand. We can borrow a hundred thou, so if we put up five thousand each, we're away. We'll get the planning consent altered a bit too, so we get two floors of office use.'

'Mm.'

'What?'

'Hugh won't approve.'

'Do you need to tell him everything?'

'No. No, I don't,' she said quickly. She had discovered that she was too used to running her own affairs to take at all kindly to joint accounting. They had resolved this, she and Hugh, by agreeing that they would contribute a set sum each to the joint account and all joint bills would be paid from there, but that they would keep other monies separate. It could not be argued that Hugh would object to her making her own investments. What he *would* mind was her going into a joint venture with Paul; in his uncomplicated, disciplined, professional way he was quite clear that you concentrated on the business you were in, and didn't mess around diversifying and doing odd bits here and there. She and Paul, who had lived less settled lives, were both interested in making a quick profit if they could and both reckoned they had more than enough energy to run another project on the side. She suppressed any qualms about being economical with the truth.

'You want a cheque when?'

'Tomorrow will do. Make it payable to Leisure Investments Ltd.'

'Do we need a company?'

'Yeah. It's all right, Sean and someone else can be directors.'

She knew she was on uneasy ground, if Paul wasn't willing to have his name on this one, but it was a good deal, and she did not doubt their joint ability to make a profit, particularly with another floor of office use. And she was just not going to ask how Paul would swing that planning consent, and he wouldn't bother her by telling her.

They kissed, to seal the deal, and she glanced across to where David Banner was. The pretty waitress started guiltily and rushed off to two tables who were waiting hopefully for coffee, leaving David turning restlessly back to his paper, looking suddenly bleak.

'Go and take him away, Paul.' She considered the scene again. 'Where are you going? No, come to think of it, don't tell me, I'd rather not know.' She waved them out wistfully before turning back to the grinding routine of running a big restaurant.

CHAPTER FIFTEEN

March 1987

Paul Seles woke with the familiar dull headache and rolled irritably away from his wife's warm body in the wide double bed. 'The baby's crying,' he said, rolling back to dig her in the ribs.

Maddy groaned and pulled herself out of her side of the bed, staggering with sleep, ungainly still from pregnancy, the blonde hair lank and showing darker at the roots, and he looked after her with longing. The baby's wailing intensified and he heard the unmistakable sound of a slap and his son Stephen's four-year-old voice raised in protest and lamentation. Galvanized, he rolled out of bed and was in the next room, tying his dressing-gown cord before he quite realized what he was doing. Stephen was wailing and hitting out at Maddy who was holding the crying baby, bleary with sleep.

'Stop it, you little bastard,' he roared, and Stephen bolted like a rabbit, the wail stopping in his throat. Paul heard the door of the child's bedroom slam and started after him.

'Paul, *help* me.' He stopped, distracted, and Maddy pushed the baby at him. 'I can't manage,' she said hopelessly. 'I must get some sleep. *Hold* her, will you, while I find the nappies? Stephen woke her up and now she's shat herself.'

'He'll get worse than a smack when I catch up with him,' Paul vowed, holding the screaming baby. 'There, there, sweetheart, Lily, baby, ssssh.'

'I'm ready, Paul. Put her down for me, can you?' They bent together over the wailing scrap, both wincing as Maddy peeled off the nappy.

'Better out than in, sweetheart,' Paul said, managing a recovery, and Maddy gave him a sidelong ghost of a smile in tribute. He accepted the nappy like a trophy and put it in the disposal bag, thankfully clipping it shut.

'What time is it?' she asked, pushing the faded blonde hair back out of her face and cradling the restored baby against her shoulder. 'Seven? I might as well feed her. Again.' She walked through to the bedroom and settled herself in bed, with Paul expertly packing pillows round her. She slid her nightdress down and opened the heavy nursing bra, wincing as the baby fastened hungrily on to her left breast. 'Oh God, it doesn't matter which side I start, it still fucking hurts. Ouch.' There were tears in her eyes and he reached over to comfort her, stroking her hair until she was relaxed. The door banged open to reveal Stephen, the baby's rattle in one hand, eyes on his mother's breasts.

'Get out!' Paul shouted angrily, taken by surprise, and Stephen, scarlet, shouted back that he wouldn't, so there. Paul disentangled his arm with a jerk that dislodged the sucking baby who howled in distress and dived over his wife's legs to get at Stephen who fled, banging the door again. Paul lunged after him but was brought up short by a phone ringing, disagreeably loud and close.

'Oh, God. Paul, can you answer it? I'll just try and get her on the other one.' Maddy was rigid with tension again and he snatched the phone up and took it outside the door, jerking at the long lead.

'Yes. 7304.'

'Paul. I'm very sorry to bother you at home, but I tried all day yesterday.'

'Who is this?'

'Michael Banner.'

'For fuck's sake, can't it wait?'

'I'm sorry, but it can't.'

Sheer surprise kept Paul on the line. The over-anxious, nervy Mickey Banner was sounding grimly determined. 'Peter is at home, ill – his wife says he's too ill to come to the phone, and I

264

can't keep the business going without any cash. We had forty-three thousand pounds in the bank last Friday but we needed every penny to pay bills. And it was gone on Monday – Andrew Small signed it away. I've spent the whole of the last two days telling people they couldn't have cheques for bills which are over ninety days old. Two of them are taking out writs and I don't blame them.'

'You're part of a group, Mickey,' Paul said, reaching for a cigarette. 'Sometimes cash is needed more somewhere else. Fucking grow up. Tell them to bugger off. You'll have some cash by the end of the month. And don't call me at home.'

'I had to. Look, Paul, no one can work like this.'

Paul felt his whole skin flush. 'You don't want to work for me, you know what you can do.'

The silence at the end of the line could be felt, and Paul banged the phone down, momentarily assuaged. He stubbed out the cigarette half-smoked, made to push open the bedroom door to return the phone, hesitated and listened, then put the phone on the floor and went downstairs to the study, switching on the coffee machine which was always clean and primed with coffee. He pressed a button on another phone, lighting another cigarette as he did so, and waited.

'Kelly,' the phone said, with the familiar closed teeth enunciation.

'Me. Paul. How are we?'

'We made de deposit. Just. An hour late.'

'Why a fucking hour late?'

'The sub-companies didn't co-operate.'

'Bastards.'

'We got dem all.'

Paul drew on his cigarette. 'I'd like to change all the mandates so that we only need your signature, and don't have to fuss with the finance directors.'

'Dey won't like it.'

'They can fucking walk if they don't like it. I've just told Mickey Banner that. Bloody cheek – I only gave him a job

265

because David asked me to.' He listened to the silence. 'Sean?'

'I tort dis was valuable and experienced management we had.'

'Get off.' Paul grinned as he pressed the button down to cut Sean off. He sat down again at the desk with his coffee and looked out unseeingly over the park, the grass white with frost and the distant trees leafless and still, no wind anywhere. He went out into the hall and picked a thick track-suit off the pegs. He dropped his dressing-gown on the floor and pulled the trousers and top on, then found a heavy jacket and a pair of boots and, turning off an elaborate alarm system, headed out through a narrow door to the terrace and started to walk down to the gravel paths to the woods beyond. It was all his land; Dellingham Hall had arrived on the market in 1985 complete with 130 acres. He had bought the lot but continued to let 125 of them to a neighbouring farmer. It didn't pay him financially, of course; he was getting less cash from letting than he needed to pay the interest on the loan, but it paid him over and over again emotionally to know that all that he could see, on three sides, was his. The garden was coming into shape, he had two gardeners, on the books of one of the companies, as were the driver, the housekeeper and both daily helps. He stopped to inspect, uncomprehendingly, a row of holes, then remembered that a beech hedge was going in there. Not the right time of year, the gardener had grumbled, but he'd been told to get on with it. He turned back to look at his house with love; Georgian with two not bad Victorian wings, and solid, with the Downs rising behind it. And under an hour from London, provided you went early before the traffic built up.

He speeded up; you couldn't jog in these boots, but he could walk fast and he felt the morning's headache ease in the fresh air. He had a spare hour this morning because he was flying up to Glasgow to see one of the companies, and he had intended to sleep in until woken up by his son. He scowled at the thought of Stephen, but this was displaced instantly by the memory of Mickey's phone call. The company in Glasgow would be squealing too very probably; they were chronically short of cash, and Sean had cleared their accounts out as well. The opportunity to buy something like Rainbow Engineering didn't come every day, you had to grab it, he told an invisible audience angrily and broke into a shuffling run as he came within a hundred yards of the house.

'Sheena,' he said without preamble, when a woman's voice answered. 'That wanker at Standard and Lloyds, one I met last week – a director. What's his name?'

'Ewen Winter.'

'Get him round for later today. Don't bother with nice, he'll wet himself.'

'Nice doesn't cost anything, Paul,' the voice said crisply. 'What time do you want him – how long do you have to spend in Glasgow?'

'I'm not going. So cancel them, set up Winter – before lunch – and you and I will have lunch, yes?'

'I thought you'd never ask.'

He had been sleeping with Sheena for three years, almost from the day she had started work as his secretary. She was a treasure, tireless, efficient, memory far better than any computer data-base, and fixated on him. She and Sean knew all his business, and they were the only ones who did.

He rang off, feeling better, and listened to the sounds of the house; nothing from upstairs but a clatter in the kitchen. He kicked off his boots and padded in to find the plump, pleasant Swedish au pair, whose name he'd forgotten again, coaxing Stephen to eat cornflakes. They both looked at him apprehensively, but he had been cheered by having remade his plans for the day and greeted the girl cheerfully and ruffled his son's hair as he passed. He poured himself a glass of milk and made to sit down, but was interrupted by the telephone again, which he snatched up, feeling his muscles go tense.

'Sean. Yes?'

'Got a writ here, Paul, which I tort you should know about before you go to Glasgow. Asking for de top company to be wound up.'

'What?' Out of the corner of his eye he saw Maddy pad into

the kitchen, her elegant bathrobe spotted with milk, uncombed hair in her eyes, their daughter clasped to her shoulder.

'It's just a way of getting us to pay quickly. But dere threatening publicity.'

'How much?'

'Four hundred and twenty-three thousand. With costs.'

'Shit.'

Maddy cast him a despairing look and he turned his back, excluding her.

'Get on to Barclays, ask the manager to come by the office.'

'I tried. De little turd wants us to come to his.'

'Right. That's him gone. I've got someone coming in this morning. Standard and Lloyds.'

'Oh, dem. Well, why not?'

He put the phone down, his headache back behind his eyes, and looked down the long table. The baby was lying back in her little canvas chair on the table with the Swedish girl cooing at her, Stephen beside her, and Maddy slumped in a chair, head resting on her hand, wearily drinking tea. A tiny movement caught his eye, then there was a wail from the baby as the chair slipped on the edge of the table and Stephen was bolting out of the room. Paul reached him in four strides and smacked him hard on the head, and the child, screaming with terror, lashed out, catching him painfully on the nose. He grabbed Stephen, turned him over his knee, tugged down his pyjamas, seized a wooden spoon from the counter and hit as hard as he could till the child's bottom was red and welted, fighting off Maddy, who was trying to stop him, and screaming at her and the wretched Swedish girl to shut up.

'Paul, the baby.' He realized his Lily was screaming her head off, clasped in the arms of the Swedish girl who was weeping noisily and looking at him as if he had grown two heads. Stephen was lying across his knees, screaming in short hysterical bursts, and Maddy was on her knees, trying to pull the child away, two ugly welts on her arms where she had got in the way.

'He hit me,' Paul said through the noise in his head, holding the child down with one large hand.

'He's only little. He didn't mean to, Paul, *please*!'

He released his son, who threw himself into his mother's arms, still screaming with shock and pain, fettered at the ankles by his pyjama trousers. The Swedish girl picked up the baby and rushed out of the room, crying. He found he was still holding the wooden spoon. He threw it away violently, breaking a glass bowl at the other end of the kitchen, then stormed out and was in the car ten minutes later, behind a stony-faced driver, cursing at the commuter traffic.

Four hours later he was greeting Ewen Winter; he had deliberately kept him waiting for fifteen minutes, sending Sheena out to apologize and explain that it was a call from Budapest that had delayed Mr Seles, but as Mr Winter would know, the lines were so bad that Mr Seles had felt he had to speak when he could. The man had swelled visibly, and the younger bloke he had brought with him had been impressed out of his mind, as Paul and Sean had been able to observe. What looked like an ordinary mirror was a device so that anyone in Paul's office could see exactly what was going on in the waiting-room.

He saw the bankers by himself, and after ten minutes, as they had arranged, sent for Sean.

'We want to take in another, more ambitious bank for this deal,' he had explained casually. 'I asked you to come in – and one or two others – because I thought you were making sense when we met the other night. We're fairly happy with Barclays, but we're expanding fast and we need someone else on board who understands the company.'

He had handed the man over to Sean after twenty minutes of this and resolutely tackled the pile on his desk, making a dozen phone calls, looking up only when he heard noises of farewell. He peered through the mirror to see Winter and his side-kick collecting coats, both clearly excited, hurrying to get back to their base.

'Gottem,' Sean reported with his customary economy, 'Gave dem de story about NatWest wanting to do de deal. Dey tink dey'll be lucky to be allowed to lend us tree million now. Decision tomorrow, he says.'

'Right. Well, let's get them hooked, then you can put the boot into Barclays.'

'Don't do dat, Paul, we can always use a spare bank.'

They were both laughing as Sheena came in. 'Excuse me,' she said perfunctorily. 'Mrs Winterton – Miss Redwood, I should say – says she has to see you, soonest. I told her you were busy.'

'I always see Jens. Tell her three o'clock.' He glanced at her sideways.

'I tried that. She wants to see you at once. In fact, what a nerve, she's here!'

They looked through the mirror wall to see Jennifer Redwood hanging up her coat. She looked at the mirror and walked up to it. 'Paul, we need to talk.'

The scene he had been trying to forget all morning rose clearly before his eyes and he felt sick. 'Show her in, Sheena. Scat, you two, I'll see you later.'

Sheena showed her in, sulking, and pointedly asked Paul if he wanted sandwiches brought in.

'Not for me. And no phones, please,' said Jens, who had not been asked, and Paul, stony-faced, deliberately ordered some for himself, feeling defensive, anger making him clumsy. She waited, equally pointedly, for Sheena to leave and close the door behind her. 'Does she listen?' she asked in the infuriating clipped upper-crust tone she used when she was really angry.

'What if she does?'

'Then she's going to get an earful. Maddy and the kids are at home. My home, I mean.'

'So?' he said, as rudely as he could. 'You can keep them.'

'If that's what you really mean, I will, and I'll take Stephen to my doctor forthwith.'

She was looking at him in the way the Swedish girl had, as if he had grown two heads, and he felt murderous rage, deeply familiar and satisfying, start to overwhelm him.

'What were you going to do for an encore, beat him with the buckle end of a belt?' she asked, cold as ice, and he lunged at her over the desk. 'Well, at least I'm nearer your size. You hit me, Paul, and I will hit you back, as hard and as often as I can. I'd welcome the excuse.' She opened her hand and he saw that she had picked up a paperweight, and he just got his right hand away as she crashed it down on the desk.

'Shit,' he said, shocked out of his fit. 'You would have.'

'Willingly. How *could* you, Paul?'

He sat, shivering, on his side of the desk, trying to revive the cleansing rage but feeling only terrible shame.

'Nothing's broken. Piss off, Sheena,' he heard Jens advise unemotionally, and heard his secretary gasp, then the sound of the door closing.

'Why did Maddy come to you?' he asked hopelessly. 'She doesn't even like you.'

'She came because for some reason she doesn't want her marriage to break up – I expect the fact that Lily is three weeks old is the sticking-point – and she thinks I have influence with you.'

'How is she?'

'Tearful.' She waited while he struggled with himself.

'How's Stephen?' he asked the desk.

'He has a fever, but that's mostly because he cried for three hours solid. His bottom is swollen and bruised, of course. We've doped him and he's asleep, or was when I left. Maddy is asleep too, and my nanny is looking after Lily. Your au pair has resigned her post.'

'Cow.'

'She did not feel able to stay in a house where the father was as violent towards his child,' Jens said in unconsciously perfect mimicry of the prim, flattened Scandinavian vowels, so that for a moment he wanted to laugh. Then the thought of Stephen weeping uncontrollably for hours filled him with despair and anger.

'I can't bear it,' he blurted out.

'What can't you? Having beaten your kid so badly that your wife felt she had to leave for the sake of his safety?'

'Yeah, that.' He tried to think his way through the darkness. 'But he's getting you all looking after him, isn't he? I mean, you fussed round him while he cried.' He looked down at his hands in surprise; he appeared to have bent the silver paper knife into a right-angle.

'Paul, he's four years old. Do you think he *wanted* any of this?'

'He was winding me up. All morning. Then he hit me.' He closed his eyes, wanting to crawl under the desk and cry, but found after a bit that he had to look at her, sitting unmoving on the other side of his desk.

'You need help with this, Paul, and I suppose I'm one of about two people who can tell you that. You've never quite told Maddy about when you were a kid, have you?'

'No.'

'Well, you don't have to now. I did it for you, this morning.' She waited, but he could not speak for a moment.

'It won't happen again,' he muttered, finally.

'Maddy doesn't feel safe and nor would I.'

'So what's she going to do?'

'What she'd like is to stay married and for you to get some therapy.'

'Maddy never thought of *that*.'

'No. She just wanted me to make you promise you'd never do it again. It was me who told her that it was unlikely you could keep that promise.'

'What if I won't? Go to a shrink, I mean. I did all that, long ago.'

'Then I will take Stephen to my doctor and that will precipitate all sorts of things you won't want. Come *on*, Paul, do you *have* to treat your own child as you were treated, for fuck's sake?'

'I want Maddy. Back at home. And the kids.'

'You can come and see her but she stays with us as long as she wants to. Or my godson wants.' She was looking at him without affection or friendship, or even tolerance, and he hated her.

'You don't know what it's like with this business,' he managed to say.

'*What* don't I know?' she said furiously, the calm exterior shattered, to his enormous, private relief. 'What it's like not being able to pay bills? What it's like having suppliers let you down? Or customers cheat you? Or being terrified of a step-father? *What?*'

'Sorry,' he said, released by her anger. 'Sorry.'

'Don't say it to me,' she said, still scarlet with rage. 'Say it to your son and your wife. And get some help so you mean it.'

'I promise,' he said between his teeth. 'Can I come round now?'

'Better not, Paul. Tomorrow would be better.' She rose to go and he managed to unglue himself from his chair. He was absolutely not going to let the day end without seeing Maddy, and Jens, always tuned to him, understood it without his saying so. 'Well, all right. Come at six. But she may not want to see you.'

He followed her. 'She has to,' he said, panicked, and she turned to look at him searchingly. The cool look, as if she had never seen him before, frightened him and he felt himself, horrifyingly, beginning to shake with the terrible sense of exclusion and abandonment that came from a long time ago.

'Paul. Come here.' He felt her arms go round him and the tears of despair he had been holding in poured out. She held him and let him cry and they ended up sitting in an uncomfortable tangle on the edge of the desk, with him gulping into her shoulder. 'Sorry,' he said helplessly. 'Sorry.'

'You ought to have done this with Maddy,' she said, pulling back to find a handkerchief, and he saw that she was crying too. 'You just looked so lost.'

'I was,' he said, taking a huge shuddering breath.

'Come back with me now,' she said suddenly. 'Just as you are.'

He nodded, unable to speak, and they went off together, past Sheena, who furiously carried on typing, refusing to look at either of them.

The lights were on, shining a soft yellow in the spring evening as David gunned the car up the drive and jumped out. 'Sorry, sorry,' he called, as he unlocked the door, looking anxiously round him. No kids, well, it was 8.30 and they would be asleep, but Ann had not come to the door. He pushed open the door to the kitchen; no sign of her and no indication of anything for him to eat. He chewed his thumbnail and turned to make for the living-room. He pushed through the door, conscious suddenly how small the house was, and saw his wife sitting on the window-seat looking out at the garden, hands still in her lap, not turning to greet him.

'I *am* sorry, darling, the meeting just went on and on.'

'So I heard.' She spoke without turning her head and he froze, the confidence draining out of him. Ann got up and drew the curtains crisply, then turned to face him. 'I know where you've been, David. There've been enough people to tell me. And council meetings don't take place at Houghton Hall.'

He felt as if his feet had become glued to the hearth-rug and made a huge effort to move and break the tension, but no words would come. She had been crying, he saw, her eyes were swollen and she looked small and tired.

'You've made a fool of me, David.'

He understood suddenly why the room looked wrong, the photographs of their wedding and of the children were no longer on the piano, and he went cold with fright. 'I've made a fool of myself,' he said, managing to get the words past the constriction in his throat. 'Annie, I'm sorry. Look, the reason I was late is ... well ... I was putting a stop to it all.' He looked into her unmoving face. 'I'd have done anything rather than upset you,' he said desperately.

'Anything except not go after her in the first place. Or any of the others?'

This was far, far worse than he had realized. He was frightened. His Ann was looking at him without affection or sympathy or warmth, and he was dead without her. He felt a flash of blinding anger at all the women who had smiled back at him, or, in the case of Sylvia, wife of the local major landowner, set out to seduce him.

'She came after me, that's why it's been difficult,' he said, his voice tailing off at her look of absolute contempt. He had to stop her looking at him like that, he had to get the house back to normal. 'Annie, God, I don't want her, I want you.' He moved hopefully towards her but was stopped in his tracks by her look of open dislike. He waited, helpless, looking for a chink of light somewhere.

'David, I've had enough. I'm going to take the children and stay with Mum while you think about us.'

'Don't do that. Please don't. I *have* thought. I'm sorry. It didn't mean anything,' he added hopelessly, hearing the time-honoured excuse echo in the quiet room.

'It meant enough for you to have made yourself conspicuous. And me. You're putting it all at risk, aren't you, David? Me, the children, and your precious seat. Don't think they can't change their minds if you're involved in a scandal, especially with *her* – with her husband on the Conservative committee.'

'I know, I know,' he said, agonized. 'I wanted to stop.'

'And she wouldn't let you? I'm going tomorrow morning, so it'll look normal and I won't have to drag the children around at night. I'm going to sleep in Caroline's room – I've put them in together.'

He watched her pause at the door and managed to get there and take her in his arms, but she was stiff and unyielding.

'I don't want that, David. And I don't want to hear about any of it. I'll come back in a week when you've decided what you want to do.'

'Oh, Christ,' he said, holding her shoulders and stooping to look in her face, desperate to convince. 'I *know* what I want to do. I want to be with you and the children, and I want to be an MP.'

'Then you'll have to decide whether you can keep your flies zipped, won't you?' Ann could be down to earth but the bitterness and uncharacteristic vulgarity shocked and frightened him, and he let go of her, watching, desolate, as she headed upstairs to the Z-bed in Caroline's little room.

He retreated to the kitchen, heart thumping, distractedly

looking for something to eat. He had gone from a meeting to Sylvia's bed, but had refused to stay and eat anything, in order not to be even later, and momentarily he felt aggrieved that virtue had been so poorly rewarded. He put the kettle on, hoping that tea would make him feel better, and resolved he would try taking Ann a cup; they usually had one about this time and perhaps it would persuade her to modify this terrifying decision. He poured out the tea and carried the cup into the hall. His foot was on the bottom step of the narrow stairs when he heard the key turn in the door of Caroline's room. He went back slowly, feet dragging, and sat at the kitchen table, staring into space, opposite the little mirror on the wall below the notice-board full of the children's drawings and the telephone numbers of the nursery school and the doctor and the plumber. He looked without affection at his reflection, seeing himself suddenly as a handsome, cheerful sham who was totally unable to give any of these women what they thought they wanted, doomed to disappoint them all, including Ann. He put his head down and wept, loudly enough so that Ann should have been able to hear and come and console him, but the house remained silent, and when he finally, wearily, went through to the living-room, feeling as if his legs were made of lead and with his face swollen, he could hear nothing at all from the rooms above.

Looking for distraction, he turned on the television for the ten o'clock news; the papers were full of speculation about an election in May, but he was not convinced by any of it. This lot in power could go anywhere up to May 1988 and they would pick the best time for themselves they could, and for his money that was the autumn. Not that any of it was going to matter to him, he thought, with a flood of pain; if Ann left him he was in no shape to fight an election and that was the truth, so all that planning and striving would go to waste.

The phone rang and he came slowly back to himself, reached for it automatically, then hesitated; anxious in case it was Sylvia. It shouldn't be – he had made it clear that he could not be telephoned at home – but they had parted on poor terms and women always rang you up after that had happened. He picked it up in the end since the ringing persisted, and gave the number curtly.

'Mickey,' he said, surprised, then wary. 'How are you? What?'

He listened, alarmed, to the stream of words.

'Hold on, Mickey. Have you actually resigned? No? Thank God for that, at least.'

The voice at the other end slowed and calmed and he listened with increasing exasperation, then interrupted. 'Mickey, for God's sake, if you throw this job up, what are you going to live on? Two children and one of your own on the way, you *cannot* be serious about walking out. No, shut up and bloody well listen, I don't want you falling into a depression again. Jean won't stand it either. Oh, she does? Well, she's nuts, tell her. Where are you going to get another job at that kind of money? Not with my lot, I can tell you.' He cradled the phone as Mickey went on about how he couldn't manage a company with no money in the account, how it was unprofessional and he wasn't going to put up with it, and what he had said to Paul Seles.

'Well, if you said any of that you're a bloody fool. Paul owns the company, you're lucky to have that job. He won't let it go bust.' His brother's voice rose to a pitch of anxiety and he waited, exasperated. 'Look, Mickey,' he said finally, to stem the torrent of rationalization and explanation, 'do something for me – and yourself. Wait a few days, Paul's promised to get you some cash. See if he does. Then just bloody *hide* some somewhere, so if you ever get this again you can cope. But don't just slam out.' He listened to the stubborn, miserable silence at the other end of the line. 'You should be in politics. If I flounced out every time anybody was bloody rude or treated me unprofessionally I'd never be there.'

He heard a reluctant laugh from the other end, but Mickey couldn't *leave* it, with a decision made, he never could, he had to go on chewing it over and worrying about his status and what to say to the creditors on Monday, and so on and bloody on. He finally lost patience. 'Mickey, this is not a good time for me. If you feel you must resign, do it, but I think it would be stupid. No, I'm not going round the bushes again. Love to Jean.' He put the phone down, feeling angry and oppressed and beset from all sides, and tried to keep himself going by feeling ill-used. But as he sat in his small living-room he felt a chill that seemed to go right to his bones, so that he could sit no longer. He went to the little cloakroom and had a pee and washed his face and hands, slowly and carefully, looking dispassionately in the mirror. He crept upstairs, like a burglar, and his heart lifted as he saw a crack of light round the door of Caroline's room, and heard the springs of the Z-bed creak. He tapped gently on the door.

'Annie?'

No answer, so he tapped louder, banking on her not wanting the treasured, fiercely protected children to wake, and heard the rustle of the bedclothes.

'What do you want?' She sounded small and cold and miserable.

'*Please* may I come in?' He waited, hardly able to breathe until he heard the key turn, then pushed through the door and seized her, hugging her hard. 'I can't bear it,' he said truthfully, holding her to him, feeling the rough wool dressing-gown under his hands. 'Please come back. Now, I mean, please don't go.' He felt her hands on his wet face and then she was holding him and crying too. He picked her up, lifting her easily, and carried her to their bedroom, tears pouring down his cheeks, and put her on the bed, kneeling beside her, holding on to her. He tipped her backwards gently on to the bed and scrambled to lie beside her, undoing the buttons on the dressing-gown, feeling the warm breasts beneath the thick cotton nightie, momentarily anxious about whether he was going to be able to perform at all, given what he had already done that day.

'Davey,' she said sharply, and he stopped, keeping his hands still where they were. 'I mean it, you know. Do you think you can stop?'

There was too long a pause before he managed to speak,

and they both lay listening to him fight for words. 'Never is a big word,' he said finally and painfully. 'But I can try. And you need never worry about looking ... about being ... exposed ... again. That won't happen.'

'You can't afford it to. Neither with the party nor with me.'

'I know.' He kissed her gratefully. 'Oh, darling Ann.' He turned sideways, still kissing her, and pulled off his belt and struggled out of his trousers. She was still crying, so he undressed her carefully and lovingly, pulling the nightie off over her head. 'I'll buy you one that isn't in decent, warm brushed cotton,' he promised, bending to kiss her breasts. 'Oh, God.'

She was ready for him, and would not let him bring her on but wanted him inside her, now, and thank God he was able to oblige, deeply moved, wondering with one corner of his mind why he'd ever bothered with the others. He made her come, twice, triumphantly, but afterwards he would not sleep until she had promised him that she would put the pictures back in the living-room and unpack her case, first thing in the morning. In the end they got out of bed and did it together, and she made him a cup of tea and took him back to bed, and he just felt her take the empty cup from his hands as he fell into a deep, exhausted sleep.

CHAPTER SIXTEEN

April/June 1987

Pregnant women were supposed to feel placid and calm and Jens decided she must in this as in so much else be unfeminine. She was driving the big Citroën station wagon that the business had bought her when William was born in 1986. She was appallingly uncomfortable and even with power-steering the car was a brute to park. Not that she was even that pregnant; the baby was due in July, a good three months away, but she had swollen like a barrage balloon just the same as last time. No one, she thought sourly, as she fought her way out of the seat-belt, would believe she still had three months to go; restaurant customers were already openly anxious that she might give birth any day.

She reached across awkwardly for her briefcase, heavy with papers. Redwood's had grown in three years from one big restaurant to seven of assorted sizes. Two of these, the original Redwood's and the second one, Redwood's II, had been started from scratch, the other five she had bought just after William had been born from the receiver of a company that had overreached itself. There had been at least nine months in the last year when she had wondered whether the five sites were going to cause the demise of Redwood's as well, but she had survived, and indeed prospered to the point where the accountants were urging her to consider putting Redwood's shares on to the stock market. She had considered the keen young men who were pushing her and taken other advice. Paul had also wanted her to do it, but in this case she distrusted him;

somehow Paul always contrived to spend more than he had, both personally and corporately, though between them they had made some good profits in property dealing. They had made five separate investments. She had managed to pay off her bank borrowings and squirrel some cash away. It had been easy money; the market had gone up steadily from a low point in 1984, and Paul had a golden eye for this as in any business matter. In one sense he did not need her as a partner, but she always had a bit of cash somewhere, and in property deals some cash was always required as seed-corn. But his principal motive, as she knew, was to stay close to her, and he had managed to find a game they could both play, which was often just on the edge of legality and which they kept a secret from their partners. A bit like having an affair, she thought, in a sudden flash, but harmless.

She had talked to Charles, who had advised her and the company since its inception. 'You've never seemed to me much of a gambler, Jens,' he had said mildly. 'What do your instincts tell you?'

'To wait until I'm quite sure we've got all the bugs out of the new lot. Not literally, of course,' she had added hastily, touching wood to avert the restaurateur's nightmare of something awful turning up on a plate in front of a customer. 'I mean the system and management bugs.'

'Then do that and wait till you're happy,' Charles had advised calmly. 'Plenty of time to go public.'

'They say now is a good time and that I'd get a good price.'

'Do you want to get out? Yourself, I mean?'

No, she had said, horrified. Security was having her own business, run as she wanted it run, beholden to no man. Charles's question had reminded her that where her money and her independence were involved she was risk-averse down to the bones; old scars ached when she thought about losing what she now had.

Her decision had not been popular, and she had just left a meeting of accountants who were openly wistful about her refusal to consider even talking to a stockbroker or a merchant bank, and only just less open about their conviction that she would change her mind when the baby was born. She had left a door open by suggesting that uncertainty about the date of a general election must be affecting the market and that the whole question could be reviewed after the election. Given that this could constitutionally be postponed until the spring of 1988, she felt she had won herself some space and could leave the meeting, driven as she was by an increasing conviction that the home front was not secure.

Her fears were justified, she understood immediately, as she turned the key in the lock. There was no sign of Hugh, and her eighteen-month-old William, who should have been in bed a good hour and a half ago, staggered along the passage to greet her, tripped and wailed with tiredness.

'Where's Susan?' she asked anxiously, picking him up.

'She's gone out, Jennifer,' her mother's voice called from the drawing-room, and Jens slumped on the seat in the hall with William clinging to her. 'I *am* sorry, Mum,' she said, pulling herself together. 'She was meant to wait for Hugh because we knew I'd be late.'

Her mother, briskly competent in a flowered apron, came through into the hall and stretched her arms out to William who promptly deserted Jens to hurl himself at his grandmother. 'Well, she rang me up and explained that Hugh had rung to say he was delayed, and she didn't seem to know where to get hold of you and this was apparently a long-standing date tonight, so of course I said I would come round.'

'How very kind,' Jens said, gritting her back teeth. There was almost everything wrong with this narrative; as Susan well knew, her secretary could always find her. Hugh, who had promised to be back, had obviously preferred to ring Susan rather than her, in the hope that she would cover for him. Susan, a tough little girl from Manchester, deeply resistant to any entrenchment on her free time, had equally unhesitatingly gone for the soft option and rung William's doting grandmother rather than get in touch with her employer. And Mary had come round like a shot. Jens had resolutely continued to keep her mother at a distance. She would have liked some help, and now that her half-brother was almost grown up her mother longed to be there. But there was still Joshua, and she could not cope with *that*, and she would have to if her mother were let into her life. And Hugh *knew* all this, he knew exactly why she kept them at a distance.

For a moment she contemplated, luxuriously, firing Susan and replacing her with someone nicer and more flexible, but the next ten days at the least required a nanny full-time, and in any case William loved her. I may be a rotten mother, she thought, but I will not remove the person he loves just because she is not disposed to do a minute more than she is paid for. And in any case this was Hugh's fault, he was supposed to be there.

'I wish you didn't have to work so hard, Jennifer,' Her mother was a contender for the world's worst people manager, having spent the last twenty years in the secure command of a husband and loving son. She would have lasted about thirty seconds trying to run a restaurant, Jens thought wearily.

'It's a bad patch at the moment,' she said diplomatically, but her mother had obviously wound herself up for a challenge and was embarked on an over-prepared and overwrought speech about how unfair it was to William and how it would, of course, all be more difficult when the new one came. 'And it's so difficult for Hugh as well,' she added incautiously.

'I earn about three times as much as Hugh does,' Jens said, as she had absolutely meant not to. 'We would be pressed to live on his money. And in any case it's what I do, and he wanted me to go on when he married me,' She stopped, shaking, but her mother had not expected to be so forthrightly challenged and had gone scarlet with rage and confusion. Jens sought to recover the position. 'It's very good of you to have come. And we must, I agree, organize our lives so that you do not get called out like this on no notice.'

It was of course too late for diplomacy, and William, over-tired, started to howl. She held out her arms for him, but her mother, still unable to speak, turned her back and carried

William away, leaving her stranded in the hall, raging and vowing childishly that the child now kicking her just below the belt should be *hers*, and her mother would not be allowed even to pick it up.

The trouble was, she thought bitterly, banging around in the kitchen to make herself a much needed cup of tea, that neither she nor Hugh had understood what having children was actually *like* when they had so cheerfully planned their future, three years ago. It was one thing to come home late by yourself to find nothing prepared and the place in a mess, quite another to come back to a reproachful mother and fretful child. And she was lucky to have a mother; she could easily have come home to a tight-lipped nanny, wishing to hand in her notice, and a cowed, neglected child. But she *had* to go on with the restaurants; her life, her security, her self-esteem, the core of her was there, for better or worse. She could not give up; the very idea panicked her.

Much, much later when she and her mother had managed to declare a truce and get William to bed, and when she had eaten two scrambled eggs and Joshua had finally collected her mother, she heard Hugh's key in the lock. She had meant to get to bed before he arrived home; she shrank from the row that badly needed to be had. Hugh was good with William, better indeed at playing with him than she was, and generally a kind father and concerned husband. But he was not taking seriously the fact that she was a substantial business-woman who could not be asked to cope with scenes like this. And she was pregnant, she thought, raging . . . did he have no idea?

He walked in looking exhausted to where she was sitting in the only chair in which she was comfortable. She kept resolutely silent, watching him fidget round the room, alarmed by the sheer dislike she felt for him.

He looked at her sideways. 'I'm sorry, but I could *not* get away.' He looked tired and stubborn and confused, and she was angered into speech.

'Why couldn't you? We had a deal.'

'I suppose you haven't seen the news. Sterling is all over the place. Election rumours.'

'And without you there it would have fallen apart?' The baby in her womb kicked sharply, as he or she was prone to do at this time of night, adding to her feeling of injustice. 'And in any case why didn't you ring me? You knew Susan was going out.'

'I'd forgotten. And it was one of those days where I had literally thirty seconds, then we had to go over to the House with the Chancellor.' He looked across at her. 'And I suppose I thought she'd ring you rather than your mother.'

It was a partial apology, but she was not mollified; she felt between them a fundamental disagreement about what he could be expected to do. If his Ministers or even his seniors at the Treasury wanted him, he abandoned any agreement made with her without seeming to realize that that was what he was doing.

'I came home to find Mum had kept William up two hours beyond his bedtime, because she wanted to play with him, so he was in a state. And then she had the nerve to have a go at me.'

'Oh, for God's sake, Jens. She bailed us out, you didn't have to pick a row with her. And it's high time you stopped being so . . . so difficult about her. It's not as if Joshua raped or beat you. Lots of children have a much worse time.'

'She bailed you out,' she shouted, outraged. 'And you don't know anything about what Joshua was like.'

He bent his head, declining the fight, and she realized she could not manage to have this battle either, her need for sleep and to get to the restaurant office the next day was too great. Raging, she went into the little dressing-room they had set up for her for the nights when the childhood insomnia had re-curred, and locked herself in, away from interruption and argument. She slid into the narrow bed, remembering despair-ingly as she fell into sleep how she had promised herself that when she was grown up she would live by herself in a little house where she would not be subject to other people's unfulfill-able demands.

*

Mickey Banner drove his treasured BMW carefully up to the garage and put his finger on the button which lowered the windows, as Susie and Samantha erupted from the house and rushed over to kiss him.

'Let Daddy out, Susie, Samantha,' he said, feeling instantly better. Whatever else had gone wrong in his life, these two were a running, breathing tribute to his qualities as a father. He had inherited them as pallid, thumb-sucking little girls of three and four and now they were lovely, tall, outgoing creatures of six and seven, who were suffering absolutely none of the miseries he had as a child. Susie, a year older than Samantha, was a little anxious, but the two girls were good friends.

'Mummy's making something special for supper,' Samantha confided, and he hugged her, both touched and worried. He looked down at his girls; both sported identical pink jeans and pink and white trainers, both, he was certain, new and expensive. He earned a good salary – in fact a very good salary for a man of twenty-seven – but there were four people to support off it and it had never stretched round new outfits for the girls every other week as well as expensive food and frequent holidays. He hoped that this particular extravagance had been financed from the dwindling remains of Jean's inheritance from her first husband, but he had an uneasy feeling that there was not much of that left.

His wife met him at the door, a small, pretty woman, glowingly pregnant, looking a good deal younger than her thirty-two years. They had meant – or at least Jean had meant – to have a child very quickly after their marriage three years ago, but it hadn't worked like that. Jean had been getting increasingly worried, though if he were honest he wouldn't have minded if Susie and Samantha were all they were ever going to have. He was, after all, the only father they now had and felt his position to be unshakeable. He folded his wife in his arms, basking in the warmth coming off her, partly the baby and partly a flush from the heat of the kitchen. He looked contentedly over her shoulder; parcels were piled on the hall table and he considered them.

'More things for the baby?'

'Only a few nappies and Babygros.'

'Didn't you have a lot left over from the girls?'

'Well, a few, but they were very tired-looking after two of them, and I thought this baby should have new things.'

She had not, he realized, taken in anything of the worries he had poured out to her only on Friday, including the possible need to resign from his well-paid job. He opened his mouth to remonstrate but closed it again, not wanting to destroy the party atmosphere or disappoint the three women clustered around him. He would try, later, to go over the whole problem with her.

'Let me take my apron off.'

He untied it for her and lifted it over her head, putting his hand on the warm swelling that was pushing out her dress. 'How's our daughter?' he asked privately, glancing round to see that the girls were not within earshot.

'Kicking me again.' They knew it was a girl; Mickey had found himself totally unable to sleep or relax when her pregnancy had first been established. Jean had intuitively understood his fears, and had the tests to assure him that the baby was not suffering from either spina bifida or Down's Syndrome. *That* had cost money too, and would cost more yet; at thirty-two Jean was not regarded as being a high-risk category by the NHS and they had had to find a private gynaecologist who had organized the tests and would deliver the baby in a private hospital.

'She's going to be the best-looking baby in the hospital. She ought to be, she's got the most handsome father.' Jean was leading him into their living-room, bright and welcoming with pretty new chintz covers and carefully, artfully arranged collections of small expensive objects, in sharp contrast to David and Ann's immaculately neat but plain sitting-room. David was making much less than he was, of course, a source of continuing private satisfaction. On the other hand he didn't seem to spend it; he had always been careful, had Davey.

He made for 'his' chair, the big comfortable armchair he

always sat in, Susie and Samantha squabbling over who should sit on the larger of the two stools beside him, and let out a long sigh; it had been another impossible day and he had had two lots of Anadin since lunch in an attempt to relieve the headache that was still located above his right eye. Susie, deftly, put a foot-stool under his feet while Samantha put a glass into his hand.

'Champagne?' he discovered, disconcerted. 'What's this for?'

'To cheer you up. I could see you'd had a bad day – I had a little bottle left from Christmas that I've been saving.'

He sipped, hoping disloyally that this was indeed a left-over and not a new piece of spending. The idea of living within a budget seemed to be one that Jean found intolerable, and he found himself wondering how her first husband had managed to control the household expenditure. But he loved her and she certainly gave good value; he had the most comfortable house and the best meals of anyone he knew, and he felt lapped in comfort and security whenever he walked through the door.

'It *was* another rotten day,' he acknowledged, glancing warningly at the children, who, secure in the knowledge that he was home, were edging towards their play-room and the second television. He waited for them to go, then smiled wanly at Jean. 'I couldn't do any work at all, I was just lying to people on the phone. And neither Paul nor Sean were returning my phone calls.' To his horror he felt tears at the back of his eyes. 'I can't do another day like that,' he said, in futile protest.

'Well, perhaps they will send some cash over tomorrow. Or someone will pay one of your bills.'

'I wish . . .' he said bitterly, 'I can't go on like this – I'll ring them tomorrow and tell them I'm resigning.' He sneaked a look at her to see how she was taking this, but her expression was carefully blank and guarded.

'You need your supper. Did you have lunch?'

'No,' he confessed. 'I couldn't eat.' He looked at her pathetically, but this time she was looking openly impatient.

'You did promise always to try to eat, Mickey. Even when you're not feeling like it.'

'Sorry,' he said, feeling both rebuked and deeply reassured. 'I just couldn't face it. What is for supper?'

'Beef olives.' It was his favourite and he thought smugly of David eating mince or cold ham, both of which seemed to be staples of Ann's cuisine. And he did feel a great deal better after a square meal. They worked together to clear the table, then he read to the children and kissed them goodnight and joined Jean for coffee by the fire.

'I'd have to look round a bit for another job,' he said returning to his problem. 'But, after all, I've got three years' experience now as a general manager. It should be much easier than last time.'

'Last time we weren't having a baby,' Jean said, stone-faced.

'That's true,' he said, looking at his hands. 'The thing is,' he said miserably, 'that I feel as if I'm going to break down again with everyone shouting and not knowing what's going on. I mean, what if the firm is bust?'

She sighed. 'You could ring David. He and Paul are close still, aren't they?'

'I can't bother him. He's fed up with me asking him to help, I know he is.' He was feeling short of breath, as he always did when he was under stress.

He pulled Jean on to his knee and leaned over to switch on the television. '. . . the general election will take place on Thursday, June 11th.' They both sat up, galvanized, and stared at the TV while the newscaster repeated and expanded on the point for the next ten minutes, with cut-in interviews with Norman Tebbit as Party Chairman and Neil Kinnock, David Owen and David Steel, all expressing confident readiness.

'No good ringing,' Mickey said flatly, turning off David Steel in full flight. 'They'll be busy. This is his big chance.'

The phone rang and he snatched it up, discharging tension by barking out the number. 'Paul,' he said, somehow finding himself on his feet.

'Mickey,' the voice said, honey-smooth. 'I just wanted to ring you to thank you personally for your understanding. You'll see tomorrow why we needed to pull in all our cash. It's a very exciting deal for me, and for all of us.'

'What is it?' Mickey asked, baldly.

'We've bought Rainbow Engineering.'

'But that's a big group.'

'Yes, it is. I want you in London the day after tomorrow, Mickey. I want to talk about the new group. All right? Sheena will make the arrangements tomorrow. How's your wife? Good, glad to hear.' He rang off crisply, leaving Mickey still struggling to speak in sentences. He put the phone down, stunned, then looked across and beamed at Jean, feeling suddenly ten feet tall with all his hesitations a thing of the past.

'Do we have any more champagne left, or do we have to make do with white wine in bed?' He pulled her out of the chair and hugged her, then bent to pick her up.

'Mickey, no, I'm far too heavy. Put me down.'

'No, you're not,' he lied gallantly, kicking the door open, but he could not manage to negotiate the stairs with her in his arms, so he had to let her go so that they could creep upstairs silently in order not to wake the children.

'David, Ann, please, just look into the camera. Thank you.'

It was a beautiful early morning in June, and the courtyard by the Members' Entrance to the House of Commons was dotted with little groups, mostly of three people, but some larger. Some twenty new Members of Parliament had been installed that afternoon and were being photographed with their wives or, in two cases, husbands, and the constitutency agent. Some new Members had brought half-grown children and, as the watching House of Commons police observed to each other, that might well be the last time the kids saw their dads for a bit. David Banner, Ann's hand firmly clasped in his, nodded politely to two new Conservative Members before dropping back to talk to the Shadow spokesman on Defence. 'Must get you along,' the man said. 'Not many people on our side actually served. Or not recently.'

'I'd like that,' David said, meaning it. He was still almost incredulous at his good fortune, totally undiscouraged by the horrible office which he was expected to share with three others, and by the small, poky flat where he was uneasily perched in a tiny spare bedroom, too small to contain both him and Ann. He was here, he was an MP, he was in, despite the party's rout at the election two weeks ago. Senior members of the Shadow Cabinet had gone out of their way to be civil to him, shell-shocked as they still were. He had privately not expected his party to get in, judging shrewdly that the presence of the hated Alliance would divert too much of the Labour vote, but next time, when he would be in the running for office, they would do it. Mrs Thatcher couldn't go on for ever and there was no quality in this Government without her.

'David. We need to go if we're to look at this place before dinner.' They were on their way to see a small flat which a Labour MP who had been unexpectedly defeated was needing to sell or let, and he bade quick farewells to everyone he knew. He was keeping a notebook with names, constituencies and a thumbnail sketch. It was the old Army trick, you learned everyone's name within a day of taking command, and made everyone feel you had noticed them particularly.

'I'm too tired, Paul, I'm sorry.'

'Oh, Jens.' It was a cry of childish disappointment, and she looked at him pathetically. She was sitting in her big black and white office on the third floor at Covent Garden, above one of the five Chez Michel's which were finally running smoothly and doing the turnover she had hoped for. 'I'm having a baby in two weeks' time,' she protested feebly.

'You can have a rest tomorrow. And we won't be late, but I want you. It's a double celebration, after all. My deal *and* David's becoming an MP. *And* I want to announce a surprise. It won't be the same without you.'

'Now, that's true,' she acknowledged. 'I'm not sure how well that private dining-room really works.' She considered the point. 'And I'm not going to find out – if you told them I'd be there. You did?'

'Of course I did.'

She grinned at him, shading her eyes against the slanting

evening sun. 'All right, I'll brace myself. Drinks in half an hour? I'll go down and have a look, see that all's well. We are . . . how many? Hugh and me, you and Maddy, David and Ann, Sean, Roger Caldwell . . . that's eight. You're booked for ten.'

'Yes. Mickey and Jean Banner. We're moving him to London. She's pregnant too.'

'Wonderful,' she said. 'We can have indigestion together. I don't know her very well. And last time she insisted on telling me all about how you had broken Mickey's leg when he was five. As if I hadn't been there.'

'I've always thought it was your stone which got him,' Paul said. He put a brotherly hand on the bulge beneath her breasts. 'What you got in there, triplets?'

'You'd think so, wouldn't you? But no. Just the one, I am told. I hope it's a girl. How's your Lily?'

'Lovely.' His face lit with pleasure.

'And my godson?' She had tried to sound casual, but his face went wooden and he turned away.

'He's fine.'

She waited, hoping he would expand, then realized he wasn't going to. 'I need help,' she said firmly, and stretched out both hands so that he could get her out of her chair and help her down one flight of stairs.

'We're doing very well, Mrs Winterton,' he called in the high, encouraging note with which people habitually address the very old and deaf, backing down the stairs in front of her. 'Do we need the cloakroom before we have our din-dins?'

'Piss off.'

'That's what I was asking,' he pointed out, and they arrived still laughing in the small, elegant dining-room, furnished in green and gold and flooded with the summer evening light, which lit brilliantly the large round table laid with white linen and silver. 'Looks good,' he said appreciatively. 'Why don't you float the company?'

'Shut up, Paul. You know I don't want all that yet. We're only just bedding down. I know it seems fun to do these gigantic deals you keep doing, but it scares me, if you want the truth.'

'Scares me too, sometimes.' He was prowling round the room, touching things, and there was a sudden clatter as a blind rattled down.

'It came off in me hands,' he said, backing away, and she slid her hand on to the buzzer underneath the table by the host's place. She indicated the fallen blind to the young man in a dinner-jacket who arrived within seconds, and he rushed over to put it right.

'Don't *touch* anything else, Paul, or I'll probably have the baby here and now.'

The young man gave her a hunted look and redoubled his efforts just as Sean slid quietly round the door with Roger Caldwell, who was not looking well. Paul rushed to get him a chair and he sat down, exhausted.

'Sir?' Paul squatted beside him, anxiety in every muscle.

'I'm just tired, my boy. It's the hip but they're going to give me a new one soon.'

'How soon?'

'Oh well, you know.' He eased himself in the chair. 'Not long.'

Paul and Sean looked at each other and vanished from the room, leaving Jens to pour him champagne.

'Where've they gone?'

'To buy you a hospital, I imagine.' She raised her Evian to him.

'They mustn't do that.'

'Give it up, Roger. I've only just managed to stay out of a private room in that place which only the Arabs can afford.'

'Oh, Lord.' He looked hunted and old and she remembered that he was in fact only in his late sixties.

'Roger, they *like* doing it. Drink your champagne and brace yourself for the next lot. Maddy and two sets of Banners. Hello, Maddy.' She was looking dazzling, Jennifer thought wistfully, no tummy and enviably slim. She levered herself out of the chair, seeing David Banner behind Maddy, the bright fair hair looking almost red in the evening sun. 'Ah, the new Member. Congratulations, David. You need to approach from the side if we are to kiss.' He managed that, laughing, and she kissed him back. He was alight with pleasure, unable to keep still, striding round the room. 'And Ann. I'm sorry to be quite so pregnant, but I gather your sister-in-law is in the same condition.'

'I am too,' Ann said, blushing.

'Oh, goodness!' Jennifer tried to remember how much older the existing children were. 'Oh, splendid. Have a chair, quick.' She turned to introduce David to Roger Caldwell and to Mickey and Jean and they all agreed that the pregnant women should sit down, now, joining the older man. Jens turned to check the preparations to find Paul and Sean on the doorstep, both looking smug.

'What've you done?'

'He's seeing Roger Britton tomorrow. Top man at Guy's, the quack says.' The 'quack' was the advisory doctor for the staff of the Seles Group.

'Will he like that?'

''Course he will.'

She watched indulgently as they converged on their mentor, and glanced at her watch. Hugh, had warned that he might be late, so she decided to start in ten minutes. She nodded to the young man serving drinks, holding the fingers of both hands spread flat, and found David Banner at her side.

'It's beautifully done, Jens. You must be very pleased with it.'

'I am.' The young man was at his elbow refilling his glass and she watched critically. 'By and large.' She swallowed some flavourless Evian. 'I cannot wait to have this baby.'

'So you can drink again.'

'So I can do *anything*. So I can get out of a chair without the assistance of two strong men. So I don't get indigestion what-ever I eat. You don't want to hear all this, tell me about your inauguration, if that's the word.'

He told her, making a good story of it, and she laughed with pleasure, stretching her back. 'Are you moving south? No? You'll need two houses then. Yes, James, we'll sit. Roger, you are to my right. David to my left. Paul opposite.' She looked to see that everyone had found their place and sank into the chair which was being placed for her. She considered the plate placed before her, deciding that the coulis could have been a tiny bit thicker, but that the design was immaculate, and nodded to the waiter who served everyone else.

'They wait till you've approved it?' David Banner said, amused.

'Well, yes,' she acknowledged, and turned to see that Roger Caldwell was comfortable. He leant across her to David, bright-eyed with interest, revived by the champagne and the affection of his boys.

'To which union are you affiliated?'

'To none, sir.' Like Paul and Sean he fell automatically into the school form of address. 'I feel rather strongly that Members of Parliament ought not to have financial ties of any sort.'

'Like your distinguished colleague, Dennis Skinner.'

'I'm afraid I'm not going quite to rise to his standards. I do intend to draw the full salary, and allowances. We just couldn't manage otherwise, brilliant though Ann is.' He smiled at his wife sitting diagonally across the table from him, next to Paul.

'Interesting decision,' Roger Caldwell said, taking a hearty and appreciative gulp of the beautiful Sancerre that he had just been poured. 'It'll put you in a very strong position in the debates your party will need to have with the unions. Pity more of them have not taken your line.'

'There are arguments both ways, of course. You learn a lot from being sponsored. And I will have to find my own briefing.'

'No, you won't.' Roger Caldwell spoke with the confidence of a life-long political observer. 'Quite the contrary. You will be deluged with briefing from them all.'

David laughed and raised his glass, and Jennifer, sedately lifting her Evian in return, decided that he had made that calculation for himself. Much less of the simple soldier than he played it, she thought as she had before, distracted by a sharp pain somewhere round her abdomen. She sighed, put her spoon down and waited for it to stop, and saw that David was watching her. She smiled briefly and looked across to check that Jean Banner was not finding the food too heavy going. She was staring round-eyed at the expensive blinds and the French china.

'Do you have this china in the main restaurant?'

'No. Different pattern and cheaper. This one is in all the private rooms.' They admired it together, white with a gentle faded design of leaves in green.

Jean sighed. 'I must get some like this, if we can. London's very expensive, though.'

'I'm afraid so. You and Mickey – I'm sorry, we all seem to call him that, even though he's grown up now – are moving down, I hear?'

'Well, we have to. We're looking in Kew.'

'That's expensive.'

Jean pouted and attacked her fish, every fibre of her rejecting the idea of anywhere that wasn't Kew, and Jens caught David Banner's sardonic look.

'Great day for you, David,' she said, conscious that she was sounding a touch jealous. Well, she was; it was impossible not to feel a bit competitive with her two closest male contemporaries. Particularly at a time when she was heavily pregnant and so tired that the idea of doing anything else other than plodding slowly on in the same deep rut was simply impossible. Paul and David were both moving on and up, and she was stuck, like a beached whale. *And* her own husband was being no help at all, either with the children or her business. She listened to David's excited account of the political set-up, trying not to look sullen but conscious only of feeling left out and unwanted, even in the middle of her own successful creation.

'Jens, can I interrupt for a minute?' Paul still behaved like a five-year-old if you didn't pay him attention the minute he wanted it, she thought, momentarily distracted from her miseries. 'I want to make a general announcement,' he said, as all the heads turned to him indulgently. 'My directors and I agreed this morning to set up a charitable trust, funding it with a percentage of the profits every year. Some of my shares are going into it too.' He paused. 'It's a trust to provide hostel places and flats for teenagers who can't live at home.' He looked anxiously across the table at Jens and she felt tears prickle, remembering Paul's teenage years in a children's home, a fate from which she had only been saved by William French. Now *that*, she thought suddenly, was not true, she could have made her own home tolerable, no one had beaten her, beyond the ability to resist, with the buckle end of a belt, no one had raped her. The baby kicked, and she tasted bile at the back of her throat. She could not, must not, spend the rest of her life in mourning for her early teenage; others, as Hugh had said, had endured, much worse. After the baby she would try harder. 'And we also agreed to ask Sir ... Roger Caldwell ... to be one of the trustees.'

Tears were standing in Old Caldwell's eyes as well, she was relieved to see, and managed to join in the chorus of approval. She was raising her glass to Paul with the best smile she could manage, and the next course was being discreetly brought in, when another sharp stab caught her, clenching the muscles in her back and stomach.

'Ow,' she said involuntarily, and sat still, breathing deeply. As the pain eased she felt David Banner's hand on hers. She clutched it and suddenly felt a painful wetness between her legs. 'Ah,' she said sharply, sitting uneasily straight in her chair. 'Help.'

Paul heard her immediately from across the table and David started out of his seat.

'It's the baby,' she said to them both, and caught her breath as the pain came again. 'Ambulance,' she said, as it eased momentarily. 'Sorry.'

The room broke into frenzied movement, people rising startled and the young manager and Paul colliding in the rush for the phone. David stayed where he was, holding her hand, not wincing as she dug her fingers into his wrist through the next pain.

'How close are they?' It was Ann, unruffled and competent.

'Feels like thirty seconds. No. Not as bad. Ow.'

297

'A minute.' David was wearing one of those watches with a second-hand, the date and very probably a device for locating buried treasure, she thought, in a moment of detachment.

'Ambulance on the way,' Paul reported breathlessly, and pushed his way in to be beside her. 'Shall we get you downstairs?'

'Yes,' she said, 'please,' spacing the words between the pain.

They set off in cavalcade, David supporting her, Mickey Banner on the other side, Paul, panicked, issuing contrary commands in front of her, and somehow got down the narrow stairs to the first landing. She indicated that she had to stop and leant against David, the pain so bad that the fact of her soaking knickers and tights had ceased to matter at all.

'There isn't room for three. You two go on and act as safety stop while I help Jens down,' David said briskly.

Both Paul and Mickey moved to obey him, Paul clumsy with anxiety, and they got tangled somehow and both tripped on the stairs, so that Paul fell sideways, getting a sickening clout on the hip as he fell. Through the pain which had taken over the whole of her, Jens just saw his face. 'Paul!' It came out as a scream, but he looked up at her and she saw him come back to himself. 'We could break Mickey's leg again and really make it a reunion,' she said huskily, on a snatched breath, and she heard them laugh, saw Mickey get up shakily, and heard her husband's voice on the stairs. After that the pain took over and the last thing she remembered was Hugh's face, white with anxiety, and the feel of David's heavily muscled shoulders as he lifted her into the ambulance.

CHAPTER SEVENTEEN

June 1990

The sloping roof of the Matthias church in Budapest came into view as Jens peered out of her taxi, exhaustion and mild terror forgotten. She gasped as the roof suddenly appeared in double image, the brown and green and white and yellow reflected in the glass of the Hilton Hotel, where she was bound. She watched it, delighted, suddenly feeling that she was truly on holiday, cheered and strengthened for the inevitable argument with the taxi driver, which turned out not to be necessary. Paul, spitting Hungarian and flanked by anxious hotel employees, erupted through the sliding glass doors. He swept her into his arms, while keen young men unloaded her substantial luggage.

'How long you staying, Jens?'

'Oh, God. I'm sorry, I was so disorganized I couldn't pack properly. I brought everything.'

'So I see. And in plastic bags.'

'Sorry, sorry.' She hugged him to her, breathing in the cigar smell of him. 'Difficult day.'

'Come on.' He stood over her while she signed the wrong bit of a form and handed over her passport, then took her up in the lift and stood back while the senior escorting flunkey demonstrated the virtues of the vast suite with its dazzling view over the Danube to Pest.

'Paul,' she said feebly, when the uniformed crew, heavily tipped, had bowed themselves out of the room, 'I thought cash was tight.'

'Cash is. This is expenses.'

It was a familiar joke and she decided to give up worrying and enjoy, luxuriously letting sheer exhaustion overwhelm her. She sank into a chair in an inelegant heap and stretched out a grubby hand for the glass of champagne that Paul was pouring.

'Oh, dear God,' she said, closing her eyes the better to savour the dry bubbles. 'I've got here. I can't believe it.'

'Difficult journey?'

'Not once I got out of the house.'

'Hugh and the kids all right?'

'The kids were.'

He looked at her sideways and topped up her glass; half of it seemed to have vanished. 'Was he pissed off at you going away?'

'No. Yes.'

'Well, he could have come too; I invited him.'

'I know you did. And I'm furious with him for not coming. But it's the usual rubbish. Sterling is going up, down, or sideways, or all three at once for all I know. And the Chancellor needs him, and so on.' She took another healthy draught of the champagne. 'But we did agree that I should come by myself; Hugh says I'm so tired I'm intolerable and I guess he's got a point. So I have abandoned husband, children, restaurant – the lot – for a week, and I just hope they'll all be all right. The restaurants will; Gerard is on deck.'

'Who is looking after the kids?'

'The nanny. And my mother. She likes Hugh much better than she likes me, anyway.'

Paul looked at her glass thoughtfully. 'I'll get some tea.'

'Good thinking, but we may as well kill the champagne.' She was ruffled by the implied criticism. 'Why didn't Maddy come with you, anyway? Or have you brought Sheena instead?'

'Maddy didn't want to come this time.' He was looking sad, and she felt a pang of conscience; no need to jab at the good brother who had brought her on this much needed holiday. 'And I didn't ask Sheena because I know you two don't get on.'

'That isn't quite true.' She stood up unsteadily and pulled off her jacket. 'I'd get on with her very well if she and you weren't lovers.'

'Don't you start.'

'I wasn't going to. I'm on holiday.'

'You and Hugh still OK in bed together?'

She wished she had kept her mouth shut on the subject of Sheena, she really didn't want to talk about her own sex life. 'Yes. We don't get there as often as we'd like, but we do get there.' She realized she did genuinely need to go to the lavatory and headed gratefully for the bathroom, stopping to wash her hands properly and comb her hair in the hope that Paul would have been distracted by the time she emerged. He was satisfactorily attached to the phone when she came out, selling something, she thought, judging from his expansive gestures and the way he had thrown himself back into the chair.

'Done,' he said, putting the phone down. 'Dinner with Nagy – he's a junior Minister in Trade and Industry. You'll like him.'

'No. I won't. I didn't come here to watch you do business.' She was cross and disappointed, but of course her good brother was not here solely for the pleasure of her company. 'I'll do something else, you eat with him.'

'Jens,' he said coaxingly. 'Just dinner, just tonight. Then you can shop tomorrow, and the day after we'll fly up to the Tatras. And I've found a new place. It's a surprise. You'll spoil it if you don't come.'

The phone rang and he picked it up, breaking into German as it squawked at him, and she watched, interested. He was hunched forward over the phone, tense, every ounce of him concentrated, and she was reminded of a picture she had once seen of a cheetah, lying along a branch, intent on some creature below working its way nervously through the forest. She saw him relax minutely, then he put the phone down with a series of carefully structured civilities and jumped to his feet to hug her. 'You have to come tonight, Jens, I need someone to provide distraction.'

301

'I can't speak German,' she pointed out. 'My Hungarian's not all that good either.' She knew about a dozen words, all of them connected to food.

'They all speak English. And I'll be doing the real business the day after.'

'I'll come if you tell me what you're doing.'

He hesitated, but they had known each other too long and she knew he could not resist telling her.

'I've got the chance of buying into one of their big companies.'

'Which makes what?'

'Well . . . chemicals.'

'What sort?'

'Darling, you don't know anything about chemicals. What does it matter what sort?'

'Do you scatter them on fields, or mix them with things, or what? I'm not as green as I'm cabbage-looking.'

He was looking distinctly shifty and she waited for an answer. 'You make explosives with them. For blasting rocks, for instance.'

She considered him, none the wiser, but knowing there was a sore point. 'What are some of them called?'

'Ah. Semtex, to name but one.'

'Like what terrorists use to blow up planes.'

'Oh, Jens. Real people use it for road-building and quarrying. It fits in with Morgan Construction, which I own – in case you'd forgotten. And it's very profitable.'

'I bet it is. It's a very useful explosive; I heard the chap on the BBC explain after that car bomb.'

'We're not going to do that. Lighten up. You're tired.' He pulled her to him and she rested comfortably against his chest.

'I *am* tired.' It was a cop-out but she needed to relax and to stop getting furious about everything. 'Do I have time for a kip?'

'You do. I'll ring you in two hours and get you up. Finish this.' He poured out the rest of the champagne and she remembered her errand and decided to get it over with. 'I've got the figures for Albany Wharf.' His pleased expression soured. 'I know, sorry, but I said we'd look at them. The auditors for the pension trustees are querying the valuation.'

'Bloody nerve.' He had gone crimson and she put a soothing hand on him.

'They only need a letter from the chap who did it. Your mate.'

'Yeah.' He read the papers with his customary speed, standing and flicking through them. 'Not one of our better ideas.'

'No,' she agreed. They had had an unbroken run of success with their joint property ventures until this one, a very large warehouse, ripe for conversion, near the East India Wharf, which they had bought late in 1988. The timing had been terrible; it had taken them eight months to get the right planning permission and by then the cold fog of recession was beginning to creep all over Docklands, and the Bank of Scotland, who had funded them ungrudgingly up till then, had refused to lend enough to do the conversion. Paul had borrowed £800,000 from the pension fund of one of his subsidiaries, paying 2 per cent over bank rate for it, so that the trustees had been glad to lend. They had relied on a valuation, done by one of Paul's old friends, which made the finished property worth £1 million. Only it wasn't. The ten flats were nearly finished but all the agents, however hungry, had advised unanimously that they would have to take a huge loss to shift them.

She would willingly have abandoned the subject; it depressed her even to think about it, but she feared they were stirring up trouble for the future. Five years before, when she and Paul had first started in property, it had seemed like the perfect way to make money, with huge gains available for doing very little, quite unlike the hard, continual, pounding effort and laborious work with recalcitrant staff that was involved in running restaurants. Indeed, when the going was particularly difficult she had comforted herself with the recollection of a steadily growing pile of money in her own building society account, which only she and Paul knew about. It was an insurance against the failure which on black days she feared, her secret fund which would save her from her mother's poverty and helplessness if she lost Hugh. It was also, she acknowledged, a way of staying close to Paul, of being his partner in a small way where she had been too ... well ... cautious to join his main company in any capacity. It gave them a private game to play, secret from Hugh and from Maddy, although when she came to think about it, Sheena probably knew. She returned, reluctantly, to the charge.

'We could just sell them for what we can, and leave ourselves with £200,000-odd each to find,' she suggested half-heartedly, realizing that *that* kind of money would mean she would have to confess to Hugh that she had been trading in partnership with Paul all these years. And worse, trading unsuccessfully; any profit she had made from these deals would be wiped out by a loss of this magnitude.

'I couldn't do it,' Paul said without hesitation, and she blinked at him.

'But what about your shares?' Paul owned 10 per cent of his substantial company.

'Not just now, anyway. Shit. Let's wait a bit on this one.'

With interest rates at 11 per cent and rising, she felt that waiting could be a disastrous strategy, but it didn't suit her to try to resolve the impasse.

'See you later,' she said, knowing she was making a mistake but too tired to go on.

'It's here somewhere. There.'

It was in a street off the park, in a plain, distinguished nineteenth-century building, and she looked at it, interested. 'Why not Gundels? Is it not still good?'

'Been taken over by an American, and I thought it might not be. In any case this is the place to go at the moment.'

She followed him, relishing being told what to do and where to go. At the door, he stopped outside to let her in first and she walked into a glittering lobby, faced with mirrors and shining brass and polished wood.

'Madame.'

She looked up at the tall man in the dinner-jacket. 'Ferenc,' she said, feeling a huge smile start to spread across her face. 'What are you doing here?' She would have kissed his cheek but he had taken her hand and conveyed it to his lips in the old-fashioned continental greeting for a married woman.

He looked older, well of course he did, it was nearly fifteen years since he had bought her a delicious lunch in a small restaurant outside Budapest, treating her as a distinguished visiting expert rather than the twenty-one-year-old raw beginner in the trade she had then been. And just as Paul had said, that night in her room in the hotel he had not made any overt sexual advances, but had been admiring and courtly and respectful.

'How are you? What have you been doing?'

They seemed still to be holding hands.

'Me? I have been away for some years . . . I was in Houston.' And indeed, now she listened, he had a faint Southern drawl. 'And now I am back. This is my restaurant.'

She turned to look at Paul who was grinning as broadly as she. 'You knew?'

'I did. I thought you'd be pleased.'

'Oh, I am.'

The whole evening went with dreamlike ease. She did not like the Minister particularly, a hard-eyed, thin, dark man in his forties, but she decided that Paul was well able to stand up to him. He was drinking too much, she thought, studying him under cover of a barrage of chivalrous toasts, but this must be a difficult deal. There was only one uneasy moment, when one of the men at the table pushed Paul a little hard on some detail of payment, and she saw the scarlet blotches above his cheek-bones which meant trouble. She cut across the conversation, asking about some detail of the next dish, so that the moment passed.

As they finished the meal, Ferenc appeared and asked if Madame – the title gently stressed – would do him the honour of looking at his kitchen. She beamed, delighted with him and the evening and looked inquiringly at her host, who leant over to her, excluding everyone else.

305

'You can manage without a chaperone this time, Madame?'

She went with Ferenc, laughing, both of them extremely pleased with themselves, and admired his kitchen and his refrigerator and his store-rooms and asked about his wife and children – joining him soon from the USA – and told him about her children and her husband, and her plans to have a few days in the Tatras.

'I had planned to go soon myself,' he said, meticulously escorting her to the table and bowing as he handed her back to Paul. 'You go when? And you are in the Grand? That is very good.'

She watched him go with regret and looked to Paul to understand what he wanted her to do. Despite the sleep she had had earlier she was worn out and would have liked a little walk to settle the digestion, and mercifully this seemed to accord with Paul's plans, so they were able to bid courteous farewells and start to walk home through the balmy June evening, his arm companionably round her. He had relaxed, she could feel from the weight of the arm, and in any case he was humming to himself in the way he did when he was pleased.

'Did you ring London?' he asked.

'No, but I must tomorrow. I can catch Hugh at the Treasury. And I must call home too.'

'Your mum there?'

'I expect she arrived ten minutes after I left. Hugh's supposed to take over from the nanny at seven-thirty, but he never gets home by then.' She did not want to think about Hugh. He had packed for her, as he always did, deploying his ability to get an untold amount into a limited space by hours of careful jiggling that left her exhausted. Both of them had been tired anyway, and both had been feeling angry and guilty for different reasons: Hugh because he had promised to take a holiday with her, and then reneged; she because she had snatched at the chance of going with Paul at a time when Hugh was particularly busy and would have real difficulty managing the busy household without her.

'I'm just tired of being the more competent bit of a badly run small company,' she said now to Paul, knowing this was treachery and betrayal, but, after all, this was Paul, her brother in all but fact. 'We don't have a marriage, we have a business partnership in which one partner brings his mother-in-law to work.'

'He shouldn't be doing that,' Paul said, immediately angry for her, and she retreated.

'It's my fault in a way. If I weren't working all day, every day, I could manage. But the kids love her and I'm not there. How *can* I?'

Paul stopped, to consider the view, pleased to be allowed into an area of her life which she usually kept barricaded off from him.

'What does Hugh earn?'

'What everyone else of his grade gets in the Civil Service. £40,000-odd.'

'Jens. Why doesn't he give it up and help with your business?'

'I actually don't want that.'

'No, you don't, do you? You like to control your lot yourself.' He grinned as she scowled. 'And why not? Nice little cottage industry you've got there – not going anywhere but nice small business.'

'Piss off, Paul. We're in there, still paying the interest even with the bloody recession.' She was almost going to cry and he was instantly contrite.

'I love you, you know I do.'

'But you like to have a jab every now and then.'

'Jens. Hey.' He stroked her face anxiously.

'You should have rung home too,' she pointed out coldly.

'I did. Spoke to Stephen, since you ask. They're all fine and my little Lily got a gold star at the nursery.'

'How did Stephen do?'

'He's seven, Jens. He's at school.'

'Maybe he gets gold stars there?'

'Not him. Can't even read properly.'

With a mother who spends her time having long lunches with her women friends, and shopping, and a father who continually presses and hassles him, this was hardly amazing, she thought acerbically. She was on holiday with every penny paid for by Paul, she reminded herself, and this was not the moment to discuss her godson. The conversation had already made him uncomfortable.

'Why don't you just sit about tomorrow? Take the camera, have a gentle stroll round, act like a West German matron. Don't try and do too much.'

'I couldn't do anything energetic,' she said. 'I must be more tired than I thought.'

'You haven't sat down since Sara was born and she's three.'

'Last peaceful week I had,' she said reminiscently. 'The one after we all had dinner. I just clung to my hospital bed. I knew that at home my mother would be quarrelling with the nanny, so I stayed put. It's been uphill at the restaurants ever since. I don't know how you manage to keep your profit up; everyone else I know in business is having a terrible time.'

'Diversity,' he said briskly. 'Lots of different sorts of companies, lots of different countries. That's why I'm trying to buy again here.'

She held her peace, knowing this could not be the whole story, but unwilling to challenge what city investors apparently found satisfactory. 'So Poprad and the mountains the day after tomorrow, right?'

She braced herself against the hill, legs trembling, and forced herself to keep going down and round the interminable zig-zag descent, sick and dizzy in the thin mountain air.

'You can see the café,' Paul shouted encouragingly, from the next corner. He had scrambled a few feet off the precipitous path in order to let the continual stream of people, both ascending and descending, get past him, and she shuffled towards him, grimly watching her feet on the hard, rocky white path, counting under her breath to keep herself going.

'*Grüss Gott, Guten Morgen, Dobry Den*,' she said with the

last of her breath, in acknowledgement of greetings from three groups toiling up past her, and slumped by Paul wondering if she was actually going to manage the remaining near vertical 1000 feet down to where the lake at Popradske Pleso glittered temptingly, with its café and hotel in a bowl of these magnificent, hostile mountains.

'It's a good path,' Paul said encouragingly, and she nodded, struggling to get her breath in acknowledgement. Given that the Austrian/Hungarian/Polish/Czechoslovakian groupings who had opened up the High Tatras had decided to make a path up a precipitous 3000-foot hill, starting from a glacial lake, then it was no doubt a good one. It zig-zagged endlessly to the top, made of carefully banked white rock, pitilessly hard on the feet. No individual bit of it was steep but it went on and on and on. She refused even to think what going up it would have been like, she was having enough trouble getting down. She and Paul had come up on the cable car, further along the narrow, beautiful High Tatras range, early that morning and had walked across below the ridge to this sharp descent. She had got tired even on the first part of the walk; her feet had hurt, she was too hot, but they had started very early and she had been confident of completing what was said to be a five-and-a-half-hour walk. This confidence was rapidly draining away, and she looked anxiously at Paul, who was sweating profusely in the hot mountain sun, and all too clearly not enjoying himself.

'I *do* know you'd rather be lying in a mud bath, Paul. I'm sorry.'

'No, no, it's fine.' He looked at her carefully. 'You're not pregnant again?'

'No. Am I being very slow?'

'Yes. And your eyes look funny.' He fished for the water bottle and made her drink. 'Better give me your rucksack.'

She hesitated. 'It's heavy. I brought a decent anorak because it said these hills were treacherous.' They both gazed at the bright sun. 'No one else is wearing anything half as warm.'

'They aren't, are they?'

They sat in contemplation of the continuous stream of walkers passing them in both directions, exchanging brief multilingual salutations as the convention was.

'The Slovak climbing dress would appear to be sneakers, shorts, T-shirt and a plastic mac,' Jennifer observed.

'That's all people here have,' Paul said sharply, and she nodded, rebuked, feeling the headache that had been threatening her for the last hour clamp down over her right eye.

'Come on,' Paul said abruptly, and she pulled her sun-hat as far forward as it would go and started wearily to slide off the rock then stopped, arrested. 'Look.'

Above them on the hill, a man was running down the path over which they had toiled, overtaking the streams of people like a dancer, putting a toe on the edge of the path then shifting his balance immediately to pass the next person. They stared at him transfixed, as he raced down from the top, totally concentrated, always anticipating the next problem, moving like a chamois, part of the hill.

'God, he must be fit,' Paul said, awed and jealous, and she could only nod, straining her eyes to watch, headache almost forgotten in the pleasure of watching this graceful and confident performance. The man turned two corners above them, jumping from one zig-zag to another, jinked round a solid Austrian group heaving themselves uphill with ski poles, cut the next corner and landed just above them, looking to see where to go next, sweating, his dark hair flopping into his eyes.

'Ferenc,' they both said incredulously. He checked on one foot, the lovely rhythm broken, shifted his weight back on his heels and stopped, just out of the way of two toiling, grumbling children and their overweight parents. He laughed, amazed, and jumped across the gap, putting a foot down on a rock to steady himself, and arrived beside them.

'What are you doing here?' he and Paul said simultaneously, while she stood, dizzy, fighting a headache, squinting at him as he stood against the sun. He was wearing the uniform shorts and T-shirt but he had expensive lightweight American climbing boots, and carried a neat rucksack.

'Jennifer, are you all right?' he asked, looking down at her.

'Not awfully.' The sun seemed to have got even hotter and her knees shook as she tried to stand up.

'Look at me, please.' He bent his head and tipped her hat back. 'You have sunstroke. Your eyes show it. Sit down again.'

She subsided, the sun hot on her head, even through the sun-hat, and he slid off his rucksack and fished in the pockets, shaking something into his hand. 'Salt pills.' She reached a shaky hand for the water bottle and he closed his hand round hers until she had a good grip. She looked for the pills, her vision blurring, and felt his hand on her chin.

'Open your mouth.' She tasted the sweat on his fingers as he put the pills on her tongue. 'Swallow.' She took a gulp of water and swallowed obediently.

'Take some more water, Jens.' Paul was crowding in at the edge of her vision and she drank carefully.

'You need something over the back of your neck,' Ferenc said. 'The sun has burnt you.' He dug into his rucksack and produced a triangular bandage and knotted it carefully round her neck.

'What else have you got in there, Ferenc?' Paul was sounding defensive.

'I always carry First Aid. Army training.'

The conversation seemed to be coming from a long way away as she sat with her eyes closed. Ferenc was standing close up against her and she realized that he was doing it so as to offer her some shelter from the sun.

'Poor old Jens. She would insist on this walk. But what are you doing here?' Paul was sounding suspicious.

'I am often here. Whenever I can. I like to climb – I mean properly, with ropes, but I have not time today, so I am walking.'

'Didn't look like walking to us.' Paul sounded only slightly mollified, but Ferenc bent down to her.

'Jennifer, can you go on, do you think?'

She considered the point; the headache had slightly receded and blessedly she did not seem to feel sick. 'Yes, slowly.'

'Give me your rucksack.' He stuffed it into his own and helped her up, stamping his boots, poised to go, and she looked at him helplessly.

'I'll lead, you follow right behind me. Don't look down, keep your eyes on me and try and keep in rhythm.'

And miraculously that was how it was. She did exactly as she was told and somehow, eyes fixed on his bobbing rucksack, the path cleared for her, she kept up a decent pace, arriving at the flat land at the bottom of the hill in a brisk fifteen minutes. There she found her legs buckling, refusing to adjust to going along instead of down, but Ferenc called a halt, and issued her with two more salt pills, gave her five minutes' rest and got them to the café. They looked, intimidated, at the swirling crowds patiently queuing for the services of a very small number of overworked waiters.

'I will go and see.' Ferenc strode off, leaving her his water bottle, while Paul found her a shaded ledge to sit on. She was still on the edge of falling over, and they sat silently watching the crowds.

'You can tell the locals from the Westerners,' she bestirred herself to observe. It was easy even on the hill to decide in which language to offer the conventional greeting. Shorts or light trousers and T-shirts were universal, but the local make was of poor material, heavily dependent on nylon, skimpily cut. The people inside the clothes looked different too; lively but somehow old-fashioned, and she realized that she was seeing mental pictures of her parents and their friends in the forties, wearing poorly fitting clothes, thin and strained from the struggle to get the ordinary necessities of life, hair badly cut or not cut at all.

'They'll all look quite different in a year or so,' Paul said, making her jump. 'I was in Poland last year and everyone looked heavy and tired and was wearing rubbish, but it's changing very fast.'

'Not an advertisement for socialism, these countries,' she said cautiously.

'Oh, there were some good things,' he said firmly. 'But it

does turn out you need a mixed economy, so *that's* got to change. What *is* Ferenc doing?'

'I have got a ride for you, Jennifer.' Ferenc, not a hair out of place, appeared from the crowd.

'They don't let cars up here, surely?' Paul straightened her hat for her irritably.

'They have to,' she said in realization. 'To keep the chalet and the restaurant stocked.'

'That's right,' Ferenc said smugly. 'We will go down with the empty bottles.'

She slept for four hours after the journey in the rattling van that smelt sickeningly of beer, and the final, painful two hundred yards to the hotel. She lay flat out in the hotel's best suite, diagonally across the nearest approach to a king-sized bed that Slovakia could boast, and woke slowly to find Paul stamping round the living-room end of the suite.

'I didn't mean to wake you. I was just leaving a note. I have to go to Poprad now, for the evening. How do you feel?'

She rolled on to her side and lifted her head cautiously. 'Bit odd. Not too bad.'

He came and sat on the bed beside her, looking anxious. 'I *have* to go.'

'It's all right. Don't worry. I'm actually hungry. I must be OK.'

'Ferenc is here,' he remembered. 'He can look after you.'

She opened her mouth to object but Paul had seized the phone and was speaking Hungarian.

'No problem,' he reported, putting the phone down. 'He will see you get dinner.'

'Paul,' she protested, 'what will he think? Indeed, what *does* he think? About us, I mean.'

'You and me?'

'Yes, idiot. Did we creep off here to be together?'

He stared at her. '*Here*? To a hotel full of East German and Polish families? After we've known each other for nearly thirty years? Not promising, is it?'

She laughed and struggled to sit up and he gave her a hand, propping all the pillows behind her and opening a bottle of mineral water which she drank greedily.

'I don't know how Ferenc keeps so fit,' Paul grumbled, checking his pockets. 'I know restaurateurs don't do any work but that's ridiculous. Anyway, I'm for off.' He snatched up two briefcases, kissed her warmly and left.

She got out of bed, carefully keeping her head low, and had a cautious shower. Even in the best suite in the hotel the water ran fitfully, and the flush on the lavatory felt distinctly insecure, so she handled it gingerly. Everything that could be done by working hands had been achieved; the room was immaculate, the bed made as soon as you got out of it, but equally, everything that needed capital investment or Western manufacturing technique, or both, was in short supply. The bathroom fittings were in cheap plastic, the towels were thin and scratchy and the carpets the sort of nylon mix that had not been seen in England since the sixties. And none of the cupboards quite fitted, though all bore the marks of patient tinkering.

She looked at the pale face in the mirror; she looked worn but not absolutely terrible as she had when she got off the hill, and that would have to do. She put on trousers and a silk shirt and sat down again feeling dizzy. She needed to eat something and, she told herself, to ask for room service in Slovakian was beyond her. The phone rang first.

'Are you well enough for dinner? No need if you are not.'

It was a very nice voice, she remembered, deep and with an attractive slight Southern twang which combined oddly with the careful European phrasing. 'I'm hungry, I think.'

'I'll fetch you.'

She opened the door to him two minutes later; he was wearing immaculate jeans and a pale blue shirt, with a sweater slung over his shoulder. He exuded health, burnt by the sun, hair still damp from the shower, bouncing with energy, and she felt tired and frail by comparison. He checked that she had her key and locked her room for her, taking charge automatically as good restaurateurs do, and she was amused.

'Your eyes are still a bit crossed. Do you still have a headache?'

'A little,' she admitted.

'You will be better to eat, although the food here is not good.' He lowered his voice in deference to a beaming, plump, middle-aged man in a too-tight dinner-jacket, who was waving them to a table in a huge room full of the pink light of the setting sun which illuminated, in loving detail, the carpet with its cerise roses alternating with bright green and yellow foliage and the unmatching pink blouses worn by the waitresses.

He gazed at the menu and ordered a Coca Cola for her. 'You will be all right if you stick to soup first, then omelettes or the Tatras Plate. The meat is good, if tough, and the soup is OK, provided only they keep the vegetables out of it.'

'Why?'

'They use tinned carrot and tinned potato for that matter.'

They looked at each other, two Western professional restaurateurs, united in horror, but the soup was all right and devoid of vegetables.

The waitress swooped on their plates the second they had finished and they looked after her, disconcerted.

'Can they be short of crockery?' Jens wondered.

'Very possibly, but I don't think it's that,' he said. 'It is very eager service because they have not any of the right materials.'

The beaming waiter arrived, followed by two of the pink-bloused waitresses bearing plates under steel-domed covers which were set ceremoniously before them and whisked off clumsily but willingly to reveal a dauntingly large collection of grilled meat, fried potatoes and gherkins for her, and some lumps shrouded in orange gravy and five slices of dumpling for Ferenc. They both gravely returned thanks and the convoy bowed itself away.

'Yours looks delicious,' she said, straight-faced, passing him the salt.

He hesitated, then attacked the first lump he could see, but had to abandon the attempt to cut it up and swallowed it whole, gulping slightly and taking a hasty slice of dumpling.

315

'Would you taste the sauce?' he asked, and she took a cautious spoonful from his plate.

'Paxo,' she reported. 'Or near offer.' She sucked the spoon, considering the aftertaste carefully. 'Bit more monosodium glutamate than Paxo usually has.'

'It will be a Slovakian version. And much cornflour.' He grinned at her.

'I feel as if I have been watching you consider some dish, with just that expression, for so many years. I am so glad that Mr Paul has caused us to meet again.'

She recognized, with a thump of her heart, the concealed question. 'My biggest supporter in every sense, is Paul. The brother I don't have, and it's the same for him.'

He had hidden two of the lumps under his fork, and was watching her plate hungrily.

'I'm not going to eat half of this,' she said. 'You wouldn't like to help out? It would save hurt feelings.'

They started to divide her vast plateful, which brought both waitresses running with clean plates and extra knives and forks. She realized heads were turning all round the dining-room, but Ferenc was accepting it as his due, joking with them in German. She caught a familiar phrase and looked at him inquiringly as the girls retired, pink and pleased.

'They ask if we are married,' he reported, picking up a forkful of potatoes. 'This *is* better. I suppose they are puzzled by you.'

'No. They wanted to find out if you were available.' She managed a sisterly smile and returned to what turned out to be a slice of liver. She ate carefully and slowly and cautiously realized that she was feeling infinitely better, but providence had better not be tempted. She sat back and watched indulgently as Ferenc finished the rest of the plate with the speed of hunger.

Waitresses swooped to remove the plates and to hand them the menus. He considered his seriously.

'The compote will be canned and sweetened with a saccharin derivative.'

'Sounds delicious,' she said firmly. 'We'll have that.' They waited while the girl retreated, both of them scarlet with suppressed laughter.

He looked at her carefully. 'Your eyes look better.'

'They are. I am.' She beamed at him in the sudden liberation from the band round her head.

'We could make a little walk after supper?'

'I'd love it.'

They chatted inexhaustibly through the compote and the coffee ('Chicory,' she had said, grinning, in answer to his raised eyebrows), and he looked round for the bill.

'Mr Seles has signed all,' the head waiter said severely, giving him a considering look so that they had to escape before they both burst out laughing.

'Oh dear,' she mourned, 'my reputation! Your reputation! Thank God we couldn't possibly meet anyone else we know here.'

'That is not necessarily correct,' he said, helping her into her jacket. 'There is no isolated place any more. I was in a terrible café in Warsaw last year – right off any tourist beat – when two of our neighbours from Houston sat down at the next table.'

'And ordered lumps of gristle in orange gravy?' She was very conscious of his hands on her shoulders.

'Of course. That is what there was.'

They set off, arm-in-arm, along the pleasant, wide pavements, full of contented people walking in groups.

'Barely a night club or a restaurant in sight,' she said, breathing in carefully in case the feeling of well-being was about to evaporate.

'Most people are on a package holiday with not much money for extras.'

'They're all having a good time, though,' she observed, nodding and smiling in return to the various multilingual greetings. Ferenc, exceptionally good-looking, and very tall, would always cause heads to turn, she realized. She could smell the pine trees still discharging the warmth of the day, and she was suddenly happy.

'This is good, isn't it?' he said, squeezing her arm. 'Can you go on? Ten minutes and we turn.'

Dispiritingly, she found herself tiring after five minutes, but he saw it straightaway and made her turn for home. 'Sorry.' She looked sideways at him, apologetically.

'Tomorrow you will be all right. What shall we do?'

She felt a great wave of pleasure. 'I assumed you were going to do another twenty miles vertically.'

'Not if I can do something with you. We will decide in the morning.' He kissed her hand and bowed her into the lift.

She thought she would not sleep but she did, waking only twice, both times out of a disquieting dream about the children. As she passed the reception desk she was summoned to receive a message from Paul; he was delayed in Poprad and could not get back until that evening. She went down and had ordered breakfast, when the girl who was bringing her coffee looked up and exclaimed, and she followed her admiring gaze to see Ferenc, carrying a newspaper.

He shovelled *The Times* on to her lap. 'It's three days old, but I hoped you'd like it. Paul is not up yet?'

She explained his absence, carefully not looking across the table, then they split the paper between them and read it avidly, passing each other bits of it. Sterling had made another of its lurches downwards; Hugh and the Chancellor would be engaged as usual in the unproductive obsessive discussions of what the Treasury and the Bank should do, not as far as she could see that any of it made any difference. He might just as well have come on holiday with her. She considered, covertly, the man who had decided to come on holiday with her. She had woken feeling tired but with her head clear, and understood, as she lay luxuriously in bed, that Ferenc's presence here was not an accident; he could not have expected to find them on the hill but he knew they were staying at the Grand and had arranged to do so too. And, if his behaviour as a younger man was a precedent, he would not push her, but he was very much there if she wanted him. Which she did, she acknowledged, considering his dark, lithe good looks, even better now than fifteen years ago. She drew breath, alarmed. She had never considered being unfaithful to Hugh, indeed had not even been tempted in six years of marriage. She tried, conscientiously, to think about Hugh, bleary-eyed, changing nappies, or taking the children to the park to give her a two-hour breather at the weekend, but it was superseded by the vision of Hugh exhausted and depressed by the latest incomprehensible shift in the currency markets, slumped in front of the nine o'clock news, ignoring her. She looked across the table at Ferenc, who was chatting in German to the manager, blue shirt open at the collar, brown from the sun, bending to scoop up bits of the newspaper with the easy suppleness of the athlete. He caught her eye, brought the conversation to an end and folded his napkin decisively. 'We go for a walk – no, I promise, not more than two miles, it's a well-known view.'

'Two miles vertical?'

'A rise of a thousand feet only. I think you can manage.'

Fully kitted up at his insistence in long-shirt with collar, sun-hat, sun-cream and light trousers, she made the distance easily, and they emerged through a gap in the pine woods to stare far across the plains beyond the hills. He found a bench and they sat, his shoulder against hers.

'You could have done a peak by now, if I weren't here,' she said, afraid of the silence.

'I would rather be here,' he said to the air, and she held her breath as he turned his head. They looked into each other's eyes steadily, then he leant forward to kiss her, his hand on the back of her neck, his mouth moving on to hers. It was pure, unmitigated pleasure, the feel of his mouth against hers and the smell of him and the warmth of his skin. She remembered, horrified, that they were visible to everyone in the café, and pulled back.

'Goodness,' she said at last.

He touched her cheek. 'Can this be, for us?'

The careful question steadied her and she looked into his dark eyes. She wanted him, she thought, reassured and cheered.

She was on holiday. It would be all right. She nodded, feeling shy.

'What are we doing two miles up a hill?' he said despairingly. 'What has made me bring you here instead of taking you to the bottom of the hotel garden and kissing you, as I have wanted to ever since I saw you on the hill?'

'Eyes crossed and about to keel over?' She was holding his hands.

'And much less frightening than the so distinguished business-woman I thought I knew.' He kissed her hard. 'Let's go down.'

They had arrived back at the hotel a great deal faster than they had gone up. He had checked, momentarily shy, but she had taken charge, desperate to be with him, and had collected her key and taken him upstairs to her suite where *she* found her courage evaporating. It was nearly punctured by a message from Hugh, which, typically of him, was prefaced by the reassuring statement that there was no emergency.

She hid it in the blotter and turned to face Ferenc, who took her in his arms unhestitatingly and started to take off her clothes for her, so that in thirty seconds they were on the hard double bed, kicking the lumpy duvet out of the way, desperate to get close to each other. He made her lie face down at first, so that he could kiss her spine, but she felt strange and self-conscious and uneasy and turned over to face him.

'I will be too quick,' he said urgently. 'Lie there.'

He was all over her, she thought, momentarily frightened dazed by the warm, hard feel of him but the whole of her skin seemed to have become wonderfully sensitive. She felt his hand move down between her legs where she was swollen and hard and wet, and he kissed her stomach, then moved down so that his tongue was on the centre of the swelling. She tensed, momentarily self-conscious, but he was so assured and so certain of what he was doing that she stopped trying and arched her back against the bed as he brought her close, then stopped, then did it again, then took her over the top so that she cried out.

'Ferenc.' She reached for him, but he had got a condom on and was kissing her on the lips, his own wet and salt-tasting.

'I may turn you over?'

'Yes. Oh, yes.' She turned over and came up on her knees, spine arched, so that he could come into her. She came again as he pushed, his hands holding her hips, and was still feeling the echoing aftermath when he came, loudly and pleasurably, ending up lying along her back, kissing the side of her cheek.

CHAPTER EIGHTEEN

July 1990

David Banner sat at his desk in his small, cluttered office, trying to ignore Michael Daws MP, his room-mate, who was losing his temper on the phone with a demanding constituent. His head ached; he had been up too late and had drunk too much the night before, as so often when the House was sitting late. He picked through his constituency mail; even the gratifying subserviency of most of the requests, coupled with assurances that only he could intervene to right this particular wrong, failed to cheer him. The truth was, he acknowledged painfully, that all he was doing – if, indeed, he managed to accomplish any of the things with which his help was sought – was to move a few pushy, demanding people ahead of an otherwise patient queue of constituents waiting for operations, jobs, houses and invalidity benefit. He could do nothing to change the system and precious little to change the way it operated; you would have to be in power to do any of that. He glanced again at the pile of newspapers, reluctant to start on his letters, and was momentarily cheered; with a 15 per cent lead in the opinion polls and the country deeply fed up with Mrs T, it could only be a matter of time before his side did have power. And he had his feet on the first fragile rung, he was part of the Shadow Defence team, a very junior part, but he was the only one with real military experience and it was a winning card every time. It ought to be good enough to get him a PPS job when they were the Government and *then* he would be a step closer to being able to change things and make policy. Hopefully it was just a question of waiting and being patient, but he had never been any good at either.

He seized his Dictaphone and dictated answers to the substantial pile of letters on his table, ignoring his room-mate. He had had to listen to him telephoning half the day, and in fact he was at it again, only this time speaking very softly, his back turned. A woman, David diagnosed instantly, someone with whom Daws was having a walk-out. He finished his letters and piled them up in a folder with the tape, then looked up to find his room-mate looking something between furtive and triumphant.

'Women, eh?' he said hopefully, watching David for a reaction.

'Problems?' David asked obligingly. He found it difficult to imagine what worthwhile bird would enmesh herself with Michael, who was about five foot five inches in built-up heels, balding and carrying too much weight, but the magic suffix 'MP' gave the most unprepossessing types an edge.

'Usual thing, you know,' the man said anxiously. 'They get bored, don't they, and they can't understand that you can't duck out of a vote to do things with them or bring them in to the House all the time. And there's the press to worry about, of course.'

It was stretching credulity too far, David thought savagely, to suppose that anything involving Michael Daws, short of Satanism in the Chamber with a coterie of much better-known MPs, would be of interest to the press, but he assented politely. There was no point in making an enemy gratuitously and the man was otherwise harmless, even if he did creep a bit to the union barons. If he wanted to feel he was living dangerously, let him.

He picked up a couple of resident difficulties out of his in-tray and decided that he might as well throw them away, there was absolutely nothing he could do for Mrs Ross and her schizophrenic son; he had already shamed the local manifestation of the NHS into doing all they were going to do. What was needed was the local mental hospital back again, so that overstretched Social Services would not have to try and deal with people who were incapable of coping with themselves outside the secure walls of an institution. One day, the Ross son, a big, strong, hopelessly mad twenty-three-year-old, would kill himself or his mother and that would resolve the situation. A solution worthy of the nineteenth century in which so many Conservative values seemed to be rooted.

He threw the letter into a briefcase; his last, best hope was that Ann would be able to think of something, or pull some local string he could not. He rang his home number, desperate for comfort. He had already talked to Ann earlier that morning, but she would not be surprised. Even when he rang several times a day she always found something to tell him, but the number rang on and he realized she must be out. He rose restlessly to his feet, suddenly maddened by the small, untidy office. He needed to get out; there were plenty of people who would have been glad to have lunch with him but he could think of no one he wanted to see. On impulse he decided to walk up to Redwood's and buy himself a bar lunch and see who was there. If Jens was around she would feed him. So would Paul, or Sean, or, of course. Mickey. He didn't want to have lunch with Mickey and be anxiously interrogated about how he was getting on, the questions charged and fuelled uncomfortably by jealousy, but he would take his chance. He checked his wallet and hesitated; lunch at Redwood's would cost him £10 whatever he did, whereas he could eat for £2 in the Commons canteen. And there he might sit next to one of the powers in the party, not the leader, of course, who hardly ever came there, but some of the Shadow Cabinet. He saw himself, just for a minute, edging closer in the queue, casually trying to find a space on this table, and rebelled; it was like school except that at school other boys had usually wanted to sit next to him.

I need a treat, he thought, I need to be asked for *Any Questions*, or *Newsnight* again, or something better than the local radio in Leeds. But none of that was forthcoming either. The telephone rang and he picked it up hopefully, but it was his mother, bored, he understood immediately, and resentful that he had not rung her for at least a fortnight. She was another of the duties that he hoped Ann had taken over, but he knew this was unreasonable. It would be impossible to explain his depression to her; she only wanted to hear good news of solid progress, so he grimly invented as much of that as he could bear to, and sent his regards to his stepfather. For whom, he reminded himself as he put the phone down, he should give thanks every day; the burden of responsibility for his mother would otherwise have been squarely his, since she did not want Mickey – and never had – and bloody Thomas had escaped to Australia straight after leaving school.

He walked to Redwood's to burn off energy and lift his depression and found his spirits raised by the purposeful pre-lunch bustle and the glittering, military neatness of the polished brass and the white napkins. He gazed round proprietorially and asked for Jens, suffering a pang of disappointment on being told that she was still away in Czechoslovakia and that Mr Seles was not booked today. He had been banking on seeing Jens or Paul and was depressed.

'David Banner.' It was a pleased, female voice, and he turned to see, moving his whole body in the relief of finding someone to lift this dark mood.

'You don't remember me.'

'Oh yes, I do. Alison. How nice to see you.' He kissed her cheek happily, unable to remember whether they were on those terms, but knowing it did not matter, no female person had ever flinched from his touch. 'But I haven't seen you for a very long time,' he said.

'No, that's right.' She was a beauty, he thought admiringly, with that black hair and long legs. 'We were in America for a couple of years. I've been shopping.' A long hand indicated a substantial pile of carrier bags which the receptionist was disposing patiently in the inadequate space behind the counter. 'I came in because I hoped to find Jens, but I understand she doesn't get back till tomorrow.'

'I hoped to find her or Paul Seles.' He hesitated fractionally.

'I'll buy you lunch instead.'

'Don't be silly, we've got an account here. But I'd *love* to have lunch with you. I was just crossly going to ask for a paper.'

He laughed, charmed and raised immediately out of his depression. 'Great treat for me too. I suppose *I* was going to go crossly back to the House.' It was automatic, he thought wryly, to remind everyone that he was a top person, a real live MP.

'Well, you don't have to do that just yet, do you?' Alison said, unimpressed, and he remembered that her husband – name like Michael – was a rising star in Shell and knew all the MPs he needed to. 'Gerard, I'm not booked, but can I have my table? You are kind. And the usual.'

The usual appeared to be champagne, and he felt the corners of his mouth lift in a smile. They talked hard through the soup and the delicious fish; they had decided to have the same thing without consulting each other and his spirits had risen even further.

'David, tell me something.'

'Anything.' He was watching her mouth, long and curvy, with a trace of dark red lipstick still adhering on the upper lip.

'When we first met – at the Frenches – we got on tremendously well, didn't we?'

'I was remembering the tennis court,' he acknowledged promptly.

'Yes.' She hesitated. 'We went out twice, then you vanished. What happened?'

It was extraordinary that this beautiful woman, who could have had anyone in London, remembered a teenage disappointment, he thought, dazed.

'Was there another girl?'

'That's right. I had a girlfriend,' he said, deciding in a split second that the truth was going to play much better than any other explanation. 'I fancied you rotten but, well . . .'

'So you didn't go on?' She smiled, looking into his eyes. 'Actually, that's rather nice.'

'I'm sorry, I didn't explain at the time. Teenage boys are pretty hopeless, though, aren't they?'

'Oh God, yes. I *couldn't* go through all that again. Honestly, David, I think I'd just skip the whole thing and wait till I was old enough to go out with men. That's what I tell my daughter, who's thirteen now.'

'If she looks anything like you, she has *absolutely* no hope of avoiding the attentions of just such gauche teenagers as I was.'

She burst out laughing through a last sip of champagne. 'Oh, Christ.' She mopped herself up and blew her nose, unself-consciously, on the napkin. 'It *is* good to see you again, David. Oh, God, it's nearly three o'clock. Michael's in Indonesia and the kids are at school, of course, but I suppose I'd better get on. And you need to vote or something, don't you?'

'I believe that the nation's business might manage to transact itself without me – at least for a bit. You wouldn't like to come for a walk?' He held his breath, watching her, totally involved and wholly alive. He had kept the promise he had made to Ann three years before; he had never, even in his desperate need to keep her, committed himself not to have another affair ever, but he had undertaken never to embarrass her again. And he hadn't; he had managed a couple of brief walk-outs with women in London, outside politics, whose paths would not cross Ann's, and she had, he was sure, known nothing about them. It had been difficult in both cases to keep the affairs sufficiently compartmentalized from his busy politi-cal life; it had required a lot of rushing about, but he had promised. But this was dangerous territory. Ali was very close to Jens and always had been, and any indiscretion would get back to her. Ali's husband was politically active and unlikely to be complaisant if he ever found out.

'Mm.' She looked into his eyes. 'Well . . . yes, I would, but I'm not going to be much use with all these parcels.'

'They'll keep them for you for an hour.' He could feel the adrenaline flowing and everything seemed suddenly very sharp and hard-edged and his heart was thumping.

'Tell you what,' she said, calling for the bill. 'Let's take them back to my house in a cab, *then* we'll have a walk. Yes?'

'Yes,' he said on an indrawn breath, knowing where the

afternoon was going to end. He went off to the Gents, a spring in his step, smiling easily at the faces turned to him in half-recognition, and had a pee and a wash, and checked that there were two condoms in the inner part of his wallet. He grinned secretly at the mirror, anxiety and depression banished, launched on a new adventure.

Paul Seles sat in his big car considering the selection of correspondence Sheena had thought he should see. The news was good, and would be better when he was able to announce the two joint ventures he had negotiated in Czechoslovakia and in Hungary. Nothing could be more fashionable than investment in Eastern Europe; bankers and consultants were everywhere this year, desperate to get into the territories that had been virtually closed to the West for so long. They were going to have some serious disappointments, of course, you needed his kind of background experience to make the right deals, but he had been in and out of these countries in the fourteen years since he was a twenty-year-old just out of Borstal. He knew what was worth buying and what wasn't, and what would be nice, but you would have to take on too many of the old, corrupt guard to make it worthwhile. It would all need cash, of course, that was why you could get the deals, people there were desperate for the hard Western currencies and for access to Western markets, but his bankers would find that he had a good story to tell them. And he knew perfectly well that they got a bang out of dealing with an ex-Borstal boy, and that they told each other that you needed someone like Paul Seles to cope with the emerging East European mafias. Well, that was true; none of these nicely brought up Englishmen would be able to deal with the people who counted.

He glanced at his watch; he and Jens had caught an earlier plane than they had planned and one of the messages waiting for him had been to say that Sheena had not managed to contact Maddy with their change of plan. She probably had not tried very hard; she was both jealous and disapproving of his wife and probably hoped that if he got home early he would find Maddy with a lover or two. He felt a momentary uncomfortable twinge and distracted himself by remembering Jens meeting him in Poprad to fly back to Prague. She had arrived in Ferenc's BMW and he had understood immediately that they were lovers; his stolid, determined sister had looked pink and pretty and relaxed. And Ferenc had been nice with her; making sure she had all her parcels and kissing her hand in farewell in the correct old-fashioned salutation for a married woman. He had teased her about it, amused, and not displeased to have something on Jens who could be intolerably prissy about his behaviour. She had been extremely self-conscious at first but had relaxed enough to tell him it had been nice and that she had liked being in bed with Ferenc. She had not asked him not to tell Hugh but then she did not have to.

Maddy's car was out, he realized, irritated, the garage left open to reveal his own car. The car they kept for the nanny was also missing so not even the children were there. He banged into the house to find it empty except for the house-keeper who was having a quiet sit over a cup of tea, and watched the driver dump his suitcases.

'I won't go into the office,' he said on impulse. 'I'll be here. I'll ring and tell them.' He accepted tea and sat on the bed watching TV while the housekeeper unpacked for him, taking everything to be dry-cleaned. Maddy was due back in an hour; she had gone to have lunch with a friend, apparently. He knew where she kept her diary and took it out to look; she was having lunch with a Diana Fell, so *that* was all right, but the name was half familiar and he frowned, trying to remember. Not one of her regular friends. He flopped back a couple of pages and found a sheet of headed paper, the beginning of a letter in Maddy's writing. It was addressed to this Diana she was lunching with and he felt his heart thump and his face go scarlet as he read. Why was the silly bitch consulting a solicitor? How did she think she was going to make *him* leave the house? She'd never prove anything, no one could know for sure about him and Sheena. And what the fuck was this about mental cruelty to her and actual cruelty to Stephen? He read the letter, which stopped after six paragraphs of Maddy's childish handwriting, three times before he grasped the full inwardness of it and then he was seized by black, wretched desolation from which the only escape was rage. *This* was why Maddy had not come on holiday with him, he raged self-righteously; she had hoped he would take Sheena and give her evidence, instead of going blamelessly off with Jens, who had, like all women, unkindly taken *her* opportunity to deceive her husband, much though old Hugh had it coming. But none of the anger was any good; it left him beached and sick, and chewing on the unmistakable harsh reality that his wife no longer wanted him anywhere in her life and had waited patiently for her opportunity to invoke professionals and strangers to help her escape.

He told the housekeeper brusquely to go, he would take the family down the road to the restaurant when they got back, and bundled the woman out, ignoring her doubtful protests. Then he poured himself an enormous whisky and read the letter again, and waited in the kitchen until he heard the door of Maddy's car slam and could see her walk slowly towards the door, beautiful, slim and desirable in the summer sun, chewing her lower lip.

'I'm having some difficulty in establishing why you are getting margins on your products about twice those of your competitors.' The woman journalist was courteous, unruffled and persistent, and Mickey Banner was starting to fray. He slid his jacket off, looking wistfully out at the lake glistening in the bright light of the early evening, and bent his mind again to the question. This was the second time this woman had rung him.

'Our finance director will be back tomorrow if it is too difficult.' A bit of well-placed rudeness seemed justified.

'Well, it *is* all a bit incomprehensible, isn't it?' The clear, educated voice was unruffled. 'I have to say that the answer is not obvious; you seem to have discovered the secret of defying gravity. Everyone *else's* margins are being hideously squeezed yet the Seles Group is sailing along still making increased profits. And yet you are in the same markets.'

Mickey leapt thankfully to the defence. 'Yes, indeed we are. Our secret — not that it's much of a secret — is that our costs are lower. We have three plants in Czechoslovakia and two in Hungary.'

'Yes.' The bloody woman sounded not at all convinced. 'I know labour costs are lower there, but your employees would have to be working for free to sustain the margins you're getting.'

'We have also had the benefit of long-term contracts to supply.' He had listened to Sean or Paul enough times to be familiar with the official line, but as he spoke the words he was assailed by doubt about which long-term contracts were yielding those margins.

'Don't understand that.' The voice was undiminishedly cheerful. 'In a recession those sorts of contracts get renegotiated. How have you managed to hold on to them?'

'I really think you would be better talking to Sean Kelly or Paul Seles. They are both abroad but Paul is expected back tomorrow.' The silence at the other end of the line was almost palpable and he cast round for some more positive way of ending the conversation. 'You can always take the view that profits are a statement of opinion. As a statement of fact, however, the company is cash-rich.'

'I suppose that's true,' Miss whatever-her-name-was said blithely. 'But I can ring Mr Seles and ask him to explain how he's managing *that*.'

The sarcastic bitch thought she was talking to the office boy, rather than the top human and public relations man for the Seles Group, Mickey thought angrily as he put the phone down. He was chronically insecure about his own status, but drew comfort from reciting a private mantra listing his £60,000 a year salary, twice brother David's, his BMW and his substantial office with its view over the lake. He had told the journalist the truth — and an important truth, too — that there was no cash shortage; the rocky days of lying to creditors were gone three years ago and these days bills were paid taking only an orthodox forty-five days' credit from suppliers. *That*, he fancied, was at least partly down to his own representations in 1987; you really could not run something the size and standing of the Seles Group with writs flying about, he had said, and Paul and Sean had listened to him for once.

He stared out of the window, still angered by his failure to deal with the journalist, deciding he must go through the accounts with Sean, so that he was able, himself, to be more convincing. The trouble was, he really did not understand the company's finances and no one would tell him much about them.

He was distracted by noises outside his office and the familiar unintelligible Irish greeting delivered with the back teeth clamped together. 'Sean,' he said, erupting from his office, 'I didn't realize you were back today. There's a journalist we need to deal with.'

Sean's habitually gloomy expression intensified as he explained the point at issue. 'I'll not ring *her*. De bitch can ring me if she wants.'

Mickey opened his mouth to suggest that this might not be the best way of handling relationships with City journalists, but was forestalled by Sean's secretary, as insularly Irish as he. 'Sandy on the phone. It's the fifth time he's rung today.' Sean's mouth compressed. 'I'll take it.' He pushed past Mickey into his own office and kicked the door shut.

'A friend, perhaps?' he suggested urbanely to Sean's secretary, who lifted her head from the desk with a look of scorn that made him wish he had kept his mouth shut. They stuck together, the Irish, it was no good trying to draw Eileen into any comment on Sean's sexual proclivities, though she knew all about them. He had once emerged very late from his office to find her watching Sean effing and blinding round the room and observing that there would be another lad along where *that* one had come from.

'You're expected for dinner, Mickey. Your wife asked if I would remind you,' Eileen said, watching him trying to decide whether to wait and catch Sean when he finished his phone call.

A crack like a shotgun going off made them both jump, and

Paul Seles shouldered his way through the door. They gaped at him; his dark hair was standing up, unbrushed, and there were patches of scarlet in his normally sallow cheeks. He strode past them both to his own office without a greeting, and the main door crashed shut behind him. Mickey, not wanting to miss a drama, stood hopefully, and Sean appeared from his office, wordlessly raising his eyebrows at Eileen.

'No idea,' Eileen said to Sean, as a further crash from inside the office made them all jump.

'I'll wait.' Sean retired to his office while Eileen returned collectedly to the task of tidying her desk, and Mickey craned to see what was going on. The door of Paul's office suite banged in his face but not before he had seen Sheena rise from her desk, startled, and take Paul in her arms, and heard, incredibly, the sound of sobbing. He stood irresolute and miserable, the childhood terror of being excluded from something that was going to matter, keeping him rooted to the spot. But there was nothing for him here, with two firmly closed doors, and Eileen collecting her coat to go home, so after a few minutes he trailed reluctantly off to his car.

Jens let herself into the house, the company driver behind her carrying a case and two bags. The children flung themselves on her and she hugged them and decided that she might not be an unnatural mother after all. Eight days away and she felt loving, competent and able to take charge of her life, she thought exultantly, as she buried her face in their warm necks and blew, in the time-honoured game, making them giggle. Perhaps that was why women had lovers, so that they could feel appreciated and central rather than appearing as exhausted, under-achieving drudges on roller-skates.

'Granny and Granpa Josh are here,' William confided in tones likely to blast an eardrum.

'That's nice,' she said tranquilly, good temper undisturbed even by this piece of news. 'Where's Daddy?'

'He's coming home soon.' Both children were watching her a little anxiously, she realized.

'Let's go and see Granny.' At least they had had the decency to let the children receive her by themselves, she thought, and set William and Sara to searching her luggage for their presents while she headed to the kitchen to find her mother.

It was due to no such delicacy of consideration that they had not come to greet her at the front door, she realized, answering their distracted questions about her holiday. The atmosphere of a row hung unmistakably in the air, try though they might.

'Where is Susan?' The most likely candidate for the other half of a row was the children's nanny, but she could give as good as she got.

'It's her evening class. We arranged to come some time ago so Hugh could go out to a reception.' Her mother had read her mind.

'The children said Hugh would be late.' She bent down to scoop up Sara who was wrapped in the piece of embroidery that had been the only thing in the Tatras she could think of to buy for a little girl. As she straightened with her arms full of child, she saw Joshua, in a black temper.

'Yes,' he said, clearing his throat. 'Yes. We won't wait for him, Jennifer, if that's all right.'

'Of course.' She helped to package them into their outdoor clothes, read to the children and unpacked and sat down in the quiet house to try to let the events of the last week settle. In the event Paul had been delayed three days in Poprad, so she and Ferenc had had an uninterrupted seventy-two hours together. They had been in bed every minute of the hours of darkness, but had spent the daytime hours outside, in deference to his need to discharge energy. No one in the hotel could have been in the smallest doubt about what was happening, but *that* did not matter. Paul had guessed immediately, and she did feel a small nagging inconvenient guilt about that, but by and large she was pleased with herself for having handled a holiday affair with poise and competence. She heard Hugh's key in the lock and went to open the door for him and kiss him.

'What happened?' she said, feeling his chest sag as he exhaled a huge, tired sigh.

'Oh, everything. I have to get in early tomorrow, sterling's still fragile. I decided to come home rather than sit and worry until Tokyo opens. The Chancellor, sensible man, went home too.'

'I'm sorry about sterling.' They had moved to the kitchen, and she was heating up the soup that had been served in Redwood I that evening.

'Yes. And I had a row with your parents.'

'I thought there was an atmosphere. A row about me, as usual?'

'No. About me. What a rotten father I was and how I neglected the children. Not you at all.'

'Why don't you just tell them to bugger off?' She was surprised by the speed of her own reaction. However cross she got with Hugh for putting the Treasury first, second and third, he was a good father, loving and imaginative and hard-working, and bloody Joshua of all people was not going to be allowed to make him miserable.

'Oh.' He looked hunted. 'You're always so black and white about it. And you've got some tiresome allies too.' He was eating in the manner of a man who had missed several meals. 'Paul, to name but six.'

She absolutely declined the quarrel, still hugging her cheerfulness to her. 'Paul does not feel free to tell me what to do with my life.' She considered. 'No, he does, but I don't feel obliged to take any notice.'

'Did he come back with you from the Tatras?' Hugh conceded the point tacitly.

'Yes. And guess whom we met out there? Our old friend Ferenc. From Gundels. Back from the USA and with his own restaurant in Budapest.' She covered the statement by spooning more soup into his plate.

'Was he walking too?'

'Not exactly walking. He was far too fast for Paul and me.' She crossed her fingers in her apron pocket as she had when she was a child being economical with the truth. 'Tell me about sterling.'

He laughed, and she saw that the worn look was easing. 'I'd much rather just sit on the sofa with you. I have to watch the news, but we could do that together. Could I have a drink? Quite right to feed me soup first, but I need a bloody great Scotch. And a cuddle.' He held out his arms and she went into them, finding with guilty interest that it was simply a pleasant experience.

The phone rang and they both looked at it inimically, but the long habit of discipline in a household with two careerists held, and she picked it up.

'Maddy?' she said, surprised. 'What's the matter? Sorry, they didn't give me the message, I'm only just back. Oh, God. Where *is* Paul? No, he's not here, I haven't seen him since we landed at Heathrow.' She listened, wretched, for what felt like several hours. 'Yes, of course you had to. I am sorry. And I will call if Paul gets in touch. Talk to you tomorrow, yes.'

She put the phone down, cold all over, and burrowed into Hugh's warm, familiar arms. 'He beat Maddy up – he found out she'd been to see a lawyer about a divorce. Then he attacked the nanny when *she* got back and then had a go at Stephen, then ran. She's changed the locks, Maddy, I mean. My poor Paul.'

Hugh held her as she wept. 'How is everyone else?'

'Maddy has a broken arm. The nanny is bruised, but Stephen is not much hurt, because Maddy and the nanny intervened, very bravely, I must say. I'm the only person who can cope with Paul in a rage.' She felt him stiffen.

'Now, that is one illusion I'd like you to abandon. Paul is dangerously violent, and I've told you that before. You two think you've got a magic relationship which no one else understands.'

'You're jealous,' she said stiffly, pulling away from him.

'Yes. And fed up with you seeing everything from his point of view. Maddy has had a terrible time with him. Anyone else would have left long ago.' He sighed. 'I shouldn't have let you go on holiday with him. It's time you both grew up. He'll *use* it somewhere, Jens.'

'You could have taken me on holiday if you feel so badly. You knew I was desperate to go away.' She would willingly have hit him in guilty acknowledgement that he was right and that she had given another hostage to fortune.

She stamped up to their bedroom, raging, the warm cheerful feeling of being loved and in control quite vanished. She sank down on the bed, cold even on this warm evening, longing to be back in the uncomplicated Tatras where no one knew who she was, where the restaurants were a distant pleasure, rather than an ever-present worry, and where she had someone whom she wanted as much as he wanted her. Somehow, with Ferenc, it had been possible to say exactly what she wanted in bed. He was, of course, skilled and interested and experienced, but above all he gave her confidence, not least because she could hardly keep her hands off him, and she had been resigned to missing that particular emotion. And it all had a great deal to do with her being uprooted, childless and single again, away from home and its heavy, ceaseless responsibilities, and having all day and night to do simple physical things like walking, having baths and making love. The classic agony-aunt response to her problem she thought, leaning against the pillow, was to use this new-found ability to get and give pleasure to the resident man, and she could start now, at least with a kiss. She pulled herself off the bed and made for the door, but as she opened it she heard the news and could see through a half-open living-room door her husband sitting tense in front of the television, portable phone in his hand. She retreated again, shutting the door on a familiar face, talking obsessively about sterling.

CHAPTER NINETEEN

May 1992

It was a bit damp on the new terrace at Dellingham Hall but, as Paul had observed, you could be sure you weren't being overheard. Anyone who wanted to talk to you had to walk twenty yards to the sheltered corner which housed a decent-sized dining table. It also meant every plate, knife or glass had to be carried some distance, but that was what staff were for.

'We must bring Jens out here next time,' Paul said, looking gratefully at the beautifully arranged plate in front of him. 'Bella really knows how to cook. Mind you, Jens wouldn't believe me. She thinks everyone from Czechoslovakia was trained in the Tatras.' He sneaked a look at Sean who was staring, unseeing, at his plate. He sighed and laid down his fork. 'Sorry, mate, but you heard the man. Production cut right back, only known customers, preferably members of the Government get any of it. And Vlad can't reveal who his ultimate customer is, now can he?'

'De factory needs de business. Dere putting yer people out of work.'

'But that's what happens when you get politicians with ideals, mate. Havel doesn't want to head a country whose principal export is arms and explosives. So he regulates where it goes, and starts off with the basic stuff like Semtex.' He lowered his voice automatically on the word.

A long, awkward silence fell, broken only by the sound of the birds singing in the trees. Paul doggedly started to eat but Sean sat staring out over his loaded plate.

'De ting is, Paul, dere's people expecting it.'

'Well, they can't bloody have it, can they? You need a permit and you're not going to get one.'

'Yer man, dis morning. Was he not suggesting dere was another way?'

Sean never missed a trick, cunning little bogtrotter that he was, Paul thought angrily. He had been speaking Hungarian with the morning's visitor whose first language it had been, but even so, Sean had managed to understand the gist of the conversation.

'It's the same way it's always been. There's a few lads in that factory in Martin who'll load a lorry after hours for you and tell the foreman several tons melted into the river in the night. But you and I are legitimate businessmen and we don't do that, not any more. Particularly not where we have a shareholding in the factory.' He looked at Sean; no stranger would have been able to sense anything from that impassive expression, but he had known him for fifteen years. 'We can't afford it, Sean. We're taking the bankers out there for a jolly and they have to see smiling faces, top politicians, get their hands shaken by Havel . . . and all that. So they go home knowing their money is safe and their good selves well appreci- ated, and they can make speeches at the Rotary about "our contribution to Eastern Europe".' His tone would have curdled milk, but Sean did not respond.

'Dere's people looking for dat stuff,' he said obstinately, picking at the edge of his plate.

'Well, you'll just have to explain. This'll blow over. Havel will stop playing silly buggers as soon as he runs short of foreign currency.'

'Dese people, dey don't understand when you explain.'

Sean, he realized, might be here in body but in spirit he was a long way away. 'What have they got on you, Sean?' He needed Sean, needed him back in action with his mind on the job. 'It isn't money, is it?'

Sean shook his head scornfully, and Paul sighed. Money he could arrange, but Sean had all the careful, prudent meanness of the peasant; his substantial earnings were carefully invested in property which paid him decent rents in good times and in bad. He had substantial shareholdings in the Seles Group as well; no, it wouldn't be money.

'It's personal.'

'How?'

Sean pushed his plate away and gazing fixedly at the spot where it had been, proceeded to explain near inaudibly while Paul, from long experience, managed to extract the salient points. It had all started two years ago when the Seles Group had bought a shareholding in a factory in Slovakia which manufactured Semtex among other things. He knew the factory well; he had been a customer when he was a freelance, barely out of his teens, and the Seles Group had done years of proper, legitimate, officially permitted business with it, before being allowed to buy a shareholding. But in 1990 Sean had inconveniently fallen in love with Sandor Thokoly, a Hungarian with a Turkish mother, a boy of twenty at the time, appallingly good-looking, with black curly hair and thick long eyelashes, six inches taller than Sean, slim and clear-skinned. Sean had obviously felt he'd won the pools, he slavered around this Sandy, who was inevitably involved with the trade in arms to the Near East. Paul had never made up his mind whether Sandy was with Sean entirely for his contacts or whether there was some real affection. Not that it would have mattered; before he had even noticed enough to utter a warning, they had become a couple and Sean had bought Sandy a flat in Budapest. They quarrelled like a married pair and went everywhere they could together which, interestingly, did not include anywhere near Jens Redwood. She had met Sandy, had memorably taken against him and was still hoping, aloud, that Sean would grow out of him. The only result of this pious hope had been to drive a wedge between her and Sean who was not prepared to tolerate Sandy being so spectacularly unwelcome. It was a nuisance and he felt Jens might have been more tolerant and less prissy, given what *she* was up to with Ferenc.

Paul had dealt with a request that the company in Slovakia

would supply Sandy's unnamed associates by introducing Sandy and a couple of more serious men, older, plainer and harder, to his biggest Hungarian customer, a man who, like Paul in his youth, would supply anything to anyone. This arrangement had presumably been operating smoothly for the last eighteen months, but the company which owned the factory was now not allowed to supply anything to anyone without a permit which specified the end-user. The Hungarian, who had enough legitimate customers to keep him going, wasn't going to risk his business by deceiving the authorities, which left Sandy out in the cold. And rather than find an alternative source, the idle, scheming, treacherous sod was putting pressure on Sean.

'Would Sandy really give you up, Sean?'

'He might not have de choice.' Paul saw, horrified, that Sean's hands were trembling. 'Dese people, dere saying dey'll hurt *him* if dey don't get supplied.'

One might have known, Paul thought, in impatient pity. Sean could not cope with the thought of pain inflicted on something he loved. There would be no point urging him to call their bluff. 'Well, we'll just have to find him another supplier, won't we?'

'Where?' It was pathetic to see the colour come back into Sean's face.

'Outside Slovakia, of course, for the moment. The Ukraine, I guess. Tell them – tell whoever – it'll take a few weeks.'

'Tanks, Paul.' He looked unseeingly at his congealing food, and Paul went over to the house and shouted to Bella to replace it with a fresh plate, which Sean promptly wolfed. 'Dat's better,' he said, pushing the empty plate away with a sideways look. 'I've been worried.'

This understatement made Paul shout with laughter so that Sean had reluctantly to join in, and they sat in amity, looking over the garden.

'Coming on well, dem trees.' Sean had the Irishman's eye for a well-cultivated piece of land and was always interested in new planting.

'Yes.' Maddy had not in the event been interested in keeping Dellingham Hall so he had bought her the house she wanted in Holland Park, near all her friends and schools for the children. He still felt sullen when he thought of it; she had chosen the house and he had agreed, expecting to finance it entirely on mortgage, but her bitch solicitor had insisted that the house be Maddy's alone, entirely free of charges. That had left him seriously strapped for cash since he was not prepared to bring any over from the East and he had had to borrow further against his own shares in the company. In futile revenge for that and for the undeniable, miserable, still unpalatable fact that Maddy no longer wanted him anywhere in her life, he had moved his head office into the wing he had intended for the children and moved Sheena into the main house and his bedroom.

'The trees were my idea. Maddy always wanted to be able to see the little hill but I wanted a wind-break.'

Sean looked at him anxiously as he always did when Maddy was mentioned. She and Paul were still enmeshed in the divorce courts, and Sean retained enough of his Catholic upbringing to be acutely uncomfortable with the whole process. 'She going on all right, is she?'

'She's trying to rip my balls off in the settlement, if that's what you mean.'

She had gone for sole custody too, refusing even to consider joint custody, and he could foresee trouble with the access arrangements. She could, for all of him, keep Stephen, but he had to see Lily, and was, as his wife well knew, prepared to pay highly for this privilege. It was a sore place whenever he let himself think about it; he wanted beautiful Maddy, who was making it quite clear that she would rather never see him again, far more than he wanted Sheena, who was doing her best to become his second wife.

He considered Sean, who had gone back to his normal sallow colour and was fidgeting. Of course he wanted to make a phone call. He himself shared Jens's views about the meretricious and beautiful Sandy, and for one pleasurable moment he allowed himself to contemplate letting whoever was behind this have Sandy, but the price in terms of Sean's grief would have been too high. Apart from the fact that he loved the little bogtrotter, he needed him to handle the substantial acquisition they were going to do, bankers permitting.

'Right. Back to work.' He too had a few phone calls to make and it was a real bugger getting through anywhere in the Ukraine.

'We would be off the record, Simon, right? Any record.'

'Agreed. This is for background, strictly.'

And that was as good as he was going to get, but it would do. This particular journalist could be trusted if you used the well-understood conventions.

'Do you want to do it over lunch, or your office?'

David considered, with hostility, his room-mate, hunched over papers. 'Lunch. I'll pay for my own.'

'You don't have to do that,' Simon Dearsley said casually. 'The Beeb do pay my expenses. Do you know Redwood's?'

'Indeed I do. Jens Redwood and I were children together. Yes. One o'clock?' He put the phone down, feeling imperceptibly less miserable. He had put a brave face on the defeat inflicted on his party four weeks before, but he had truly believed that they were going to make it, just, and possibly with a helping hand from the Lib Dems, and he was still recovering from the shock of finding the old guard with an overall majority. He walked into Redwood's and saw his host perched at the bar, reading three newspapers at once, just like a politician. He greeted the man cordially, straightening unconsciously. You did not see on the TV that this chap was a good two inches taller than him, moving easily inside his expensive clothes which hid a bit of a bulge at the belt; well, none of these media people took any real exercise. He ordered the steak and refused alcohol; he had found himself drinking at lunch ever since the election, and however friendly an interview this was, Simon Dearsley was fundamentally the enemy and alert for signs of weakness.

343

They chatted through the first course, exchanging details of families and background; Simon Dearsley had been at Winchester and had all too obviously just about heard of David's old school, Ashford, but that was par for the course and, indeed, one of the reasons why he had joined the political party he had. But they were the same age and their children were as well, and inevitably they knew a lot of the same people.

When their steaks arrived, Simon Dearsley visibly but inoffensively shifted gear and started to probe for David's views on the April débâcle.

'Well, it wasn't as bad as you're making it sound,' he protested. 'We managed to reduce a majority of over a hundred to twenty-one. They're going to find *that* difficult to work with – and the Lib Dems fell apart.'

'They always get squeezed in a tight election. No, I agree; it wasn't the Yellow Peril that caused the Labour Party to lose this time, when every economic circumstance meant they should have won.'

David took a long drink of mineral water to give himself time. 'It's possible that the very dreadfulness of the economy worked against us.'

'It was a great help, of course, to propose a major tax increase four weeks before the election. So people who were already struggling to keep their heads above water could see themselves drawn under sure as fate,' Simon Dearsley said, swift as a snake.

'There was *that*, of course,' David said, at last feeling the adrenalin start to dissipate the depression. 'That went over big. And then there was Sheffield, where we had the drinks and stood down the sentries a week before the battle.'

The long-nosed, serious face relaxed into a smile of great charm. 'Did you think you were going to win?'

'Yes, I did.' It was a sickening relief to confess, rather than to follow the carefully agreed line. 'We bloody deserved to. Neil deserved it.'

'Why did he let Smith produce that Shadow Budget, with all the vote-winning tax rises?'

'Oh, Simon, Christ! You've been a political journalist long enough. It was Agreed Policy, that we would raise child benefit and the old age pension. It was agreed in 1988.'

'When things looked rather different.'

'They did, didn't they? It looked *outrageous* then to drop the top tax rate down to forty per cent, and it seemed absolutely reasonable to shift it back up again to fifty per cent and put a bit more on National Insurance to pay for children and the old.'

'It wasn't a bit more, it was nine per cent. On people who hadn't been anywhere near the top rate of tax.'

'Simon, don't go on. I couldn't bear it.'

The man laughed and finished his steak, unhurried and watchful. 'I'm going to have coffee; I've got a dinner and I can't eat two puddings a day. But I am going to have a brandy, how about you?'

'Yes.'

'A stonking great brandy?'

'Absolutely.' They grinned at each other.

'So what happens now, David? To you, I mean?'

Ah, he thought, warmed by more than the excellent brandy. This is not just a discussion to enable a journalist to add another mind-blowingly tiresome piece about whither the Labour Party to the ever-growing pile. He rolled a sip of brandy on his tongue and put the glass down; he would need to concentrate.

'Well,' he said, trying to get the length of the bowling, 'there's a lot to do.'

'And not many good people to do it. What are your plans, David? Spokesman for Employment?'

Well, *that* was clear enough, and he decided on a small gamble. 'I think I've probably done all I can as a Defence Spokesman.'

'I agree. You did it very well; you sounded much more convincing than the Shadow Secretary when the Gulf War was on.'

'Well, I had served of course.'

'As I'm sure we all remembered.'

Fuck, David thought, then managed a grin. 'Yes, well, *that's* a good reason for moving.'

'Quite, or you'll get stuck. Well, you've done DTI as a junior as well. Will you make the Shadow Cabinet?'

'Not this year.' He had done his calculations. 'For that I need another job.' He paused. 'But not Employment.'

'Too close to the unions?'

The man was alight with interest and he felt his heart thump. 'That's right. If we're ever to be elected again we have to distance ourselves.'

'They could bury you, David.'

'Risk I'll have to take.'

Simon Dearsley took a small sip of his brandy; he, too, David saw, was going very carefully.

'Of course you're not sponsored, are you, David? Now, *that* was a good move. Leaves you in the perfect position to take a detached view – you know, unions are excellent things, important role to play in society but need to be independent.'

'Between ourselves, Simon, I tend to feel they should be abolished and their leaders – the ones who lost all the jobs in the seventies and are still there drawing fat salaries – drowned in the Thames.'

'Now, *that* you had better not say, not even to me.' Simon Dearsley was laughing. 'Can I suggest you try for Environment? Then when you get into the Shadow Cabinet you need one of the big ones, *not* DTI but one of the big three! How are you on economics? Worth learning some – enough for *Question Time* anyway.'

'Thanks Simon. I'll do that.'

'I'm writing something for the paper. It may help you. Another brandy?'

'Sofe. Lovely to see you. Smashing suit.'

Jens embraced her, casting off her various cares. They were in the office above Redwood's, the mother-ship. She stood back the better to admire her friend, who was still the same stocky shape she had always been but whose taste in clothes was so good and so developed that she always looked right. Sofia had skipped entirely the year's tentative attempt to make long skirts fashionable and was wearing a neat, knee-length skirt, beautifully cut, with a cardigan top, a silk shirt and wonderful jewellery. She hitched up her own long split skirt – at five foot eight inches in her socks she had felt she could afford to follow fashion, but seeing Sofia she wished she hadn't bothered. Sofia, who never paid a compliment unless it was sincerely meant, was at that moment engaged in exclaiming over a paperweight on her desk, so she wasn't overwhelmed by the long skirt either. Admitting to herself that she was hobbled by it and mentally consigning it to Oxfam, she smiled in real affection.

'Lunch now? How is John?'

Sofia had married the year before, just when they had all begun to feel that marriage was something she was not going to attempt. John was a fellow academic, ten years their senior, in a field of mathematics that Sofia had explained to her several times without leaving her any the wiser. It did not matter; the point about John was that he, although barely an inch taller than Sofia and slight, was emotionally another version of William French, kindly, clever, all-observing and infinitely tolerant, and they had all loved him at once.

'And how is Hugh?'

'Busy.' She considered, wearily, the old battleground; she ran a company with a turnover of £30 million but she had to get home to let a nanny off the hook while Hugh, who only ran an office, albeit that it was now the Chancellor's Press Office, seemed to consider himself excused from doing anything domestic. 'Do you know, Sofe, I think I've spent my entire married life chained to the pound.'

'That could go on,' Sofia said slowly.

'It could. He says it's very rocky – shaky, I mean. Much under pressure. In fact it's good that you're here today. You know I've been collecting advice on floating the company. It's beginning to look as if it won't work. I mean, everybody was very cheerful for about three weeks after the election, but bloody sterling is depressing them again. Or at least I *think* that's what they're saying.' She started to laugh. 'I forgot – you'll like this, Sofe – one of those sixteen-year-old yobs the brokers seem to employ told me earnestly that I'd need a lot of balls to float in this market. Then he remembered who he was talking to.'

'Dear God.'

'I know. They're all rather like that, except of course dear Charles. But anyway, Sofe. I'm afraid we may not be able to buy our diamonds this year.'

'That's all right. We can wait.'

That would be true, Jens thought, relieved, now that Sofia had her John who made very good money doing whatever it was he did.

'What about Lucy?' she asked, dreading the answer. 'I mean, I never expected she would have to wait more than ten years to get her money back.'

'Oh, but she did,' Sofia said, surprised. 'She always said it would take you longer than you had thought because you would be terribly anxious about letting go of control. Don't look like that, Jens, she also said that because you are as you are you wouldn't lose it for her, or let it moulder in things that were never going to be any good, like her wretched trustees.'

'Mm. Well, at least she's always had reasonable dividends. Except in 1988 of course,' she added guiltily. 'But look, I could find someone to buy some of her shares now, at a decent profit, if she is short.'

'No, she's OK, really she is, don't worry. You don't need cash, do you?'

'Well . . .' She thought of their sizeable mortgage, and with real unease of Albany Wharf with which she and Paul were still stuck. It would not sell nor let and there was no way it was worth anywhere near the value of the loan. She had always comforted herself for this folly, and avoided confessing it to Hugh, by promising herself that when Redwood's went public she and Paul would sell enough shares to pay off the loan from his pension fund, so that it would not nag away at her. Well, it would just have to wait; it had become £500,000 now, and she could not find even her half share. She knew, because she had had a row with Paul a few days ago, that he was in a worse situation than her. 'No, I could have done with it, to pay the mortgage. And the company needs to reduce debt so we can all get a decent dividend. And Paul always needs cash.'

'But your mother doesn't?'

'No. Joshua did very well right through the recession. And Sean, of course, is *very* careful.'

'Poor Sean.'

'Yes. Come on, lunch. I thought we'd eat downstairs if you don't mind. We are, as usual, short-handed and I didn't want to take someone off the floor to serve us up here.'

They headed into the restaurant to be received with the customary flourish accorded to the proprietor and she asked, as her custom was, to eat what Chef recommended. Any conscientious restaurateur had to know what Chef considered his best shot for the day and mercifully it was skate with black butter.

'That's David Banner over there, isn't it?' Sofia asked.

'I haven't got my glasses.' She could see perfectly and read the smallest print up to a range of about ten feet but beyond that things got a little blurred and she had to wear glasses to drive, but never seemed to have them outside the car. She squinted, recognizing the way the blond head moved.

'I'm very cross with him,' Sofia said severely, and Jens sat up, alert. Sofia was virtually never ruffled.

'Why?'

'Because of Ali.'

'What because of Ali?'

'Jens, can you really not have noticed that she was having an affair with him?'

'What? No! Is she?'

'Not any more. He dropped her. Not a word, not a phone call, after nearly eighteen months.'

'No!' She was utterly taken aback. Davey, whom she thought of as a brother, and Ali who was her friend. She gazed wildly down the restaurant as if illumination might be there, then pulled herself together and looked at Sofia.

'They both did their best to keep it from you, I expect,' Sofia said astringently, 'but I am still surprised they succeeded.'

'I've been so busy,' she said, thinking guiltily of the time she had spent with Ferenc over the past two years, then stopped in mid-bite as the implications of what she was being told came home to her.

'But that's awful of him,' she said childishly.

'Indeed it is. Dreadful for Ali.'

She and Sofia both knew beyond any need to refer to it, that Ali for all her dazzling looks had absolutely no real self-esteem and was liable to severe depressions.

'How is she?' she asked apprehensively.

'On anti-depressants again.'

'Oh dear. Oh, I am *sorry*, I'll go and see her.'

'Jens. What would be more to the point is to get David Banner to go and see her and explain himself. He said, apparently, that they would have to be very careful over the election period and of course he was right; there were some very dirty games going on, John says. But he never even phoned and he hasn't since.'

'And you want me to tackle him?'

'Somebody needs to, for Ali's sake.'

And as Sofia knows, Davey and I are close, Jens mused or I thought we were five years ago after Sara was born. She thought back to 1987, just after another general election when she had very nearly had Sara in her own private dining-room and Davey, strong and careful, had got her downstairs and lifted her into the ambulance. He had appeared in her hospital room the next day, Sara snuffling in a transparent plastic cot at the end of the bed and she sitting up in bed feeling pleased with herself. He had kissed her warmly and made rather proprietary overtures to Sara.

'You'll have another little someone of your own in six

months' time, Davey,' she had said amused but he had looked suddenly bleak and she had called for tea and admired the flowers.

'Is yours an unexpected pleasure?' she had asked, deciding the direct question was always better, and he had confirmed her guess. 'You'll like it when it gets here,' she had said, firmly, but he would not smile.

'We can't really afford another,' he had said abruptly, and she had tried to cheer him up, suggesting alternately that another baby wouldn't really cost anything, or not for years, given that Ann was already at home full-time, or that he could get a second job as many MPs did. 'Is Ann pleased?' she had asked finally, feeling suddenly tired and wishing he would either cheer up or go away, so that she could get a rest.

'Yes,' he had said wearily. 'Yes, she is. She wanted another one and I was in no position not to agree.' He had looked at her sideways and she had considered him, tiredness forgotten.

'Oh, *Davey*. What have you been up to?' She had known from Paul that Davey was given to women and extremely successful with them, but she had never really thought about him in that context; obviously too busy getting married and having children myself to be interested in other people's sex lives, she had reflected.

'Oh, the usual. Or to be fair a particularly ill-considered version of the usual. More or less on my own doorstep.'

'And Ann found out?'

'It wasn't very difficult, I'm afraid.' He had looked tired, discouraged and older, and a bit hung-over, and the bright hair was dull and flattened. 'Sorry, I shouldn't be burdening you with this when you've just got a lovely daughter.' He cooed at Sara, who had opened one eye and closed it again, definitively, sucking her fingers. 'Oh God, she's not impressed with me either.'

'Oh, Davey, I'm sure she will be, but she's a bit young yet. Have some more tea. Well, it's much better than ending up divorced, isn't it?'

'Oh, yes.' He was drinking tea and the colour was coming back to the fair skin. 'I could not have borne that.'

'Davey, why did you do it? Have an affair I mean?'

'Oh, she was *there*, and I was feeling down and frustrated. And she was very pretty.'

'A male thing, I suppose,' Jens had said disapprovingly, but feeling stirrings of jealousy; he obviously found it all so easy and pleasurable. 'But you'll have to stop. I mean . . .' she had checked herself, realizing she was in unknown territory, and he had patted her hand.

'Dear Jens. I *do* find that depressing.'

'Yes, I see that,' she had said, rallying, 'but what can you do, Davey? Will something else not work? Cold baths?' She had considered him, thinking about herself. 'Or a bit of success?'

'Ah, now.' He had sat up, life visibly returning. '*That* would help. If I could only get somewhere in politics, be a minister, then I think I could manage without all the nonsense. If I could *do* something like you do, for instance. You've got the restaurants which *you* created – I mean, but for you they wouldn't be here.'

Yes, she had said, and meant it. Whatever the difficulties, the restaurants with their several millions of turnover and even then just under a hundred employees and the endless customers had been willed by her, they were her creation and *that* was a lasting monument.

She returned abruptly to the present problem. I owe too much to the Frenches not to intervene, she acknowledged, remembering William and the patience and affection he had lavished on Ali and of which she had been mindlessly jealous. This one I have to do, she thought, remembering with a little smugness the stylish farewell scene she and Ferenc had managed three months before.

'I don't know that I can get him back for her,' she said slowly.

'Not necessary. In fact much better not, but she does need to be said goodbye to in good order. Then she might stop beating herself up.'

'Bloody men,' Jens said, trying to lighten the atmosphere.

'No. *A* bloody man. Don't generalize, Jens, think of our husbands. Neither of them would do that.'

'No. That's true,' she admitted, understanding that Ferenc had behaved much better as well. 'I'll try, Sofe, I promise. I understand what you're saying.'

They finished lunch, gossiping placidly about other things, but she was badly cast down both by having had to acknowledge to Sofe and to herself that Redwood's was still probably stuck as a debt-burdened private company and by finding that David had been capable of behaving in this way to a girl she regarded as a sister. And, let her admit it, that they had managed to hide the whole thing from her; it meant that she was either less intelligent or less close to both of them than she had hoped.

'In fact,' she said abruptly, cutting across Sofe's admirable description of the Turkish hill forts she had just visited, 'I'll try and catch Davey now, if I can get rid of whoever he's lunching with. Excuse me, Sofe, but I'm miserable about this, and I'd like to fix it.'

'Do you know what you're going to say?'

'No. But I'll manage.'

Sofia had always complained that Jens rushed into situations without quite knowing how she was going to get out, but sometimes it was the only way you could cope at all. She marched up the long restaurant steps, constrained by the fashionable skirt, to David's table, automatically counting the numbers lunching and stopping to straighten a cloth. She looked inimically over the back of a dark head into Davey's familiar blue eyes.

'Jens.' He bounced to his feet to kiss her. He'd been in a lot since what must have been a crashing disappointment and the staff were instructed not to bill him if he were by himself, an arrangement which he had, this time, tacitly accepted. He was slightly flushed; alcohol always showed immediately on that fair skin. She considered him without affection and he, quick as he always was to reflect emotion, looked back, instantly wary. She turned politely to greet his companion and found herself looking at a familiar face, with an unfamiliar, tentative smile.

'Jens, this is Simon Dearsley.'

'How do you do?' Crumbs, she thought. Oh.

'Is that the time?' Davey had seen his chance. 'I must go, I'm so sorry, Simon. May I run?'

'Of course.' Simon dragged his attention back to his guest and said his farewells while Jens stood furtively straightening the skirt and wishing she had stopped to put her lipstick on again. 'Have you time to have coffee with me?' he asked, and they both of them considered the table, littered with coffee cups and brandy glasses.

'I have a guest. I left her only to have a word with Davey.'

They looked at each other, unsmiling.

'Lunch tomorrow? Or Friday? In someone else's restaurant to give you a break?'

'Yes. Yes, I can do that.'

'I'll ring your office and fix it. It was a very good lunch.'

'Thank you. I'm glad to hear it.' Her feet seemed to have stuck to the floor. 'Till tomorrow then,' she said, and managed to get herself back to explain to Sofia that Davey had fled and that she would faithfully find another opportunity to tackle him.

The Saturday morning sun was warm on Mickey's back as he decided to cut through Kew Gardens. Jacinth loved the garden, and he smiled proudly as she danced away from him across the grass, tall for four and fair like him and his brothers, though it was David's curly hair rather than his own straight floppy mop that she had inherited. She cannoned into a tall man who caught her and set her on her feet.

'I'm sorry,' Mickey said, rushing to his daughter who was looking baffled, then saw who the man was. 'Dr Daiches! What are you doing here? How are you?'

'Mickey! Michael Banner. Well, I'm blowed. I'm a Visiting Fellow near here. Do you live here? Yes? Is this little one yours? What a pretty girl.' He smiled kindly on Jacinth who bridled and clung to Mickey's trousers.

'I've got two stepdaughters too,' he boasted, wishing they were here to help impress Dr Daiches, who was looking much older, and more tired and smaller.

'You're still working for the Seles Group, then?'

'Yes, yes. It's going very well,' Mickey added automatically, careful not to say anything which could anticipate next week's news.

'I'm so glad. And you're settled yourself?'

'Oh, yes. We had to move to London because the Group was getting so big, and Paul wanted me here. We've got a very nice house.' To think, he marvelled, that this pleasant, middle-aged – no, actually, more nearly old – man had once been so important to him, and so powerful. He might still be important in his own world, but he probably didn't earn as much as the chief of staff for the Seles Group.

'I'm semi-retired now,' Dr Daiches was saying placidly and without seeming to feel this was other than a pleasurable time of life. 'And how is the rest of your family? Is your mother well?'

'Oh, very. She's staying with us now as a matter of fact. She wanted to see Davey do *Question Time* and of course Davey and Ann can only afford a tiny little flat in London. So she comes to us.'

'That must give you pleasure. To be able to provide in that way.'

'Yes, it does.' It did, even though he knew his mother would not have bothered to come to them except for her need to see Davey and share in his success. But it still made him feel grown up and real, providing a comfortable suite for his mother and listening to Jean telling her not to worry, the housekeeper would do whatever was required. It was a long way from the miseries of his teens.

'I see your brother's doings in the newspapers every now and then. And I saw him on *Question Time* last week. He's very persuasive.'

'Davey always was. I'm not sure it's all going to get him anywhere, though, given the mess his party is in.'

The doctor considered him in exactly the thoughtful, comprehending way he remembered. 'Tell me more about yourself, Mickey. Are you happy?'

Both of them were watching Jacinth who was squatting in the grass, unmoving, fiercely concentrating on a squirrel who was picking up lumps of bread thrown for him by a devoted old lady.

'Very. Three girls to spoil me, a lovely house, Jean, a good job. Sometimes it seems too good to be true.'

'Oh, enjoy it, my boy – sorry, that slipped out, you'll have to forgive the maunderings of age. Happiness is a good thing to have in the bank, as it were.'

'You always said that a happy patch early in life was a strong foundation,' Mickey said, suddenly feeling easy with him.

'I still do. It gives people something to hark back to in bad times. Gives them confidence that they can be happy again. But you've done well, Mickey.'

'I'd like another of my own,' he felt able to say, lowering his voice so Jacinth could not hear. 'It just doesn't seem to have happened.'

'Your wife is older than you, I think I remember.'

You couldn't expect them to remember every detail, Mickey reminded himself. It was eight years since he had seen the man. 'Yes. She's thirty-seven.'

'And has had three children.'

'Yes.' He remembered, sharply, this man suggesting to him that his mother was not too old at forty-four to want a new life, and the distress that this had caused him. But dislike it as he might, Dr Daiches was right, time was not on his and Jean's side and he must persuade her to go and see someone.

A piercing shriek from Jacinth made them both jump. The child was bolt upright, bristling with indignation. 'Daddy! The big squirrel chased away the little squirrel and took his food.'

'I'm sure the little squirrel will come back,' he said hastily picking up his daughter, and saw Dr Daiches' wide smile over her shoulder.

'Nice to see you, Michael.' He waved and was gone, and Mickey watched him walk away with regret before turning his attention to what could be done about the naughty, naughty big squirrel.

CHAPTER TWENTY

June 1992

There were nineteen people in the Seles Group boardroom, three more than Paul had expected, and he frowned at Sheena who should have told him exactly who was coming. She ignored him in favour of chivvying a secretary to provide more chairs. She was now his Personal Assistant and had two secretaries in the office with her to do the typing and the heavy-duty telephoning. The bankers, it transpired, had turned up in greater force than had been expected, and he braced himself for trouble; these were not bag-carriers but senior directors of his own merchant bank and two clearing banks. With the usual army of lawyers and accountants it made for a very expensive meeting. He looked in inquiry at the most senior director of his merchant bank.

'Bit of difficulty, Paul. So we've got everyone here, so they can all speak up. I think we're all right but I want everyone inside the tent now.'

'Good idea.'

The man acknowledged the heavily ironic comment without being deflected and Paul sat, tense, ready to do battle. He tried not to fidget; he had hired Frank Stenhouse for the smoothness of style which enemies had described as being carried over the Niagara Falls in a barrel of honey, but he had heard the story too often and he wanted to get on. He had *made* the deal, and these wankers were here to help organize the money, not pick over something they were clearly not going to understand. Stenhouse had taken them through the paper, and was now summarizing with unbroken smoothness.

'So. Paragon is capitalized at two hundred million at mid-market price yesterday. Our view is that we can get it by offering two Seles Group ordinary shares plus cash of three pounds for every five of theirs. Leaves us needing a hundred million to finance the purchase, plus another fifty million to get Paragon's gearing down to fifty-four per cent or the same as ours. New borrowing of a hundred and fifty million. Murchiesons will underwrite the whole of the rights issue on that basis, provided always the share prices stay within the range you have at page five.'

The senior Standard and Lloyds director cleared his throat and said that they had run the numbers again, following the most recent forecasts for the Seles Group, and he had to say they would prefer to reduce the gearing by some £30 million. Paul knew enough not to be fooled by the way this was put as a preference; it was in practice a condition, and Frank Stenhouse had made it clear that some very hard bargaining had taken place. Even on the basis of £30 million the rights issue would be substantially more difficult to bring off and Murchiesons were hesitating over the underwriting.

'I have already undertaken to take up the full extent of my rights,' he said on cue, and Sean piped up as well, adding an undertaking to take up a further £200,000-worth. The roomful of men brightened up at this point; it was always reassuring for bankers to see directors putting their money where their mouths were, as Frank Stenhouse had put it, his customary smoothness momentarily deserting him in a difficult interview late the night before.

Paul sat watching the room, seething with impatience, as the juniors scribbled and the seniors sat and thought. Sean had stopped listening, you could always tell. Mickey Banner, who was there so that he understood enough to be able to answer questions about redundancies when they put the two companies together, was looking uncomprehending – well, he wasn't meant to be a finance man. .

And Sheena, unforgivably, had been on the bankers' side from the first. 'It's a big group, Paragon,' she had said, sitting up in bed, scolding him. 'And it's got a couple of companies – the Hungarian ones – which need cash. You can't afford to gear up that much. You'd be better with no acquisition debt at all.' Well, he had let her try that thesis on Frank Stenhouse, so she could discover for herself that there was no way of doing this as an all-share deal, Murchiesons could not get it underwritten. 'Subject to documentation,' the Standard and Lloyds man said into the silence, 'and subject, of course, to Murchiesons getting the underwriting, I can go with this.' The man from the Royal Clydesdale nodded slowly, with the air of a great power adding his signature, although as Paul knew, he was clinging anxiously to Standard and Lloyd's coat-tails.

The room broke up into a series of huddles as the bankers picked up points with the lawyers, and the accountants and the merchant-banking team cleared figures with each other. Frank Stenhouse withdrew with Paul and Sean who sat and watched him stonily.

'We really don't know a lot about the two Hungarian companies, in the sense that they are both dependent on Government contracts, and we haven't been able to do much due diligence on those.' He looked anxiously at Paul.

'They're five-year contracts. The Hungarians won't break them, they can't afford to have foreigners ticked off with them.'

'I'm sure that's true, but the payment terms are a bit, well, discretionary. And the turnover.'

'Defence contracts look like dat.'

Frank Stenhouse thought about that for a bit, without Paul or Sean contributing further.

'But these are people you know well?' he asked, dredging for comfort.

'Yes.' Paul took pity on him. 'Relax, Frank. It's legitimate business, and very profitable. *I'll* write the words in the document for you.'

'Well. We'll agree something. All right. I'll just go round the bases again and confirm with you tonight.'

An hour later all the visitors had gone; Mickey had returned to his own office to recheck the redundancies likely to result from combining two head offices, and Sean had gone off to rejig the computer program to take account of £30 million less borrowing in the numbers. Paul, restless, decided to phone Jens but found Sheena sitting on his desk between him and the telephone.

'Paul. I want you to think about calling this deal off.'

'Why?' He knew why, she had had a go at him before.

'It's too big,' she said patiently. 'Paragon is big and it's not well run, we *know* that, that's why our engineering companies have been taking their market.'

'So what? With them under the same ownership, not buggering up the market with funny prices, we'll make double the money.'

'Not true,' she said grittily. 'It's not as simple as that, you *know*, we'll lose some of the customers we have in common, because they won't want to be dependent on a single supplier.'

This was irrefutable and he was nettled into continuing the argument. 'The Hungarian companies are two gold mines. They don't show a quarter the profit they make in the Paragon accounts.'

'That may be this year, but that profit's not reliable, and you have to spend to get it.'

He had kept Sheena well away from his dealings in Hungary, and he was seriously disconcerted. 'Who told you that?'

'Oh, come on, Paul, I watched you with those men. I've seen you do that before.'

He felt himself go crimson and fought for control, but she wasn't finished.

'And the two newspapers. I know why you want them and you'd do better to pay a PR agent if that's what you want. You need to know about businesses like that, or the journalists will rob you blind.'

'How the fuck do you know so much?'

'Paul, I'm thirty-five and I've worked since I was eighteen. You and Jens Redwood think you're so clever – well, you are, you've managed to get your own businesses, but you could be throwing yours away.'

He had hit her across the face before he had realized his hand had moved, and she had staggered back, holding her jaw. Her eyes focused again incredulously, and she snatched the heavy paperweight off the desk and had clouted him with it before he could duck, catching him excruciatingly on his nose. He pinned her against the door with one hand, blind with rage, and pulled back his fist to break her face for her, but somehow she managed to turn her head so that she took the blow on her cheek, screaming for help. He tugged at her hair, willing to kill her in that moment, but Sean had his elbow wrenched behind his back, still strong as a bloody ox, so that he had to let go and see Mickey Banner take her away, weeping with pain and misery, all of them knowing that there was no way back.

'No, I'm going out to lunch, thank you, Gerard. Let my table go.'

It was a good day when Redwood's had to take over the table normally kept for Jens and any guests of the house. She was checking automatically the take figures for the day before, but her brain was not engaged; she seemed to be able to think of nothing but Simon Dearsley. She stared out of the window and tried to decide what to do; in her present state of mind she would find herself launched on an affair with a high-profile journalist, in her and his home town, a bare three months after she had decided to bring her affair with Ferenc to an end. And she had reached *that* decision because she felt the affair was beginning to cause comment and was very difficult to continue, with them both owning restaurants some 2000 miles apart. She gave up; she felt totally, wonderfully better than she had done for months, her life seemed to be transformed, with the disappointment over the postponement of the float, her permanent state of exhaustion, and Hugh's continuing intransigence over an underpaid, grinding and pointless job quite forgotten. It gives you new hope, having a love affair, she thought, and hastily made for the kitchen before considerations of how ephemeral all this might be could intrude. It is simpler than that, she decided, in the middle of agreeing with Chef that the steaks should be returned, with contumely, and a 'special' involving chicken be substituted – she *had* to have Simon, if he was available. Like with Ferenc at the beginning.

It was finally noon and she was able to get her make-up on and her hands washed. She took her driver but told him not to wait, understanding that she was committed.

Simon looked just as good, she saw with relief, as he stood up to greet her, a smile spreading right across his face. Not as classically good-looking as David, the nose a shade too long and the dark hair going back at the temples, but he filled the eye just the same, a big man, large-framed and somehow already familiar.

'I expect you know this place?'

'Not well, because the trouble with being a restaurateur is you tend to eat in your own, if you have any spare time. But she is very good.' She smiled politely to the chef and owner who bowed to her before disappearing sharply into the kitchen.

He had chosen carefully, she saw. It was a fashionable but casual place, with a lot of faces semi-familiar from the television and the backs of books. Half the room greeted Simon and four people came up to talk to him, all of whom he received with patience.

'They want to appear on your programme.' She had watched it guiltily last night; he was the host on an arts programme as well as a regular programme on politics.

'Most of them have,' he said easily, and she understood he was somebody who kept his own counsel and did not gossip. He looked across at her. 'Never mind them, tell me about yourself. How do you know David Banner so well?'

She told him, watching him tuck the facts away, and found herself telling him about Paul as well.

'And you all still know each other? I don't have any friends left like that. Are you a gang, one for all and all for one?'

363

'Most of the time. Paul and I are ... partly, I suppose, because he isn't married at the moment. And of course I see a lot of David because his wife isn't in London.'

'Can't afford it, I suppose.'

'Doesn't like London, I think.' She hesitated. 'Are you a Londoner?'

'Yes. My wife, like David's, prefers the country, but she comes up for the odd night.' He was crumbling a roll and she watched his hands, wondering dazedly what it was that had brought on this excess of pure lust. He felt her watching him and looked across at her so that she blushed and sat back, feeling confused, happy and much younger than her thirty-six years. 'Jens. Does everyone call you that or only David and Paul? May I?' He hesitated. 'Look, this doesn't happen to me all that much.'

'Nor to me.'

'Oh, good. Then we can discuss freely whether we leave now or finish this blasted meal sedately in good order.'

'The second. I could never live down walking out of Clarke's after one course. The repercussions are unthinkable.'

'I'm sorry, how stupid of me. I'd just not thought. War to the death?'

'I'd spend the rest of my life explaining to the Chefs' Mafia.' She was hardly able to breathe between happiness and panic; this, as she had told herself in the middle of the night, was truly madness. Simon's face was far too well known, heads turned wherever he went, she had already seen. But he was irresistible, the whole thing was, and she grinned at him.

And with the short-term future settled, amazingly they both enjoyed the food and each other, squashing hours of conventional conversation into two courses and pudding. He was very well paid indeed, she understood, and very influential, already near the top of his profession and aiming for the heights, at forty-two, six years older than her. They finished their sorbets together and sat peacefully looking at each other.

'Will they be mortally offended if you skip coffee?'

'No. Just so long as we walk, not run.'

He burst out laughing, the long serious lines in his face breaking up, and she watched him, charmed and hopeful. He paid the bill and they dawdled luxuriously in the sunshine.

'How much time have you got?' he asked, a little tentatively, and she gave her mind to the problem.

'If I make a couple of phone calls, I could skip going back to the office. Then all I absolutely have to do is to get home for six-thirty. The nanny goes off.'

'I'd forgotten all that. My youngest is ten and away at school. But I have a programme to do and I need to be in a studio at six. Is that all right?'

It was more than all right, she thought then, and later when they were lying side by side in his bed. She had not managed to come, overwhelmed by the strangeness of a new body, but that hadn't mattered, and he had not, she thought, noticed. And she was hooked by his charm and energy, by the speed of the mind, and the sheer ease of being with him. She thought momentarily of Ferenc, but it all seemed a long time ago and nothing like as exciting as this man. He turned his head to look at her.

'I can't believe those quasi-brothers of yours have never tried to seduce you.'

'I tried once to seduce Paul but he wouldn't.' She told him about it, laughing, because the memory no longer hurt, but he was touchingly horrified for her.

'Have you ever tackled your stepfather?'

'No. I can't.'

'Come back here. Darling, sorry, you practically leapt out of bed. Forget I spoke. Why not David?'

'Oh. Because he was on the other side when we were little. Because he was a much too cocky schoolboy, when we met again. And he didn't fancy me. And now we're all grown up, and I like him most of the time, neither of us fancies the other.'

'You were cross with him yesterday.'

'You're so smart.' She wrapped the sheet round her for warmth in the air-conditioning. 'I cannot believe it was only yesterday.'

'That we met?' He accepted the deflection. 'Nor can I. Have I . . . that is, did I? Sorry.' He held his head.

'You mean, have I got another lover? No.' She tucked the sheet round her, suddenly conscious of how little she knew him. 'What about you?'

'Also no. I have had, but not now.' He looked at her anxiously. 'We did get into this a bit fast, didn't we? But I have never wanted anything so much.'

'What did you say your name was?'

His face broke up in laughter in the way she liked so much and he held her and kissed her. 'Oh, very good. Darling, I'm giving you a cup of tea, then we're going to discuss logistics and time-tables, and so on. *Somebody* has to organize round here.'

He had organized to some purpose, Jens thought, sitting demurely at home some two weeks later, having been dropped there by Simon's driver in good time to get the nanny off, supervise the kids' supper and read to them, so that she was now waiting for Hugh to come back so they could eat together. It was amazing, she thought, how much better she felt having Simon, having someone to giggle with to whom she was obviously and gratifyingly of key importance, and whose whole attention she had when she was with him. They had had four afternoons together, having managed to establish that Tuesday and Thursday afternoons were clear, or could be cleared, for Simon and that she, as the captain of her ship, could take time off then as well. It wouldn't work for ever, of course, and she was already feeling guilty because her beloved daughter wanted Mummy to come to her Thursday ballet class, but for the moment Simon took precedence. It was like winning the pools, well, no, it wasn't because it had to be kept secret. For her the need for secrecy was galling, for Simon, she knew, it added to the charm of the affair. She considered, just for a few seconds, the divergence between them and buried the thought, choosing instead to contemplate, pleasurably, her projected visit to Simon's art show, as a guest. This was undoubtedly dangerous, but she liked having a man whose face was so well known that he, and she by extension, attracted attention everywhere they went. It was power, of course, infinitely soothing when she was feeling a failure in business and discontented as a wife.

'Jens?'

It had been Hugh's key she had heard and she went down to kiss him, noticing with sympathy rather than exasperation that he was looking worn out.

'You saw the papers?'

'With Paul's deal? Yes, I did.' She had seen the hoardings on the newspaper stand as she and Simon had left his flat, and rushed to buy a paper. She had been relieved; despite the near-overwhelming distraction of having Simon, she was always uncomfortable when Paul was missing or too preoccupied to talk to her.

'Did you know?'

'Only that he must have been doing a deal. I mean, I haven't seen him for two weeks and I had to fix his birthday party on the phone.'

'I agree that's unusual,' Hugh observed acerbically. 'It must have leaked from somewhere, in fact. Jump in the other company's shares.'

'You get that with recommended offers, I am told.' She reached for the paper. 'Puts another fifty per cent on his turnover. It *does* make my little company look like a cottage industry.'

'What does Paragon do? I don't know them. Engineering?'

'I think that means what it says rather than selling arms, but I couldn't be sure.' She sat down, the better to concentrate.

'Nothing wrong with selling arms provided you stay out of the prohibited list. I take it Paul does?'

She was hunched over the paper. 'Interesting. I had an early edition, but now it's more written up. You can see the *Standard* doesn't like it; thinks it might be an acquisition too far. And his share price is down a little. Nothing to speak of but he must have hoped it would go up.'

'The market's off, generally. Sterling's under pressure again.

We really have not managed to convince the world that we are serious about defending our ERM parity.'

Hugh was sounding exhausted and she turned her full attention to him, alarmed. 'Don't drink that tea.'

'Why not?'

She popped a thermometer into his mouth by way of response and counted under her breath, using the trick the Girl Guide movement had taught her long ago to count seconds – 'Sixty rickety buckets' she announced triumphantly, and took the thermometer from his mouth. 'A hundred and one plus. Oh, darling. Can you stay at home tomorrow?'

'I have to go to the shop. Sorry, I'll flop for tonight, but tomorrow I have to get in. I will try and look in at Paul's birthday party.'

'Can't you stay in bed and let your office cover?' She hated Hugh being ill, it brought back unacknowledged childhood terrors. However much she reminded herself he had always been strong, and was not actually suffering from a long-standing illness, she was always so alarmed when he was sick that she was barely able to look after him.

'It's only a cold,' he said blearily, blowing his nose, and pulled her on to his knee, keeping her facing away from him. 'It'll probably be better tomorrow.' She leant against him, resentful, but drawing consolation from the solid feel of him.

'You'll get a tremendous turnout for Paul's birthday anyway. I suppose he timed the deal as a present to himself. You know he's invited the Chancellor? He might even come, he always likes eating at Redwood's.'

In the event the Chancellor failed to appear the next day, but the Financial Secretary and the Permanent Secretary arrived and both rushed to kiss her. For men dedicated to public service they were both very keen on her restaurants, she thought, amused, and on that thought she saw David behind them, handing over his old navy jacket, the fair hair ruffled. He kissed her too, easily. 'Sorry. Am I late? I walked. Unlike these types with the official cars.'

'Get a policy, David, and maybe you'll get a car next time,' the Financial Secretary suggested.'

'Oh, we've got a policy. Not that we'll need it if you lot go on the way you are. I take it you are going to be the next Minister for the Heritage?'

'Gentlemen,' Jens said primly, 'there's some lovely champagne about, just next to you. Now, let me see, who do you know?' she asked the assembled grandees and introduced them firmly to the two people nearest to them, one of whom turned out to be David's sister-in-law, somewhat over-excited by the number of well-known faces present. 'Jean's husband is part of the Seles Group and as it turns out we are celebrating not just Paul's birthday but a new acquisition.' She looked round for David to help, but a girl from Paul's PR firm had fastened on to him and was guiding him away. She took Jean with her and introduced her to an actor, part of the crowd which was beginning to assemble round a spectacular buffet with an ice swan as its centrepiece, melting rather faster than Chef had calculated. She glanced up and saw a waiter with a mop waiting his chance, and moved away, reminding herself not to get involved with ice sculpture another time. It made a good photograph, though, or would, provided someone moved quickly enough. She signalled to the PR girl who abandoned David with visible reluctance, and between them they got Paul to pose for photographs, making quite sure that the boy with the mop was out of shot.

'Paul,' she said crossly, watching him fidget. 'Put that phone down.'

'I can't, Jens. I *have* to know what my share price is doing.'

'What is it?'

'Going down, fuck it.' He gave her a harassed look and turned his back on her and the crowded room, the phone clamped to his ear. 'All right, all right. Buy at four hundred and forty. Yes.' He pushed the aerial in and turned, obviously not pleased to find her still there.

'You OK, Paul?'

'Yes, should be. I may have to buy a few more.'

'You're a director. People will know.'

'That's all right. The lads say there are others waiting to buy. They're just hoping to get them a bit cheaper. Don't worry, Jens, it's all under control.' He pushed the phone into the pocket of his loose jacket; he had put on a couple of stone since they had gone to Slovakia together two years ago, and he had given up the struggle with conventional tailoring in favour of the unstructured look. He too, she noticed, was making a beeline for the blonde PR girl; Simon, she thought smugly, preferred them dark-haired.

'Darling?' It was Hugh, showing no signs of pursuing PR girls, blonde or dark. 'Congratulations, it's a lovely lunch.'

She looked into his eyes. 'You're worse.'

'Yes. I'm going to creep away. I've just seen David. He believes we ought to be out of the ERM – I asked him if that was Labour Party policy and he said absolutely not, he just thought that if the Germans wouldn't drop their rate it would all happen anyway.'

'Is he right?'

'No. Whatever it costs we defend sterling. They'll get tired of pushing. But we do not need people like David, who are quite important these days, trying to sabotage the policy. Get him to shut up if you can.'

'Darling. *Please* go home. I'll come – oh, damn, I promised to go and see this thing at six o'clock.' Hugh was much too incisive and clear-headed normally to believe that anyone could persuade the Opposition not to do their best to sabotage any Government policy even if they agreed with it. That was what they were there for, to oppose, and the Press Secretary to the Chancellor, of all people, knew that. It must be 'flu rather than a feverish cold, and her heart sank; she needed to see Simon, but she could not do it if Hugh were going to be miserably tossing in bed, needing drinks and aspirin and comfort, none of which the children's nanny would feel it her place to provide. She saw him into a car, then went back to the party, elation quenched, knowing that she would have to cancel seeing Simon and miss seeing heads turn for them both, as she skated gracefully on the very thin ice of being a friend of Simon Dearsley's, a power in her own right and not just a hanger-on. But she did not allow herself to consider leaving Hugh literally to sweat it out; she knew beyond a doubt that something awful would happen and Simon would vanish or turn out to be a fantasy. She looked despondently round the party and saw David, and remembered as if it had all happened months ago that she had promised to get him to talk to beautiful, grieving Ali. Well, she could do a good deed and ruin someone else's day.

It took a little time to detach him from the crowd and she understood that he was quite as well known to the general public as Simon. His looks were distinctive, of course, but even a year ago it had been possible to have a quiet drink with him in one of her own restaurants without being accosted or stared at. But this was what David wanted; like her, he drew nourishment from people's admiration. And fair enough, like her, he tried to justify their homage, he wanted to give them what they craved and both of them would work all the hours God had sent to do it. To an outside eye they looked to be pursuing different goals, but the difference was much more apparent than real; she pursued money because she needed to be independent, he didn't go for money only because he had decided that freedom lay in not spending it. A photographer called to them both and they smiled uniformly for the cameras.

'Davey, I need to talk to you for a minute.'

'Oh dear. Sounds ominous.'

She glanced round, and turned her shoulders forbiddingly to shut out a young man who was hovering. 'Well, it is a criticism. You've made our Ali miserable.'

He looked at her sideways, his mouth pinching into a straight thin line, and she understood this was going to be difficult.

'Good idea to stop, and no one thinks otherwise. You can't afford an affair, nor can she,' she said, deciding that her customary directness was the only way to go. 'But you can't stop without saying goodbye, without explaining yourself. She thinks it's all her fault – Ali always does, as you must surely know, and she's wretched.' He was flushed across the cheekbones and looking mulishly stubborn, fidgeting to get away from her. 'Davey, it's bad manners, my love.'

'Christ.' He moved too quickly and a glass fell off the table. 'Shit.'

'No, no, it's just a glass.'

He laughed shortly and reluctantly, not meeting her eyes, and she understood she had not achieved her objective.

'Dearest Davey, how do you usually end an affair?'

'I don't have very many,' he protested, alarmed, looking over her shoulder.

'No one can hear us, unless you're going to shout. How do you end the ones you do have?'

He was silent and she thought he had not heard her, then she understood he was struggling with himself.

'Badly, I'm afraid. In fact I'm terrible at it. I never do it well.' He looked up, scarlet and sulky. 'There isn't a good way.'

'No. But just stopping dead, never ringing up, is terrible, as you say.' She felt a pang of cold terror; surely her lovely Simon would never behave like that. 'I mean, you could manage some graceful lie, couldn't you? Like Ann was getting suspicious.'

'That's not a lie.'

'Ah. Then you could tell the truth. Just experimentally, you know.' It was, she thought, fascinated, like dealing with a twelve-year-old, or with Paul, come to think of it, trying to justify some idiocy. 'What *happens*, Davey? Ann gets suspicious and then you stop? Or do you get fed up? I mean, if you knew that, then you might manage to stop more gracefully.'

'I get too busy doing other things. And they get cross and disappointed. And I get tired of making excuses. I know, I know, the answer is not to do it, but . . .'

'But what?'

He looked at her with dislike. 'It's different for you; you've got something of your own, you've got these restaurants, you're not hanging around waiting to be allowed to do what you know you can do and make things better for people. You can do it all, you've got your own power-base, you've built something.'

'But you've got a lot of what you want too, haven't you? I mean, when we talked . . . after Sara . . . in 1987 you'd had an affair which I . . . well, which I understood about because you were hanging about, waiting to get into Parliament. But since then you've been going steadily up, haven't you? Even Hugh says you're important and influential, and he's professionally on the other side, working where he does.'

'That's *very* nice of Hugh. Yes, I suppose I am getting somewhere, but it's so slow and so . . . well . . . chancy. That's why I gave up Ali.' She saw that he thought he had scored a point.

'You could tell her that,' she agreed drily. 'But Davey, between us, if . . . when you go on to someone else, is it not a terrible risk? I mean, *really* not worth taking. In terms of your career and Ann?' She was, she understood, asking because she needed to know for herself.

'Yes, it is, of course it is.' He was looking agonized but there was something else there, she saw, fascinated, his eyes were bright and the corners of the long mouth were being tugged upward.

'The risk is part of the fun?' she asked incredulously.

'No. Yes, I'm afraid there is a bit of that.' He looked at her, mock-hangdog, and she gazed back unseeingly at the bright, handsome face. 'Jens. What? You're looking terribly worried all of a sudden.'

'A ghost walked . . .' she said, returning to herself. 'Do you feel you have to snatch at what is on offer in case it never comes by again?'

'Something of that sort,' he agreed, interested. 'And I get low, I suppose, and nothing else seems to be working.'

'So you go for what has always worked for you.'

'Christ, Jens.'

'Sorry,' she said perfunctorily, still thinking, frightened of her instant, unhesitating rush to Simon's bed. 'Sorry,' she said again, making a huge effort, but it was too late; Davey had always been uncannily perceptive, it was part of his considerable charm.

'You too, Jens?'

'Me too, yes,' she acknowledged. 'Not the risk-taking, that's not me. But, yes. What's the matter with us, Davey? You, me and Paul? Why *do* we do these things?'

'Paul's not all that much given to women,' he objected.

'By comparison with whom?' she asked swiftly, and he winced. 'No, sorry Davey, forget that. But you take these risks with your political career, *I* can't seem to stick to being a successful restaurateur and mother and wife, and God knows you'd think all *that* was enough. It's not exactly an empty life. And Paul, wildly much more successful than either of us, is always doing idiotic things. What is it? Why do we all feel we have to have things that really don't go with what we are trying to do?'

'Childhood insecurity?'

'It seems a bit simple, doesn't it?' She saw that he was looking anxious, and sullen and fidgety and made a final effort.

'Davey, for all of us – and for you – ring Ali up, buy her lunch and bloody well explain why you had to stop. It's not her fault you had to run for cover. You'll feel better too.'

'I would,' he acknowledged. He leant over to kiss her. 'If I'd had a sister like you I'd have been better,' he said hopefully.

'You probably wouldn't have listened to a word,' she said into his ear, liking the feel of his arm round her.

'Hey, put her down, Davey, this minute.'

They turned to see Paul and Sean. 'Look, your bloody swan's melting, go and do something. Can't think why I didn't hold the party in a decent restaurant.'

'What happened to your face, Paul? I've just noticed. Did you have a black eye?'

'Two. Banged my nose on a door. Will you go and sort that swan before it disappears out the front door?'

He watched her go and lowered himself on to a table, poised

374

to move at any moment, while Sean retired three tables away to make a phone call.

'Wanted a word, Davey.'

'Oh, not you too.'

'Jens upset with you? Ah. About Ali?'

'Christ. Does *everyone* know?' He moved hastily to change the subject. 'Congratulations on the deal anyway. You've got a really big company now, haven't you? Is Mickey being useful?'

'Oh, yes. He's a good lad.'

'Well, I'll always be grateful to you for *that*. Where's Sheena?'

Paul stared at him and he felt a chill. 'Gone. Left.'

'What, just like that?' He was truly startled, he had assumed that she and Paul were going to marry, not least because of her quietly proprietary air. 'Well, you'll miss her, won't you?'

'No. She'd got too fucking bossy.'

Something had gone very wrong, and David could not resist trying to find out what had upset his friend and rival at this enviably successful moment in his career. 'Jens didn't tell me.'

'Jens doesn't know yet. I'll get an earful when she does. She thought Sheena would be good for me – I mean, she came round to the idea after Maddy left.'

'Ah.' He had learned from journalists that an encouraging monosyllable could elicit miraculous confidences.

'Oh, sod it, Davey, you know me. I lost my temper – she was getting at me – and I thought, I don't need this, a woman always telling me what I was doing wrong, and that I couldn't do things I wanted to, and getting in the way.' He was banging the table with the edge of his hand, and Davey waited out a considerable pause. 'So I told her she'd better go,' Paul said, without looking at him.

'Has she left the company too?'

'Yes. We gave her a proper pay-off.' There was a further long pause. 'Jens will be pissed off with me. She always said Sheena was the brake I needed. She told me when I was going over the top.'

'You've got Jens as well.'

'Yeah. But Sheena knew the business. Well . . . this won't get my share price up, I'd better go and chat up a few of the wankers here. Come with me, Davey, it'll get you a few Brownie points, they'll think you know something about industry or defence.'

'Get off.' But Paul was right; it would help to be seen to be close to a real industrialist and exporter, such as his party would need on their side, and so he followed, smiling and shaking hands, easily putting on his careful, controlled public front.

Jens meanwhile was contemplating a surrealistic half-melted ice swan. Disaster had been averted by the simple dint of turning off a radiator which she had not noticed was on, and her chap with the mop was busily deployed, but it did not look much like anything except melting ice and she decided to have it removed. She issued orders and looked up to see Roger Caldwell, sitting by himself, watching her with affection. She looked for Paul and Sean, both of whom were separately deployed, found a cup of coffee and sat down with him.

'Lovely party, Jens. It gives me such pleasure to see you doing so well.'

'Not as well as Paul, of course. Even if I ever do manage to float, this little company will be worth, oh, twenty million or so. Now, Paul's is worth nearer four hundred million.'

'It is remarkable, isn't it?' Roger Caldwell said seriously. He hesitated, looking at his glass. 'He's been more than generous to me, you know.'

'He loves you. And he is a kind chap.'

'To you as well?'

'Well, when I let him. I've always earned good money.'

'And invested it wisely, I daresay.'

'I wouldn't claim that,' she said, thinking about Albany Wharf. 'Most of it is in the company and when we float I'll pay off the mortgage and pre-pay the kids' education. But my pension is with a boring insurance company, or rather two.'

Roger Caldwell smiled at her and she saw with a pang that he was truly getting old, that underneath what the lads referred to, with love, as the OAP impersonation he was now a man of more than pensionable age. He was in his early seventies, of course, and not in particularly good health despite the operation Paul had bought him five years ago. 'It is always interesting to me how you became what you are – intensely self-contained, careful, professional – and Paul is so passionate and profligate.'

'I was middle-class deprived, and that makes a difference. In any case I had a much easier time than Paul – he spent six years with a monster.'

'Yes. Truly a child of a harsh winter, as is Sean. I see your friend David is here.'

'Yes. Well, there's another sign. Paul is being courted by the Government side as well, you know.' She was aware of sounding jealous and blushed for it.

Roger Caldwell considered her. 'Which brings me to something I've always wanted to ask someone sensible who understands business. How exactly does Paul's company make as much money as it does? I read the Annual Report, of course I do, but I cannot see how he manages to make quite so much profit.'

'I never could either.' She signalled for a waiter, the champagne had gone straight to her knees, and she needed a clear head. 'Do you own shares?'

'Some.'

'Don't own too many.' She met his startled look squarely. 'I love him too, but I'm telling you, don't bet the farm. Don't take up your rights for a start.'

He looked suddenly old and tired and anxious.

'Keep some,' she advised hastily, 'but when you can, sell enough to make sure you've got everything you need, house, pension, rainy-day money.'

'Without Paul I wouldn't have had enough, you know. I supported my parents for a long time, so I couldn't save, and my FSSU pension would have left me pretty uncomfortable.'

'*Don't* tell him when you sell, and if he asks, just say you wanted to pay off a debt.'

'What sort of debt?'

'The one you ran up gambling on the dogs?'

'Of course. Or the night club which failed, I'll think of something. Sorry, unimaginative of me.'

She was reminded, painfully, of William French, as they giggled into their drinks.

'So, my dear Jens, explain to me, since you have already said so much, is Paul's business, well, fraudulent?'

'Not necessarily. I'm not even sure about all of this. I do know the profits are not made where they are stated to be. The engineering companies are fairly profitable. But the money really comes in from, well, selling arms – or near arms – machine tools, and the like.'

'So the Seles Group owns companies that trade in arms?'

'Two, but both are quite small, and they're well reported and legitimate – I mean, one's a joint holding with the Slovaks. Paul owns other companies outside the group, which do make a lot of money, but probably not all of it kosher. And in a year when the public company is struggling, I think he pushes some of his own cash into it.'

They looked at each other, Roger Caldwell's hands moving anxiously on his napkin. 'Is that illegal?'

She sighed. 'Yes, if you do it secretly, because you are misleading people lending to the company and your shareholders about what is in the company. I nearly did it, you know, in 1989. The bankers were threatening to pull in an overdraft and I wanted to put in some money Hugh and I had saved. Charles told me I couldn't unless it was all disclosed and went in as a loan. I told Paul all this – he's a shareholder – and he just made one of his bankers restructure us and give us a proper loan.'

'But you think he did not behave in the same orthodox way with his own company?'

'I'm sure of it.' She looked into his concerned face. 'Roger, don't look so worried. I don't know that he did it very much or for many years, and he's probably stopped now.'

'But people may have lent money or bought shares on a false understanding?'

'I wish I hadn't told you.'

'I must talk to Paul,' Roger Caldwell said.

She thought with a sinking heart of the conversation she would have to hold with Paul first. He would be furious, and justifiably so. Roger was his father-figure, not hers, and she should not have felt it her responsibility to protect Roger from the winds of old age and economic recession by telling him that his security might be built on sand, particularly when she had no proof. Unless, of course, you counted having known Paul for most of his thirty-seven years and being closer to him than a brother for much of it.

'Roger, there's no suggestion that Paul took money out of the Group. *Au contraire*, as it were.'

He was not reassured, she saw, and she abandoned the attempt in favour of urging him to have a brandy, and found Sean for him so that she could escape and explain, sadly, to Simon or more probably to a secretary that she would have to go home rather than see him.

CHAPTER TWENTY-ONE

January 1995

Five Star Launch for Redwood's
Restaurateur Jennifer Redwood set a pretty dish before the City
yesterday when shares in the company, which bears her name
and in which she retains a 15 per cent stake, shot to 193p, a
premium of 63p over the opening price of 130p. 'I'm very
pleased for all my investors and for all the management,' she
said, pictured here in the kitchen of Redwood's I, the first of the
fifteen restaurants in the Group which she opened in 1983, just
twelve years ago. At yesterday's closing price, the company is
valued at £30 million and the shares are on a fully taxed P/E
of 10.

'You haven't lifted a saucepan in that kitchen for years,' Paul
objected, looking over her shoulder.

'That's the press for you. I agreed with the PR people that I
would do whatever I was asked, provided it didn't show my
knickers.' Jennifer was pale and tired and suffering from a
sense of anti-climax. She was also furious; she had sold shares
at 130p and had then watched them go to 60p more on the first
day. 'No one ever went broke taking a profit, Jens,' Joshua
had said, laughing, when she rang up to commiserate with her
mother. 'Just you remember *that*. No one ever came unstuck
by paying off debts either. Congratulations, you did brilliantly.'
Startled, she had thanked him and put the phone down with an
unwonted sense of regret; had he only been able to keep his
hands to himself, she might have had a serviceable stepfather.

'Sofia and Lucy must be thrilled.'

'They are. There's one debt I've really been able to pay off. To William as much as to them.'

'What are they worth?'

'Same as yours. About seven million between them.'

'That'll pay for a few nursing homes.'

'You have to remember Lucy is thinking of twenty years in one. Her mother died at a hundred and two.'

'Dear God,' Paul said, shocked into piety.

'Anyway, tomorrow's your big day, yours and Sean's. I know you wanted to do it the same day as my float but I'm glad you didn't make it. The lads tell me a rights issue of the size you're doing could frighten the market.'

'You haven't told anyone?'

'Of course not.'

'Well, after you decided to scare poor old Roger about the company last time we did a deal, I wondered. Those days are past, you know. I've had people crawling over the companies with a nit-comb, it's all kosher.'

'Glad to hear it.'

'In fact, I only sold as many of my Redwood's shares because I want to take up all my rights.'

'They're your shares, Paul, and a good and loyal shareholder you've been.' She had regretted her conversation with Roger Caldwell two and a half years ago, uneasily conscious that she had been relaying things she could not prove if push came to shove. 'Should you be here?'

'No, I should be with the bankers. I just wanted to give you a cuddle.'

She walked into his arms, laughing, and he scrubbed his cheek against hers.

'Paul.'

'I know that voice.'

'Yes, you do. Look, I want us to pay the loan on Albany Wharf back to your pension fund. It worries me. It's over a million now.'

'The property's worth that.'

'Rubbish!'

He pulled away from her, and she saw the flush on his neck. 'I need it all, Jens. I have to take up my rights. We're stretching it as it is.'

'If we repaid half we'd be OK. That's two hundred and fifty thousand each – for heaven's *sake*, Paul, that's not all that much.'

'I'll see. OK? Nothing to prevent you putting in your two hundred and fifty thousand if you want to waste your money. We'll be able to sell it all soon, Eddie was telling me just the other day.'

'Eddie is a crook or a useless wanker, I'm never absolutely sure which.'

'I have to go.' He pulled away, then turned back to her. 'Give us another kiss and wish me luck.'

She did both, not wanting him to face a difficult world without what comfort she had to offer, but she found herself furious. That loan was a running sore, but she was damned if she was going to put money in when Paul, whose company was many times the size of hers, was too mean to do so. In any case she had sold all the shares she could, she had agreed with the promoters not to sell more, and while she could have borrowed £250,000 she would probably have had to tell Hugh. And if she told Hugh he would insist, she knew uneasily, on the whole loan being repaid whatever the consequences, financial or emotional. She had enough difficulty in quelling Hugh's misgivings about Paul as it was.

'I'll have to throw another party of course,' Paul said coaxingly.

'The more the merrier. I know an excellent restaurant. Fifteen of them, in fact.'

'Get off.' He gave her a final squeeze, reclaimed his portable phones and lumbered down to the waiting car.

'And last, on my left, the Labour MP for Barnsley who has been going up like a lift in the Labour Party since his arrival in Parliament in the 1987 election. Only eight years later he has been a member of the Shadow Cabinet for a year and is currently Shadow Secretary of State for the Environment, following a long spell on Defence, an eminently suitable job for one of the very few MPs in the House with actual military experience. He has another claim to fame; like Dennis Skinner he lives on an MP's salary, refusing to accept outside jobs or sponsorship . . . David Banner.'

The round of applause was considerably greater than that for any of the three preceding panellists, as David smiled cheerfully into the camera. He was nervous but not unduly; the Conservative representative was one of the old stagers dragged out of deserved obscurity to prop up a declining Government, and the Liberal Democrat was a decent, readily confused life peer. The outsider presented the only challenge; an articulate and pretty economist with strong views on welfare payments, some of which he had cautiously pillaged. She could probably be charmed into agreeing with him; she had flirted with him easily in the hospitality room before the programme while the Conservative addled his never enormously clear brain by scrambling through a foot-high pile of departmental briefing, and the Liberal Democrat peer joked nervously with Simon Dearsley, now a formidable and unimpressible presenter.

The first question was a gift – about the soaring crime rates announced that day. He might have written it himself. He listened with pleasure while the Conservative went on far too long and was ruthlessly checked, mid-sentence, by the presenter, the Liberal Democrat flannelled, and the pretty economist answered succinctly but nervously, not making the most of her sound points. He himself had recognized the middle-aged woman questioner as a plant, a victim of a particularly unpleasant burglary, and commiserated with her on her experience before even trying to answer the question. He waited out the round of sympathetic applause before giving his answer which neatly linked Conservative economic policy, an inept and careless administration of welfare benefit and a set of criminal cases which had been so administered by the Crown Prosecution Service as totally to demotivate any police force worth the name. It was money for old rope, given the mess the

Government had got itself into, but he did it well and as he caught Simon Dearsley's approving eye he decided it was going to be his night.

And so it was; the next question on Northern Ireland was not an easy one but he managed it infinitely better than the Conservative. The audience, to judge from the applause, agreed with him. Three out of the next four questions were also easy for him, and the final, frivolous question about fellow-passengers on the lifeboat he had anticipated and got another round of applause for including Ann. He retreated to the hospitality room and modestly accepted a glass of acid white wine of a sort that Jens Redwood would never have allowed across the threshold of any of her restaurants. He raised his glass to his Conservative opponent.

'Awfully good, David,' the man said sourly. 'What's your next job? Leader of the Opposition?'

'How very nice of you. We have a leader, and after the next election I was rather hoping for your job.'

'Bed of nails, lad, I assure you,' the man conceded gracefully. 'Where's my PS? I'm sorry, everyone, I'll have to go. Things to govern, but David here will keep you all amused.' He was gone, trailing a private secretary and a Special Branch bodyguard, and David felt a pang of longing so intense that he could taste it. This lot were resilient, as he was always warning, they weren't going to give up the power and the glory easily, however badly things were going.

'Were you pleased with it, David?'

'I was, Simon, thank you. And I thought Ellen here did awfully well.' He smiled into her eyes. 'Mind you,' he added modestly, 'it's like shooting fish in a barrel at the moment. They cannot get *anything* right, can they?'

'They've been in too long.' She reminded him of Jens, direct and succinct, not a politician at all. 'And they can't stay in much longer, can they? Running twenty points behind in the polls, and scraping through with the odd vote.'

'Well, they've done the bit where you change the leader,' he said, laughing. 'And much good *that* did them. No, they are bankrupt. Can't even get the economy right.'

'Could you fight a general election now if it came to it, David? Financially, I mean?'

Simon also conducted a major political interview programme every week on which he very much wanted to be again soon. 'Yes, we could. We've made tremendous progress over the last two years.'

'Even if the unions decided *not* to fund the party?'

'Yes. People need to understand that if they want a Labour Government we have to get financial support from individuals. As we should. We've got lazy; we've depended on the unions who have been extremely generous.'

'You don't bear them a grudge?'

'No, I don't, Simon, you know that, we've talked about this before. I've always believed that the TUC should be an independent force, like the CBI, speaking as an equal to Government, of whichever party. And we're getting there.'

'What about you, Francis?'

The Liberal Democrat peer coughed on his dose of BBC battery acid and managed two conflicting sentences about the readiness of his party to win an election by themselves, tomorrow, and their willingness to contribute to a government of men of good will.

'What about a new Lib–Lab pact then, David?' All the political journalists saw themselves as power-brokers, he had observed, and the thing to do was to let them believe *that*, while making sure you yourself were on the record.

'Come on, Simon, you know we have to win as the Labour Party, with a clear set of policies. I think Francis probably agrees with me that trying to mix our fortunes in 1992 was a bloody disaster.' He had learned years ago always to use Christian names, and always to suggest that there was agreement on a key point. He was distracted by the thought of Jens and Paul, who had seen right through this; their imaginative representation of him sorting out policy at Redwood's ('Now, Gerard and Xavier, I think we *all* agree that lower wages right through the kitchen are a good thing and a change we are going to have to make if this country is to have a future') had made him laugh so much he had fallen off his chair.

'But if you were twenty people short of an overall majority you would cut a deal?'

Not if I had anything to do with it, and if in fact we got anywhere near 50 per cent of the vote we wouldn't need to, he thought, smiling cheerfully back at the persistent presenter. 'I'm not much good at hypothetical questions, Simon. And besides, I really want to ask Ellen about her Transferable Benefit idea.' And then ring Ann to make sure she was going to sit up to watch when the programme went out an hour later; she ought to be pleased by the reference to her. Jens and Paul would be watching too; he might ring them later.

'Good, wasn't he?'

'David?' Jens asked cautiously.

'Of course David. No one else was much good, except I suppose for Simon Dearsley who always does it very well.' Paul was not looking at her but she felt uneasy; she hoped he did not know about Simon, but was not confident.

Paul and Roger Caldwell were sitting in Jens's living-room, the men drinking brandy, she tea. She had a slim tolerance for alcohol of any sort and rationed herself strictly.

'Do you Londoners think this Government is going to fall?' Roger Caldwell had always maintained that London was a country of its own, particularly remote from the preoccupations of rural Somerset to which he had retired.

'David thinks they'll come unstuck on Northern Ireland, if nothing else.' Paul reached for the brandy and poured himself a hefty second helping; he was drinking too much and was putting on even more weight.

'No,' she said impatiently, having absorbed Simon's view. 'Not before 1996 at the earliest. They've still got a majority after all.' She understood she was sounding abrupt, but she was permanently uneasy about Simon these days.

'How is Sean? Is he still with Sandor?' Roger Caldwell, always sensitive to anyone's feelings, was changing the subject.

'Yes,' she said. 'I'm sorry, Roger, I know you'd have liked to have seen Sean but I will not invite Sandor here. We manage when it's the restaurants – well, I couldn't not, he's a customer, but I can't stand him.'

'Is it because he's gay?'

'No. Or I don't think so, because I've never had any trouble with Sean.' She fidgeted under Roger's bright, inquiring glance. 'Yes, I see what you mean. Sandor is after all what Sean is really about. In fairness to me, I think he is truly awful – manipulative, and a sponger. I mean, he doesn't work, able-bodied though he is. Sean keeps him.' There were plenty of rational reasons to object to Sandor and she was not going to offer the irrational truth which was that he frightened her; inside that graceful exterior there lived, she was sure, something deadly and fundamentally hostile to all of them.

'What would an election do to business, Jens?' Roger was seventy-four now, but his interest in life was undiminished; and she thought about the answer.

'It must help. Uncertainty is the killer for consumer spending. Hugh would agree and, of course, he's in a big business now.'

'Doing very well,' Roger said warmly, and she smiled at him.

'I'm sorry he isn't here. They hold every third board meeting abroad, in order to keep everybody's mind focused. They're in Warsaw this time. He rang earlier and sent you his regards.'

'He doesn't regret leaving the Civil Service?'

Hugh had left the Treasury two years before in the aftermath of the British departure from the ERM, to go on the board of a fast-growing transport company which had decided to attack the new East European markets. He had gone with the then Chancellor's blessing, but Jens was still not really sure what had enabled him, suddenly, to move out of a job and a situation with which he had been increasingly and rationally dissatisfied and which was causing trouble in his marriage. But Hugh was like that; when he changed he did so completely and unhesitatingly, leaving no little bits of himself adhering on the path. Unlike David, whom you could see reforming himself, carefully, but who remained absolutely planted in his original certainties, including the wife to whom he had so carefully made reference on the air, or Paul, who did not change.

'Hugh was fed up with the Treasury. He felt that they – I mean the officials – kept offering the wrong advice and that the country was actually just getting further into the mire. And he has always believed that we have to make things here and sell them abroad, not just graft off our talents for servicing other people.'

'So he decided to go and do it?' Roger Caldwell nodded. 'I'm very sorry to have missed him. I'm an old man, Paul. Time for bed.' He was staying with Paul, as he always did.

'I'll get your coat, Roger. You know where the loo is.' She waited for him, like the good hostess she was, and helped him into his coat. 'Paul is telephoning someone. As usual.'

'He's not well, Jens.'

Her first reaction was to be angry; she had enough to bear at the moment without having to be responsible for Paul, but she was instantly ashamed of herself. 'He isn't, is he? I don't know why, Roger, I've been so busy we haven't seen much of each other. He is putting on weight which is always a bad sign with him.'

'I don't think he and Louisa are getting on very well.'

Louisa was the second Mrs Seles, a not very bright but extremely beautiful model, some ten years younger than Paul, cut from the same pattern as Maddy but without the grit which had enabled Maddy to remake her life and look after Paul's first two children.

'He'd have been much better off with Sheena,' she agreed. Sheena at least had known the business and could have talked sense to Paul, but that too had ended in violence. Then Louisa had turned up, and Paul had fallen like a truckload of stones, showered her with gifts, and married her three months later.

'I am afraid this marriage isn't going to work. It is still Maddy whom he hankers for.'

'Oh dear,' Jens said, sadly, recognizing the truth. 'Well, I think he really can't go back there, she won't have him. And I know she's got someone else, someone new, married, I fear, but still . . . Poor Paul.'

'He walks around at night. I know because I can't sleep

through the night either – it's one of the great curses of old age, Jens. We had a cup of tea together at four o'clock this morning, but I'm not sure he managed to go back to sleep. Is it the business?'

She thought about it. 'Paragon is still a problem, you know – the business he bought in 1992. It has never made the money he hoped it would, and so he's stretched. I've been there, when I bought five restaurants at once and then the recession hit. It *is* awful, with a load of debt on your back, but the bankers all seem to eat out of Paul's hand and I assumed they were happy to finance him. Of course he's having to do a rights issue and his share price has hardly gone up at all in three years. No, I suppose that's not all right.' She looked at him apologetically. 'I've been busy, I'm sorry.'

'My dear Jens.' He pressed her hand. 'I never know how you fit it all in, what with a business and children and now Hugh away a lot. But Paul does listen to you. More to the point, he talks to you and he isn't talking to me at the moment.'

Paul emerged into the hall and she looked at him carefully. He was not with them, now she came to consider him, he was in a world far away.

'Paul?' He looked at her and she saw him come to himself and remember her.

'Jens. You seen David at all, recently?'

'You mean not on the telly? Not for a couple of weeks.'

'I haven't either, and I'd like to talk to him.'

'He turns up at Redwood's because it's convenient for the House, and he may easily be in this week.'

She stood on the step to watch them go, Paul fussing round Roger as he and the driver helped him into the car, thinking how many times over the years she had watched just that scene. Fortunate Paul, to have an adopted father whom he loved unequivocally.

It was still bitterly cold in the street and Jens shivered as she looked out of the window. She was in the company flat, which had been a self-inflicted management problem for the five years the company had owned it. It came with the fifth restaurant, one of the Chez Michel's, in the sense that the restaurant occupied the ground floor and basement and a small sub-office on the first floor. The two floors above that had been crudely converted into a three-bedroom flat, and had seemed to offer the possibility of housing a general manager or three senior waiters and relieving the perennial difficulty of keeping staff in central London. This had proved to be a dangerous illusion, and after three court-authorized evictions in five years Jens had decided that she would run restaurants and let others get on with providing housing for her staff. But something had to be done with two floors of usable space, so it had been converted, expensively this time, into a very good flat, just in time for the worst of the recession. Being still unsaleable at a price which would recoup conversion costs, it was intermittently let and was at the moment between tenants. She was in no hurry to find one either; the flat was barely ten minutes from Simon's office and while they could not go on doing this forever unremarked by restaurant staff, a few weeks must be possible. And it allayed Simon's anxieties about always using his London flat.

The bell rang sharply, and she pressed the entry code, and put away the set of accounts she had brought to look at. It had become much more difficult having an affair than she would have believed, had she felt free to tell anyone in the world about it. Simon was now infinitely busy and his days were planned to a time-table, he filled every moment, seeking always for what would be useful. He had risen fast, there was no doubt about *that*; he had two major political weekly programmes of his own and he was making a film as well.

She moved to the door to let him in so he would not have to ring when he got to the third floor, but she had underestimated the speed with which he took the stairs. He was alight with pleasure, she saw.

'I've been asked to do *Newsweek*. Take it over, I mean.'

'Oh, darling, that *is* good.' An audience of seven million, as he had taught her, was well worth having. 'Well, you deserve it. You were very good last night. And so was our Davey, I thought.'

'Yes. He's going to the top if he keeps that up.'

'If they get in.'

As a long-standing employer of catering labour, she was not at all hopeful of persuading employees to vote Labour. They all still seemed to believe, whatever the evidence to the contrary, that they would be worse off, that Labour would make them pay more tax.

'I know that I have somehow enmeshed myself with an unregenerate capitalist despite your good father but Labour will get back, you know. If only because this lot are making such a cobblers of it. I'd love a cup of tea.'

'Coming up.' She pressed the knob on the electric kettle which she had boiled before he arrived. He lived on cups of tea, and she always tried to provide something nourishing to eat. She just hoped he noticed some distinction between the beautiful food she gave him and whatever snack his assistants snatched off shelves for him.

'Can I eat it in bed?' he asked, taking a mouthful of Chef's baking and shooing her upstairs.

'Of course you can. What's a few crumbs between friends?'

'Depends where we put them, of course.'

She undressed, regretting momentarily the early days of the affair when he had always taken her clothes off for her before tearing off his own.

'Nice to go to bed in the afternoon,' he said, undoing his shoes with the hand he was not using to eat a second slice of pie.

He was, a wonderful lover, she thought, relaxing under his touch; it never seemed to matter if she had arrived with her nerves jangling and her head full of a dozen separate worries from staff shortages to the Inland Revenue – they just vanished; the day changed colour when she was going to see him. It was probably because she could not do so as often as she wanted; they were only managing to get time to go to bed together every other week. He was fond of her, he liked going to bed with her, but his career – every detail of it – mattered far more than she did, and mostly she accepted this. Because she had to, those were the terms.

'Hey. What's happening?' He always knew where she had got to.

'Sorry, sorry, just shedding rubbish. Come here and I'll lick the crumbs off, that'll make me concentrate.'

'And it'll make me come. You just worry about yourself.'

She concentrated to some purpose, so that she came unexpectedly and before she could warn him. 'Damn.'

'Darling, what? Not all right?'

'I wanted you inside me.'

'I'll tell you something about men,' he said, leaning on one elbow to fit a condom. 'It's actually quite nice for them if the woman comes first, then you can just pitch in and have a good time without worrying about her.' He slid adroitly into her and grinned down at her.

'I know that, I suppose. I could come *again*, you know. Women are capable of it.'

'And very nice too if you can.' He nipped her ear. 'But I'm going to anyway, really very soon. Ah, ah, aah.' His head went back so that the muscles in the throat stood out, and she closed her legs round his back, so that she could feel him as far inside her as possible. He finished and eased himself over, so that his full weight was off her, and kissed her. He always seemed contented with her, but she worried that she was not sufficiently adventurous or interesting in bed; well, Joshua had put paid, somehow, to all *that*, but at least she liked doing it. She knew she was lucky to have found men to get her over that hurdle, even if she still had problems.

She turned her head to kiss him, but his eyes were closed and he looked suddenly exhausted. It wasn't physical weariness with him ever, unless he was ill, and she held him closer. 'Flash of depression?'

His eyes opened. 'No. Yes. Just for a minute.'

'Don't move, tell me. A trouble shared . . .'

'. . . is two people made miserable.' It was an old, double-edged joke between them; both of them highly sensitive to other people and, as they had been able to admit to each other, prone themselves to hours and days of depression, they both functioned by using energy to cheer on themselves and those who surrounded them. 'It's not any one thing.'

She waited, stroking bits of him while he rearranged himself for comfort.

'Oh, Christ. Is that really the time? Can I have a shower?' He always asked – like a visitor – and it always hurt. He could have had anything he wanted, he was her lover, but he always maintained his sense of place. And he was right, she reminded herself, they were both married, and not unhappily. But Simon, it turned out, was not just a lover – if there was such a thing – but part of her life.

'You got your company floated, at least,' he said, returning from the shower, hair still wet, towel tucked around his waist. 'Were you worried?'

'No.' She had painstakingly taught him about financing. 'My merchant bank advisers – none of whom is more than about sixteen – are very pleased, and everyone's made a nice profit.'

He was, as she well understood, jealous of her; himself a very highly paid professional, with an income higher than she took from the restaurant, he had all the insecurity of the highly paid hired hand. In common with everyone she knew in the media and creative professions, he spent a lot of time trying to work out how to build up enough capital to be confident of being well off for ever. But it was difficult, it was the administrators and the businessmen who had made the real money out of television. The well-known, well-paid presenters and interviewers, with a few distinguished exceptions, were still salary-men, as he bitterly complained. And now she, his lover for three years, had joined the ranks of those who had made real money, a decent sum of capital, and he did not much like her for it. She tried to find a way of making him feel better.

'Well, the company was very much in debt. And we weren't allowed to sell very many of our own shares. Just enough to pay off our mortgages and send Sofia to Islamabad. You'll probably be setting up your own company or something equally grand.'

His eyelashes flicked. 'Actually, you're not far off the mark there.' He was watching his reflection in the mirror as he did his tie. 'Look, it's going to be a week or so before we can meet again.'

Dismayed, she closed her mouth on the observation that three weeks had elapsed since she had last seen him. He was watching her in the mirror and she felt a chill in the warm flat.

'I'm sorry, my love, but I have to keep pushing on this deal – no, I don't want to tell you about it, I daren't tell anyone, but you were close, OK?' He turned to look at her, ruefully. '*I* want to make my drop-dead money too.'

'Oh, *that* I understand.' The cold feeling in the stomach would not go away but she was not going to plead, and she got out of bed to put her arms round him. 'When you can, my love, I've got more time now the float's over.'

She watched him as he ran down the street and scrambled into a passing taxi. The driver would know his face, as they always did, and favour him with his views on the future of the BBC, as they all seemed to, and he would be surrounded and busy all the rest of the day and wanted in a dozen places at once. She packed up her briefcase, made the bed, and fled from the quiet, warm flat to the noise of her own office, telling herself there were a hundred things she had to do before going home to the children.

CHAPTER TWENTY-TWO

February 1995

'David! I saw you on the box last night and you were *great*.'
He always remembered to pay his brother a compliment when
he wanted something. 'Have you got a few minutes later
today?' He listened, enraged and anxious, as Davey explained
that a few minutes was all he had, and would not tomorrow
do. He'd got very grand, had his brother, but this was family
and he *must* help. He nagged on until he got the promise of a
meeting in ten minutes and managed to override his anxieties
long enough to make two more phone calls before leaving his
driver waiting just out of sight of Davey's office.

'That was quick.' Davey was all too clearly not pleased to
see him, but politician-like introduced him punctiliously to the
union riff-raff which was just leaving his office.

'Coffee, Mickey?' He saw David's weary conspiratorial
glance at his secretary and ground his teeth. 'So, what's the
problem?'

'I'm worried about the Group.' This was more baldly stated
than he had meant it to be, but Davey's open impatience was
rattling him.

'What is it that you think I can do?' Davey was sitting in an
easy-chair, so was he, but he might as well have been on the
other side of a desk.

'I need to talk to you.' His brother's guarded look told
him something was wrong, and he realized he was twisting
his hands. He unwound them and carefully placed them on
the arms of the chair. 'I'm not really sure what's going on,

everything looks all right, but there's something up. And cash is tight again.'

'So you think something may be wrong?'

Davey's elaborate, hostile patience made him want to scream but he leant forward, shoulders rigid, desperate for reassurance. 'Yes. If the rights issue goes through we should be all right. But the share price keeps going down . . . just a little.'

'That always worries people in business.' Davey had actually looked at his watch, but he wasn't going to get him to leave, not until he had made him somehow understand the panic he was in.

'Paul's a friend of yours, isn't he? And I'm your brother. If we are in trouble you may find yourself involved.' He saw with an easing of anxiety that Davey's knee literally jerked.

'Not my field. I'm not a City expert.'

Davey was so confident, he thought numbly, that he just felt inadequate and hopeless, trying to make him do things. 'Davey, I need help.' It came out in a rush, and he hated his brother heartily for the instant alarmed withdrawal he could see on his face.

'Wait a minute,' David said slowly. 'Jean was having some tests, wasn't she?'

'How did you know? Oh, she told Ann, I suppose, and Ann tells you everything.'

'Come on, Mickey, that's marriage. And family. So what was the result? I'm sorry not to have asked straightaway.'

'The smear test showed irregularities. That's what it said and they want her to have a hysterectomy. Now. This week.'

'You must be very worried.'

He was, of course, distracted and miserable. And so was Jean. clinging to her older girls, tearful and needing him to come to all the doctors with her. She had no women friends, well, he didn't have any men friends either. They had each other.

'Had she not had a smear test before?'

'Well, not for years. Not since Jacinth was born. She went this time because we'd hoped to have another one, before it was too late.'

'I always forget Jean is Ann's age. Yes, of course. And you found this. What rotten luck. I am sorry. Can I help with hospitals?'

'No, thank you. We're insured and I think we've got the best chap.'

The secretary put her head in – prearranged, that, he realized angrily, but Davey waved her away, asking charmingly if he could have another ten minutes, he could be late for lunch if need be.

Mickey gritted his teeth and tried again. 'It isn't just Jean, I mean that's awful, but that only happened last week, and I was worried before. I've been getting calls from suppliers and the VAT people. Paul and Sean won't ring them back. And we're supposed to be making *profits* . . . something's going on.'

'Have you talked to them?'

'They won't stop long enough to talk to anyone.' No one would, he thought, with savage despair, seeing Davey just glance at the large square watch that his company had given him when he left the Army . . . what . . . twelve years ago. 'I know you think it's just Jean, and I *am* very worried about her and I know I'm not very good when something goes wrong with her, but that isn't it, Davey.' He looked at his hands, they had twisted themselves in his lap and he realized he was going to cry. Well, he would just let go, make Davey realize this was serious.

'Oh, for God's sake, Mickey. Seriously, what do you expect me to do? What are you asking for?'

'Help.' He found a handkerchief, and heard Davey sigh.

'What you're saying, it seems to me, is that things are going badly at the company, and Paul and Sean are working flat out to put them right. They don't have time to talk to you.'

'No. That's not all I'm saying.' It was time to get out his deepest fear in the hope that Davey would be able to reassure him. 'I think they're doing something illegal. I think they're making the profits look more than they actually are.'

'You mean they're deceiving shareholders?'

He looked helplessly at his brother; there was, as he had known, no comfort there. 'Well, yes. I suppose so.'

'Look, Mickey, if you really think there's something criminal going on you must not be involved with it. I mean, you have to resign, now.'

'I can't.' He looked at his brother appalled. 'I can't.'

'Mickey.' At last he had Davey's full attention. 'This is how you got into such a mess at university, wasn't it? You should then have stopped going round in circles getting yourself into trouble. If you're right, you'll be involved in someone else's cheating this time.'

He winced. Davey would use words like cheating.

'Why can't you resign?'

'I can't afford to.' The very idea filled him with terror; the bills came in every month, and he always seemed to be a bit behind, and now Jean was ill.

'Come on, Mickey. You've got that lovely house and that must be worth a bit. And Jean can go NHS – it's actually still good in an emergency like this. Bit rough and ready but she'll be well looked after, and there I can help a bit.'

He hated his brother then, as he sometimes did, the efficient, saving Puritan who was never behind with his bills, who lived, uncomfortably, on half nothing, whose house was bracingly cool and where it was difficult to get a square meal.

'I'd never get another job.' This was at the core of his terror; Paul Seles had taken him on as a favour to Davey and kept him for reasons he never wholly understood, and no one else would ever do the same.

'Paul Seles doesn't run a charity. Someone else will hire you to do the same for them.' Davey was scowling in the way he remembered from childhood, and he felt a pang of secret relief; his big brother might be pissed off with him but he was hooked, he would help. 'I don't want to talk to Paul about this,' Davey said slowly. 'If something is wrong he's not going to tell *me*. I can talk to Jens and she might be helpful. She knows him very well.'

'I'd be very grateful,' Mickey said, relaxing back into the chair. 'I don't feel I know Jens well enough to ask her – I mean, I've known her for years, but she's always so busy.'

'Leave it with me, Mickey. I don't know when I'll be able to get in to see her, or even if she's in London.' He looked down as he always did when he was not quite telling the truth, but Mickey would have to settle for what he had got. Davey didn't want to talk to Jens Redwood, but he would fit it into his schedule somewhere.

'Can you do it this week?'

'I'll try. Now, you go back and look after Jean. I'll be in touch as soon as I can.'

The room looked like a Renaissance drawing, its architecture and fittings controlled and formal, the faces of the three men in it still and watchful, their sombre suits relieved by bright flashes of silk at the neck, no relaxation in their bodies despite the easy-chairs in which they sat and to which he was courteously motioned.

'Tim, I've asked Jonathan and Peter to be here as well because we all need to be clear about what we're doing, as a house. I see we've bought another fifty thousand Seles Group shares this morning. For whom?'

'For the Growth Fund. We decided to buy some more whenever the price goes below four fifty-six. It doesn't very often. We're not the only buyers at that sort of price.'

'Who are the others?'

'A couple of Swiss groups. And let us be clear, we know who they are, inasmuch as they are entities with whom the lads have done business before, and they pay their bills. As I do not need to remind you, Swiss law prevents anyone from identifying the investors in these companies.'

'They are, to coin a phrase, anonymous. Yes.' The Hon. Marcus Widnell, senior partner in Brandes and Jones, hesitated over his next question. 'We have no reason to suppose there's anything going wrong in the Seles Group? My pa says there's a lot of gossip in the House about arms sales in Eastern Europe. People selling to terrorists in the Middle East, threatening the Agreement.'

'I asked Paul Seles a month ago to assure us that his

companies weren't involved. Of course, he's also got shareholdings in a couple of associated companies, which he doesn't control. He was a bit, well, unforthcoming about them.'

'Did you minute this conversation?'

'Of course I did.'

'Right. Right. Jonathan? Peter?'

'Do it *again*, Tim. Hold the conversation again, would you, and come back and talk to us? We'll do the note together this time.'

David walked up to Redwood's I, moving quickly; he needed the exercise, relishing the instant recognition he was attracting, and thinking furiously. It was a warm spring day again and despite the difficulties of the unknown ahead of him he was glad to be alive; this morning's news meant change and movement, and made him realize how trapped and depressed he had been feeling. He bounced into the restaurant, dead on time as usual, and twinkled at the pretty receptionist, who took him personally down the long restaurant to the table where Jens was chatting to a well-known American actor and his press agent whom she left as he arrived. He bent to kiss her, noting that she was looking tired and strained.

'How are you, Davey?' she asked, when he had been provided with a drink and a menu. 'There's a decent steak if you're hungry.'

'I am. It's sandwiches tonight.' He felt himself relax; he was always comfortable with Jens. She was acknowledging without in any way encouraging greetings from several well-known faces.

'Haven't seen you in ages, except on the box.'

'I'm sorry. Life is just intolerably busy at the moment.' It sounded lame to him and her considering look told him she was unimpressed too. He sighed and looked round him. The tables were well separated anyway but the two nearest ones to them were empty, as they always were when Jens was lunching. 'I needed to talk to you. I'm getting rumours about the Seles Group.'

'Where from?'

'Mickey for one. And now in the House.' Jens was always direct and he found it possible to be the same with her. He relayed the substance of his conversation with Mickey. 'He's in a panic, Jens.'

'That's because of Jean.'

'That doesn't help, but there's something else.'

Jens knew how pressured and burdened he felt by Mickey, and indeed it had been she who had pointed out that Mickey would be all right while Jean had everything she wanted. She sighed, 'I saw Paul last night. I agree he's worried. But Mickey is in a far better position than me to know what's going on, surely.'

He cut gratefully into the thick steak that had arrived in front of him. He had run out of everything at the flat and had not wanted to eat the pastries his secretary had provided; he was putting on a bit of weight and he would be forty next week.

'Oh, Jens, Mickey's the office boy there.'

'I do know. He's not stupid, though, and he's likely right. So what do you hope I will do?'

'I suppose I want to know whether Mickey's just in one of his panics or whether it's for real.'

'And if it's for real?'

'Well, I'd then urge Mickey to have it out with Paul or resign, and I suppose I thought you'd like to know.'

'Not awfully.'

'Have you quarrelled with him?' Paul and she often did, like real siblings, even though they were thirty-nine and forty years old.

'No. I'm just busy and harassed. Hugh's away.'

He looked at her carefully; preoccupied though he was, he could see there was something dragging at her, but he needed her to pay attention to him instead of whatever it was. She would now talk to Paul, that was his mission accomplished, but he needed her for something else as well. 'I'm sorry, love, I know that's always difficult.' He paused. 'Things are happening back at the funny farm.' He longed to tell someone and he could usually depend on her being interested. 'Jim is ill.'

'He was before, surely?' She was gratifyingly distracted.

'Really ill. Having-to-give-up ill.'

'What rotten luck for him after all that. What does it do to you?'

'Moves me up.' There was never any need to pussyfoot around with Jens.

'Gives you a crack at Shadow Home Secretary?'

'Yes. I've got the support, the problem was always that no one was prepared to ditch Jim.' He looked down at his plate, he seemed to have finished his steak and he reached automatically for the next lot of food.

'Those were my chips.'

He ignored the familiar protest. 'With Jim gone, you see, the whole structure moves; everything has to shift.

'Crumbs.'

'That's why I'm busy.'

'And that's why you need to sort out Mickey. I'll talk to Paul and try and form a view.' She flipped open the five-page/five-week schedule she always carried and made a note. 'If I can find him I'll do it later today. Do you want pudding? The torte is good.' She ordered it and sat quietly, taking a gulp of wine. She did not usually drink at lunch, and he watched her uneasily, trying to distract her with an account of the morning's meetings.

'Are you all right?' he asked, finally and reluctantly.

'Not really. Don't ask. I will talk to Paul. I know it's important.'

He watched her anxiously, hoping for a bit more reassurance, but her mind was not on him.

'Aren't you eating?'

'Later.'

He saw her hands clench on the edge of the table and automatically reached over and put his hand over hers.

'I'm OK, Davey. My lunch guest has arrived, I must go.'

He let go her hand, and watched, alarmed, as she straightened the table-cloth and rose to go. He stood up for her automatically and leant over to kiss her, so that she would have to acknowledge that he still existed.

'Relax, Davey,' she said, touching his cheek. 'I would like you to be Home Secretary one day. Think how useful we would all find it.'

She walked off, straight-backed, and he watched to see who she was meeting, recognizing the man and the situation in a flash of illumination. He hesitated; he badly wanted a casual chat with Simon Dearsley, but he just did not dare interrupt, needing Jens to talk to Paul as he did.

Paul was sitting in the back of his big car in the usual traffic jam, finding it a relief to curse at the traffic. He was exhausted; he never seemed to get to sleep these nights, and was seriously overweight; Jens had suggested a week in a health farm and offered to go with him, and for a moment he let himself consider it. A week in the country with Jens would be wonderful; he could really talk to her if he could get her away from her restaurants and that stupid affair which was now so obviously going wrong. Women like her shouldn't try it, she took it all far more seriously than that elegant, clever, conceited television commentator did. She would have been better to stick with Ferenc if she needed a lover.

'Paul.' It was his driver, one of the other people who had been with him from the beginning. 'There, look, isn't that Mr Banner?'

'Oh Christ, yes. Hoot at him. Then you get out, I'll drive him, I need to talk. Take a phone. Get yourself lunch, I'll call you later.' He opened the door and heaved himself out just ahead of his quarry. 'Davey!'

'Paul, good to see you.'

Not at all what Davey meant, he thought grimly but being a politician trapped you in a habit of being polite and welcoming to people you would very much rather not see.

'Hop in a minute.'

'I'd love to but I'm running late.'

'We'll take you.' The driver was holding the door for him.

Wooden-faced, Davey got in, moving neatly as he always did, not a hair out of place, making Paul feel tired and breathless as he flopped into the driver's seat.

'Where to, guv?'

The old joke made Davey smile briefly and reminded him as it was intended to of the many times Paul had driven him on some pleasurable and unpublicized expedition.

'The House. Please.'

Well, that was all right. The traffic was bad enough, so they would have at least ten minutes.

'Davey, this time *I* need some help.' It was a bit crude as an opening, but he was desperate and it would do no harm to remind Davey that he had kept his younger brother from being a burden to him all these years. He glanced sideways and saw that his old mate was braced for trouble; somebody had got there first.

'Is it the business?' Davey of course was a politician, he had no idea what it was like to have not one but a dozen businesses, all tugging at you, not one of them running smoothly.

'Not exactly,' he said, swallowing bile, and bringing the big car up with a jerk just short of the bumper of an erratically driven Fiat. 'It's Sean, as a matter of fact.'

'*Sean?*'

Ah, now that had come as a surprise to Davey. He'd been expecting something quite different. He saw that he had made another mistake. Mickey must have run to his big brother with some garbled story. He should have made time to sit down and feed Mickey some garbage reassurance about the Group's finances, he would have known no different and he would have felt better. Even more important now to get Davey into action where he needed him, and keep him out where he would rather not have him. 'Yes, Sean. You know he's got this boyfriend – Sandor.'

'The one Jens can't stand?'

'Yeah, well, he's not my favourite person either.' This was better. 'But the point *is* Davey, as we now know, he's also a crook, he's in with some very nasty people indeed in the Ukraine. And he's managed, God knows how, to involve one of my factories in Slovakia.'

He saw that something had rung a bell with Davey.

'Your lot have been asking questions in the House – quite rightly – about the factory in Slovakia. We knew already and I was dealing with it – I tell you, Davey, it's stopped, there is nothing going out of my factory. I wouldn't touch those people with a barge pole.' He was telling the truth, he had been utterly shocked and had felt even worse when he discovered where the Semtex was going, straight to one of his adopted country's worst enemies in the Middle East.

'So how did it happen?'

He hesitated; it had of course involved Sean. The fucking Ukrainians – worse than the Mafia – had decided to squeeze Sandor out and cut off his supply. And his customers – well, their intermediaries – had put pressure on Sandor, who had in desperation used Sean to get two deliveries out of the Seles Group factory in Martin. All *that* would have been a problem at the best of times, with Davey's lot asking questions – and God knows where they got their information – but *now* with everything else going so bloodily wrong and the share price shaking, this trouble could simply not be afforded.

'Was it Sean only, Paul?'

'What? Yeah. I'm involved in sorting it out of course, because I have to be. What did you think?'

'I didn't know it was your factory.' Davey had gone chalk white, he saw, amazed, the sunburn looking yellow. 'It's me asking the questions, Paul – Peter Fountain, you remember him? My mate from the regiment. He's still in the Army of course, in Jordan, advising, like most of the senior blokes. He told me one of the nastiest terrorist gangs in the Middle East was being supplied by a British company. I was bloody going to find it for him and get it stopped. I didn't know it was the Seles Group. I've got a Question down for next week.'

'Can you withdraw it? It's *over*, Davey. It's gone, it can't happen again.' He had moved too fast and clumsily, he saw, but he was tired to the bone and he had a million other things to do, to fight off the remorseless pressure. He ploughed on. 'You won't find anything because there won't be any more to find, that I swear, Davey. I'm sending Sean to America and nobody need worry about Sandor, ever again. And you could hurt the Group badly.'

'Paul, Paul. You're asking me to do something I can't do.'

'Don't you believe me?'

'Yes.' The swift reply was not convincing and Paul winced; it was a dreadful story and he might not have believed it himself. 'I believe you Paul, I've known you too long not to. But I'm not sure you're in control out there.'

Paul felt the blood beat in his forehead and controlled himself, breathing deep. This was his life and he could not afford to let go; just for a fleeting moment he thought of Roger Caldwell. 'I'm in your hands, Davey,' he said carefully. 'You and I go back a long way, and we've always known everything about each other. You ought to know I'm telling the truth. And will go on telling it.'

You could have choked on the silence in the car, he thought, feeling the man next to him understand that he was playing in the big leagues. This was the real world here, not that Palace of Varieties down the road which they all thought was so important. He waited, patient now, the big car inching forward.

'I can't do it, Paul. I can't withdraw the Question. Too risky.'

Davey's voice was devoid of tone, dead level, and Paul knew he had reached the bottom line, the irreducible truth, always recognizable when you got to it; it had a different ring from a negotiating point. But he had to try. 'I know about you and Maddy.'

'I'm sorry about that, Paul. She said you wouldn't care, not now you were married again.'

'Oh, I still care.' He had known Davey far too long not to admit that. 'But that isn't the point. Ann will care. So will everyone else. And the press will enjoy every minute.'

'Bugger that.' The colour had come back, patchily, to Davey's face but he looked utterly different, all the animation gone, staring through the windscreen. 'You'll have to do whatever you want, Paul. It won't do any good. And, as you say, we are in each other's hands, all three of us, you, me and Jens. You think about that. I'm getting out.'

He had the door open and was gone, moving quickly through the groups on the pavement, unmistakably a man running from disaster. Paul turned the wheel savagely, but just too late to avoid the bumper of a taxi, manoeuvring slowly round a blocked corner.

'Miss Redwood, Mr Seles.' The secretary was new and anxious and did not quite know which calls to let through, but Jens did not usually ring up idly.

Paul burped. The hamburger for lunch had been a bad idea. 'Put her on.'

'She's here, Mr Seles . . . sorry. In the waiting-room.'

He lumbered to his feet and went over to fetch her, heart in his mouth. 'Jens, is it the kids?'

'Oh, darling, *sorry*, no, nothing like that. No, it's business. I was passing and I need to see you.'

He called for coffee and told the girl to hold all the calls, and looked at Jens carefully as she sat down. Even through his own misery and stress he could see she was in trouble, pale, drawn and pink round the eyes. 'What's the matter?'

'I have a cold.' She had rubbed her eyes and her mascara had run, and he advanced on her and wiped it off with a handkerchief, drawing comfort from her familiar perfume.

'Don't ask,' she said between gritted teeth.

'I wasn't going to,' he lied. 'To what do I owe the honour?'

She looked at her hands, the firm jaw set, the whole of her achingly familiar, and he watched her with love. 'I came to ask whether you were in trouble. The business, I mean.' She looked him in the face, her blue eyes wide, and he flinched.

'No. Yes.'

'What sort of trouble? Cash?'

'Isn't it always?'

'Not with a profitable Group, no. Is there anything I can do?'

'A loan of twenty million quid wouldn't come amiss.'

'Oh God, Paul.'

'We'll get by, or we would if people stopped selling the shares and the wankers in Parliament would keep their noses out so we could get the rights issue away.'

It was gratifying in a way to see Jens knocked out of her customary composure; she had gone white with shock. 'Which wankers?' She still asked the right question first, though, but he didn't want to answer it, not yet. She saw his hesitation and was in like a knife. 'What particularly are they asking?'

He got up to avoid answering and prowled towards the filing cabinets, just hearing through the thick door the noise of the phones. 'The Opposition. They're shit-stirring, asking about arms exports. I need to sort David out.'

'Why? Paul, dearest Paul, it's *me*.' It was their code but he didn't listen. She was looking at him as if he'd grown two heads, as she had when he'd beaten Stephen, but he wasn't going to collapse in tears this time.

'You could ask him for me . . . David, I mean,' he said.

'Why me? What about Mickey who works for you and whose brother he is?'

'He won't do it for Mickey. No point in trying.' He'd thought of that, as Jens should have known, he never neglected the obvious. She was looking at him stupidly, and he wanted to shake her. 'Jens, now is the time for all good women . . .'

'Paul, just tell me, how bad is it, what are you *doing*? Can we lend you some money?'

He looked at her, his mind wearily churning. 'Yes. It would have to be kept quiet, though. I mean, your board wouldn't have to hear about it.'

'I can't *do* that, Paul, not again. *I'll* lend you some, personally.'

'You haven't got enough.'

'What about your Redwood's shares?'

'Them? I've borrowed against them. Twice.' He started to laugh and stopped angrily, in the face of her obvious horror. 'What I need is a few days. I need the Labour lot to ease up, just for a while.' If he could just have *that* pressure off, so Sean wasn't in a state all the time. The stupid bogtrotter, to get a Seles Group company to supply Sandy's friends ... 'Just the once', he had sworn ... and the whole pack was coming tumbling down.

'Paul. Come home with me. You're not making sense.'

'I can't, Jens.' He felt suddenly immensely exhausted. 'If you can raise me some cash, I'll be grateful. It's like the old days here, I can hardly sign a cheque and I need to pay a few school fees. If you could see your way to fifty thousand in cash?'

'I'll do that.' She would too, without asking anyone, and he kissed her. 'I'll call you.'

He walked her to the office door, gathering himself to face his anxious staff, and watched as the driver took her away.

CHAPTER TWENTY-THREE

February 1995

'Can I have a quick word with David? He is expecting me to ring. No, you are kind, there really isn't a way of leaving a sensible message.'

She was ringing later than she had promised, but it had been an impossible morning. Her bank had behaved as if the withdrawal of £50,000 in cash threatened their reserves. It had taken her an hour even to organize it, and she was having to wait until 2 p.m. for them to arrange a series of loans from other branches, or some rigmarole along those lines. The chef at Redwood's II had come in belligerently to resign and she had spent another hour soothing ruffled feathers.

'He will ring you back, Miss Redwood, he has people with him.' David's secretary was sounding disapproving.

I don't like you either, little girl, she thought sourly, on edge and wretched, but your boss asked me to do something and I have, as usual, done it. She sat resting her eyes on the flowering cherry outside in the road.

'Jens.'

'Are you still surrounded? I've seen Paul.'

She heard him laugh, a short unamused bark. 'So have I. Yesterday. And I saw Sean today.'

'Oh.' She thought about that. 'I was going to tell you on the basis of yesterday that I thought our worst fears were justified and that Mickey would be better out.' She was always careful on the telephone; the people who had installed the system that linked all fifteen restaurants had explained to her that *any* phone call could be overheard, somewhere.

'I agree.'

She listened to the silence, puzzled. 'Is there anything I can do?'

'Not at the moment, no. I will ring you if ... if I think something can or ought to be done.' He was sounding utterly wooden, the normally warm, inflected voice dead level. 'Events seem to have overtaken us. Yesterday doesn't seem to matter now. I'm sorry, I must go.'

The phone choked down and she stared disbelievingly at the hand-set, as if it could tell her something. She looked up to find her general manager hovering in the doorway.

'Hugh rang.'

She looked at him blankly.

'Your husband, Hugh. From the airport in Warsaw. He'll be home this afternoon, the meeting ended early.'

'Thanks, Joe. Sorry, I was miles away.' She felt a rush of reassurance and pleasure. Hugh was coming home, she could tell him about Paul and he would help, no matter how much he disapproved. And he would never put the phone down on her abruptly because it was awkward for some reason. She would meet him; Heathrow was not far from Paul's headquarters and she could drop off the cash on the way. If he ever found out Hugh would be furious but it was her money after all.

Paul was not at his office, but had left instructions that the packet she brought was to go into the safe. It seemed a lot of money just to leave, but she was running late. She asked for Sean but he had gone out as well.

She waited for ten minutes in Terminal 2, straining to see Hugh. He walked out, slightly stooped, a familiar stocky figure with sandy hair and glasses, accompanied by a woman of about her own age but blonde and very good-looking. His face lit up when he saw her and he steered the blonde across to meet her; a fellow economist, he explained cheerfully, as the woman left them. Jens hugged him; she had not, she realized,

411

for one moment thought the woman was other than a casual friend. Her Hugh had always been absolutely trustworthy with women; he loved her and his family and did not need the reassurance of having something else on the side. She stopped suddenly, seeing Simon and herself through a different glass, as insubstantial and unreliable.

'What's up with friend David?' Hugh asked, putting his case down to change grip, and she took a moment to collect her thoughts.

'With David? What do you mean?'

'Just like when I was a Press Secretary.' He fished the *Evening Standard* out of his briefcase. 'Look at the sub-headline about "unnamed Opposition politician in sex scandal", plus a picture of David Banner doing something perfectly ordinary. Same technique as with all those chaps last year.'

'I don't quite understand,' she said, and he patted her shoulder.

'They've got something they can't use, or they *think* they've got something. So they publish the allegations and put a picture of the chap they think it is on the same page, doing whatever he usually does, so he can't complain.'

'You didn't do that sort of thing in the Treasury, did you?'

'No, of course not, but it was done unto us – or rather the Government as a whole – and there was bugger-all we could do about it. How're the kids?'

'They're fine.' In truth she could barely remember where they were or what they were doing, and she needed to sit down and think. Her Hugh was typically very much more interested in hearing about his treasured children than anything or anyone else, and she managed to produce a coherent account and to get to the car which was lying in wait for them with the engine running.

'Hugh,' she said, as soon as she decently could, 'Paul is in trouble.'

'Oh, no. Not again.'

'Yes. I'm afraid it may be bad.' She huddled up to him and told him all she knew, carefully leaving out the £50,000; she just was not ready to admit to that, and besides, it might come back before she had to.

'It sounds as if he's been lying about profits to get the rights issue away. You didn't buy shares, did you, Jens?'

'Well, I've got the ones I've always had. And I took up the rights last time.'

'But none bought recently? No? Did he ask you to?'

'Yes. But not very seriously and I didn't.'

'You didn't lend him money either?'

She found she could not tell a lie direct, not to Hugh, and told him about the £50,000. 'You think I won't get it back? But I know that, and it is mine.'

'I think that may be the least of our worries.' He was looking a good five years older and weary, but her heart was warmed by the use of 'our'. 'Depends what he does with it.'

'He wanted it for bills and school fees.'

'What's he got there, a tribe?' She was near tears and he saw it. 'Darling, it's all right. He's a bloody nuisance, but he's your family, I know. Come on, don't cry, I'm home.'

She sat, the next morning, in her office with eight daily papers spread out in front of her and the door forbiddingly closed, looking for news of the two men she knew so well and who had both stopped talking to her. Nothing in *The Times* nor the *Financial Times* about the Seles Group or David. The *Telegraph*, however, carried an article about freedom of the press which made open reference to a political scandal affecting a senior Opposition politician being hushed up opposite a picture of David launching a research paper. She looked anxiously at the picture; he was looking past the camera, chin propped on his right hand with the fingers spread out to cover his mouth, a pose that William French had explained meant you were trying to conceal something, or not to say it. William had turned it into a game, she remembered distractedly, and they had all had to register an emotion, using only body language. Sofia's own rendering of covetousness had been particularly striking. She reached for the phone, but checked; if the press did suspect him of having a girlfriend, all the situation needed was for her – or any woman – to ring up. The *Daily Mail* had a little piece on the Seles Group, suggesting it might be going to make less profit than forecast, but otherwise there was nothing. She picked at the blotter in a state of indecision, then dumped the paper in the waste-paper basket and started to do those things which could not do any harm, like finding out where Paul Seles was and what he was doing.

She drew a blank at his house; Louisa was out too, presumably raiding Harrods, and the office had no idea where he or Sean was. She hesitated, but the phone rang.

'Mickey,' she said, relieved. 'Just the man I want. Do you have Paul or Sean with you?'

'No, I don't. I hoped you had.' He sounded quite despairing, as if he were alone in a desert.

'They can't be far,' she said, bracingly.

'I can't cope here,' he said suddenly. 'I get frightened.'

She looked at the phone disbelievingly and remembered her conversation with David. 'Hang on, Mickey. Tell me about Jean. When's the operation?'

'Tomorrow.'

'No wonder you're worried,' she said encouragingly, but was met only by a silence, heavy with anxiety.

'Jens,' he said in a rush, 'Paul saw Davey yesterday. Then he came back here very late. I asked him if he wanted anything and he told me to go home, he was going to make some more calls. There's someone from the *Telegraph* who said he spoke to him yesterday and he asked if I was Davey's brother and could I comment. Then the *Daily Mail* rang and asked about the company.'

'What did you say?'

'I said someone would ring the *Daily Mail* back. But they keep ringing. Oh . . .' His voice rose hysterically. 'That may be Sean. I must talk to him.'

The phone went down without ceremony in a crash which hurt her eardrum. She sat, panicked, knowing only that she must get out of this office. And do what? She looked up to see the door opening a crack.

'Jens? I am sorry.'

'What?'

'It's me, Sofia.'

'Sofe?' She realized she sounded unwelcoming. 'Sorry. Glad to see you – just surprised.'

'Jens, have you got a tape-machine here?'

'You mean one of those with news announcements? Yes. Over here.'

She punched in the code and turned to Sofia in mute inquiry, but she was closing the door carefully, so she turned back to the screen. *Shadow Cabinet Member admits affair*, the screen said, and she stood, mouth open, as the text rolled on. It was not a long statement, short enough to fit on to the screen in its entirety, and it ended with the announcement of a press conference to be given by David Banner in an hour's time.

'The *idiot*. How could he be so *stupid*?'

'Do you know her? The girl, I mean?'

'Juliette Templeton. She's part of the lot that do Paul's financial PR. Dear God. She rang me up a year ago to explain that she'd left and gone somewhere else, but we never bother with PR normally, so I didn't listen properly. Jesus. I suppose she went to the press. He seems to have ditched *her* as he ditched Ali. Men! They're all the same.' She found she was crying helplessly, and that Sofia's arms were round her, as William French's would have been.

'I'm sorry, Jens. It's Simon, I suppose.'

She could not turn to look at Sofia. 'How long have you known?'

'Oh, Jens. You're not invisible, you know, and these television people are conspicuous. For a couple of years at least.'

'You never said.' She shivered and felt for a chair. 'Because you disapprove?'

'Yes.' Sofia never forced her views on anyone, of course, but she never lied either. 'And I ducked talking to you about it. I hoped you would stop.'

415

'Well, that's what happened. Or rather Simon stopped. The day before yesterday.' She felt very cold and huddled into the chair to get warm.

'Perhaps it was *his* wife who made him stop?'

'Perhaps. It's not very good, is it?' She saw in a dizzying kaleidoscope quite how unattractive it was. 'Oh, God,' she said, agonized.

'Jens.' Sofia pulled a chair over and covered her cold, clenched hands with her own. 'You've got Hugh. And you must have been taking terrible risks – well, you were. Do Paul and David know?'

'I hoped not. But if you'd noticed, Sofe, then I'd have to think they did too. *They'd* never tell.'

Sofia was pressing buttons on the machine. 'I don't think it was the girl herself who gave it to the press.'

'Must have been.' She was too sunk in misery to care.

'Jens, concentrate. It might be important.'

It could have been William French speaking, and she forced herself to absorb the text. 'Evidently not. The editor is being very shifty about it.'

'If it's not her then somebody else had it in for him. A political enemy?'

'Oh, he's got a few of those. Some of the present Government would jump at anything that discredited David's lot.' She thought of the last time she had seen him. 'And there's movement among his own lot too – he's got enemies there, and the Labour Party hasn't changed much since my pa was in it. More fun to stab one of your own than win an election.'

'Might it have been Paul?' Sofia was sounding overpatient, speaking as if to one slightly deaf, and she tried, obediently, to think.

'Why Paul?'

'Ali says David is seeing Maddy. And Paul *is* in trouble isn't he?'

'Oh God. Yes. Press the button, that one,' she said, distractedly. The Seles Group share price was 10p off, while the rest of the market was up a bit. 'Paul's got £50,000 in cash,' she said urgently to Sofia's anxious, uncomprehending face. 'Where has he gone? I won't get through to Mickey, will I? He's David's brother, and all sorts of people will be ringing him. And where the hell is Sean? Look at that!' The screen was flickering, and a run of figures was appearing beside the Seles Group share price: 461, 59, 57, 55, 51.

She pressed a button on the phone. 'Jennifer Redwood. What's happening with the Seles Group?' She forced her voice into a semblance of calm. 'No, I've just seen it on the screen. No, it's all right, John, I'm not trying to sell, I've had those shares for ten years and I bought them at twenty pence, a bit of a bump doesn't matter, I just wondered. No, I haven't seen Paul for a couple of days and I imagine his phone will be engaged. I expect you're busy too. Yes, do ring me if you hear anything.'

She put the phone down and stared at her friend. '"Can't get a price", he said. Shares are going down like a stone in a well.' They both stared at the screen, hypnotized, as they dropped below 400p.

The screen went blank and cleared again. 'Quote suspended,' Sofia said. 'Someone's on deck, then. Jens? You all right?'

'No.'

'Did you have a lot of shares?'

'No, no, it's not that.'

The door opened behind them. 'I'm terribly sorry, Jens, but we're getting a lot of calls from newspapers, asking about Mr Seles. I've said you're not here.'

'They're all about Paul Seles?'

Her general manager looked at his list. '*News of the World* wouldn't say, the *Sun* asked if David Banner was a regular customer and wanted you to call back.'

'Thank you, Joe. Ring the respectable ones and refer all calls about Paul Seles to Charles – I'll talk to him now. We won't, of course, call the *News of the World* or the *Sun*, and it's the usual line if they ring back – we don't discuss our customers. Ever. I want the car and you just tell everyone I'm in transit somewhere – Manchester perhaps.'

The door closed and Jens started mechanically to check her handbag, hands shaking.

'Where are you going now?' Sofia asked, worried. 'Would you like to hole up at my flat?'

'I'm going to find Hugh.' She stared, wide-eyed, at Sofia's uncomprehending face. 'Don't you see? Everything's coming unstuck. I have been so stupid. How could I not have seen what risks I was taking? I've always been quite ready to tell those two – Paul and Davey – all about their conduct.'

'But whatever has happened to them, you're not involved, are you? Jens, you didn't have an affair with Davey? No? Thank God for that. And you're not involved in the Seles Group, you've just told me you're not. Darling, try not to panic.'

'I'm not. Or not much. I just know Sofe, as surely as if I saw it written down, that this is the end; we three have always been in each other's hands and it's come unravelled. I must get to Hugh before anyone else does and tell him about Simon.'

'Oh, Jens. Must you? I mean, if it's over.'

'It would be even worse to have Paul or David or a news-paper tell him.' She stopped stuffing things into a handbag and started to take them all out again. 'And he will defend me – us, the kids, everyone I may have involved – more efficiently if he knows the full strength.' She looked distractedly at the pile. 'He may want a divorce, but he'll stick by me now, for the children's sake if for no other reason.'

'He is, of course, a good man.'

'I know what you think, and I wish I were dead. And where is Paul?'

'*Merci*, Mr Kelly. *Vous avez un limo? Bon.*' The small, square man took him to the door of the bank, as befitted a good customer, and he eased himself into the waiting car, slinging a heavy briefcase ahead of him on to the back seat.

'Cointrin,' he said, resisting the temptation to open the bag again and check. He left the driver at the airport with a muttered word of thanks and looked round for the man he was meeting.

'Monsieur Thokoly?' It took him a second or so to react, then he smiled and handed the man the Hungarian passport and followed him through the buildings to where a small plane stood waiting.

He was strapped in and given coffee by a solicitous young man, and the passport was returned, and as the plane taxied to the end of the runway he let out some of the tension in a huge breath. An English evening paper had been thrust on to the plane at the last minute, the front page entirely taken up with a picture of David Banner with his arm round his wife, both grimly staring at the camera, and on page two a smaller, old picture of Juliette Templeton, short-skirted and smiling. Served David Banner right, he had turned out as a cunning politician who would not lift a finger to help an old friend out of trouble. He had had the letter by him for six months or so. David Banner had turned white when he had produced a copy, and tried to say at first that there was nothing he could do anyway to call off his political friends, whatever the Seles Group threatened him with. But at the end he had stood firm, refused to intervene and told him to publish and be damned. He was a tough bastard, that one, tougher than he'd realized; denying calmly that there was anything between him and Maddy and daring him to prove otherwise. Which he couldn't; he'd never tried to get any evidence because Maddy was Paul's wife. A name caught his eye and he turned the paper sideways to look; *Seles Group shares suspended at 379p.* He read it unmoved; after all the year-long struggle they were free. A lot of people were going to catch a cold, all the greedy buggers who had fought to lend him and Paul money in the good days. He looked at his watch, it was at least two hours to where he was going and where he would meet Paul, and he loosened his belt, composed himself for sleep, huddled in his overcoat, as the plane swung to face the runway.

'Mr Michael Banner?'

'Yes.'

'I am Detective Chief Inspector Warren.' The man flicked

open a wallet and Mickey stared at it blankly, two phones shrilling unregarded around him.

'Can you answer these? Someone? Eileen? It might be about Jean, you see. What is it?'

'You are a director of this company?'

'Yes, I am. And I have no idea where any of the other directors are. I've been looking for them since yesterday. They've left me here, and I don't know what to say to anyone.'

Eileen, tight-lipped, blatantly unimpressed by Chief Inspector Warren or his two silent acolytes, pushed past them all. 'You ought to see this, Mickey.'

He couldn't take it in at first, and when he understood he turned a face of such desolation to the policeman that the man took a step forward.

'Mr Banner?'

'That's my brother.'

'The MP?' The policeman took the paper gently and surveyed it swiftly but comprehensively. 'I see.'

Something in his face made Mickey look at his own hands. He was rubbing and twisting them and he did not care, everything was gone, including Davey. How could he have been so stupid and so irresponsible? 'My wife's in hospital,' he said, with the last of his strength. 'It may be cancer. I must get there. I'll tell you anything I can but I must go there.' He rose, steadying himself on the desk, and walked to the waiting police car without a backward glance at the office where he had spent nearly fifteen years, or the policemen methodically searching it, or Eileen, or anyone at all.

'If you want to divorce me, I shall entirely understand,' Jens offered, stiffly, wedged into the furthest corner of the sofa, as far from Hugh as she could get.

'You might well understand it. How *could* you be such a bloody fool? All those media people gossip, you could have been found out any time.'

'We were always very careful.'

Some small part of her mind told her all was not lost; Hugh

420

was concentrating on the risk to himself and the children, rather than on her betrayal of him. He had hit her when she told him, and she had felt it was the least she deserved.

'I don't want you to divorce me. I am very sorry.'

'If it's him you want you'd better go.'

'Actually, it isn't.' She had understood this truth, it seemed to her now, a long time ago without being prepared to admit it. She thought about how to explain. 'I used to have fantasies – when we were fighting over my parents and your job – about marrying him, but they always frightened me. I always knew it wouldn't do. For either of us.' She looked at her husband's unyielding, angry profile and thought again what a formidable personality he was. 'I should have stopped. It is you I want.'

'You should never have started.'

'Well, that too.' In a disaster, she thought exhaustedly, there was a lot to be said for the habit of rational discussion, and not letting go and saying the most awful things you could think of. If Hugh left her, she would die. There were truly, as William French had said long ago, some mistakes that were irrecoverable and could forever make your life worse. The affair with Simon, if Hugh did leave her, would be one of those, she realized, as the menacing headache closed in on the other eye.

'He would presumably be embarrassed if you turned up wanting to marry him.' Hugh wasn't looking at her, his jaw set.

'Desperately,' she said, as steadily as she could. 'It is not me he wants; it is his wife. She is what he needs, as you are for me.'

'Why the hell did you do it? For fun?'

'Something like that,' she said drearily, and they sat in miserable silence, she not daring even to reach out a hand. The phone rang, and she looked at it, exhausted, then stretched out to touch him, unable to tolerate the silence between them.

'The office is full of policemen. I thought I'd warn you.' The normally unperturbed Joe was in a panic.

'Policemen?' She looked automatically to Hugh for help.

'What sort of policemen? What do they want?'

'They're asking about Paul Seles.'

'We'll deal with this from your office, not from here. Ring Charles and get him round,' Hugh said crisply.

'We'll come in, Joe,' she said, the 'we' echoing in her ears.

Under Hugh's direction they delayed long enough to give Charles a chance to arrive, so that it was with Charles and Hugh at her back that she faced the three plain-clothes police-men in her office.

'We have a warrant for the arrest of Paul Seles,' the senior man said briskly, putting his cup down. 'We believe you saw him recently.'

'The day before yesterday.'

'On what charge? The warrant?' Hugh leant forward, calm and formidable.

'Supplying arms to people on the prohibited list,' the senior man said, after a protracted pause.

Jens kept her mouth shut and watched Hugh.

'You visited his office yesterday, Miss Redwood? Sorry, Mrs Winterton. And left him a package?'

'Oh, crumbs,' she said, startled into speech. 'Yes, but it wasn't arms, for heaven's sake.'

'What was it?' She slid a look at Hugh, who nodded. 'It was fifty thousand pounds in notes. It was a loan.'

'You usually make loans in notes?'

She could hear Charles objecting, but she had thought her way through that and told them what Paul had said about not being able to write a cheque.

'Are you suggesting my client has committed an offence, Chief Inspector?' Charles asked.

'Obstruction, perhaps. Assisting Mr Seles to avoid police inquiries.'

'Where *is* Paul?' The headache had lifted a little, she could see again, and there was something about the tucked-in corners of the man's mouth that was worrying her. 'Can't his office tell you? Michael Banner or Sean Kelly? Or, I suppose, Sandor Thokoly who shares a flat with Sean?'

'A man giving the name of Sandor Thokoly flew into Geneva this morning, then took a private plane from there.'

'Oh,' she said, and realized that she didn't understand at all. She looked to Hugh.

'A man giving the name, Chief Inspector? With a passport in that name, you mean?'

'Yes, sir.'

'Where did the plane go to?' Charles was asking, he and Hugh both leaning forward.

'Not very far. It blew up on the runway at Cointrin, killing both pilots and the passenger.'

'Couldn't happen to a nicer chap,' she said viciously, releasing tension, and realized all four men were watching her. 'Sorry. Couldn't stand him. What?' She appealed to Hugh.

'Who was the passenger, Chief Inspector?' She felt his warm hand clench on hers.

'Identification is not yet final, but we believe it to be Sean Kelly.'

The room spun before her eyes and she heard Hugh call her name. 'But Paul Seles? He wasn't ... he didn't ... he isn't?'

'He was not on the plane, Mrs Winterton.'

'Thank God for that. My poor Sean. But where is Paul?'

'We hoped you could help us. We believe he has left the country.' There was a long pause. 'Do you know where he could have gone?'

'Anywhere,' she said, desolate. 'In several countries.' She felt Hugh's hand on hers. 'I truly do not know, Chief Inspector. I'm not saying I'd tell you if I did, but I don't.'

'He may get in touch with you.'

'Yes,' she acknowledged. 'He may.'

'I am sure my client intends to co-operate with your inquiries.' It was Charles, of course, there to remind her of the duties owed by the chairman of a public company. And Hugh's wife and William and Sara's mother.

The police left after a while, presumably, as Charles warned, to get authority to tap hers and the restaurant's phones. Then, finally, Charles went back to his office and it was just Hugh and her in the big room full of flowers.

'I'm sorry. My poor Jens.'

'This is much worse than anything.'

He understood her immediately and they looked at each other seriously. 'Because Paul has actually gone?'

She had, she understood, destroyed his trust in her to the point where she had to spell this one out. 'He matters much more than Simon. I love him.'

'He loves you too.' Hugh had always been generous, she thought desolately.

'Yes, he does. He could have sold me to the newspapers as well. He never even threatened it.'

'You *told* him about Simon?' His face was naked and young in disappointment.

'No.' She reached out to him. 'But I've been kidding myself. He knew, of course he did. I'm afraid a few people must have guessed.'

'We're not out of that wood yet.' He was looking grim but he was still holding her hand, and she tried not to move. 'Come on,' he said, pulling her up, 'let's go home; the kids will be back from school.'

CHAPTER TWENTY-FOUR

February/March 1995

'David? I'm ready.'

He shot up from the sofa, scattering newspapers which he folded up again. He looked at her as she stood in the doorway, small and compact, the square jaw, which had become more prominent as they got older, set. He rushed to help her on with her raincoat; it was a dreary, wet day outside, soaking the grey streets. He rested his hands on her shoulders, deeply grateful to her for being who she was.

'Anyone outside?'

'No. They must have got tired of it.'

For the last three days, ever since he had faced the cameras to explain Juliette, photographers had waited outside the flat. He had always courted publicity, but the last three days had produced the sort of reporters he had never seen before: shouting, noisy men, who didn't mind what they asked, and laughed or stared at him incredulously when he suggested they were overstepping the mark. Ann had been brilliant; she had always disliked publicity and always known that reporters were awful people, but had walked through it all, grimly and exclusively concerned with protecting him. She had understood without being told how betrayed he felt and how helpless, and how much he needed to explain, and had stopped him doing any of that. 'David's said all he's going to say and so have I,' she had said to the mob, silencing in the end even the most persistent. There had been a brief flare-up the day before, when Juliette Templeton had surfaced with her solicitor to confirm the story and be photographed. She had behaved well too, playing it down; she had, of course, a career to protect too.

He bent to kiss Ann, bracing himself for the day's task. The car was outside, looking particularly old and scruffy, but he was not going to find the cash yet for a new one. He could see, resentfully and anxiously, that he might have to do something for Mickey's family. Mickey wasn't going to be able to get a job at that level again. Or possibly at all. He thought briefly of Jens Redwood, but reality reasserted itself; she was in deep trouble as well.

'Not a good day for Sean Kelly's funeral,' he said, this being as close as he dared come to comment.

'No. I feel badly not going.'

'We can't, Annie,' he said, alarmed.

'Oh, I know.' She patted his knee comfortingly. 'We agreed, and so does Jens. I did ring her. She understands. She's reckoning the press will be there in force, and she says it would be even worse if we were there.'

'I'm afraid that's right.' He had not told Ann about his brief affair with Maddy, deciding that there was nothing that could not be denied, and Maddy would protect herself and her family fiercely, as he was doing. And, more compelling than these cool calculations, he was terrified that Ann would leave him over that one; it was possible to pass off a couple of months of passion with Juliette as a one-off aberration, but not if he had had to confess to Maddy as well. As he might in the end have to. He wished, momentarily, that it had been Paul Seles whose funeral Jens was now arranging in the teeth of public anger about the facts of the Seles Group's collapse which were now emerging. Ironically, she and Hugh had been in the papers almost as much as he and Ann had, getting on and off aeroplanes and in and out of grim offices. Jens had arranged for Sean's body to be brought back after the autopsy, or whatever there was to bring home; he thought of the pictures of the blackened wreckage; the just discernible outlines of black skeletons still strapped into their seats were quite as bad as anything he had seen in the Falklands.

There were a lot of things he wasn't going to be able to do, he thought, momentarily desolate, but checked himself. He was lucky to be here in this car with Ann, with his treasured political career derailed temporarily but still with a fighting chance. He had gone, with gritted teeth, to see the Leader as soon as his solicitor had confirmed that there was absolutely nothing he could do other than in the very short term to keep the affair out of the papers. The man who had been, he saw, forewarned already somehow by somebody, had listened to him in cautious, censorious silence.

'Well, I'm very sorry, David,' he had said, when Davey had finished his careful, contrite statement. 'I'd prefer to regard all these things' – the single dismissive gesture put him in a collection which included homosexuals, cross-dressers and party members who appeared with both eyes blackened, blinking in the light of day outside German night clubs – 'as strictly personal. But that's not the way the game is being played, and you'll not be surprised that I'll not feel able to put you in charge of one of the more sensitive portfolios when I rearrange to take account of Jim Bryan's illness.'

He had come out with a half-promise of Social Security, and knew that he was fortunate to have *that*. It had been made very clear that if there were any more revelations about what the man insisted on referring to as his 'personal life', then he would be dropped from any Shadow spokesman job. He would also, he understood, need to work extremely hard to hold his place in the Shadow Cabinet. Indeed, his best hope now probably lay in an election postponed to 1997, which looked like an eternity from where he was. Just underneath his enormous sense of relief at still being in the game was a sense of considerable misery; not to be able to find another adventure, to have to give all *that* up, was an unexamined but considerable grief.

'And you have to visit Mickey today,' Ann said firmly. That was right too, of course, and the psychiatric hospital in which Mickey was immured was an appropriate place to be on the morning when what remained of Sean Kelly was buried.

He put a tape in the machine, and drove steadily, soothed by Mozart, Ann quiet at his side.

'We're here, darling. Turn right.'

'Good God.' The car swerved right and he switched off the tape, shaken.

'What?'

'He's been in here before. When he was first ill, as a kid. Sorry, it gave me a turn. I didn't recognize the name.'

'It used to be St Charles's.'

'*That's* right.' He pulled into a space and sat staring at the well-remembered facade.

'Come on, Davey, we have to go on after this to Jean's.'

The one bright spot in all this was that Jean's lump had turned out to be a benign cyst, requiring a ten-minute excision. The news had come too late to help Mickey who had collapsed when he understood that the Seles Group was probably insolvent, drained of cash. The Group was still trading with the indulgence of its bankers, somehow. And the pension scheme, which the bank's accountants had rushed to look at first, was all right, to everyone's relief and surprise. So Mickey was not absolutely destitute; there was provision for him which could be used if he was going to be too ill to work, provided of course he stayed out of jail. Jens had told Ann that it was clear that even if he had known some of what was going on he had never *done* any of it, so with luck that hurdle could be surmounted. Paul Seles and Sean Kelly, those shrewd, tough operators, had had more sense than to trust Mickey to be near the real action, a dispensation for which David was now thoroughly thankful since it would enable him to distance himself from anything that had been going on.

'Mr Banner?'

'Oh God, Dr Daiches.'

'I'm sorry, it must give you a sense of *déjà vu*.'

'To say the least.' He rallied. 'But it's good to see you and I'm sure Mickey is pleased you're here.' He stood distractedly, observing the man. He'd grown a bit since he was a teenager, but the man still topped him easily, although he must be nearly seventy. 'How is Mickey?'

'Come into the office a minute before you see him.' He sat them down and gave them coffee and David's heart sank. Ann touched his hand gently and he felt better.

'He had a collapse.'

'Like when he was a child?'

'Yes, David – if I may? But he isn't a child and he has an adult's resilience. How quickly he gets back into action depends on how much support there is. From his wife, principally, since he is so dependent on her.' He was addressing Ann, David realized, choking back remembered rage and panic.

'Jean's frightened,' Ann said bluntly. 'She can't cope with him weeping and twisting his hands all the time.'

'A breakdown is a frightening thing, but he has recovered before.'

'I'll talk to her.' Ann never wasted words and David felt a rush of love. 'We'd better go and see him.'

They all three rose and David found Dr Daiches at his side as Ann headed down the corridor with a nurse; she had visited every day and knew the ropes. 'I'm not being very good about this,' he heard himself say.

'You were young when Mickey first broke down, and struggling yourself. So it does frighten you. But you have married well.'

'I have, haven't I?'

'How is your mother?'

'Oh, she's here. I mean, she's staying with Jean. Flew down to support her boys.' He considered the statement. 'Came down to support *me*, only I don't need it. I mean, I only need Ann.'

'Mickey would find it very useful if she would support him.'

'We all would . . .' He looked up at the man, feeling eighteen again. 'We'll manage. Thank you, Doctor.'

'Good luck.' Dr Daiches stopped, indicating that he should go on, and he ran to catch up Ann, gripping her hand as they turned to face the room in which Mickey was.

The rain fell unremittingly on the crematorium at Golders

Green, and on the crowd of bedraggled photographers wearing a wild assortment of raincoats, the precious lenses shrouded in plastic bags. Jens hesitated, uncertain which waiting-room to go for, and three of the press crew told her; they had been following her and Hugh and had become a familiar background. She felt Hugh take her arm. She was cautious herself about touching him; he was still very angry with her and she did not wish to push her luck. He was not going to leave her, that much she knew in her bones; it was not in him to leave the wife and children to whom he had committed himself, as she should always have known, but his trust in her was fractured and he was deeply miserable.

She walked into the waiting-room, not knowing what to expect. Louisa, Paul's wife, had declared her intention to stay away, but in fact had arrived, and Maddy had come with the children. None of the Banner family was present, but Sofia and Lucy were there and so was Roger Caldwell, looking small and pinched and yellow. She rushed to kiss him and his arms went round her convulsively. She felt the tears on his cheek and she gave him a handkerchief automatically.

'Sit with us?' she asked, and he nodded wordlessly as they were called to go into the chapel. In the end the front row contained Maddy and Louisa, looking disconcertingly like sisters, both blonde and spectacular in black, separated by Stephen and Lily. On the other side of the aisle Jennifer, Hugh, Sofia, John, Lucy and Roger Caldwell completed the family mourners. The rest of the substantial audience was an injudicious mixture of police, reporters and a few bewildered Seles Group employees.

It was not a long or inspiring ceremony. The service was taken by a Catholic priest, since Sean had always maintained his allegiance to that faith. Indeed, Jens had identified, in Geneva, the crucifix he wore round his neck and his signet ring, there being nothing else that anyone other than a forensic scientist might recognize. She read Psalm 100, the priest spoke a few final words and she sat waiting for it to be over in a state of willed disengaged calm until the moment came when

430

the coffin containing the blackened, disconnected bones, which was all there was left of Sean, shuddered into movement towards the flames that had already consumed his flesh.

She sat for a few minutes at the end with Sofia shielding her from the curious, until she could go outside into the rain which fell blessedly on her swollen face. The police had somehow dealt with the reporters and most of the congregation had gone. She drew a deep breath, kissed Sofia, John and Lucy and saw beyond them Roger Caldwell, standing under a tree, infinitely pathetic. Hugh was with him, having, she understood with love, seen someone even more in need of protection than his wife.

'Roger,' she said, catching up, 'will you come back with us?'

'Please,' he said, pale and old and shrunken, and she braced herself to deal with another of the disasters Paul and Sean had left behind.

'Did you have Seles Group shares?' Hugh was asking, as the driver hurried them back to the restaurant.

'Yes. Jens advised me not to hold them all, but I never felt able to sell. But I also have shares in you, Jens, more than enough to live on. Paul gave them to me. I feel I ought to return them.'

She opened her mouth, agonized, but Hugh was ahead of her.

'When did he give you them? Three years ago? No, no, you don't need to at all. Either legally or morally, that predates any raiding of the company.'

'I am relieved,' he said bleakly, after a pause, and a silence which she was too unhappy to break fell between them.

'All your pretty chickens . . .' Hugh said, and she held her breath.

'That's what I was thinking,' Roger Caldwell agreed exhaustedly. 'We tried, we all tried. First us at Woolverstone Hall, and then Sean and he had the great good fortune to find you, Jens.'

'And none of it was any good. To him or to Paul.' It was a relief to say aloud what she had thought so often in the last week.

'They were both very badly damaged, of course, as children,' Hugh observed gently.

'Yes. Yes, and some damage cannot be restored. I gather Mickey Banner is in hospital?'

'Yes.'

'And yet his brother from the same background is a survivor. As you are, Jens. Of course you were both fortunate in your marriages. No, I won't come in, Jens, or not yet, I want to go into St Martin's for a little.'

They watched him go, a small, huddled figure who stumbled going up the steps.

'He's lost an awful lot,' Hugh said, watching his back.

She sat, straight-backed, finally able to measure the full extent of her own loss: Sean dead, Paul apparently beyond recall, Simon lost beyond even friendship on the other bank of a river, divided from her by every convention, and David too enmeshed in his own problems to help. And worst, Hugh estranged from her. Of all this, what would *not* be tolerable would be to lose Hugh, that steady, consistent, loved rock on which her life was built, and she should never, ever have put that at risk. She looked helplessly at his profile; he looked weary and heavy and spoke without looking at her.

'I'll go and sit with Roger and bring him home for supper. He shouldn't be alone.'

She watched him walk into the church and sat quietly, staring out through the windscreen. There were things she could do, other than pray for Sean's soul, and those she would do. Even if they were no use.

It was still snowing and bitterly cold in Prague as darkness fell; no hint of spring in the air, unlike England. The big man in the car was sitting next to the driver, the car phone crackling between them on its stand.

'She's gone in, Paul. Give us five minutes.'

It was a long five minutes and he could feel his heart thumping irregularly as he waited it out, neither of the other men in the car daring to break the silence. 'She's still clean. No followers.'

Time then to take the risk. He pulled on his hat, extracted thick gloves from his pocket and buttoned his coat to the neck. The second man in the car leapt out of the back seat to open the door for him and accompany him across the corner of the old square to the massive, beautiful baroque church, timing their arrival so that they went up the steps and straight in through the doors at the end of a queue of American tourists, booted, hatted and oblivious to everything except the need to get out of the cold. He waited till his eyes adjusted and then saw her where she had been told to be: on the end of the fourth pew. The dim lights dimmed further, leaving the improbable flying cherubs glittering in the half-dark, and he stood in the shadows and listened to the introduction in Czech, German and English. It was a concert for trumpet and organ, and the audience was about 80 per cent tourists, as these musical evenings in Prague's churches usually were. The light dimmed again, the audience settled down, and into the silence a trumpet spoke from the gallery, high and clear and impersonal, and he caught his breath, momentarily unable to move for pain. Sean had loved trumpets; they spoke to something in him and he had always had baroque music playing in his car. The man with him touched his arm, bringing him back to himself, and he moved silently under cover of the organ entry to the seat she was keeping for him at the end of the pew. Her jaw was set rigid with tension and her shoulders were hunched. He slid a hand into her pocket, covering her clenched cold fingers with his own, and felt the answering, grateful pressure as they sat in silence listening to the unbearably eloquent trumpet, like a human voice but without a human personality.

'Jens, did you come alone?'

'Yes. That's what I said.'

He felt warmth go right through him at the familiar irritable impatience which she only displayed when she was nervous.

'But I have this feeling of being watched.' She was speaking without moving her lips, under cover of the organ, and he was reminded again of Sean.

'That's my people. Come on, let's get out. Give me three

minutes.' He slid out of the pew and emerged into the dark square, looking for the watchers who signalled that he was clear, and waited, eyes on his watch. She emerged, as he knew she would, precisely on time, huddled into her coat, looking round for him, and he reached out for her and held her in his arms.

'Does Hugh know you're here?' he said into her ear.

'Yes. I don't do things any more without telling him. He sends his love.'

'Why have you come?'

'I am a messenger. Can we sit down inside somewhere?'

He led her off the square and down below street level to a crowded, expensive tourist trap and ordered coffee and brandy in English for them both.

She looked thin and tired, he thought with anxious love, and her blue eyes had lines round them that he had never noticed before. She was looking back at him, unsmiling, and he held both her hands, desperate for her not to be angry with him.

'Oh, Paul. I am so glad to see you.'

He realized he was going to cry and let go of her hand to find a handkerchief, turning his head into her shoulder. She reached round to hold him, ignoring the waiter who was putting coffee and brandy down for them. He sniffled and took a huge slug of the brandy, feeling it burn inside him.

'From whom are you a messenger?' he said, when he could speak, with the grammatical precision Old Caldwell had instilled in him.

'From lots of people. We want you back, Paul. The Seles Group is still trading. The banks have put up enough cash to keep it going and they've put in their own bloke.' She was looking at him with the familiar careful, searching expression. 'I expect you know all this. You won't like the bloke but he's good and, what's more important, he is *desperate* to have you back, because only you can tell him where everything is.'

'He won't get far without me or Sean, that's for sure.' His voice went rough in his embarrassment and he looked away, and she covered his warm hand with both of hers.

'It was Sandy's fault Sean died, I assume.'

'No.' He was having trouble getting the words out and he tightened his grip on her hand. 'No, it was mine. Sean had agreed to let Sandy's people have another delivery of Semtex. From our factory – on a one-off basis – because Sandy was being threatened. And I stopped it. Our people – MI6 – were after me and Davey's lot were too, but I wouldn't have it anyway, not for Sandy's people. I wouldn't have them mess us up.'

'So they killed Sean, thinking he was Sandy.'

'Yes. The careless, idle buggers didn't even *check* at the airport, just blew him away.'

'"Revenge is mine, saith the Lord."' She was watching him, eyes wide.

'Not in this case. Sandy and his backers are six foot under.' She tried to pull her hand away but he held on. '*No*, I didn't do it, but I told someone who would. They were glad to know.' He had shocked his sister, he saw, but for the moment he did not care. He was an exile and an outcast, but he had avenged Sean, as he had had to, or be unable to go on living with himself.

'All right. So you've done that,' she said, surprising him. 'You can come back, and take your chances.'

'No, I can't.' He could not look at her. 'I couldn't face it.'

'Not even for Roger Caldwell?'

'For Sir? How is he?'

'Desolate.'

He shivered and called for more coffee and brandy, in Czech this time, so that the waiter looked at him sharply.

'Shit. You shouldn't have come.'

'Charles knows I'm here. He says that if you come back there's actually not all that much they can charge you with. After all, you didn't take money out of the company or out of the pension scheme – not like Maxwell.'

'Except that Albany Wharf loan.'

'I paid it off. All of it. For both of us.'

He felt himself turn scarlet, between relief and embarrassment. 'You needn't have done that.'

'Oh, yes, I needed. We were committing a fraud on your pension scheme as we stood. I did it to save my neck.'

'Why the fuck did you pay off all of it?'

'Joshua told me to.'

'*Joshua?*' He stared at her in wild surmise. 'Since when do you consult him?'

'Since you buggered off and left me with Sean dead, your company bust, and nobody else to ask.'

He choked on his coffee and recovered to see her glaring at him, flushed across the cheek-bones. He sat looking at her, a great sense of peace and relief spreading through him. 'You're pissed off with me.'

'No, no, not at all. Bloody furious are the words you want.'

'Tell me about Joshua,' he begged. 'This I have to hear.'

'Well.' She was looking suddenly less tired. 'I needed a property man, and it was no good asking that set of crooks you consulted. And I couldn't risk asking a professional to advise me for fear of exposing both of us. *And* I had to go fast because the team the banks put in were moving very steadily and there are armies of them. So I rang Joshua.'

'And?'

'He came straight away and he spent the whole morning. Not that he needed to, he knew the building, he just didn't know we owned it. He says it will sell at about seven hundred thousand if we use a decent agent, but not for more. So our loan is gone.'

'Only half of it. You didn't need to repay it all.'

'Shut up, Paul, and *listen*, dammit.' He subsided, reassured. 'I repaid the lot because Joshua pointed out that any investigation into the loan would reveal a ... well ... none too scrupulous history in which I was involved. And at a time when Hugh was still in the Treasury. And I *did* know all along, Paul.'

'Yes.'

'He pointed out that if the loan had been repaid no one would have to do any investigation at all, even if they wondered why the money had come back a bit sharpish at this particular point in time. They've got other things to worry about. *And* he lent me it, as a bridging loan, until next year when I am allowed to sell enough of my own shares.' She was looking very pleased with herself but he was horrified.

'Jens. What did you have to do?'

'Now comes the best bit. He tried it on – a quick grope, I mean – while I was thanking him for helping. So I said that while I was truly grateful for present help, he could bugger off if those were his terms. *Then* he said he didn't mean anything and I said yes, he did, it was bullying and harassment. And I didn't cry.'

He stroked the back of her hand, unable to speak, and she smiled at him. 'I told him he had messed up my life as a teenager.'

'And thereafter,' he said carefully.

'As you say. But I understood, Paul, that I had been stupid to let it get to me, and it wasn't going to any more. So I told Joshua that too.'

'What happened?'

'He apologized. He said he hadn't understood it was upsetting. Well, of course he understood it, but I thought I'd got as far as I needed for one day. So we shook hands on the deal.'

'What made you able to do all that?' He was suddenly bitterly jealous.

'You, you idiot. What you had managed to do coming from where you came. I suddenly thought where do *I* have the right to be such a wimp about Joshua when you had your guardian to cope with?'

'But I've fucked it up, totally.'

'Not true. You built up a marvellous company there; you just never had good enough financing or advice. Because, of course, you don't trust easily, and Sean, God rest him, whom you did trust just wasn't good enough. Too introvert, too . . . well . . . untrained. You needed somebody like my Joe. And my Charles as a lawyer, rather than that set of crooks you use.'

He stared at her; she was looking young and determined. 'I've blown it, Jens. I can't come back. I can't go to jail.'

'You've been there before.'

'Well, thank you very much.' They glared at each other, then both burst out laughing.

'I tell you something else amazing,' she said, revived. 'Mickey!'

'Mickey Banner?' he asked, with a sinking heart.

'He's all right. In fact he's more than all right. Once he found Jean was going to be OK he came whistling out of the bin he was in, and went back to his desk and is working twelve hours a day with the bankers, keeping the company going. Tower of strength, apparently. I mean, he doesn't know all sorts of things, including how the finances work, but he knows the people and he can lay his hand quickly on contracts and documents. Interesting, isn't it?'

'Davey always said he was amazingly good in an emergency.' There was a pause during which he felt increasingly awkward. 'And Davey? *He* won't want me back.'

'You aren't his favourite person at the moment, I agree. I managed a drink with him in the office at Redwoods. He was very low but he does know that it was Sean, not you, who sold him to the papers.'

'I didn't even *know* about Juliette Templeton.'

'Me neither. He just sneaked that one past both of us. But he knows you didn't even try and use him and Maddy, whatever you may have threatened.'

'I never would have, but not to spare him. I wouldn't have my kids dragged through that.'

'Ah, of course.' She smiled at him. 'So you aren't even a successful blackmailer.' He grinned back sheepishly. 'So the news on Davey is that he lost a step and he'll have to be the world's most faithful husband, which he'll find difficult. But he's there, he didn't compromise, he'll fight another day even if he doesn't get to the top.'

'He won't quite, will he?' he said, suddenly seeing it. 'He'll do something every time to louse it up for himself. Not necessarily an affair, but *something*. Like all of us.'

'I've stopped doing that.' She looked exactly herself at nine

438

years old, jaw set. 'I've got a good small business and a lovely husband who is at the moment justifiably miserable, but who has stuck by me and the kids, and I'm never going to risk that again. And you can stop doing it too. Your kids need a father, not a fugitive from justice, and Roger Caldwell needs his adopted son, and I just plain want you back.'

'Don't go on.'

'I wasn't going to.' She blew her nose. 'I have to get the last plane; Charles advised this should be a quick trip.'

'I can't come to the airport, but my driver will take you.' He got stiffly to his feet to make the necessary arrangements and to button her into her coat.

She leaned over to kiss him on the lips and pulled back, hands on his shoulders, so that he saw again the nine-year-old on the building site, squaring up to defend him against all comers.

'Go carefully, my love,' he said unsteadily.

She was trying not to cry as she had tried thirty years before, and he pushed her into the car and watched until its tail-lights vanished quite away.

READ MORE IN PENGUIN

In every corner of the world, on every subject under the sun, Penguin represents quality and variety – the very best in publishing today.

For complete information about books available from Penguin – including Puffins, Penguin Classics and Arkana – and how to order them, write to us at the appropriate address below. Please note that for copyright reasons the selection of books varies from country to country.

In the United Kingdom: Please write to *Dept. JC, Penguin Books Ltd, FREEPOST, West Drayton, Middlesex UB7 0BR.*

If you have any difficulty in obtaining a title, please send your order with the correct money, plus ten per cent for postage and packaging, to *PO Box No. 11, West Drayton, Middlesex UB7 0BR*

In the United States: Please write to *Consumer Sales, Penguin USA, P.O. Box 999, Dept. 17109, Bergenfield, New Jersey 07621-0120.* VISA and MasterCard holders call 1-800-253-6476 to order all Penguin titles

In Canada: Please write to *Penguin Books Canada Ltd, 10 Alcorn Avenue, Suite 300, Toronto, Ontario M4V 3B2*

In Australia: Please write to *Penguin Books Australia Ltd, P.O. Box 257, Ringwood, Victoria 3134*

In New Zealand: Please write to *Penguin Books (NZ) Ltd, Private Bag 102902, North Shore Mail Centre, Auckland 10*

In India: Please write to *Penguin Books India Pvt Ltd, 706 Eros Apartments, 56 Nehru Place, New Delhi 110 019*

In the Netherlands: Please write to *Penguin Books Netherlands bv, Postbus 3507, NL-1001 AH Amsterdam*

In Germany: Please write to *Penguin Books Deutschland GmbH, Metzlerstrasse 26, 60594 Frankfurt am Main*

In Spain: Please write to *Penguin Books S. A., Bravo Murillo 19, 1° B, 28015 Madrid*

In Italy: Please write to *Penguin Italia s.r.l., Via Felice Casati 20, I–20124 Milano*

In France: Please write to *Penguin France S. A., 17 rue Lejeune, F–31000 Toulouse*

In Japan: Please write to *Penguin Books Japan, Ishikiribashi Building, 2–5–4, Suido, Bunkyo-ku, Tokyo 112*

In Greece: Please write to *Penguin Hellas Ltd, Dimocritou 3, GR–106 71 Athens*

In South Africa: Please write to *Longman Penguin Southern Africa (Pty) Ltd, Private Bag X08, Bertsham 2013*

BY THE SAME AUTHOR

The Highest Bidder

Success in making the winning bid in the Government's sale of a construction company depends on power and influence with the people who matter. And for four of the players, the outcome could mean brilliant success – or ruinous scandal.

'Janet Cohen moves adroitly between the civil service, business sharks, bankers and dirty dealings ... the old power game handled with aplomb' – *The Times*

Janet Cohen has also published four acclaimed crime novels under the name Janet Neel:

Death's Bright Angel

Winner of the 1988 John Creasey Award for the best first crime novel

'A very well-written novel about big business shenanigans, with a splendidly forceful heroine ... The writing throughout is sharp, intelligent and amusing' – *Independent*

Death on Site

'It is no mean achievement to make a building site seem both interesting and sinister ... a splendid follow-up to Neel's cracking first-timer' – *The Times*

Death of a Partner

'Neel's insider feel for the subtle undercurrents of Whitehall and the boardroom combines with precise plotting and believable characters ... A winner' – *The Times*

Death Among the Dons

'Probably the best crime novel set in a women's college since Dorothy Sayers's *Gaudy Night* ... it combines an intriguing detective story with a serious consideration of some of the problems confronting women in academic life' – T. J. Binyon